Nohemi,

Enjoy a little
Romance Novel
in your very
little Spare
time

nice to Meet you

Pat Ser

Jennifer
mom

TRAVEL AGENT ESCAPADES
Adventure and Romance Around the World

COPYRIGHT © 2021 Pat Seiler

Manufactured in the United States of America

ISBN: 979-8481814-49-0

For more information,
write to the author at
P.O. Box 573
Helena, MT 59624

Published for Pat Seiler by
BLUE CREEK PRESS
Heron, Montana 59844
www.bluecreekpress.com

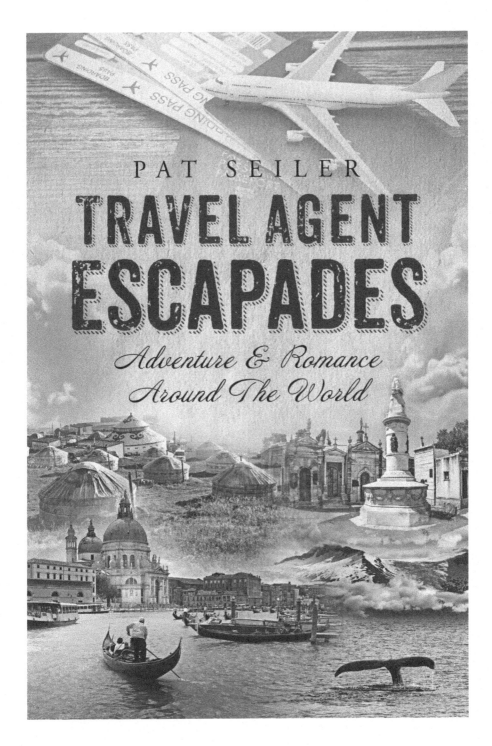

PAT SEILER

TRAVEL AGENT ESCAPADES

Adventure & Romance
Around The World

IN MEMORY OF
MARY JANE, BEVERLY
AND VIRGINIA DARING

PROLOGUE

With a sigh of relief, Ginger began gathering her belongings to exit the plane in St. Louis. She had planned to take the morning flight so she would have plenty of time to meet her friends for their annual social get-together. It was a sacred tradition. They always met for happy hour in the lobby bar of the convention center hotel the night prior to the American Society of Travel Agents conference. As the owner of her own agency, Ginger was always up against deadlines, which seemed to consume every available minute. There was the meeting with her manager on staff vacations, quick calls to new corporate clients to thank them for choosing her agency, and the submission of her weekly radio talk show agenda.

Growing up as the oldest child in a middle-class working family, she was always striving to be reliable and steadfast. Perhaps the Catholic school nuns also imparted a bit of guilt. She was constantly trying to please others by taking on more than she should. Arriving on time, she said to herself, *I did take a risk today in booking the afternoon flight, and it worked out just fine. Maybe I should continue to loosen up a bit. It just might produce some unexpected surprises.* Checking her watch, Ginger smiled when she realized she had an hour to spare. She was becoming convinced that it was going to be a very good day.

Seated in the taxi, she reminisced about the first time she had met her friends. It seemed impossible to believe that several years had passed since they were assigned to a brain storming panel at the conference. As complete strangers from states miles apart, there was something special about the instant attraction they felt for each other. They even teased and called themselves the "Renegade Team." They were always ready to push the envelope in making revisions to industry regulations that they felt needed updating or changes. In just a few short years, they had made a name for themselves as leaders at the conference. The Renegade Team had been appointed to various influential committees and drafted numerous proposals, earning the admiration of their peers. However, the upcoming happy hour gathering was not intended for industry business. It was a chance to catch up with each other's personal lives, sharing the warm and caring bond that they had so easily developed as friends.

Ginger mused at how different each of them was yet how closely they were connected. Victoria was sophisticated and gorgeous. Her long, dark hair was straight and shining, her makeup flawless. At 5'9", she always wore the newest trending fashions. Having been raised in a wealthy East Coast family, she shared the fact that her parents constantly reminded her that they had spent a fortune to send her to private schools and an ivy league college. They were disappointed that she had not put her college major to use by following a career path offered to her with a prestigious advertising firm in Boston. She would laughingly remind her parents that she was putting her marketing degree to good use doing what she loved. Her brother had joined an international investment firm, and she never failed to mention that her income was equal to his. Victoria had built her agency to be a profitable and successful business. Her clientele were affluent travelers who flew first class, booked the best resorts and always remained faithful to her agents. Having several of the nation's top universities and museums as clients also gave her the opportunity to plan exotic expeditions to remote places on the globe. Whether it was bird watching in Borneo, communing with penguins at a research station in Antarctica or discovering lost civilizations in Peru, Victoria was always up for planning unique adventures.

Jessica was the most intellectual of the crew, but as strange as it may seem, they called her the wild one. This was not because she acted inappropriately, but that she was a risk taker who would branch out and try things that the rest of the group would never dream of doing. Her wavy, naturally red hair and flawless skin were a tribute to her Norwegian heritage. At 5' 6", she was a stunning woman with a great sense of humor and an engaging personality.

Jessica had a twinkle in her eye and a playful nature. The group loved hearing of her romances. Men were always falling in love with her, but she was fiercely independent.

The fourth woman in the group was Emily. Although she was younger than the rest of the Renegade Team, her wisdom was beyond her years. She was a natural beauty, only 5'2". Her long blonde hair was often worn pulled back in a casual clip. Her athletic figure was a reflection of her morning routine of swimming laps before her young sons were awake. Always on the run, keeping up with her busy family, she was the only one married with children. She was madly in love with her husband, Tom, who owned one of the most popular, high-end restaurants in Los Angeles. Emily worked part time for her aunt Marjorie's travel agency. With a degree in accounting, she was invaluable in navigating the challenges of the travel industry's ever-changing financial requirements.

As Ginger wheeled her new fuchsia suitcase into the hotel lobby, she caught a glimpse of herself in the ornate wall-sized mirror. Somehow, she had been able to keep her New Year's resolution to work out and eat sensibly, and it showed. She was 5'7", and slim, but with curves in all the right places. Her brunette hair was styled in a modern bob that was layered to swing around her cheeks as she moved. She lived in Seattle, where it rained constantly, so she had chosen a hairstyle that was easy and carefree.

In her hotel room, Ginger took a few minutes to sit down and unwind. It had been a hectic day. She then freshened her makeup and slipped into the fashionable red dress that she had purchased especially for the occasion. It was tight-fitting, a bit off the shoulder and just short enough to be noticeably stunning with her high heels.

As she walked through the lobby, she heard a familiar voice. "Hey, pretty lady. You are looking fabulous as usual."

She spun around and found herself in front of Brian, her Delta Airlines rep. "I'll take a compliment from you any day," she laughingly responded. Brian had been calling on her agency in Seattle for over a year now, and his engaging personality had won over her entire staff. He was tall and good-looking, but never acted the least bit cocky or conceited. Brian had a wholesome, boy-next-door charisma that made him extremely likable. In fact, Ginger had to admit she felt an attraction to Brian. And they were both single.

Brian kept the conversation going. "That red dress looks great on you,"

"Glad you could make this convention," Ginger replied. With a little gesture, she touched his shoulder. "Umm, cashmere. I also like that navy jacket on you!" They both smiled broadly and shared a warmhearted hug.

Brian then spoke in a more measured tone., "I was wondering if there is any chance you might have dinner with me tonight? There is a charming Italian restaurant up the street, and I thought we might get to know each other a little better."

"What time do they usually dine in Italy?" she asked with a twinkle in her eye. "Actually, I would love to, but it would have to be eight-ish. I'm on my way to the lobby bar to have a reunion with some women friends. We need at least three hours to catch up with each other's lives and escapades."

"Escapades?" He laughed. "Well, I certainly would not want to interrupt this gathering. Although I would love to be a fly on the wall during the conversations!"

"I'm sure you would." Ginger flashed him a big grin. "But, alas, it is girlfriend talk and oh, so private. But if you can wait until 8:00 pm, I would love to join you for dinner tonight."

"Great. And since I can't be that fly on the wall, I guess I will just have to use my imagination. Have a good time. See you later."

Everyone else was present when Ginger arrived. Her friends had captured the perfect table — somewhat private and next to a large window overlooking a lovely garden. There were warm hugs all around as everyone got up to welcome Ginger. "Wow! Looking mighty good," Jessica exclaimed as she stepped forward to take a closer look at her friend. "I've never seen you wearing that alluring red color before, and it suits you."

The three friends laughed as Victoria added, "Jessica, is there ever any doubt that you, of all people, would comment on red as an alluring color." This brought even more laughter as they settled into their seats.

"Sorry I'm late," Ginger apologized. "I ran into my Delta rep in the hallway."

"I hope he's single," Jessica couldn't resist commenting. "Especially since you are wearing that hot red dress."

"As a matter of fact," Ginger shared, "He is single and very attractive, and I have a late dinner date with him tonight." She went on to tell them that Brian admitted he found it intriguing that four women friends faithfully gathered yearly to catch up on each other lives. And she explained that, "He confessed he wished he could be a fly on the wall to listen in on the conversations."

As the waiter delivered elegant, long-stemmed wine glasses to the table, Emily explained that husband Tom had arranged for the delivery of two premium bottles of wine, compliments of his newest restaurant. Emily was especially proud and delighted when the manager stopped by their table to share his compliments regarding the exceptional vintage. The glasses had hardly been filled when raucous laughter erupted from the table.

"No way! This is hysterical," Ginger exclaimed loudly. "How can this be?" she said with a look of shock on her face. The waiter was dismayed to think he had done something wrong, and the neighboring tables looked over to see the source of all the commotion. There, perched on the rim of Ginger's glass was a fly. Brushing it away, the waiter was aghast and profusely apologized. It flew off and landed on the windowsill nearby. Emily quickly and politely explained to the waiter that the group was not upset. It was just an in-house joke amongst her friends.

"Well, that good-looking rep of yours is most definitely interested in our conversation," Victoria said after all of the commotion died down.

Before they had taken the first sip of wine, Jessica chimed in with a mischievous gleam in her eye. "I have an idea. Instead of relating war stories about the busy days at the office or personal accounts of fender benders and water heater leaks, why don't we spend this year doing something different? How about delighting our friend Mr. Fly by sharing the most romantic interludes we have encountered while traveling around the world."

"Are you kidding?" Emily protested. "Those are secrets we don't tell anyone!"

"Tell anyone? We aren't just anyone, " Jessica exclaimed defensively. "We are dear friends, and it will definitely be a bonding experience. Besides, Ginger is the one who unknowingly invited Mr. Fly to the party. And look, there he is sitting on the window ledge waiting patiently."

"Actually, it might be a revealing exchange," Victoria said, "and there is something intimate about sharing encounters few, if any, people know about us. We trust each other implicitly. The only thing I insist on is that we are careful not to compromise the confidentiality we pledge to our clients. I will even go first because I had the most romantic experience on an archaeological dig."

Although always somewhat reserved, Victoria did have a clever sense of humor. As she poised herself to begin, she picked up her wine glass and slowly blew mist onto the edge of the rim, where she made an imprint of a kiss. "My story starts with the planning of an archaeological expedition to a far-away site in Mongolia."

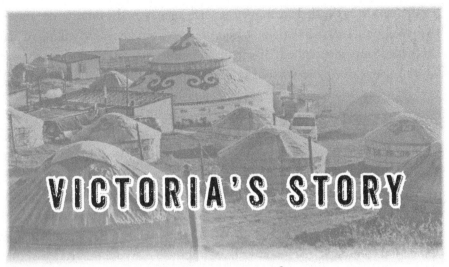

VICTORIA'S STORY

Mongolia

Victoria had taken on one of the most complicated and risky challenges of her travel career. She was to plan an archaeological expedition to Mongolia, not for a group of scientists or graduate students, but for a group of well-traveled, wealthy patrons of a prestigious museum. It had all started a year before when the director of her city's natural history museum contacted her to inquire whether her travel agency might be willing to plan an expedition to Mongolia. There was a group of sophisticated intellectuals who expressed an interest in having their local museum archaeologist, Dr. Mark Shelby, escort them to a remote site in Mongolia where research was already underway excavating a recently discovered tomb which had gained international attention.

Dr. Shelby had extensive experience on previous excavations abroad and was particularly interested in the project in Mongolia. The museum director explained that because of Dr. Shelby's contacts, the group would have an opportunity to participate in fieldwork at the site for four nights. They would be working alongside a famed Mongolian archaeologist whose discoveries had been published worldwide. After their authentic excavation experience, the group wanted an extended tour to include major sites in Mongolia and an extension to visit the Terra-cotta Warrior exhibit in Xian, China.

Victoria was thrilled to think that her agency had gained a reputation that prompted such a prestigious request. "We would be most willing to plan this expedition," she replied. "It will be an honor, and you can be assured that we will take care of every detail so that your group returns home with only rave reviews of their experiences in Mongolia."

After graciously agreeing to plan the expedition, Victoria ran into her first major hurdle. She had not realized that the country of Mongolia was under Communist rule. No American travel tour companies were allowed to conduct business as ground operators in Mongolia.

She had thought it would be easy to contact a reputable national company to assist, but after calling several, she got the message: "You will have to work with the state-run agency in the capital city of Ulaanbaatar, and good luck if they respond to your request. They are almost impossible to communicate with, and who knows if they can be counted on to follow through. You know, you will be dealing with a Communist country which has strict restrictions and limited western style services."

Just as Victoria began to panic, she had a stroke of uncanny luck. To her good fortune, she was provided a credible contact by a friend who was the president of her local university. He had become acquainted with Charles, a New York City businessman representing Mongolia in reciprocal programs with universities in the United States. As a native of Mongolia, he had many contacts in his country. Her friend advised Victoria to inquire to see if this man might be able to be of assistance.

Victoria's spirits began to lift after she had a lengthy conversation with Charles. He was enthusiastic and explained that his country would soon be gaining their independence, and that his cousin was planning to start a travel company offering ground operations to international tourists visiting Mongolia. He convinced her that she would not be disappointed and his relative could handle the job. He offered to be her interpreter during the planning process since his cousin spoke limited English.

He explained that it would be a costly endeavor. The tents and supplies would need to be shipped in from other countries. Charles emphasized that his country would be coming out of hard times after being under Soviet rule and did not have an infrastructure comparable to services offered in the United States. Victoria assured him she understood, and her agency was prepared to provide ample financial resources to the expedition. Although she knew it was a substantial risk to contract with an inexperienced ground operator, it was her only alternative.

As she hung up the phone, Victoria wondered if she had gotten in over her head. She would be working with an inexperienced tour operator in a remote country that would be gaining their independence only a few months prior to their arrival. She knew that scientists were willing to accept modest accommodations on far-flung expeditions. It was to be expected. But, to bring twenty-four upscale travelers to a remote site with limited infrastructure, security, sanitation and sleeping accommodations seemed daunting. If not for her unwavering tenacity, she may have reconsidered. Her reputation was now on the line, and there was no turning back.

Finally came arrival day came. As the somewhat worn Mongolian Airlines plane landed on the runway in Ulaanbaatar, Victoria let out a sigh of relief. Because of the caliber of the participants and the multitude of unknowns, she had decided to personally escort the group. If anything went wrong she would be there to deal with it. *It would be unfair to expect one of my agents to be responsible*, she thought as she gathered her luggage from the overhead bin.

"Please be here to meet us as planned," she whispered as they approached the terminal. The owner of the local tour company had promised he would meet the group and escort them to the hotel upon their arrival.

A pleasant, middle aged man approached the group entering the terminal. "Hello. I am Altan," he said. "I am the owner of your local tour company, and I will also be your guide." He spoke limited English, but to Victoria's relief, he was dressed nicely and appeared confident. She introduced herself, and he seemed genuinely happy to meet the person whose name he had heard numerous times throughout the many months of planning. As Altan was explaining that the motor coach would take the group directly to the hotel, a most attractive, tall, sandy-haired man came forward with an engaging smile on his face. He was wearing a khaki safari shirt with rolled-up sleeves that showed his muscular tanned arms and hiking boots.

With a most charming British accent, he said, "Welcome to Mongolia. I am Phillip Doyle, an archaeologist from London, I am here doing research for the summer. I thought I would come out to the airport to welcome Dr. Shelby and your group. I do hope you had a good flight."

Victoria assured him that the flight went well and stepped aside as Mark came forward. He greeted Phillip warmly.

"This is a pleasant surprise. When we visited at the meeting in Berlin last year, I never dreamed we would be here in Mongolia together. I'm very much looking forward to working with you."

Mark turned to the group which had gathered. "Everyone, I would like you to meet Dr. Phillip Doyle. Phillip and I have logged many hours together at archaeology conferences throughout the years. He has published some incredible work and made quite a name for himself."

Phillip seemed almost embarrassed by Mark's glowing accolades, but he turned the moment into one of humor by replying, "I think he is trying to butter me up so he can have the best tent in camp!"

Everyone laughed, and Victoria took a deep breath. She was appreciative that Dr. Doyle had broken the ice so beautifully and put everyone at ease.

As they settled into their seats on the motor coach, Victoria took a few minutes to finally look over her travel group in detail. They were mostly in their fifties and sixties. For all of their obvious life accomplishments, they seemed engaging, kind and particularly easy-going. She was well aware that the main reason they were willing to pay such an exorbitant price for the expedition was precisely because of the few days they would spend in actual fieldwork with these archaeologists of unrivaled expertise. The participants looked forward to having scientists share insights into the past lives of the nomadic cultures in the vast region of Mongolia.

Her clients knew that this was an incredible chance to uncover authentic artifacts, something that very few tourists have an opportunity to experience. It was indeed a one-of-a-kind adventure. *But not too adventurous,* she secretly hoped.

Somehow, though, she now knew that these spirited travelers would be willing to endure conditions that were not up to Western standards. They would accept roads that were rough and bumpy, tents that were modest and food that was foreign. They were the adventuresome kind that was interested in authentic experiences.

As Victoria looked over at Mark and Phillip deep in conversation, she smiled. How fortunate she was to have such charismatic and likable scientists in their midst. She could have had a stern, serious professor type as their leader, but here she was with two men who were relaxed and easy going. She hadn't known Dr. Shelby before planning this trip, but her meetings with him were always pleasant. She had heard from a friend who volunteered at the museum that all of the docents had a crush on him. He had an image likened to *Indiana Jones*; he was not too gregarious, a man of few words, yet most approachable. There was a magnetism that drew women to him. It was subtle and hard to explain. He wasn't a lady's man kind of guy, but a gentle and thoughtful man with definite sex appeal.

Then there was Dr. Phillip Doyle. As Victoria looked at him, she could feel a definite spark of interest. It was an instant attraction. She had always loved a British accent. The British actors in movies have been some of her favorites, so when he smiled and welcomed the group at the airport she was instantly charmed. Not only did he have a captivating accent, he was also extremely good looking. Victoria noticed how easily he endeared himself to her travel group. She liked his quick wit and playful nature.

Since their local tour guide Altan spoke little English, Phillip was kind enough to stand in the motor coach and give a little commentary on their way to the hotel. Everyone enjoyed his British expressions as he informed them that they would be "motoring straightaway." En route, he explained that Mongolia, lying between the Soviet Union and the Republic of China, had only gained its independence a few months prior. Peering out of the windows, everyone could easily recognize decades of Russian rule in the stark bunker-like buildings that lined large open squares of concrete. It felt as if little had changed for these people in several decades.

He had been in the country for a while, and Phillip willingly continued to share facts that he had learned about Mongolia. He explained that the country was one of the least densely populated in the world with just a little under three million people, eighty percent of them under the age of 38. There were only five people per square mile.

"It's pretty uninhabitable out there," he said with a smile. "More sheep, camels, horses and wild critters than people in a rugged landscape. But don't worry, we won't encounter any wild animals, only hospitable locals who make their living as herdsmen." He explained that because of climate conditions and the terrain, the dominant economic activities centered around livestock breeding. They would certainly catch a glimpse of herdsmen tending to their livestock on the drive to the archaeological camp the next day.

At that point, Victoria raised her hand and stood to briefly share that she had arranged for the group to visit the home of a nomadic family on their way to the camp. She explained that since animal husbandry was the main livelihood of Mongolians, she thought it might be interesting to see first-hand how locals lived and worked as they raised their horses, camels and goats. "We will have a demonstration of archery and horseback feats, and best of all, we will be invited to actually ride a Mongolian horse if we choose. It's purported that the horse originated in Mongolia."

As Victoria finished, she noticed that Phillip had suddenly taken note that she was the tour leader. A glimmer of curiosity came over his face. He was obviously pleased that this attractive woman was part of the team. When she caught his look of interest, she pressed on to ask a question.

"Have you ever ridden a Mongolian horse, Dr. Doyle?"

He tossed his head back with a hearty laugh and shot a question back to her, "Have you ever seen the size of these stout little Mongolian horses? Being six-foot-four, I'm sure my legs would drag on the ground."

With that, everyone burst into laughter.

"I'm sorry. I didn't get your name," he said when the laughter died down. "Victoria," she said, and thought to herself, *This guy is indeed charming.*

"Well, Victoria, I look forward to seeing you riding one of the Mongolian ponies when we visit the nomadic family. By the way," he continued, "I hear that they milk the mares and ferment it to make a type of alcohol. Now, that might be something I could participate in."

Several of the group members cheerfully agreed, and Victoria playfully promised to see if she could arrange a "tasting."

When they arrived at the hotel, Victoria explained that although it appeared modest, it was the top hotel in Ulaanbaatar. Everyone assured her that it was going to be just fine. She grew a smile of relief knowing that the travel group would be accepting of whatever came their way. There was a noticeable, contagious sense of anticipation growing.

Before departing the motor coach, Phillip took the lead again." Altan will help you check in, and then you can go directly to your rooms to rest and freshen up. You will meet our local host archaeologist, Dr. B., over dinner in the hotel at 7:00 pm He's a most likable man. Not only does he have a worldwide reputation, but he has a very pleasing personality."

"Is his name really Dr. B.?" one of the women in the group inquired.

Phillip laughed. "No, but if you look at the length and spelling of his name in his biography you will know why he cheerfully encourages visitors to simply call him Dr. B. I think he actually likes it. It's similar to the nicknames you give each other in the States, is it not?"

Everyone nodded in agreement and Victoria saw a couple people taking material out of their backpacks in order to read Dr. B.'s bio.

"In fact," Phillip continued, "I have been at international conferences where colleagues come up to him with a warm greeting and introduce him to their fellow colleagues as Dr. B. Am I right, Mark?"

"Yes, you are correct." Mark replied. "You will get an indication of his playful, engaging demeanor tonight. He's quite a character and far too humble for the magnitude of his accomplishments and discoveries."

With everyone checked in, Victoria began up the staircase to her room. She glanced back and noticed that Phillip was watching her ascend the stairs. She would have stayed to visit, but she desperately needed some time alone. After the stressful year she had just gone through, she wondered if it was the right call for her to take on the complexity of escorting this expedition. She felt a bit scattered and exhausted. It was unlike her. She was usually brimming with confidence and positive energy. In her room, she set her alarm clock for an hour later and within minutes she was asleep.

The sound of the alarm woke her. She showered quickly and dressed for dinner. She decided on a vibrant sapphire-blue blouse, a black skirt with a belt that matched her boots and an interesting shawl she had purchased in India. As she went down the hall for dinner, she felt appropriately dressed for the occasion — unassuming but fashionable. The hotel had set up a modest dining hall with round banquet tables. Everyone had already gathered and seated themselves when Victoria arrived. She took an empty chair at one of the tables and joined in the conversation.

When Dr. B. entered the dining hall, he immediately made his way across the room to greet Mark Shelby. They were well-acquainted from various international meetings. She overheard Mark explaining to Dr. B. that while his plans were to stay for a month at the site doing research, he was pleased to be bringing a travel group of twenty-four museum patrons who were interested in archaeology but not experienced in the field. He shared that this group would be at the site for four nights before touring Mongolia. Dr. B. seemed genuinely pleased that the group had come all the way from America to participate in the excavation. He said he looked forward to getting to know them and would be happy to assist wherever needed.

Mark introduced Dr. B. to the group and made reference to the fact that everyone had already met Phillip Doyle. Dr. B. then offered a warmhearted welcome. With a twinkle in his eye, he explained that since his name was difficult to pronounce, "Please just call me Dr. B."

He was a handsome man. He appeared to be in his mid-sixties, although Victoria found it difficult to know for sure. His hair was graying, which gave him a distinguished look. It was well over his ears and Victoria thought that was a statement that he was casual, confident and an individualist. Though short in stature, his physique was becoming with broad shoulders and a flat abdomen. He looked hearty, and she was certain it was due to the exercise he must get combing the mountainsides in search of excavation sites.

Dr. B. apologized for his modest command of the English language, but his humility simply added to his charm. He actually spoke English quite well. He gave a brief overview of the research being done at the site where the group would participate in the field work.

"I'm sure you all know that archaeology is the study of human history and prehistory through the recovery of artifacts. How do you say it — clues? Yes, we are looking for clues into past cultures. Our country is rich in archaeological sites. Primitive man appeared in what is now Mongolia 300,000 to 350,000 years ago. We have sites from many different historical periods of human life, dating from the stone age to 17th and 18th centuries. People are especially interested in the valuable findings discovered from our sites associated with the period of the Mongolian Empire."

Victoria looked around the room and noted that Dr. B. had everyone's full attention. He continued. "When we study the past we have an opportunity to discover fascinating facts about how humans used to live. We are looking for clues as to their diets, what clothing and jewelry they wore, how they cooked their food, and also how they erected shelters. I'm especially interested in the way they commemorated their dead." He chuckled and added, "It's not, of course, because I'm the oldest archaeologist in this room!" Everyone laughed but quickly became quiet at his closing remark, which hit a cord with Victoria and her entire group. With passion in his voice, he said, "I suspect when we discover the past, it helps us better understand our own societies and those of other cultures on our planet."

At dinner, Phillip seated himself across from Victoria. The conversation centered around participants getting to know each other. Everyone shared a little about themselves. One of the group members, Georgiana, asked the question that most interested Victoria.

"Dr. Doyle," she prompted. "Do you have a family back in England?" Victoria held her breath waiting for his answer. She had felt an undeniable attraction from the first moment they met in the airport.

"I was married once," he said. "We were graduate students in archaeology and ready to go out together and discover the greatest treasures the world had to offer. But she immediately got a fabulous opportunity to join a team in Greece for a year while I stayed in the UK to finish my doctorate. Then her next assignment was in Jordan, and I was on my way to Romania. Those are pretty long commutes," he said with reflection in his voice.

"We were young, and it just didn't work out. We have remained friends. She married a good chap, and her sons actually refer to me as their uncle. You can't get much better than that," he said with a satisfied sigh. "My lifestyle wouldn't be an easy one to juggle with marriage and kids. Archaeology is my passion, and we all know that most people don't get to truly follow their passion in life. I travel the world working with the top archaeologists in the field and return to the university when time permits to encourage and teach young people who are the next generation in our quest."

As the evening was coming to a close, it was Mark Shelby's opportunity as the group leader to give a brief description of what was expected of everyone at the excavation site. He shared some important do's and don't's. The protocol was very precise and exacting. If someone was fortunate enough to come upon an artifact, it was critical that the rules were followed. Patience and care were needed in removing the artifact. Equally as important was measuring its proximity to other items that may be buried nearby. Everyone listened intently, and the look on their faces convinced Victoria that they were going to take their four days at the dig site very seriously.

As Mark concluded his remarks, Phillip Doyle stood to propose a toast. "Here's to the success of our excavation and to your very best health. Down the hatch." He raised his glass with the formality of a proper English gentleman, and downed his drink with the gusto of a Brit in a local pub. The group participated with enthusiasm, and Victoria smiled. There was no doubt that his being in Mongolia at the same time as her group was a bonus, not only to the educational aspect, but most definitely to the entertainment.

As everyone departed the room, Victoria came over to talk to Mark. "Dr. Shelby, I am so glad you are the archaeologist leading this expedition. Thank you so much for giving us a briefing regarding our time in camp."

"You are most welcomed. In many respects, you're the one doing all the work. And after offering my services as your group archaeologist for just a few days, I will have the incredible opportunity to stay on and do fieldwork and research for a month. It's something I've been wanting to do for a very long time. I must admit I'm a little jealous that I won't be going on with you to tour the Gobi Desert and especially Karakorum, the former capital of the Mongol Empire. But honestly, Victoria, as enticing as that is, I gladly gave it up to be working with Dr. B. here in Mongolia. And Phillip Doyle is here too. It's like getting a second Ph.D.!"

Phillip came up to join their conversation. Mark said, "I was just about to tell Victoria that I hope she will feel free to join the group in hands-on excavation work at the site."

"I most definitely agree." Phillip said enthusiastically.

"For a city girl who has never been on an archaeological expedition before, I'm fortunate to be going first class under the direction of you two internationally known scientists." Victoria replied. "Thank you for the invitation. I accept".

"We will try not to disappoint you." Dr. Shelby smiled. "By the way, Victoria, just call me Mark. Even though you consider me a top internationally-known scientist, please do drop the title!"

They all laughed. Victoria briefly shared the next day's itinerary, which included local sites and the visit to the herdsman's homestead.

Phillip explained that even though he had been in Mongolia for several weeks, he had not had an opportunity to visit the actual home of a local herdsman and his family. He expressed gratitude for the opportunity to participate and jokingly added, "Besides, I am looking forward to seeing our travel planner ride one of those stout Mongolian horses."

Victoria replied, "Well, I may not have excavated for archaeological artifacts before, but I am actually, familiar with horsemanship, so you may just be surprised. Too bad you are too tall to ride with me," she teased. "If you recall, that was your assessment not mine."

The next morning, everyone was rested from their long flight and ready to explore Ulaanbaatar. Mark and Phillip decided to join the group. The first stop was the National Library of Mongolia. In doing her pre-trip research, Victoria had learned that Mongolia had been able to preserve and store 11th-century Sanskrit manuscripts and priceless books despite all of the wars the country had endured.

Inside the library building, the group was spellbound by the collection on display. *Eight Thousand Verses* was a book written with gold embossing, and *Belief* was embroidered in multicolored threads of cloth. The *Biography of Mother-Dara* was the smallest book in the library. It was composed of twelve pages written on paper less than five by three inches. The museum guide willingly brought out books wrapped in animal hides and bound between boards with ropes. She even showed them a book written with gold powder on black papers.

Kit, a travel group member, stepped forward to ask a question. "I have come to your country especially interested in seeing the book *Jadamba*. I understand it is written with the powders of nine jewels and precious metals, including gold, silver, coral, pearl, turquoise, lazulite, shell, steel and copper. Is it possible that you could please show it to us?"

"I am so sorry, Madame," the museum guide explained. "We are not allowed to handle this book; only our museum director has authority to do so, and he is not available today. It is indeed a beautiful and unique treasure."

Kit looked extremely disappointed, but being the gracious woman she was, she smiled and thanked the guide.

Back in the motor coach, Victoria remembered that her clients Peter and Jenni had a large family, so she announced, "If any of you have children or grand kids who are interested in dinosaurs you will find our next museum of interest. Mongolia's natural history museum is known for its incredible dinosaur exhibit. Don't skip seeing the notable nearly complete skeleton of a late Cretaceous Tarbosaurus and a nest of Protoceratops eggs. In doing my research, I learned that one of the most famous, well-preserved, dinosaur discoveries in the entire world is housed in this museum. The fossil is referred to as the 'Fighting Dinosaurs.' In 1971, a Polish-Mongolian team discovered two dinosaurs captured in a fighting position. They believe that a sudden sand flow may have buried them. The fossils were found perfectly embedded in a white sandstone cliff in the Gobi Desert where we will be visiting later in our tour."

The last stop in their city tour was Victoria's favorite. She was so pleased that Altan's company was able to arrange a private meeting with the Abbot of Mongolia's oldest Buddhist monastery, Ganden Monastery, where over 100 monks still reside. He had also provided an English-speaking guide to assist the group. The guide explained that the word "Ganden" was actually short for the longer version of its name, Gandantegchinlen.

Its first temple was constructed in 1809, but only one wooden pillar now remained. When a new temple was built, the Dalai Lama stayed in residence there in 1904. Sadly, in the 1930s, the Communist government of Mongolia, under the influence of Joseph Stalin, destroyed all but a few monasteries in the country, and killed over 15,000 lamas. The Ganden Monastery survived and reopened in 1944. It was allowed to continue as the country's only functioning Buddhist monastery, and now, as the country gained its independence, restrictions on worship had been lifted. For that reason, the guide explained that the travel group would be able to meet with the Abbot for a blessing.

After quietly and reverently visiting the school where young monks were deep in study, the group entered the main building where the Abbot would receive them. Many candles flickered inside, and several monks, clad in their orange robes, were busy assisting with directions. The Abbot sat on a chair against a wall lined with several vases of flowers. He had a peaceful, loving energy surrounding him. Victoria's group lined up. When it was each's turn, they leaned forward and the Abbot put his hands on the sides of their head and offered a blessing. She felt her emotions come to the surface and tears began to swell in her eyes as she received her blessing. She also noticed that Phillip appeared touched in the same way.

When the group gathered later in the exterior courtyard, one of the men in the group, suggested they take up a collection for a donation to the school. Everyone agreed that it would be a thoughtful gesture, and Ken passed his hat to collect the money, which he presented to one of the monks as their interpreter explained the intent of their gift. The interpreter spoke with the monk for a few minutes. She then came back to the group and relayed his message.

"The monk said to tell you that the Tibetan translation of his monastery is 'Great Place of Complete Joy.' He says you have brought joy to this place with your generous donation, and he hopes that your visit here will bring blessings of joy to your hearts."

Everyone acknowledged the monk's kind words with tender, loving smiles. It truly was a touching moment.

Back on the motor coach the group was noticeably quiet. Victoria could see that they were genuinely touched by their visit to the monastery. As they pulled away onto the modest, semi-paved highway, she allowed everyone time to process for a few minutes in silence before she stood from her seat in the front.

"Unfortunately, the infrastructure is somewhat lacking in this country. The microphone is not working, so I hope you can hear me in the back," she began. As an expressive affirmation came loudly from the last row, and Victoria continued. "My staff and friends say my voice carries miles, maybe even continents!"

Everyone laughed as her engaging humor eased them back into a lighthearted mood.

"I mentioned yesterday that we will be stopping to visit the homestead of a nomadic family on our way to the archaeological site. I understand that in Mongolia it is considered extremely rude and bad luck to ask when we will arrive. However, keeping that in mind, I can give you a hint. Depending on the condition of the jaw-jarring potholes in this road, the drive should take us approximately one hour."

Victoria realized that the group might be wondering why Mark and Phillip were no longer with them in the motor coach. The vehicle shook from side to side as they hit a huge rut in the road, and she found her perfect opening.

"I think I already explained that the infrastructure in this country is modest at best, she said." Everyone smiled and nodded their heads in agreement. "Don't worry," she continued. "If our coach breaks down, we have a backup plan. Dr. B., Mark and Phillip are traveling behind us in a Jeep. I'm not sure if it's out of chivalry or simply their desire to 'talk shop,' but in either case, I am glad they are there!"

As they travelled along, Victoria gave an overview of the country from notes of the extensive research she had done during her months of planning. She invited Altan to contribute his local perceptions, but she knew he did not speak much English. She would be careful not to embarrass him with questions from the group. He was doing an exceptional job fulfilling all of her tour requests and she was most grateful for his service.

"We are going to visit a herder's homestead for several reasons," Victoria explained. "We will learn about how the herdsmen and their families live in this country. Livestock husbandry is key to their economy. We will also visit the inside of a *ger* and become familiar with their everyday clothing. You will notice that both men and women wear a loose, calf-length tunic made of one piece of material called a *deel*. Each ethnic group has its own individual style, distinguished by cut, color and trim.

In case you might be wondering," Victoria continued with a mischievous grin, "both men and women wear trousers or shorts under their deel. I am also told that the Mongolians are known for their gracious hospitality. We will most likely be offered salted yak milk tea, and it is impolite not to accept. This stop will give us an opportunity to see many of their daily activities such as milking the mares, making cheese and roping their horses. You will find the way they rope to be interesting. It is done by lassoing the animals with a noose attached to a long wooden pole. Do keep your cameras ready if some of you wish to accept an offer to ride their Mongolian horses."

Altan, who was sitting next to Victoria's seat, indicated he wanted to add something. Instead of standing before the group, he shared it with Victoria, and she translated it from his charming broken English. "Altan wants you to know that the horses are safe to ride. He says his grandfather often took him on trips to the high country when he was a little boy. It was there that he learned horses have all sorts of characteristics. Some are easy going and some are temperamental, but the ones you will be riding at the homestead are friendly."

She liked Altan's use of the word friendly and included it. She noticed by his smile that he was pleased with her interpretation. "Altan also tells us that it is courteous to ask if you can take a photo of a person in his country. However, he wants you to know that this family is now welcoming visitors, and they are happy to have you take photographs of their family members so please do not feel shy." Altan smiled again at her use of his words.

As the motor coach dodged multiple ruts in the road, Victoria braced herself, held tight to her notes and continued to share information regarding Mongolia. The country is one of the largest and emptiest in the world with ninety percent comprised of desert or steppes, which are the level grassy, unforested plains.

She confirmed that Mongolia had a population of less than three million people and was one of the lowest population densities in the world. There are only five people per square mile. She laughingly noted that she had relatives who lived in Montana, and she had thought that seven people per square mile seems remarkably remote. It was her example of a comparison with Hong Kong that grew gasps from the group, though.

"Hong Kong has over 68,000 people per square mile as the eighth most densely populated country in the world. How many of you have been to Hong Kong?" she inquired. Most of the hands in the coach went up.

"Quite a contrast. Wouldn't you agree?"

Victoria was glad that she had taken the time to research so many facts prior to coming to Mongolia. The group was intelligent and curious. They welcomed information. She pointed out that the ancestors of the herdsman's family they would soon visit were originally nomadic, raising horses, goats, sheep, camels and yaks. For thousands of years, they have moved several times a year in search of pasture for their animals. The lifestyle was a precarious one. The constant migrations often prevented them from transporting reserves of food and necessities.

"Can you imagine not having a permanent home, and just moving your herd from place to place every year?" Victoria asked, engaging her audience. She went on to explain that under Communism, livestock husbandry was based on herders employed by the government who kept collective stock for a monthly salary. They also had quotas that they had to fulfill each year. Now, herdsmen owned their own livestock. With the reduction in the price of meat and milk, nomads have started producing more cashmere wool to subsidize their livelihoods.

"You will also have your first opportunity to see an authentic ger at the homestead. I'm sure you all know that they are likened to the Russian yurt. If you have read books on Genghis Kahn, you may remember references to him as being a leader of people who lived in felt tents called gers. Interestingly, many people in Mongolia still live in gers. However, today, most are made of white canvas, which you will see as a stark contrast to the green pasture lands."

Victoria began to wrap up her information sharing. She said, "Let's give a hand to Altan. His tour company actually constructed a large dining ger at our archaeological camp site."

Everyone clapped loudly to show their appreciation.

"Would you be interested in a few more pieces of information before I sit down and give your ears a rest?" With nods indicating approval, she continued. "I have a suggested list of courtesies that one should adhere to if invited to a local home in Mongolia. One should always say hello when one arrives." Turning to Altan, Victoria asked, "Please, stand up and tell us how to say 'hello' in your language."

He stood proudly and said, "*Sain bainuul.*" Several group members asked him to repeat the words. They hoped to speak them correctly while in his country.

Victoria continued to read from her list. "Always bring a gift." She assured everyone not to worry because she had already packed a gift bag to present on behalf of their travel group. It included children's mittens, some warm scarves, men's and women's socks and some American treats like trail mix packets.

She went on to give other tips. "Always accept food. Take a bite of offered items, even if you are not hungry. Always receive objects with your right hand and keep your whole palm facing up when holding cups. If you are wearing a hat, please leave it on when entering the ger. Men enter to the left and women to the right. Never point at anyone with your index finger; instead, use your whole palm.

In a gentle voice, Victoria added, "I know that is a lot to absorb, but as we all know, a smile goes a long way in a foreign country." Everyone nodded in agreement. "Okay. Here is the last tip, one you will not have to concern yourself with it today." Victoria grinned as she read from her sheet of notes. "Always sleep with your feet pointed toward the door of the ger!"

As she sat down, the group erupted into an enthusiastic applause. Several members shared their appreciation, and Georgiana said, "That was a fabulous overview. What a great introduction to our next stop. We do appreciate knowing the customs of a country."

For the rest of the drive, Victoria talked with Altan about the provisions he had arranged for in camp. Each tent had two cots, air mattresses and a lantern. Instead of sleeping bags they would have a pillow, coverlet and a locally-made, heavy woolen blanket. The cook was already in camp with two helpers, and the local dishes would be prepared carefully. They had factored in extra portions for the graduate students, and the dining ger was equipped with tables and chairs as well as a modest set of dishes, silverware and coffee mugs.

They turned off the main road and approached the herdsman's property. Everyone could see the stark white ger shining in the sunshine. There were several men tending to the livestock, and some were on horseback. Altan helped all of the guests depart from the motor coach onto the uneven grassy ground. Group members smiled as they were greeted by the herdsmen, and a few who were adept at languages even spoke the local greeting, "*Sain bainuu!*"

Everyone began mingling around the property, taking in the demonstrations of archery and the milking of mares. Victoria felt a tap on her shoulder. It was Phillip. "I have heard many glowing compliments from your group members about the fantastic presentation you gave on the way out," he said with an engaging smile. "That was a good idea, Ms. Travel Planner."

"What makes you think I'm a Ms. and not a Mrs.?"

"I inquired last night. But I must admit it did not seem professional to ask whether you were seeing anyone seriously," he said in a joking manner. But it was obvious he was curious.

"Single and not attached," she replied, amused by his forward and engaging personality.

The Mongolians were every bit as hospitable as Victoria had heard they were. As she walked among her group members, she reminded them, "Don't forget you are welcome to enter the ger to see mare's milk being fermented and cheese being made. The women of this family may also invite you to milk a mare if you so choose. And don't miss the opportunity to ride a Mongol horse. They are the native horses of this country, and they say that the breed is largely unchanged since the time of Genghis Khan."

Dr. B. was kind enough to interpret when needed and seemed to rather relish the chance to get out into the countryside with the locals. The most popular experience was riding one of the short, stout Mongol horses with their decorated wooden saddles. Everyone lined up for the experience except Phillip, who had already assured Victoria that, at well over six feet, he would look ridiculous.

Victoria wandered over to three little children who had been curiously watching her every move. They were dressed in warm knitted sweaters, and one was wearing colorful, rubber rain boots. It was easy to tell that they had been playing out of doors as their tiny, round, pink cheeks were splattered with dirt. One little girl picked a flower and shyly brought it over to her. When Victoria bent down to accept the flower, she heard the click of a camera. When she turned she saw that it was Phillip photographing her.

"I would love to have that photo," Victoria said. "Have you changed your mind about riding one of the horses? It certainly seems more inviting than milking a mare, wouldn't you say?"

Phillip emphatically shook his head. "I must decline a horseback ride. I would not want to taint the macho reputation of true cowboys. But I'll have my camera ready when you get in the saddle. I'm anxious to see if you are as spontaneous and adventurous as you appear. Or are you just a big city girl from Boston who doesn't want to get her boots dirty?"

"Are you daring me, Dr. Doyle?"

Victoria walked toward the horses, and a handsome, young herdsman came quickly toward her with reins in hand. She noticed he did not hurry away, but lingered to arrange the reins and be sure she felt comfortable in the saddle.

I'm sure these herdsman don't get to flirt with women every day, she chuckled to herself.

"Wait a minute," she said as she turned toward Phillip. "I need a photo to show my friends back home that I have taken your suggestion to heart." With that, she guided her horse around to face Phillip's camera. She then urged her horse into a slow gallop across the grassland with confidence

When Victoria returned from her ride, everyone was in the ger, presumably watching the cheese making demonstration. As she turned to join them inside, she saw a herdsman arriving with three camels. He was gesturing to her that they were available to ride. These camels were the perfect size for a tall, handsome Englishman! She stepped inside the ger and whispered to Phillip, "I have a surprise for you outside." She motioned with her hand and led him toward the doorway. "Give me your camera," she asked. "Your photo op awaits you."

Phillip could not believe his eyes when he saw the gigantic camels standing outside the ger. He laughingly mounted one of the camels just as all of the group exited the ger.

Victoria had another idea. "Hey, Dr. Shelby," she called to Mark. "Why don't you and Dr. B. get aboard the other two camels so we can have a group photo of our three expedition archaeologists?"

Everyone loved the idea and prodded them on. With encouragement and a playful, willing nature, they obliged the group for the most delightful camera shoot of the day. It generated such a wave of enthusiasm that everyone wanted a photo of themselves on a camel with the ger in the background. The sound of laughter delighted Victoria. Despite her raw emotions, she knew that she was keeping her feelings in check and doing a good job as the escort of the expedition.

Everyone bid the herdsmen and their families goodbye and climbed aboard the motor coach bound for the camp site. Victoria was surprised to see that Phillip had come on board too. She had moved to the back of the coach and he came to where she was sitting and asked if he could join her.

"I decided to let Mark have a little private time with Dr. B.," he said. "And, by the way, thanks for arranging that great opportunity to get to know the local people. You are good at this travel planning business. I was surprised to learn that as the owner of the travel agency you also escorted groups. Do you do this often?"

Victoria explained that it was rare that she takes time to leave the office. With seven agents, a sales team and support staff, the responsibilities usually kept her tied to her desk. On occasion, she explained, she would escort a group she found particularly interesting or a destination that she had been longing to visit.

"I wasn't going to lead this group," she admitted, "but it became such a challenge, and there were so many things that could go wrong, I changed my mind."

"As far as I can see everything is not only going smoothly, but very well. I am most grateful for the blessing from the Abbot today. His peaceful, loving energy touched me."

Phillip turned toward Victoria and noticed that she was looking out the window and seemed almost on the edge of tears. "Are you okay?" he asked in a tender tone.

"Yes, I'm fine, just a little distracted is all," she said with a smile of appreciation for his concern.

When they arrived at camp, the setting sun was starting to cast a soft pink glow over the landscape. Victoria's admiration for Altan was instantly confirmed in spades. There at the modest excavation site was a most beautiful large dining ger, an open white canopy for shade, and brand-new tents scattered in a grassy field nearby. It was the perfect setting for their four nights in camp. Victoria gave everyone their tent assignment. She paused a moment to talk to Kit Dennison.

"Kit," she asked, "is it alright that you and I are tent mates? We don't have enough tents for single occupancy, and I thought we could bunk together?"

"That would be nice." Kit replied. "I look forward to getting to know you better."

How fortunate, Victoria thought, *that Kit would be my tent mate*. She had liked Kit from the first time they met. Kit was a classy, educated woman with a spirited nature and a practical wisdom that made her liked by everyone in the group. In conversation, she gave you her undivided attention. It was as if talking to someone was the most important thing she could imagine herself doing at the moment. Victoria guessed Kit to be in her sixties, but her energy level made her appear as though she was in her forties. She was a beautiful woman with big blue eyes, a blondish braid that cascaded down her back and a most engaging smile.

Victoria announced the dinner hour and went to find Dr. B. with an invitation. "I would like to invite the graduate students to dine with us while we are in camp. I asked the cook to be sure we had extra provisions for them, and it would be our pleasure to get to know them better."

"What a thoughtful gesture," Dr. B. replied. "Our meals here in camp are very modest, so I am certain that they will greatly appreciate your kind invitation. The graduate students speak very little English, but when I told them we had guests in camp from a prestigious museum in America, they were all very enthusiastic. Please call on them for help whenever it is needed."

"Thank you. They have already endeared themselves to several of the group members by carrying their luggage to the tents. I'm sure their expertise in excavation will also be greatly appreciated. I have arranged for beer and wine during dinner. Will that be a problem?" Victoria asked.

He laughed. "Not a problem, unless they drink too much and can't do their work in the morning." He then added, "Seriously, they are very hard-working young men, and it will be nice to see them having some extra enjoyment in camp."

The first evening was everything Victoria could have hoped for. The interior of the huge ger was spectacular with towering wooden poles and lanterns hanging from ropes. The setting was almost out of a movie scene, and it added much to the ambiance. At dinner, Dr. B. welcomed everyone to camp and introduced the graduate students. He thanked Victoria profusely for her gracious gesture to include the graduate students at meals.

"We often have bread and cold meats for our dinner so having this traditional lamb stew with sweet biscuits, paired with wine and beer, makes us feel like we are in Genghis Khan's court!"

Maury, one of the group members, quickly stood to add something to Dr. B.'s comments. Maury was an older gentleman who was well-read, intelligent and witty. "Dr. B.," he began, "your delightful words may be truer than you realize. I have read that Genghis Khan had six wives and over five hundred concubines. Geneticists estimate that 16 million people alive today are probably genetic decedents of Genghis Khan."

Everyone found his comments interesting as well as amusing. There were warmhearted exchanges at dinner. The students learned a few words of English, the archaeologist shared scientific facts, and everyone reminisced about the day's activities. When the evening ended everyone bid each other a good night and headed to their tents filled with anticipation and knowing the next few days would be spent excavating at a noteworthy archaeological site. Victoria did not go directly to her tent. She didn't want to disturb Kit, and she needed some time alone.

A bit later, as Phillip left the dining ger, he saw someone sitting on a rock outcropping a short distance away. The person was sitting all alone in the dark. His first thought was not to intrude, but his caring instincts prompted him to see if someone needed help. When he got closer, he realized it was Victoria. She was slumped over and looking forlorn.

Since she appeared to be an extremely proud person who kept her emotions inside, Phillip intuitively knew that if he asked if she needed help she would be embarrassed and turn him away. He simply walked up quietly and sat next to her on the large, flat rock.

After a few minutes, he spoke. "I'm sorry to see you so sad," was all he said. Victoria simply acknowledged his kindness with a weak smile. At that point, Phillip put his arm around her shoulder. His sweet gesture of comfort brought down the protective barriers she had built to keep her emotions in check. Tears gently started rolling down her cheeks. After a few minutes, he pulled a blue bandana from his pocket. "It's clean. I just put it into my pocket this evening."

She accepted the bandana and began to wipe the tears from her eyes. "I'm sorry to be falling apart like this. It's just that I'm feeling a little overwhelmed right now."

He smiled kindly but did not pull his arm away from her shoulder. He simply sat with Victoria in silence. After a bit, he asked, "Is there anything I can do to help?"

"No. I have had a lot happening lately, and my emotions just seemed to spill over tonight. I didn't want to wake my tent mate, so I came out here."

"Sometimes, shedding a few tears is the best way to get it all out," Phillip said with a gentle smile.

"I do feel better," she replied with a sigh. "I'm sorry, I don't want to burden you with my problems."

"If you want to talk about it, I don't mind. I'm actually a good listener."

"I know it may seem childish and silly, but at the Boston airport on our way here, I bumped into the man who called off our wedding two years ago. I hadn't seen him since then and all of a sudden, there he was in the coffee shop where I was waiting for my flight. Not only him but also his new wife, which somehow upset me. They had been in Boston to celebrate with his parents the news that she is pregnant. They are going to have a baby!"

Victoria told Phillip the entire story. She and Roger had lived together for five years. They got along so well, enjoyed the same food, old movies, travel destinations, and holidays. Everyone said they were the perfect couple. In many ways, they were best friends. They never argued and allowed each other lots of space to pursue their own interests.

It was comfortable, and neither of them made any moves to make changes. But their parents started prodding them towards marriage. The idea wasn't on their agenda because they were doing just fine and saw no reason to alter their lifestyle. But, as months went on, their parents' enthusiasm won out, and they began planning a wedding. A week before the invitations were to be mailed, Roger confessed that although he sincerely cared, he was not deeply in love with her. He felt that one should only enter into marriage with a person they were madly in love with. One who they couldn't imagine not having in their lives forever."

"That must have hurt you terribly," Phillip tenderly said.

"To tell you the truth, as strange as it may seem, he did us both a big favor. My intuition kept screaming at me that Roger was not my forever love, either. We just got swept up in the moment. I know I wouldn't have had the fortitude to call off the wedding. Roger was the brave one. It took courage, but it was the right thing to do."

Victoria admitted to Phillip that it did hurt her feelings at the time, and that she was embarrassed when friends started calling to say how sorry they were to hear the news. But deep inside, she secretly knew it was best for both of them. Thankfully, they parted without bad feelings. Roger took a job in another state. They hadn't seen each other again until the unexpected meeting in the Boston airport on her way to join the travel group for this archaeological expedition.

"I don't know why it upset me so much. I guess it's because he looked so happy. He truly did look like a man in love. I didn't feel jealousy towards his new wife. She seemed like a good person and was most adoring of him. I suppose my feelings of sadness are because the realization it suddenly hit me that I have not been able to find the happiness he is now experiencing."

Victoria paused and took a deep breath before she continued.

"It has been a tough year. My dearest friend was diagnosed with a terminal illness. My mother was in a serious car accident and broke both of her legs. After rehab, she needed assistance, so I moved into our family home to help her in the evenings after work. My father is appreciative, since he was in the midst of a huge international merger of his company. I never told him that my travel agency was in the middle of negotiations to win a lucrative government contract. Somehow, I got through it with the help of my dedicated staff."

"We secured that contract and two more, but it stressed me to my limit. Not to mention that just two months ago my new town home flooded, causing major damage and repairs. I guess seeing Roger again was just the straw that broke the camel's back."

Phillip nodded and she continued, "With so many things happening at once, I've started to feel overwhelmed and a bit shaky. I'm even beginning to doubt myself, wondering if I should have come as the escort for this very important travel group."

"Victoria, I think perhaps you are being too hard on yourself. All of those challenges in just one year would cause anyone emotional stress. Don't forget you are human."

"Allowing myself to be imperfect is not one of my strong suits," she admitted. She was feeling better and more like herself.

"Maybe not, but as one with a scientific bent, I can inform you that all of us carry characteristics of being human. It's not a weakness; it's just part of being alive."

Victoria paused to let his words sink in. He was right. Being vulnerable was not a weakness. Unfortunately, she had been taught that one needed to always be in control, be strong and never let one's guard down. She began to realize she was living much of her life in that exact fashion. Phillip was right. If she could accept her own humanness and not be so hard on herself, then she could be open to more freely to accept it in others and, most importantly, in herself.

"Your words make sense." Victoria smiled. "I truly appreciate your kindness tonight. I don't know how I can ever thank you."

"Then don't try." He smiled as he helped her down from the rock ledge. "Let me walk you back to your tent. Even with all of these bright stars, it is still dark out here."

As they came around the corner of the ger, they saw a most beautiful shooting star streak across the sky. "I suspect that is your little sign that everything is going to be just fine," Phillip said with a gentle smile.

The next morning, breakfast was a hearty fare of dark brown bread, potatoes, tomatoes and eggs. Again, Dr. B. expressed how grateful the graduate students were to be invited to meals. With a twinkle in his eye, he said, "Can't you stay with us for a few extra weeks?"

Victoria felt it a small gesture to improve camp life for the hardworking students. It delighted her watching them interact with the group. She saw that although they did not share the same language everyone had warmed to the students. They were so hospitable, opening doors, lending a hand serving the meals and pouring coffee. *If one can call this bitter, weak drink coffee,* Victoria thought.

She laughed to think how much she missed fresh ground coffee beans from her espresso machine at home. Perhaps she should change to tea, the staple of this country. But who could start a day without coffee, even though it tasted dreadful? Besides, she knew how hard Altan was working to provide their creature comforts. She was definitely not going to complain.

As she departed the dining ger, Victoria was struck by the realization that her participation in an authentic archaeological dig was about to begin. She would never have dreamed that she would look forward to digging in the dirt, but this wasn't just any dirt. This was a site of great significance, and who knew what they might discover.

The sadness of the night before seemed a distant memory. She was feeling better and centered, thanks to the kindness of a man she hardly knew.

Everyone arrived on time at the site with all of their gear: jackets, hats, gloves, and a great deal of anticipation. Dr. B. and Mark reminded the group that their careful attention was needed, and to be sure that they remembered the details of the directions they had received. Patience was of the utmost importance. They were to carefully use their brushes to sift away the dirt a small portion at a time. Members were advised to alert one of the archaeologists or graduate students if they thought they had uncovered something.

As the group began to disperse, Victoria heard a familiar voice. "I hope you slept well." It was Phillip.

"Thank you. I did, and about last night…"

He held up a hand.

"We all have those times in our lives. I'm just glad I was there to listen. I'm especially pleased to see you feeling better today."

"I do feel more like myself. In fact, I'm feeling very positive and full of energy. I've never done this before, and I'm excited to get started."

"I'm glad to hear that joyful enthusiasm back in your voice. We can use some extra hands to help us make progress before we close up for the season. Here is an extra pair of smaller gloves that I found in the Jeep. They might come in handy. And you won't be needing that jacket now that the sun has come out. Her's a brush and a piece of canvas to kneel on while you work."

Victoria was surprised at the sense of enthusiasm she felt at being invited to be a member of the team. There were a couple of women in her group who had participated in excavations before, and she sought them out. She positioned herself between Judy and Mary for guidance.

After a few hours of kneeling on an old piece of canvas and sifting away dirt, Victoria came to the conclusion that the profession of archaeology was not an easy one. Carefully sifting through the earth for clues from the past was tedious, back-breaking work. But she looked around and saw that her group members were not in the least bit dissuaded. Kit was digging next to Dr. B., who was smiling and explaining every detail.

Why not? Victoria thought to herself. Kit had those beautiful blue eyes, which she focused on Dr. B. as he spoke. And Mark was being very attentive to the group; moving about, answering questions and giving encouragement.

The afternoon sun got hotter, and Victoria shed her safari shirt. She was grateful that she had thought to dress in layers. After putting sunscreen on her bare shoulders and chest, she could now work in her tank top.

After a bit, Victoria got a strange sense that she was being watched. As she was pondering the cause of her uncomfortable feeling, she heard a familiar voice whisper something over her shoulder. It was Phillip. "You are driving the graduate students crazy," he said. "These young blokes rarely see an attractive woman out here and especially one bending over in a red, lacy bra."

The graduate students had moved to a section directly across from her.

Victoria looked up in horror and embarrassment! She had not considered what she might reveal while kneeling in the loose tank top she was wearing. She decided to play it cool. She jumped up and went for a drink of water in the dining ger. When she looked back, the graduate students were laughing, not so much at her personally, but at her reaction to finding out that she had been putting on quite a show for young men who rarely had tourist women in camp.

Victoria's cheeks were bright red. How could she have not noticed what position she was in as she dug in the dirt? *For heaven's sake,* she thought to herself, *this is a serious scientific endeavor.* She vowed to be more careful when she chose her attire the next day.

By lunch, Victoria had regained her composure, and she stood to make an announcement. "I have a surprise. Today is the wedding anniversary of our friends Jim and Joanne. To help them celebrate we are going to have a special Mongolian barbecue dinner and a dance right here in our ger. The graduate students have graciously loaned me their boom box for the music tapes I brought from home. They are old fashioned love songs."

Everyone clapped and Victoria continued. "Peter has agreed to be our master of ceremony and DJ for the evening. I apologize that we were not able to get French Champagne shipped in, but we still have a good supply of wine and beer. So, be sure to save a little energy for our festivities tonight. We will move our dinner hour back to 8:00 pm with dancing to follow."

As everyone headed for their tents to gather their gear for the afternoon, Phillip came over to Victoria with an invitation.

"How about coming with me today?" he said. "I'm driving back to Ulaanbaatar to pick up Dr. B.'s niece so Dr. B. can stay in camp with the others. He's become noticeably committed to this travel group, and I suspect it's because of your pretty, blue-eyed tent mate's attention. The fact that she is so interested in his work is flattering, and I'm sure it added to his request that he stay in camp, and I pick up Chimeg. One of the graduate students could pick her up, but I need to make a couple of calls in town anyway. I thought you might enjoy a little break from your responsibilities."

The idea of skipping the rest of a day of work under the relentless beating sun was inviting. Mark would only be with the group for a few more days, so she decided to accept Phillip's invitation. "I'd love to go with you."

"Chimeg is who is also an archaeologist," Phillp said. "She couldn't join us earlier because she was teaching classes at the university. She will be in camp for the rest of the summer season. It will be great to have her here with your group because she speaks fluent English. After earning her bachelor's and master's degrees in New York City, she has returned to work with her uncle as she finishes her doctorate degree. Chimeg is extremely intelligent as well as great person. You'll like her."

"She sounds interesting. I look forward to meeting her."

"Great. I was hoping your answer would be "yes." We'll be back in time for dinner and your anniversary gathering — a very clever and thoughtful gesture on your part. Can you image the photos Jim and Joanne will have to share with their family and friends? They won't believe they were dancing on the dirt floor of a ger in Mongolia on their anniversary."

"Let me take a minute to check with Mark to see if he wouldn't mind taking responsibility of our group in case there was an emergency in my absence. Since there is an extra Jeep in camp it should be fine."

Victoria explained the situation to Mark, who said he was most happy to assist. "After all," he reminded her, "I am grateful that you will be taking the group for two weeks without me. I'm learning so much from Dr. B. He has a strong feeling that this could be the site of a tomb that he has been hoping to uncover for a couple of years. That would make my stay even more remarkable. I really appreciate this opportunity. You have made that happen. Thank you."

Victoria smiled. She liked Mark. His relaxed nature, engaging smile and passion for his field made him endearing.

"Thanks for holding down the fort while we pick up Chimeg in town," she said with a wave.

"Who is Chimeg?" Mark asked.

"Dr. B.'s niece, an American-educated and accomplished archaeologist who is coming to join you in camp for the rest of the season," Victoria replied.

"I like the sounds of that." Mark gave her an engaging grin.

Victoria stopped by her tent to freshen up a bit. As she changed into a clean plaid shirt, she smiled. She was still wearing the infamous red bra that had caused such a stir at the excavation site. She laughed to think that she had come on expedition to a rugged wild part of the world and had not brought sensible underwear to match the occasion!

Phillip was in the Jeep and ready to go. Victoria noticed the wet curls on the back of his neck. "I had the time to take a quick shower. The water in our portable outdoor shower was warm today. It felt great. I never thought I would be so grateful that the sun shines here 250 days out of the year." Phillip commented.

"Is that an actual fact?" Victoria asked.

"It is. Mongolia only gets 14.9 inches of rain per year." Phillip shifted into gear and settled back into his seat. Victoria took a deep breath and for a few minutes she relished the silence. No responsibilities, no decisions to make, and in a way, not a care in the world. It felt good. She looked over at Phillip, who gave her a gentle smile as if he had read her mind and was glad she could enjoy a few peaceful moments.

Victoria broke the silence. "Tell me more about yourself."

She learned that his father was Irish, hence his playful sense of humor. His mother was English. They met as college students on a holiday, and after getting married, his mother encouraged his father to make London their home. He had an older brother and younger sister, which he said gave him the reputation of being the unruly, middle kid in the family. He told her funny stories about his big extended family and all of the crazy reunions they held throughout the years.

As they drove on, they talked more about themselves, their growing up years, places they had lived and silly stories about their escapades in college.

At that point, Phillip's demeanor became more serious. "I'm glad you felt comfortable sharing your feelings last night."

"I was going to apologize this morning," Victoria replied, "but I got to thinking about your comments on being human. It's true that no one is perfect and if we can accept our shadow sides, along with our positive traits, life might be an easier journey."

Phillip was touched that she had taken his comments to heart.

"I actually think you have far more positive traits than negative ones. You are not only a most attractive woman, you're smart, and you seem to have an abundance of compassion, kindness and good judgement. I especially like your sense of humor and your positive energy."

As he said this, they approached the crest of a steep hill. "I want to show you what I personally find extremely meaningful here in Mongolia."

Victoria could not imagine what it could be in such a remote, uninhabited location, but she sensed that it was important to Phillip, and she waited patiently because he wanted to share it with her. He turned onto a modest country road. It got narrower and more rutted as they climbed in altitude. They came around a sharp turn, and there was something most unusual alongside the road. It was an ancient spiritual mound made of stones, earth, and branches. Scattered on it were various objects—bottles, coins, blue scarves and small pieces of cheese.

"What is it?" she whispered in reverence.

"It is called an *ovoo*," he explained. "It's a shrine that local families or travelers erected to show gratitude, respect and to honor the spirits."

"Long ago," Phillip continued, "the people of this region believed in a god that was somewhat like a Hindu god or a Buddhist spiritual entity. This god presided over the many spirits of the trees, rocks, rivers, storms, and all kinds of natural phenomena. The prehistoric peoples not only believed in the countless spirits but also in the ability of shamans to contact them and seek their healing powers. The reason these shrines are often found in higher mountainous regions is because it was believed that higher places were closer to the gods."

"From here, protection and good fortune would be more readily granted. This one is a perfect example because it has several blue scarves hanging on it. The scarves are known as *khadag*. They are the traditional ceremonial scarf of Mongolia, and their blue color represents the sky. Notice how they flutter in the breeze. It is said that when the wind blows them, it creates energy to be used by the traveler."

Victoria was spellbound. It was like no other shrine she had ever seen. She had seen offerings at various shrines around the world, but this setting seemed so private, sacred and safeguarded in the high mountains. Much different, she remembered, than shrines in India where thousands of people gather to worship.

Phillip continued, "The people here still believe in spirits. In many ways this shrine is a place to ask for safety on one's journey. I have some coins in my backpack. Would you like to place one on the mound? You can simply make an intention, or you can ask for healing and good fortune. These shrines are a way of communicating with a higher power. It can be anyone of your choosing."

"I would love to get out of the Jeep and place a coin on the shrine. In fact may I have more than one?" Victoria was visibly moved. He did not know if she would embrace the experience, but he could easily sense that it was meaningful for her. They got out of the Jeep, and Phillip explained that they were to circle the shrine three times in a clockwise direction before leaving their offering. As they walked silently around the shrine, Victoria thought about the people for whom she wished safety and good fortune; she included her parents, her brother, and her dear friend who was ill. She sent an intention for peace and the elimination of hunger around the world. As she bent down to place her coins on the shrine she was overwhelmed by emotions, thinking of the many women, who, just like her, had left their intentions at this very spot.

Phillip stood quietly watching Victoria. He instinctively knew that stopping at the shrine was more relevant for her than he could have ever imagined. He was touched to see this spiritual side of her. She felt comfortable communicating with those from the beyond. She believed, and her open, accepting nature was a beautiful trait to him. As Victoria turned to walk back to the Jeep, she instinctively put her arm around Phillip's waist. He responded in kind to let her know he felt the intimacy too.

At the Jeep she turned to him, "This has been such a treasured gift. You have no idea what it means to me to have had a chance to see this spiritual mound."

As Phillip reached to open the Jeep door they were standing very close. Victoria could not hold back the impulse to kiss him. There was something so meaningful in their recent experiences that it just came out of nowhere. It seemed so right. As she leaned forward to kiss him, she had no assurance that he would return her kiss, but she was willing to be honest in wanting to show her affection. Affection for the man she felt a spark of attraction for when they first met, affection for the man she playfully teased at the herdsman's homestead, affection for the kind loving man who held her in her tearful moments, and affection for the man with whom she felt a strong, growing connection. Phillip did not pull away from her kiss. It felt like a magical moment, so natural and trusting on one hand, and so romantically passionate on the other.

When they arrived at the University, Phillip went in to make a few calls and find Chimeg. "Are you comfortable waiting here in the Jeep?" he asked. Victoria assured him that she was and told him to take all of the time he needed. As she waited in the Jeep she noticed a vendor selling scarves on the corner. She immediately saw the blue color. They were ceremonial scarves like the ones that had been placed on the spiritual mound. Victoria was out of the Jeep in a flash. She was grateful that she always carried a small amount of cash when she traveled. Fortunately, the woman was willing to accept American dollars. It would be a surprise for Phillip. It would be her goodbye gift.

When Phillip and Chimeg returned to the Jeep, Victoria could not believe her eyes. Chimeg was one of the most stunningly beautiful women she had seen in a long time. Her long dark hair was piled in an informal knot, but it still shone like silk. Her complexion was flawless with a creamy pinkish tint on her high cheekbones. Her figure was like a miniature fashion doll. At 5'4", she was well endowed with a tiny waist and the most perfect proportions. She was wearing a tight-fitting silk vest embroidered with a subtle but colorful pattern and tan colored jeans that accentuated her petite frame. Her eyes were sparkling as she approached the Jeep with an open, engaging smile.

"Hello, I'm Chimeg. And you must be Victoria. Phillip tells me you are the travel planner in camp. It is so nice to meet you." She slid into the back seat while Phillip put her bag into the Jeep.

"It's nice to meet you too," Victoria replied. "I understand that you studied in New York City. I would have been your neighbor to the north. I'm from Boston."

"I loved visiting Boston. It is so historic, and your research universities are fabulous, not to mention that wonderful soup. Is it called clam chowder? I could have eaten it at every meal," Chimeg said enthusiastically.

Victoria liked Chimeg immediately. Her personality was vivacious and energetic. Victoria wondered if Chimeg had any idea of how breathtakingly beautiful she was. If so, she certainly did not show it. There was something natural and lovely about her. She had a striking elegance that would definitely turn heads any time she walked into a room. And Phillip was right, she spoke flawless English, which would delight her travel group. By now, Phillip was at the wheel again. Victoria noticed that he seemed, all of a sudden somewhat quiet, different than earlier in the day.

As they drove back, Chimeg directed a question to Phillip. "How's it going in camp? My uncle tells me that the guests are delightful, and he is enjoying their company and especially the food!"

"Yes, it is going well. The travel guests are not experienced in fieldwork, but they are intelligent and interested in the excavations."

"There is an archaeologist from the United States leading the group right?" Chimeg inquired. "My uncle knows him from international conferences, and he likes him."

Phillip looked toward Victoria to answer Chimeg's question.

"Yes, his name is Dr. Mark Shelby. He is great guy, and I'm sure you will enjoy working with him. He will be staying on at camp as I take the group touring your country and on to Xian, China."

Chimeg expressed enthusiasm in hearing that the group would be going to Xian. "You will find the Terra-cotta Warrior exhibit fascinating. Can you believe that there are so many Terra-cotta Warriors still buried at the site? When the warriors are removed from the earth, the colors quickly fade so the excavations are slowed until they can determine a way to preserve the pigment."

"I didn't know that," Victoria replied. "It seems that Xian will be the perfect finalé for our archaeological expedition." Chimeg and Phillip nodded in agreement.

"How long will Dr. Shelby be staying here in Mongolia?" Chimeg asked.

Phillip explained that Mark would be staying for a month. They would overlap for a few weeks before he returned to London. "My university classes just ended," she continued. "I'll be staying in camp for the rest of the season. I'm looking forward to working with both of you."

Victoria tried not to smile noticeably as she thought ahead to Mark's facial expression when he met Chimeg. "I'm sure Dr. Shelby is looking forward to getting to know you too," was all she could say. Chimeg seemed pleased with her comment. Victoria continued, "We are having a little party in camp tonight, and I hope you will join us. One of the couples in our group is celebrating their wedding anniversary, and we are making it a festive occasion. We have actually planned a dinner dance in our ger, and our cook is making a special Mongolian barbecue."

"I would be delighted to participate. Thank you for including me. My uncle tells me that you have invited the students to join you for all of your meals and they are thrilled. Our camp food can be quite modest and bland. Wouldn't you agree, Phillip?"

"Absolutely. Can you imagine, we also have beer and wine at dinner."

"My uncle already told me, and he loves it. Victoria, that was so nice of you to include the students. They will most definitely miss you when you depart."

Victoria found Chimeg easy to converse with, and her lighthearted, breezy manner was enjoyable. Unfortunately, she noticed that Phillip continued to be distant for some reason. She could not understand why, but it was most noticeable. Perhaps he had received bad news during his phone calls, but her intuition prompted her to think that it had something to do with their kiss that afternoon at the spirit mound. Putting her thoughts aside, the drive back to camp seemed to go by quickly. Chimeg told Victoria about her time in New York, and confided that although she loved it in the United States, Mongolia was her home and where her heart belonged. For that reason, she came back to teach at the university, and do field research with her uncle as she completed her doctorate degree. She wanted to know more about Mark. Victoria explained that Mark was the Dean in the university's archaeology department, and he consulted with the museum in which the travel group of patrons was affiliated. He was respected and was an accomplished, published scientist. "You'll easily see how passionate he is about your field of archaeology as you spend time with him."

As their Jeep pulled into camp, several of the group members came to announce that they had uncovered several meaningful artifacts, and Dr. B. believed they were reaching the entry chamber of the tomb. It was that moment Mark walked up to the Jeep. He directed his comments to Phillip who was still behind the wheel. "I think you'll be amazed at the artifacts we uncovered this afternoon."

As Phillip climbed out of the Jeep so did Victoria and Chimeg. Victoria could not help but notice the look on Mark's face when he first saw Chimeg. He kept his swagger, but she saw his eyes widen and a smile come across his lips.

"Mark come meet Chimeg," Phillip said as he made an introduction.

Chimeg walked directly to Mark, held out her hand to shake his and said, "Hello, Dr. Shelby. I'm so happy to meet you. I understand you have been doing extensive work in South America, and I am anxious to learn more about your research."

"It is very nice to meet you as well," Mark replied. "Your uncle tells me that you will easily surpass his achievements before you reach his age. I understand you studied in the United States. I admire you for coming back to your country to assist on these most important excavations."

"Thank you. You are most kind, but I'm sure you realize my uncle is undeniably biased."

"I've never heard him utter a word that was not true," Mark shot back in a most charming fashion. "And, by the way, since we will be working closely together, please call me Mark."

"Thank you. I will," Chimeg responded with one of her charming and most engaging smiles. "But right now, I am off to find my uncle. In addition to being my mentor, and apparently an avid supporter as well, he is my dearest relative, and I want to give him a great, big hug." Everyone laughed as Chimeg so naturally radiated a playful nature.

Victoria lingered for a few minutes thinking Phillip might acknowledge their special time at the spirit mound, and the romantic kiss they had shared, but he just gave a casual wave and walked away. There was definitely a cool distance between them now. She wasn't sure why, but she found herself disappointed. As Victoria headed to her tent to drop off her bag, she started to ponder what might have gone wrong. She now regretted initiating the kiss, although she knew he returned it. She thought, maybe he just returned her kiss because he felt her ego was fragile due to the breakup with Roger. He may have wanted her to believe she was still attractive to men. Or, maybe the kiss just did not resonate with him as much as it did with her. Sadly, her last consideration was the most painful of all. Perhaps, he had someone special back home in London. She had never asked him if he was currently seeing anyone.

It was time to get ready for the party. Stepping into the dining ger, Victoria was amazed. It was transformed into a lively decorative space. Her group members, Sue and Carol, were finishing wrapping the poles of the ger with fresh green branches and bits of fabric from ribbons that people had tied onto their suitcases for identification. "Well, I am almost embarrassed to think that the top interior decorator in Boston is now reduced to working with such meager decorations," Victoria said to Sue. "You and Carol have done a fabulous job of creating a most festive atmosphere. I know Jim and Joanne will appreciate it."

"We enjoyed doing it. The graduate students moved the tables to create a space for our dance floor, but we are sorry to admit that we were not able to get it waxed and polished in time," Carol teased. "However, our husbands admitted that dancing on a dirt floor, in a ger was going to be an unforgettable experience."

"And that Mongolian barbecue smells mighty good," Victoria said. "I had better go dress into something more suitable. Be sure to introduce yourself to Chimeg. We just picked her up in Ulaanbaatar. She is Dr. B.'s niece and an accomplished archaeologist in her own right. Plus, she speaks fluent English. And those are definitely not her only appealing traits. Chimeg is an absolutely stunning woman. You'll find her as beautiful inside as she is on the outside."

Back in her tent, Victoria decided to wear black jeans, a long-sleeved copper-colored top and a fringed, black suede wrap. She had checked on the preparations for the celebration, and everything was in order. She was pleased that her sophisticated travelers had embraced the evening's festivities with such enthusiasm. The fact that they actually unearthed some significant artifacts that afternoon undoubtedly added to the high spirits which were pervasive everywhere. When Victoria entered the ger for dinner she scanned the room to see where Phillip was sitting, but he was nowhere in sight. She saw Dr. B. and Kit seated with Chimeg and others, and also a table where Maury, Georgiana and Judy were talking science with Mark. The guests of honor were at a central table that was decorated with items that Sue and Carol had gathered from the group. A colorful scarf as the table runner and some meager flowers from the surrounding landscape completed the setting.

Victoria sat at the table with Kit, Dr. B. and Chimeg. The discussion centered on the political climate of Mongolia's neighboring countries. She noticed that Phillip came in minutes before dinner was served and sat at a table with Mark and others. He was facing her, but he never made eye contact. As the dinner ended their group member, Peter stood to start his duties as MC for the evening. He asked everyone to raise a toast to congratulate Jim and Joanne. He then acknowledged Chimeg as being the newest member to join camp and also thanked Dr. B., Mark and the graduate students for their guidance in helping everyone participate in a most exciting afternoon of discoveries. Everyone cheered and clapped to show their appreciation. Upon Victoria's request, he also invited the cook and kitchen crew to come out for a bow. It was obvious the applause pleased them very much.

Peter announced that the anniversary couple would share the first dance. The boom box was turned up full volume as the "Anniversary Waltz" was played. It was truly a touching moment with everyone snapping photos of Joanne and Jim dancing on the dirt floor of a ger in Mongolia. When it was time to open the dance floor to the group, Victoria smiled to see Mark walk over and invite Chimeg to dance before anyone else had an opportunity to ask her. The graduate students thought it was so much fun to be invited to dance by the women in the group, and they blushed as they put in great effort to not step on their toes. Victoria was asked to dance by a couple of the graduate students. She was the one blushing as she danced with them fearing they might be wondering if she was wearing her red lace bra. Looking around the room, she noticed that Phillip had slipped away. Sadness and disappointment flooded her thoughts as she had hoped that they would enjoy the evening together. With the emotional experience they had shared at the spirit mound, she truly felt they were beginning to create a romantic connection. As the day's light faded, the lanterns began to cast a warm dim glow in the ger. A few of the group members had called it a night, but most were still dancing to the old tunes of the past. Victoria delighted in watching the exchange between Dr. B. and Kit. He had not danced until she came across the room and prodded him onto the dance floor. Actually, Victoria was impressed to see that he had great rhythm. As she stood watching, Victoria felt a hand around her waist. It was Phillip gently steering her onto the dance floor. To the music, of a beautiful slow song, he held her very close without speaking.

As the song ended, she started to talk when he said, "I just want to hold you and dance. I promise I will explain everything later. Is that alright with you?"

She nodded as they continued. At 5'9", Victoria was a perfect dance partner to Phillip. She had her head on his shoulder and they seemed to be dancing as one entity, very close and ever so romantically. When Peter, their MC, announced the last song, they continued to dance, and Victoria noticed that Phillip's demeanor was more like the man she had been with earlier that afternoon. She was confused by his change of heart, but he had promised that he would explain later. She wasn't going to diminish the romance of the last dance with worry. She was surprised when he bent down and discretely kissed her on the neck. "Let's get a couple of mugs of wine." Phillip said as the dance was over. "I know a great rock where we can sit and talk."

After getting settled on their old familiar rock ledge, Victoria said, "I'm really sorry, I was so forward this afternoon. I don't know what came over me. Maybe it was the touching experience at the spiritual mound."

"Please, don't apologize," Phillip began. "Your kiss was wonderful. It made me realize how truly special you are, and how much stronger my feelings for you are growing. There is something important I want to share with you. I pulled away tonight because I just don't want to risk having you hurt again. Ever since you confided in me regarding your engagement breakup, it has haunted me. If it did not work out between us, I would be adding to your pain again."

"It is so very thoughtful of you to be concerned for my feelings," Victoria replied. "It makes me see the depth of your integrity. However, Roger and my relationship was more of a deep friendship. The pain I felt in seeing him again was an unmet longing to find that kind of love for myself. I sincerely appreciated his bravery in setting us both free to find the person destined for us."

"Yes, I do understand, but let me explain why I am so hesitant and unsure of going forward into a relationship with you. Believe me when I say that I wish I could cast my apprehension and fears to the wind. I feel something special for you, but how can we be sure it will last?" Phillip seemed so sincere in wanting her to know how he felt.

Victoria could hear the genuine concern in his voice, but she still did not understand what was troubling him. What could be making him so leery of giving their relationship a try? She decided to remain silent so he could fully express his feelings.

Phillip went on, "I have had two very difficult breakups in the last few years. They really shook me to the core because I felt so badly that I had hurt someone. It's not like me. I've always thought of myself as a compassionate, good man. It's hard to explain, but let me try to clarify it by first relating what it's like to be away on a lengthy, archaeological excavation team assignment.

Imagine a young, healthy group of professional men and women being thrown together onto a deserted island for eight to ten months. The experience takes on a life of its own. Since everyone works closely together, relationships begin to form rather quickly. I guess you could say people begin pairing up. Before you know it, you find yourself moving into each other's tent. Then, within weeks, you are in an exclusive, committed relationship. There is also a lot of lovemaking going on in camp, which I have often thought might have created somewhat of a false sense of intimacy. As the months pass, everyone settles into a comfortable rhythm. In the evenings, we couples would play games, drink beer and share stories. There wasn't a lot of outside contact on these remote sites, so we became an island unto ourselves."

Victoria could tell that Phillip really wanted her to fully understand where his hesitancy was coming from, so she listened carefully and gave him her full attention.

"I met Ingrid on an eight-month international project in Egypt. She was pretty, athletic and several years younger. We shared a strong commitment to the project and the thrill of discovery. When the contract ended, Ingrid said she was in love with me and decided not to go back to Finland. Even though I knew I did not feel as strongly about her as she claimed to feel about me, moving into my flat together seemed like a natural transition. From the start, my inner voice kept telling me that it wasn't a good idea, but Ingrid was so persuasive and excited about our being together.

"I thought there would be time to see if our relationship would deepen. Unfortunately, our differences quickly became apparent. I was teaching full time at the university. She could not find a job in our field, so accepted a lower-level position in an advertising firm. She was bored, and I was stressed. Sadly, we drifted apart. To the very end, she was convinced that she was truly in love with me. She cried and cried when I finally made the move to end the relationship. Ingrid returned to Finland heartbroken. I felt so badly that I had hurt her that I actually started questioning my self-worth as a compassionate and unselfish person. I did not date for an entire year because I couldn't bear the thought that I might hurt someone again. I started doubting my judgement when it came to relationships."

Victoria remained silent as he continued. "To make this long story short, it happened again two years later when I accepted a position to manage an excavation project in Italy. I meet Elaina and again things began moving quickly. When the assignment was over, I insisted we take our time, live separately and see if we were truly meant for each other. Again, I heard my inner cautionary voice, but I did not listen to it. When Elaina lost the lease on her flat, she asked to temporarily move in with me. Within a few months, she wanted to get married and start a family."

"I remember the night I had to tell her I couldn't marry her. It seems like it was yesterday, even though it was eighteen months ago. She was devastated. Elaina kept calling me and pleading to give our relationship another try, but I knew I was not deeply in love with her. Elaina was a very caring and nice person. Many men would have been thrilled to ask her to marry them. I was sorry, but it could not be me. She married within six months. Soon afterwards, there were various phone calls and pleas telling me of her failing marriage, and asking if we could reunite. I had to explain to her that although I was sincerely sorry to hear of her unhappiness, my feelings had not changed."

Phillip was now looking into her eyes. "Victoria, these times were gut wrenching for me. The guilt almost destroyed me. My friends kept assuring me that I wasn't an awful person. They said if I was unfair or insensitive, I would not have felt so badly about hurting someone. In time, learning to accept my part in not setting stronger boundaries, I forgave myself, accepting that everyone is human. It made me painfully aware that when relationships don't work out, it is devastating for the one who feels rejected. In reality, also for the one making the decision to end it."

Victoria sensed that Phillip was being completely honest and sincere. No wonder he was worried about getting to know her on this brief four-day encounter in Mongolia. She was torn because she felt they had a genuine connection that was worth pursuing. But, on the other hand, she did not want him to compromise what he thought was right for himself.

Gently, she replied, "Hearing the pain in your voice makes me realize how difficult it was for you. I only wish that Ingrid and Elaina felt about you as I did about Roger. I can see why your breakups were so agonizing. These women believed they loved you and you knew that you were not in love with them. I now understand. Our intuitions and our hearts don't lie. I admire you for not misleading these women. As difficult as it was, you showed integrity in not going forward."

Phillip interrupted her, "Thank you for your understanding, but I have more to say. Although I wanted you to know why I am leery of relationships, I also want you to know why I came back tonight. When I went to my tent I realized that meeting you was extremely magical. I felt it when we met at the airport and somehow cannot ignore the magnetic pull I feel towards you. Even though I'm in a quandary, I can't imagine never seeing you again. Perhaps it is destiny that we met this week in Mongolia. All I know for sure is this, I fear that if I walk away from getting to know you, I will forever regret it."

Victoria took a few minutes to gather her thoughts. She knew the only thing to do was to express her feelings in total honesty. If admitting that she also had feelings for him caused him to retreat, there was nothing she could do about it. She would risk telling him how she felt. She also did not want to live with regret. In a gentle voice, she began, "Phillip, I want you to know I feel exactly as you do. I also felt an undeniable connection when we met, and it has not lessened in these past three days. If anything, it has grown stronger with your compassion during my melt down, your spiritual moments with me at the mound and our sweet first kiss. You might not know this about me, but intimacy is scary for me. I have a tendency to run from it. I suppose it is one of my shadow sides." She paused with a tender smile. "But this time, I don't want to run. I also cannot imagine walking away from a chance to see if our meeting and attraction could develop into something much more. It is true that we live on different continents, but we live on the same planet. We are smart, mature people, we should be able to find a way forward. Whatever the future holds, you and I can work it out together if we promise to keep our communications clear and our hearts open to the possibilities. There is no way of knowing if it would develop into a lasting love. Perhaps, it just requires our gathering up the courage to give it a try. I'm willing, if you are."

Phillip reached over and gave her the most beautiful kiss, and she definitely kissed him in return. "I would also very much like to give it a try," he whispered.

The next morning, as the sun started to cast beams of light into her tent, Victoria slowly opened her eyes. She had slept peacefully knowing that she and Phillip had now made a commitment to pursue a relationship. As she turned over, she saw that Kit was already awake and reading a book.

Kit greeted her with a smile. " Good morning. You certainly seemed to be having a good time dancing with that good-looking British archaeologist last night."

Victoria loved Kit's charming, open nature. You never needed to guess what she was thinking. "I certainly did, and I noticed that you even got Dr. B. out onto the dance floor. I'm not sure why I initially thought differently, but he is actually a very good dancer."

"Yes, I am discovering that Batu has many wonderful hidden talents. He is an interesting man," Kit replied.

"Is that Dr. B.'s first name?" Victoria was extremely animated, almost as if she had discovered some hidden secret. "I have never heard it before, so it took me off guard."

"Yes, I supposes he is a bit of a private person, but that is his first name. It means strong, so it is a good name for him."

As the two women continued to visit about various aspects of the evening Victoria paused to ask Kit a more serious question. "Kit, do you have a few minutes to talk with me? You seem like a wise person, and I could sure use a little bit of advice. I hope I'm not overstepping any boundaries as the tour leader, but I need someone to talk to right now."

Kit responded, "Heavens, no, you are not overstepping any boundaries. I'm not sure if I have any great wisdom to share, but my mother always said that a lot can be learned by hearing ourselves speak out loud."

"Before we start our talk, can I go over to the ger and get us both a cup of coffee? If that is what we can call the bitter concoction they serve in this country." Victoria laughed.

"I like the idea of visiting over coffee," Kit replied. "But just bring us two cups of hot water. I have some packets of good, Italian roast, instant coffee in my luggage."

"You have already made my day!" Victoria exclaimed as she headed out of the tent. As they settled in, Victoria told Kit about her feelings for Phillip and his admittance that he felt the same about her. She explained that she sensed an undeniable attraction the minute they had met. Kit listened to her explanation of how comforting Phillip was when she shared her past hurts, and how admirable it was that he did not want to hurt her if things did not work out between them. "Do you think it could work out between us?" Victoria asked. "I know we have just met, and we live continents apart.

However, we both feel that maybe there is some destiny at play in our meeting."

Kit acknowledged her question with a very tender expression that seemed to indicate she knew what Victoria was going through because, perhaps, she had also been there at some point in her life. "Victoria there are no guarantees in life, and there certainly are no guarantees in love. But I do believe if two people feel that magical pull towards each other, it may be a sign from the universe that should not be ignored. It is, in many ways, a very precious gift. Do you know how many people never get to experience it? If real, it needs time to nurture and grow."

Victoria was listening intently to every word as Kit continued. "It's interesting to think about the wide spectrum that exists in the realm of relationships. You know, after the war many soldiers came home and married the woman who wrote them letters while they were gone. Maybe, they were girlfriends, but often they were a neighbor, their sister's best friend or a volunteer sending supportive mail to the troops. These young men and women entered into a lifetime commitment with someone they hardly knew. And guess what, many of these marriages were not only successful but extremely happy. I suspect it was attributed to their unquestioned commitment, and to their desire to start families, build careers and stayed married to the end. I believe that there are many possibilities when it comes to relationships. Have you ever heard that commonly used phrase, 'some for a reason, some for a season, and some for a lifetime'?"

"Yes, I have heard it and I believe it is true," Victoria replied. "As I think back I am certain now that my relationship with Roger, my former fiancée, was intended to be for a season. It doesn't mean it wasn't special. It just wasn't meant to be forever."

"That could certainly be true, Victoria. So, which of the three do you think applies to you and Phillip?"

"I'd like to think ours could last a lifetime. He has all of the qualities I admire in a man. He's kind, understanding, has a great sense of humor, and he's also intelligent, responsible, and steady. I think we share the same values, and I feel that I am beginning to really know him. There is already a bond between us. I hope it will become something more."

"Well there is your answer," Kit replied with a reassuring smile. "Remember, Victoria, when destiny steps in to show you your true love it would be a shame to deny that it is real. Be careful not to let it slip away. My instincts tell me that Phillip is a good man."

Breakfast was well underway when Victoria entered the dining ger. There was a lightness in her step and a cheerfulness that was noticeable to everyone at the table. "You look in a particularly good mood this morning." Her traveler Jenni commented. Victoria smiled just as Phillip approached their table and took the only empty seat that just happened to be directly across from her. Because the excitement was running so high from the discoveries of the prior day, everyone had technical questions to ask of Phillip, and he willingly answered them all. Victoria noticed his sweet gesture when he tapped her foot under the table.

Dr. B., Mark, and Chimeg were already working at the site with the graduate students. "I had better get to work," Phillip commented after a quick cup of coffee accompanied by a bread and cheese sandwich he had put together. "If any of you have questions please just come over and ask me at the site. This could be another very good day since we have begun to excavate the first chamber." He then turned to Victoria. "See you later."

The morning was a flurry of activity with everyone participating in the excavation efforts. As she knelt working on her pad, Phillip came by. "I have a surprise for you at lunch; meet me at our favorite rock."

At the lunch break, Phillip was waiting for her with a backpack over his shoulder. "How about a picnic? I found a great private spot just over the ridge."

"Sounds romantic," Victoria gave him a big smile. "I love it. I had better tell Mark before we go so, in case of an emergency, he will know where to find me."

"I already spoke with Mark. I told him I would cover for him next time," he said with a playful grin.

Phillip had located a shady spot out of sight, over a high ridge and near one of the few tall shrubs that existed. He had even managed to squeeze a blanket in with their lunch items. "You have thought of everything," Victoria said as he pulled her onto the blanket to share several passionate kisses. She thought it was so touching of him to take the lead in planning their spontaneous picnic together. She sensed that he no longer felt hesitancy in their relationship.

Back in camp, Victoria spent an hour going over the plans for the evening's musical entertainment that she and Altan had planned as part of their cultural event. He had arranged to bring out several men who played the horse fiddle, and one who was well known in the region for throat singing. They decided it would be memorable to have the performance out-of-doors after dinner, around a bonfire. Altan had thought of everything. There were original camel bags for sitting on the ground, the fire pit was already prepared, and since he would be staying to take the musicians back, he would tend to the fire.

For just a moment, Victoria smiled remembering her concerns about entrusting her travel group to an inexperienced local ground operator. "Altan, I cannot begin to express my satisfaction with the meticulous service you have provided." As she saw the puzzled look on his face she realized that a person who was not fluent in English might not understand the meaning of the word "meticulous." Immediately, she continued, "You have done a fine job, and I am most happy with your services. Please let me know if I can provide a recommendation or put in a good word for you as you plan more tours."

Altan burst into a big smile and shook her hand, which made Victoria even more charmed by his appreciation. In reality, she knew that she had been extremely fortunate to have found him.

The afternoon flew by quickly. It was obvious that the group had, in just a few days, become much closer. Many of the participants did not know each other prior to signing up for the expedition, but they now seemed to be old friends. Before dinner, Dr. B. and Chimeg gave a brief overview of the artifacts the group had uncovered that afternoon and followed up with a heart-wrenching explanation of the challenges facing their work in Mongolia. They explained that the looting of archaeological sites was becoming a serious problem and threat in their country. Chimeg added that most people were not aware of the fact that climate change was linked to the increase in looting.

"Nomadic herdsman have been impacted by a decrease in the quality of the grasslands where they have traditionally grazed their livestock. With the economic decline, they have taken to looting to supplement their income." She explained that they were gathering precious artifacts and selling them on the black market. Dr. B. looked both concerned and forlorn as he told of several significant ancient treasures that had been sold to illegal antiquities dealers. He explained that the antiquities were considered especially valuable because Mongolia was one of the largest land empires in the history of the world under

Genghis Khan. "Because our country is a large land mass of plains, deserts, and mountains you can understand how difficult it is to protect the many scattered archaeological sites," Chimeg continued. "Imagine the artifacts we have uncovered in just the last few days in this tomb. If looters had found it first we could not do the scientific research we are doing today. It is so very devastating for all of us."

Maury, one of the group participants, asked, "Are there no laws to protect these historic treasures?"

"Even though our country has reasonably good laws in place regarding the protection of our cultural heritage, it is impossible to enforce these laws with such a vast land mass and so few enforcement officers, due to our meager financial resources. The worst thing is that these looters are primarily looking for gold, silver, and gemstones. In the process, they trash so many of the artifacts that would help us learn how the Mongols raised their food, fed their families and conducted their everyday lives. We must find a way to stop them. These relics are part of the soul of our country," Chimeg said with deep concern and tears welling up in her eyes.

As Victoria looked around the room, she saw how deeply moved the members of her group were by Chimeg's sincere emotions. They had grown to respect and like her. They knew that with her reputation, talent, and personality, she could have easily secured a prestigious job anywhere in the United States. Instead, her dedication and passion prompted her to return to her country to try to make a difference. And, as the group was now learning, it was a race against overwhelming odds. Victoria also glanced over to see Mark's reaction. She sensed that he was not only dismayed by the issues facing his professional colleagues, but the look on his face was also one of concern for Chimeg. He surmised that she was a strong-willed and passionate woman who could be harmed if she were to run into a confrontation with looters. Following Chimeg and Dr. B.'s brief presentation, Victoria instinctively knew that everyone realized that their work at the excavation site counted. They could easily see the challenges ahead for their two new friends and the graduate students who would follow them in their mission to preserve Mongolia's artifacts for future generations.

Victoria did not want to change the subject, but it was time to announce the evening's menu since she knew the cook had put considerable effort into making it special. She explained that it was their opportunity to sample several of the different kinds of meat raised by the local herdsmen. The cook had prepared a buffet of camel meat, mutton, and yak. All were accompanied by a large platter of the local cheese, carrots, and potatoes. "I saw some of you participating in milking mares at the herdsman homestead. Therefore, I asked our local guide to be sure that we had fermented mare's milk available tonight for you to sample." She then hesitated, with an amusing look on her face. "And I did not forget Dr. Doyle's request for local vodka. You may find it interesting to know that they actually produce a premium vodka here in Mongolia. We have several bottles available tonight."

With that information, Peter, from the group spoke up. "Any chance you have tonic water?" His humor created a round of laughter throughout the ger. Victoria enjoyed watching her clients playfully trying the local products. The mare's milk was most definitely an acquired taste, as was the strong, pungent cheese, but the yak meat was tasty and a big hit. As at previous meals, the students waited until the guests had filled their plates before they came through the buffet and scooped up every last morsel with gusto.

When she returned to her table Phillip said, "You have thought of everything. Great planning, Victoria."

She could tell that his compliment was given with the utmost admiration. It made her feel especially proud knowing it came from him. "And how about the fact that I remembered your request for vodka?"

Phillip leaned back in his chair and gave a hardy laugh. She loved seeing him so relaxed and happy. For some unknown reason, she turned to make eye contact with Kit, who gave a playful wink. After dinner everyone gathered around the bonfire to experience authentic Mongolian music. They seated themselves on the camel blankets that circled the fire, already crackling and burning brightly.

As the sun went down the wind was blowing slightly so people wrapped in blankets to stay warm. Since Mark was sharing his camel blanket with Chimeg, Victoria felt comfortable sitting with Phillip. She noticed that no one in her travel group was the least bit concerned. The expedition had far exceeded their expectations, and, in many ways, they had bonded into a genuinely caring team that wanted the best for each other.

The performers were dressed in local costumes. The men wore deels, the traditional calf-length tunics. Their blue and red hats, with cone-shaped tops, were made with thirty-two colorful stitches, symbolizing the unification of the exact number of Mongolian tribes. Perhaps, the most distinctive items of their attire were their boots with the upturned toes. They were tall and made of unbending leather and decorated in various colors. Most interesting was the fact that the right and left boots were shaped exactly the same and could be worn by either foot. The name for the horsehead fiddle was *morin khuur*. Everyone learned that this fiddle was an important musical instrument of the traditional people. It was a symbol of the Mongolian Nation. Victoria was impressed with the beautifully carved image of a horse's head, located at the top on the fiddle. She wanted to remember to ask Chimeg where she could purchase one to take home.

She looked across the flickering flames and smiled. Mark and Chimeg had a big blanket wrapped over their shoulders, as if Mark wanted to offer her protection, given his concerns for her safety amongst the tomb looters. Joanne and Jim, the anniversary couple, were still toasting each other with cups of wine, beer or vodka. She was quite certain it was not the bitter mare's milk they had all obligingly sampled. The graduate students were scattered among their newfound friends in the group. It touched her to see Kit and Dr. B. deep in conversation as he pointed to the singer explaining how throat singing was accomplished.

Victoria had read about the unique style of throat singing they were about to hear. Phillip confessed that he found it to be haunting the first time he heard it performed in Ulaanbaatar. Also called overtone singing, a single vocalist activates different combinations of muscles to manipulate the resonating chambers of the vocal tract under sustained airflow from the stomach and chest. It almost sounded like a husky chanting and was considered one of the oldest forms of music in the world. The group was totally fascinated by the performance.

All could see why the technique required years of training to master. Victoria was so pleased that she was able to share the unique experience under a blanket of stars around a roaring bonfire. As the performance ended, a roar of applause went out to show deep appreciation for the talent of these gentlemen who had come all the way out to the camp site to entertain the expedition group.

"Hold my seat," Victoria asked Phillip. "I have a gratuity to share with the entertainers, and I want to discuss something with Altan. I'll be back soon."

When she returned the fire embers had dimmed to an orange glow and almost everyone had gone to their tents for the evening. Mark and Chimeg had come over to visit with Phillip. Victoria joined them.

"Where are your cups?" Phillip asked all of them as the four sat together. "I have a pleasant surprise for you." Phillip pulled a large water bottle out of his backpack. "You won't believe how much better vodka tastes with lemonade. Lacking a stem glass and crushed ice, it's still pretty darn good." He poured them all half a cup full, added vodka and waited for their assessment.

"Oh, my goodness," Chimeg exclaimed with enthusiasm. "It is so good. It reminds me of the fancy drinks I enjoyed in the swank New York City bars." Mark and Victoria agreed hardily.

"How did you pull this off?" Mark inquired.

Phillip explained that he learned long ago to bring comfort provisions to the excavation sites. "I got to where I always brought a stash tucked in with my clothing. Mostly, things in little packets like orange spice tea bags, chicken broth, sugar, salt, honey, and lemonade!"

Everyone thought it was ingenious, and Victoria told them that Kit also carried packets of high-end instant coffee.

"I would die for a decent cup of coffee," Phillip replied. "It is awfully weak and bitter here in camp, eh?"

Victoria commented that she noticed his alliance to his Queen in ending his sentence with a familiar Canadian "eh!" They all began to laugh, nodding their heads in agreement.

On a more serious note Victoria wanted to speak with Chimeg. "I was most touched by your words tonight before dinner. I am so sorry to hear that your country's artifacts are being sold on the illegal market. It must be so discouraging."

Chimeg looked hopeless as she responded. "Our artifacts mean so much to all of us, and it is heartbreaking that these treasures will be lost forever." Mark reached over and put his arm around Chimeg as a gesture of understanding.

"I wish there was more that could be done," Victoria shared with sympathy. "This truly is a tragedy. I can see why you are so devastated."

As Victoria looked over at Chimeg, she was struck again by her undeniable beauty. She had dressed for the occasion in a native costume, a gorgeous silk deel of embroidered colors of turquoise, black and gold. Her large gold earrings shone against her flawless complexion and on this evening she had used an eyeliner to accentuate her eyes in an exotic fashion. They were always stunning, but in the fading light of the bonfire, they were mesmerizing.

Chimeg was definitely a bright light on the stark landscape of this very barren country. There was something about her that transcended her beauty. It was an authentic humility and goodness.

Dr. B. and Kit came walking out of the darkness. With noticeable animation in her voice , Kit said, "You must go farther out from the bonfire to see the most incredible stars. They seem especially bright tonight. They almost appear to reach down to the horizon. Batu was showing me how clear the Milky Road is in these dark skies. I told him we call it the Milky Way in our country, but I find his description of a road to be more charming. Do be sure to take a look before you all retire."

"Who is Batu?" Mark asked as they have moved away.

"It's my uncle's first name," Chimeg giggled. "Didn't you know that? "

"No, I guess I have never heard him referred to as Batu," Mark replied. Phillip nodded in agreement.

"Actually, in our country the Mongols have only one personal name, which remains the same throughout their lifetime. Some of us who publish abroad have chosen first names to make things easier."

"What do you call your uncle?" Mark inquired.

"Dearest Uncle," Chimeg teased.

Mark gave her a little light tap on the shoulder in fondness. He explained that sleep was calling to him, and since he would have many more nights for star gazing, he was ready to retire for the evening. He hesitated a moment to say, "Phillip, you should take Victoria out to see the stars since she is leaving soon. Those of us living amidst the bright lights of the city never get to see something this spectacular."

Phillip and Victoria took two camel blankets with them into the darkness away from the tents and camp. Lying on a camel blanket, side by side on the ground, they covered themselves with their extra blankets. Phillip put his arm around her, and she laid her head on his shoulder. The stars were every bit as brilliant and breathtaking as Kit had described.

"There is Batu's Milky Road." Phillip smiled as he pointed to the Milky Way.

"I can't imagine calling Dr. B. by any other name," Victoria replied. I did look up the spelling of his name on his bio. How do you actually pronounce it?"

"Honey, how would I know?" Phillip replied with a lighthearted laugh.

"I'm so pleased. That is the first time you have called me honey."

Phillip pulled her closer to him. "I can assure you it will not be the last time," he said as his lips met hers. They enjoyed romantic kisses under the most incredible blanket of stars. Phillip whispered, "I can hardly believe you are leaving camp in just two days. Victoria, remember, this is definitely not goodbye. I would like to invite you to come to London as soon as I return. My flat is not palatial, but it is comfortable, and I have a balcony with a fabulous view of the London Bridge. I'm not teaching at the university next semester so we will have lots of time to be together. It will just be the two of us for as long as you can stay. I simply cannot wait to introduce you to my friends and show you all of my favorite haunts in the city. We will be together without any responsibilities or peering eyes."

"I am thrilled! You can't begin to imagine what your invitation means to me. I'm so looking forward to being together again, just the two of us. I will be counting the days." She reached over and gave him the longest hug and the most passionate kiss.

Phillip smiled as he replied, "I'm going to take that as a "yes" that you will come to London. For now, perhaps, we should head back so you do not wake Kit as you return. She was the one who suggested we come out to see the stars, but I am not sure if she intended us to stay for almost two hours."

When Victoria stepped into the tent she was surprised to see that Kit was still awake reading her book by the light of one of those clever personal head lamps. "Thank you for suggesting that Phillip and I go out in the dark to experience the night sky. The stars were so brilliant; they seem twice the size of those back home. We also had time to plan our reunion in London next month. Phillip has invited me to come for a visit. I am so grateful for your wonderful advice. It made a big difference in my decision to follow the destiny that you so wisely described. Did you and Dr. B. have a nice evening? You seem to be having a lovely time together. I'm sure you will miss him when we leave."

Kit again gave Victoria one of her gentle smiles of wisdom. "Remember when we spoke of differing relationships? One for a reason, one for a season, and one for a lifetime?" Victoria nodded as Kit continued. "I have always enjoyed the company of men who have depth and character. They are confident, interesting, and most stimulating. There is always something to learn from these intelligent lovely men. I must admit, I gain something even more from them. I come away feeling noticed as a woman. There is something precious about being in the presence of a man who truly enjoys your company. Batu has offered that to me these past few days. He is self-assured and charming. The time and attention he has given to me has been so very special. I will never forget my time spent with him here in Mongolia. You see, Victoria, it is far different than the committed, loving relationship that you and Phillip might experience in the future. I suspect that, unless Batu comes to the East Coast, our paths might not ever cross again. This does not diminish the magical times we have shared and the sense of the gratitude I feel."

Victoria sensed the sincerity in Kit's voice. She wanted to also convey her thoughts. "I will tell you without a shred of doubt in my mind that you gave him a gift in return. I am certain that your genuine interest in his work, the way you smiled at him with your beautiful blue eyes and your caring sweet attention these past few days have meant so much to him. I saw it in his eyes when you asked him to dance at the anniversary party. As you two swayed to those sweet old love songs, he was standing a little taller. In a sense, he was a man desired by a woman. You both may have met for 'a reason,' and I am sure he is also most grateful."

The next morning at breakfast, Victoria stood to address the group. "I can hardly believe this is our last night in camp. I'm sure you will all agree that it has been an experience that we will never forget." She then turned toward Dr. B. and Chimeg. "We were particularly moved, last night at dinner, to hear of the challenges you face with the looting of your artifacts. This morning our group met and decided we would like to help in your efforts. One of our members has a foundation in the United States. She will be contacting you Dr. B. to make a five-year commitment to hire additional enforcers in your country. Dr. B. looked stunned. Chimeg excitedly gave him a hug. Still in shock over the magnitude of the gift, he eloquently shared his heartfelt appreciation, "Your generosity has taken my breath away. It will make a huge difference in our efforts. Thank you so very much."

"And that is not all," Victoria continued. "We understand that your university's archaeology program is desperately in need of new computers, so our entire group is donating the funds to purchase five new computers for your department." The look of the faces of Dr. B., Chimeg, and the graduate students was still one of awe and amazement. They were noticeably touched by the generosity of visitors they had only met a few days earlier. "And I have one last thing to add. Since we will be departing early in the morning, I want to take a few minutes to thank all of you graduate students for being so helpful and attentive throughout our entire stay.

Even though we don't share each other's language, we have learned a great deal from you. Dr. B. has come to me on several occasions to tell me how much you have appreciated the warm food that our cook has prepared. As a little thank-you from my travel company, I have made arrangements for the cook to stay on at camp for an extra week. The supplies and food will be delivered when the motor coach arrives in the morning."

Victoria then turned to look directly at Phillip. With a twinkle in her eye, she added, "And since you will have Phillip in camp a while longer, in honor of the many hours he has undoubtedly logged in London pubs, I have ordered two extra cases of beer. It is the least that my company and I can do to show our gratitude for a most incredible four days."

The students cheered loudly, and when Victoria caught Phillip's eye, she could tell he actually enjoyed being singled out by her.

"Well, that calls for a toast," Phillip said, putting extra effort into accentuating his British accent. "Please, raise your coffee mugs. Dr. B., Mark, Chimeg, the students, and I are truly overwhelmed by all of your generosity, and although we will miss you terribly, we will finish excavating this tomb in your honor."

"Shall we get back to work?" Mark suggested. "We are not going to let twenty-four sets of helping hands get away from us until tomorrow!"

Everyone put in extra effort on their last day of excavation. They had become a well-oiled team as they brushed away the soil, hauled dirt from piles and carefully lifted artifacts to the table where Dr. B. was cataloging the items. In the mid-afternoon, Kit came and asked Victoria if she could speak to her alone.

"Let's take a break from the sun and meet in the dining ger," Victoria suggested. After being seated she asked, "Is there something I can help you with?"

"Remember our first day of touring when we visited the Mongolian National Library?" Kit began. "I'm not sure if you recall my asking the guide about a book which were kept in the library. It was written with powders of nine jewels, including copper, silver, and gold."

"I vaguely remember, but please go on."

"It was because of this book that I requested you include the national library on our tour of Mongolia. Seeing it is a main reason I chose to come on this expedition. I have been reading about this unique treasure for years, so you might imagine how heartbroken I was when the librarian explained that it could only be viewed with special permission in a private showing supervised by the Director of the library. I was very disappointed knowing I will probably never see it. I suspect I will not return to Mongolia again."

"I am truly sorry that you are so disappointed," was all Victoria could think of to say. She liked Kit very much and wished that there was something she could do to rectify the situation.

Kit continued, not sadly, but with a big smile on her face. "Just when I resigned myself to never being able to see this precious manuscript, something wonderful has happened. I'm going to have a private showing tomorrow!"

Victoria looked puzzled. Kit continued, "I told Batu about my disappointment over dinner last night. He knows the library director very well and will arrange a private showing for me in the morning. You do know that he has to leave camp right after dinner tonight to drive back to Ulaanbaatar for an early morning meeting with his staff?"

"No, I'd not heard about his departure, but I am thrilled that he could make these arrangements on your behalf," Victoria said.

Kit continued enthusiastically, "I will ride with him into Ulaanbaatar after dinner, and stay at the hotel where we spent our first night. Batu will take me to the library after his morning meeting, and then I can meet up with all of you in the afternoon. I wanted to let you know of my plans since I will be leaving camp and not sharing the tent with you tonight."

"It certainly is good news but there is one problem," Victoria said with a serious look on her face that initially puzzled Kit. "I'm jealous that you will be at the hotel, getting a long, hot shower before any of the rest of us do!"

They had a hearty laugh and a hug before Kit gave her parting words. "I hope you and Phillip will continue to follow your hearts. Don't let your head get in the way, my dear."

As Victoria returned to her excavation mat, she smiled to think of how fortunate she was to have chosen Kit for her teammate. She was so appreciative of Kit's wisdom and reassuring advice. It had made all the difference. She looked up from her work to gaze across the excavation site at Phillip. He seemed even more attractive than she remembered when they first met. His wavy hair, muscular stature, and expressive eyes were so captivating. However, it was not only his good looks that she found appealing. His kindness, protective nature, and sincere interest in her feelings made her realize that he truly was an exceptional man. She was thrilled to think he had invited her to London.

Victoria was touched to see Phillip being noticeably attentive to all of her clients. He knew it was their last day in camp, and he wanted to answer as many last-minute questions they might have about the excavation. At one point, he dropped by to see how she was doing.

"Dr. Doyle," she teased in a low voice, "Are you coming by to be sure that I am not putting on another embarrassing demonstration in my lacy red bra?"

"Not at all, but I do hope you are wearing it because it will give me something delightful to fantasize about this afternoon."

"Perhaps, you will not have to fantasize. I have something very interesting to tell you. Kit will not be sharing my tent tonight."

"Are you serious? Come take a break with me. I want to hear how this has come to be." He had a most interested look on his face.

They walked into the dining ger and sat at an empty table. Victoria explained about Kit's disappointment in not seeing the precious jeweled manuscript and her good fortune that Dr. B. had arranged an early morning viewing for her with the director of the library. She would be staying overnight at the hotel in Ulaanbaatar.

Phillip burst into laughter. "Well, that sly fox!"

"No, it is not what you are thinking at all," Victoria replied emphatically.

"How do you know?" Phillip asked with one of those men-know-men grins. He was, however, quick to change the subject. "I must say that this is unexpected good news. The idea of being alone with you on our last night in camp is truly unbelievable."

As Phillip departed, Victoria took a minute to ponder Kit's good fortune in getting to finally view the library treasure that she had come all the way across the world to see. She was happy to know that it was the charming Dr. B. who was making it happen. They had shared so many delightful times in the last few days. She only had to close her eyes to visualize them enjoying each other's company. Her imagination went a little wild wondering if Phillip could be right. She smiled and decided that everyone had their own private journey, and at the moment, she was concentrating on her own anticipation of the evening ahead, being alone with Phillip in her tent.

Chimeg entered the ger for a break. Victoria greeted her warmly and found it a good time to ask her for a favor.

"Shopping is on the agenda when we get back to Ulaanbaatar tomorrow afternoon. Could you recommend a place where we could buy some local items? My travelers are interested in purchasing horsehead fiddles, pointed hats, saddle blankets, those Mongolian boots with the turned-up toes and, of course, cashmere is high on the list."

"Absolutely," Chimeg said, "I will give you the name of several shops and be sure to tell them I sent you. They are friends of mine. They sell quality products, and they will treat you fairly."

"Perfect," Victoria exclaimed with gratitude in her voice. "We will do our part to help boost the economy, hoping to keep those locals from looting your tombs." But as quickly as her attempt at humor crossed her lips, she realized it was inappropriate. She immediately changed her light-hearted tone to a more serious and sympathetic one. "I didn't mean to make light of the challenge you face. I am sad that this is happening in your country. You are a remarkable and brave woman to come back to Mongolia to try to protect its great antiquities. I wish you success and safety."

"I know you were just express a bit of humor. You have such a big heart it was obvious that you meant no harm. I will miss you, Victoria. Perhaps, when I come to Boston, we can get together. Mark has invited me to participate in his museum presentation on this expedition. I have also always wanted to visit Quebec, and he has offered to take me there while I am in the States."

"You will enjoy visiting eastern Canada, and I'm sure Mark will make your trip special."

"I like his personality," Chimeg added. "He is confident and humble at the same time. There is just something about him that makes me want to know him better. He seems to have a good heart. I am looking forward to spending the next month with him here at camp. Did he tell you that he has been able to carve out a few extra days so I can take him to see the Gobi Desert and Karakorum before he leaves?"

"I know he really wanted to see those sights. I am pleased to hear that he will have this opportunity before he returns to Boston. How lucky he is to have you as his personal tour guide."

Chimeg appeared to blush as she replied, "He said those exact words to me."

"Well he's a smart man. I understand that your uncle has to return to the city tonight."

"Yes, that is true," Chimeg replied. "But I am happy he will not leave until after dinner. The cook is preparing steamed dumplings. I love them. They are one of my favorite traditional foods. They are called *buzz* and are tasty little meat pockets filled with mutton. In Mongolia, they are a delicacy at our Lunar New Year celebrations. I am certain everyone will enjoy them."

The afternoon hours seemed to fly by so quickly as the team's efforts uncovered several important artifacts to add to their collection. When the dinner hour arrived, and everyone was comfortably seated Maury stood to ask a question. "Chimeg, could you tell a little more about your customs?"

"Yes, I am happy to share," Chimeg said with a smile. She looked especially lovely this evening wearing a turquoise tunic top with an elaborate silver belt around her slim waist. Her earrings had tiny turquoise stones that dangled as she laughed and tossed her head. Her silky hair was twisted up in a bun and secured by hair pins studded with stones to match her earrings. Victoria knew it would be a long time before she would see a more naturally beautiful woman. With enthusiasm Chimeg went on to explain some of the customs of Mongolia. A child's first big celebration was their first haircut, usually at the age of three to five years. Wedding ceremonies traditionally included the handing over of a new ger to the marrying couple. Birthdays were not celebrated in the past, but today birthday parties were popular. Buddhism was the main religion in Mongolia. It is practiced by ninety percent of the population.

"I understand you visited our monastery." Chimeg was pleased to learn that they had received a blessing from the Abbot. "The Soviet's repression of our religion was terrible, but today many of our monasteries are being restored and are once again filled with worshippers." She went on. "Shamanism also has a strong presence in our daily lives. One ritual includes rubbing holy stones together to honor the spirit guides. Do watch for spiritual mounds as you travel throughout our country. They are made from branches and stones and called *ovoo*. These shrines were erected by local families and travelers to show gratitude, render respect, and honor the spirits of the surrounding land. If you wish, you can leave a coin or small item on the mound for a safe journey."

Victoria glanced over toward Phillip remembering the day he had taken her to see an *ovoo* in the mountains. It was such a heartwarming experience and the location of their first kiss. His eyes met hers with recognition and fondness. Chimeg retained her captive audience. Everyone was enthralled, not only with her charm, but with the traditions she continued to share. They coaxed her to go on. She went on to tell them that they may also see a traditional blue ceremonial offering scarf on the mounds. *Khadag*, the name of the scarf, was used for centuries to symbolizes purity and compassion in Tibetan and Mongolian cultures. Made of silk or a silk-like material, it is always blue. Often, it is given as a hostess gift at the end of a visit. It is always offered with arms outstretched."

Judy, a group member, asked, "Is there somewhere that we can purchase these traditional blue scarves in Ulaanbaatar?"

"Oh, yes, you can buy them from vendors on the street, but if you wish to find one of the highest quality silk, there are lovely shops in the city. Victoria has already spoken to me regarding shopping opportunities, and I have given the names of several shops where you can purchase all of the traditional items you have been admiring in our country."

"Victoria, you are a woman after my heart," Jenni exclaimed. "I was so wishing we would have time to shop, and you have already covered the bases. Thank you."

Victoria humbly acknowledged their appreciation. She was deep in thought regarding the blue Mongolian scarf she had already obtained to give to Phillip. It was a spontaneous impulse on her part to purchase it in Ulaanbaatar the day they picked up Chimeg. It was to be her surprise farewell gift, but now it would be more meaningful. It would be a symbol of their decision to continue into a relationship. She could hardly wait to give it to him in her tent that evening.

Chimeg noticed that the graduate students were getting ready to serve dinner. "I see that dinner is about to be served, so I will wrap up my comments by saying Mongolians have often been described as being frank, honest, hospitable, fun-loving, hardworking, self-reliant, gracious, curious, independent-minded, and having a good sense of humor. Doesn't that perfectly describe my uncle and the graduate students?" she asked with a laugh. Everyone agreed with enthusiastic applause.

Victoria stood to thank Chimeg and continued to speak to the group, "I want to inform you that Dr. B. will not be able to join us after dinner. He has an early morning staff meeting to attend in Ulaanbaatar. Since our group is leaving early in the morning this will be our only time to say goodbye and thank him for his hospitality. Directly after dinner, we will have a few minutes to bid our farewells. For now, is anyone hungry and ready to try the dumplings which are Chimeg's very favorite traditional dish?"

The laughter and playful dinner conversations were especially heartwarming for Victoria. She was convinced that this was one of the best travel groups she had ever escorted and also one of the best destination experiences. To think that she had also met Phillip in Mongolia made it all the more rewarding.

As the dinner began to wind down, Dr. B. stood to address the group. "Since I will be leaving camp shortly, I want to take this opportunity to express my feeling about our time together. I am speaking from my heart when I say that I have never experienced a group like yours. You are not trained in our profession, yet you seem to share our passion for saving the antiquities that provide us an opportunity to understand how our ancestors lived for many centuries before us. We appreciate your working alongside us to lend a helping hand with this excavation, and your generous financial gift has left me speechless. I will never forget you, and I hope that someday our paths may cross again. It is your friendship which I cherish most. Take care of each other."

As he looked to the top of the ger, his expression was soft and tender. "I leave you with a Mongolian proverb. 'Posts support a ger, but friends support a man.' Let us toast to our friendship with a very old custom that is still practiced by the nomadic people in my country. As we make the toast, we dip our ring finger into the alcohol and flick it once into the air to honor the sky, a second time for the earth and the third time for the wind.

"Very good," he said with a big smile. "Now, you can return to my country so we can again renew friendship together."

Everyone gathered around Dr. B. to thank him and share their good-byes. When it was Victoria's turn, she was overwhelmed with emotion. She stepped forward and gave him a long, warm hug. With tears of gratitude welling up in her eyes, she said, "We will never forget Mongolia, and we will never forget you, Dr. B. Thank you for everything you have done for us. I personally feel so fortunate to have met you."

Kit had just finished packing her belongings when Victoria stopped by the tent. "I have so appreciated your wonderful advice these past few days. Phillip and I have no more hesitation. We are going to take it one step at a time, but I am feeling confident that things will work out for us."

"I hope your relationship with Phillip will be of the forever kind. With that rosy glow about you, I believe that chances are very good that I might even see Dr. Doyle in Boston sometime in the coming year."

"Yes, I think you just might!"

They exchanged a warm farewell hug, and Victoria said she hoped that seeing the manuscript would be as special as Kit anticipated. She wanted to say something more about enjoying the evening and the drive back with Dr. B., but she thought it best to keep that to herself. She did notice however that Kit looked particularly lovely. She even had on a hint of blue eye shadow that matched her blue checkered shirt.

Back at the ger it was obvious that no one was ready to say good night. Since it was their last night in camp they continued to enjoy their beer, and wine as well as each other's company. Georgiana stood up to speak. "Dr. Shelby, I can assure you that after this experience, none of us will be missing your lectures at the museum and certainly not the one on this expedition."

Everyone smiled and shouted, "Hear! Hear!"

Joanne said, "Dr. Phillip Doyle, we have so enjoyed meeting you. Since we are leaving tomorrow, could you share a few of your prior experiences with us? I understand that your expertise is in Egyptian discoveries, and several of us are planning to join a tour to Egypt next year."

Phillip smiled and said he would be happy to speak. He stood in a relaxed manner where he would not have his back toward any of the group. When he began his informal presentation, Victoria was impressed beyond belief. She knew she was biased, but she was totally dazzled. It was as if a wise sage had come on the scene. She had no idea of the depth of his accomplishments. And not only did he participate in the fieldwork, but he was the lead scientist on many of the expeditions.

Although his scientific endeavors had taken him to several continents around the globe, Egyptian sites were his field of expertise. He presented a brief description of some of the remote sites he had worked on over the past years. As an accomplished presenter, he sprinkled in general facts to keep people's interest. He explained that archaeological sites could include villages, stone quarries, elaborate tombs, rock art, megalithic stone monuments,and even sites as small as a pile of chipped stone tools left by prehistoric hunters. When asked about the oldest archaeological site in the world, Phillip explained that,after several decades of research and excavations, it had been revealed that humans were living in the Theopetra Cave in Greece over 135,000 years ago.

He asked if anyone in the group had seen the Lascaux Cave paintings in France. Several hands went up. "Imagine," he said. "They are only 17,000 years old in comparison."

As Phillip continued to speak, Victoria was mesmerized. She was not familiar with his professional background and talents. From the minute he had begun, Victoria noticed that he had garnered a compelling command of the audience. This was not in a boastful or authoritarian way, but in one disseminating information with accuracy yet enthusism and humor. He was relaxed and put the audience at ease while piquing their curiosity. Hearing him speak gave her chills. He was brilliant. Not somewhat brilliant, but amazingly so. She could see the faces of the members of her group as it registered with them that this playful, charismatic British archaeologist had far more experience, intelligence, and depth than they had seen since arriving in Mongolia. And then it dawned on Victoria that he had played down his achievements because he was a guest of Dr. B. who was the expert in his country. She knew it would be just like Phillip to be modest and unassuming. The depth of his character made her adore him even more.

Within minutes, she felt a twinge of insecurity surfacing. "She wondered how anyone as worldly and accomplished as Phillip could be interested in her. Could she live up to his expectations?" As the thoughts began to flood her mind, she remembered Kit's wise words as they had parted, just a few hours earlier. "Don't let your head get in the way. Go with your heart." She knew exactly what her heart was saying, and it was unwavering. Meeting Phillip on this trip was not an accident. The mutual feelings of instant chemistry were undeniably strong. She had always believed in serendipity, and now she knew without a shred of a doubt that the Universe had a hand their meeting. As Victoria became more centered, she thought about what a relationship with Phillip might be like. She smiled to think of the many attributes she would also bring to their union. She was smart, kind, dependable and loyal. These were traits that came naturally to her. Plus, they both shared a strong physical attraction. She looked forward to their romantic and sensual times together.

Phillip chose to wrap up his comments on a subject that pleased Victoria. He spent a few minutes giving the group several tips on seeing the ancient sites when traveling to Egypt as tourists. He said that the famous sites like the pyramids and the Sphinx were well worth seeing. He cautioned the group to use a reputable tour company as Egypt was a country where danger could be of concern. He said it was amazing to see what good shape the Great Pyramids of Giza were in, given that they were 4,000 years old. He advised that the pyramids were best seen in the morning hours. Since they were located so close to the city of Cairo, the thick smog from the traffic often created a haze later in the afternoon. He recommended his favorite monument, the Temple of Horus in Edfu on the West Bank of the Nile. Built between 237 and 57 BC, he considered it to be one of the best-preserved monuments in all of Egypt. As Phillip ended, the particularly long and enthusiastic applause given by her group made Victoria realize they too greatly admired his talents and accomplishments.

Before retiring, Victoria advised everyone that breakfast would be an hour earlier the next morning, and that everyone had to have their tent emptied and bags packed to depart when the motor coach arrived at 8:30 am As Phillip walked over to her, she began to tell him how impressed she was with his commentary and his many accomplishments. He just gave her his humble smile, and thanked her. "How about we go somewhere to talk in private while everyone finishes visiting and settles in for the night? I would rather join you in your tent when it is less conspicuous. Let's go up and sit on our favorite rock. It has become a special place given that we have had some pretty meaningful talks up there. I'll grab a lantern and my backpack and be with you in a few minutes."

As she and Phillip settled onto their ledge, he pulled opened his backpack and said, "I have a surprise for you. I know you enjoy wine, so I slipped a bottle into my backpack earlier tonight. We can toast our last night in camp." Pulling the bottle out of his pack, he noticed that he did not have his knife to open it. "Can you wait here while I go back to my tent and get my knife. It has a corkscrew attached."

"You are in luck, my dearest," Victoria said in a sweet playful tone of voice. "I just happen to have my Swiss Army knife in my fanny pack."

For some reason, Phillip found the fact that she carried a Swiss Army knife to be endearing. "You are resourceful, in addition to being intelligent, alluring, and so very beautiful. What a combination! I am most certainly a lucky man." As Phillip pulled the two coffee mugs from his pack, he said, "I promise that, when you come to London, I will serve you vintage French wine in fine crystal." He paused for a moment, took a sip of his wine, and continued, "Do you know what I like best about our relationship?" Victoria waited for his answer. "It is the way I feel when I'm with you. I find myself smiling for no particular reason. When you come into sight I feel my heart skip a beat. I know it may sound sentimental, but I'm serious."

They shared a lingering kiss before Victoria confirmed that she felt exactly the same way about him. She then reached for her bag. "I have something special for you. You need to close your eyes, and, in the proper Mongolian tradition, you must receive my gift with outstretched arms."

Phillip was intrigued, but he complied willingly. When he opened his eyes, there was the blue Mongolian scarf draped over his arms. "Where in heavens name did you get this? It is just like the ones we saw on the spiritual mound in the mountains."

"I was so moved by our time at the site that I secretly purchased it from a street vendor when we went into Ulaanbaatar. I wanted you to have it as a symbolic gift from me. When we walked around the mound that day I also made a wish that the strong attraction I felt for you, when we first met, was real. Somehow, this scarf is my way of saying I hope we both take a corner, hold it tightly and never let go of each other. You mean a lot to me. I have never experienced such strong feelings before, and I couldn't be happier."

Phillip looked into her eyes. "Remember when you told me that you had inherited a sixth sense from your great grandmother? And I shared that I have also been blessed with it? Both of us now have a strong knowing. My instincts tell me that this relationship is the right one for us. They say intuition does not offer an explanation. It simply points the way. Victoria, I believe our path is clear. As far as I am concerned, it continues in London and far beyond."

Phillip stood as he put his scarf around his neck and took her hand. "And, now, speaking of pointing the way, I am reminded of an empty tent awaiting our arrival." As they began to walk, he said, "Look how bright the full moon is tonight. We can walk to your tent without a lantern."

"Is it really a full moon?" Victoria asked.

"Yes. This is the exact date," Phillip replied. "We will need to remember that our first night together was on the evening of a full moon."

As they approached her tent, Victoria was glad that she had made the decision to place hers away from the rest of the group. Mark's tent, next to hers, was the only one nearby. She looked over, but there was no light coming from his tent. She assumed that he and Chimeg had gone off to do more star gazing.

Inside her tent, Phillip said softly, "Isn't it romantic to finally be all alone? It is just the two of us tonight."

Victoria nodded and offered a little suggestive gesture. She unbuttoned her shirt just enough so Phillip could see her lacy red bra. As she moved slowly toward him she asked, "What side of the bed do you prefer?"

Phillip loved her sense of humor. "Tonight, I am definitely joining you in the middle," he replied unlatching his belt buckle. Suddenly he stopped to whisper, "Did you hear that? I think someone is next door. I hear noises."

As they opened the tent flap, they could not believe their eyes! In the light of the full moon, Mark's tent was swaying.

"I know that cadence," Phillip chuckled, with a twinkle in his eye.

Victoria gave him a knowing look that conveyed she too knew what it meant. They quickly closed the flap, and both stepped back inside laughing. But, within seconds, their emotions changed from humor to passion. Phillip pushed the pillows aside and gently lifted her onto the blankets. Who would have imagined that a rocking tent could become a powerful aphrodisiac, arousing such intensity and desire? But it had, and Victoria would always remember that night, under a Mongolian full moon.

GINGER'S STORY

Italy

I t was a beautiful sunny morning in Italy. Ginger had assisted the last of her travel clients as they disembarked the cruise ship and boarded the motor coach for the airport. She waved good-bye and gave a sigh of relief. The cruise had been a rousing success. There had not been one glitch in the entire fourteen days. She smiled with gratitude to think that she had permitted herself the luxury of adding six extra personal days to her trip. As a workaholic, she rarely took time for herself.

Venice was one of her favorite European cities. She never tired of wandering the little back streets, crossing the bridges along the canals and people-watching in St. Mark's Square. There was no doubt in her mind as to why Italy was one of the most popular travel destinations in the entire world. Besides, Venice was the perfect city for photography, and she was anxious to try out her new high-tech camera.

Photography had always interested Ginger. She had enrolled in classes at her local college, hired a professional for private lessons and even attended a photography workshop on her recent cruise. She never dreamed that she would pay such an exorbitant price for a camera, but she knew that with one of the best lenses on the market, her photographs would be far superior to those she had taken in the past with her modest camera. The shop where she purchased it suggested that she use it for a month before seeking further instructions. This trip would give her a great opportunity to become familiar with her new equipment.

She made her way to the hotel she had booked in Venice hoping it would live up to its reviews. When she entered the lobby, with its attractive wood paneling, oriental carpets and cozy furniture, she knew her research had paid off. The young man at the front desk welcomed her warmly in fluent English. As she checked in, she glanced and saw a Rotary International plaque on the wall behind the counter.

"Is your hotel the site of Rotary meetings?" Ginger inquired.

The young man explained that it was not, but that the hotel owner was a dedicated Rotarian who genuinely felt it was an exceptional organization.

"I think he is right," she readily agreed. "They have a dedicated mission of eradicating polio worldwide. I belong to Rotary. My chapter is in Seattle, Washington, in the United States. Being in the travel business, I have had the pleasure of attending chapter meetings in several countries around the world. I always carry a Rotary flag tucked in the side pocket of my suitcase, just in case I have an opportunity to attend a meeting."

The young man, impressed by their conversation, replied, "You should attend our meeting here in Venice."

He enthusiastically shared that the city's weekly Rotary Club was attended by prestigious businessmen. They met in the most elegant hotel in the entire city.

"In fact," he noted, "it is located only a few blocks from here and they meet today at one o'clock. Since your room will not be ready until 4:00 pm, perhaps you might enjoy attending. We rarely have hotel guests who are members of Rotary International, so you may not want to miss this opportunity. If you like, I would be happy to call our owner to see if he might be free to escort you to the meeting."

Ginger took a few moments to reflect on his comment and agreed that it would indeed be a great experience. Given she had the time, it would also be an opportunity to meet local Venetians.

"Yes," she replied. "I would appreciate the opportunity to attend the Rotary meeting." She remembered that she had a classic calf-length dress with a matching jacket and heels in her suitcase. They would be well-suited as business attire. She knew how impressive it would be to present a flag from Venice, Italy at her next local Rotary club meeting. After a brief telephone conversation, it was confirmed that the owner of the hotel would be most happy to introduce her to his club. He would arrive shortly before one o'clock to escort her to the meeting.

"Is there a place where I might change my clothing?" Ginger inquired.

"Absolutely, signora, we have a large, lovely women's toilette near the lobby. I will put a Do Not Disturb sign on the door so you can take as much time as you like."

"That is most kind of you. And what is your name?"

"My name is André," he answered with a big smile of appreciation that she had sincerely inquired.

"Thank you, André. You have been particularly helpful, and I appreciate it very much."

In the women's room, Ginger carefully opened her luggage to confirm that she had indeed packed a Rotary flag and was relieved to find it in its familiar side pocket. She was also relieved that she had folded her clothing carefully at the end of her cruise. Her camel-colored dress and matching jacket were almost wrinkle-free.

She checked herself in the mirror and was pleased. At 5'7", she was fortunate to have a perfect figure. Long legs and a toned body made it possible for her to look good in anything she decided to wear. She was glad that she wore a classic bob hair style. It was easy to manage, and she often had a few highlights added to her natural brunette color. As she glanced in the mirror one last time, she sensed that her outfit needed something more.

What was it? she pondered. *Ah, yes, the stunning, turquoise necklace with the Native American silver pendant.* It would be a lovely statement representing the American West where she grew up. She was grateful that her college roommate was a talented jewelry designer. It was the perfect touch. She felt professional, and even somewhat elegant. She left the room confident and self-assured.

As she re-entered the lobby, André gave her a compliment by saying, "You look magnificent in that dress." With his emphatic comment, she hoped that she was not overdressed but decided it would match the meeting setting that André found so impressive.

"André, could you put my suitcase in storage?" she asked. Ginger was sweetly touched that he appeared proud to be addressed by his name. He quickly accommodated her and asked if he could get her a cappuccino while she waited in the lobby.

As she settled into a comfortable chair, Ginger began browsing through a travel magazine on the table nearby. It was then that she saw an image that took her breath away. It was a photograph in an article regarding an ancient monastery in Italy at a place called Lake Maggiore. The setting was spectacular. The monastery hung from a sheer cliff above the crystal-clear blue water of a lake below. The balconies were impressive, as was the ancient beauty of the 13th-century architecture. "The Hermitage of Santa Caterina Del Sasso," it read, "is one of the most intriguing destinations on Lake Maggiore."

The story told of an Italian merchant who was shipwrecked in the 12th century and took refuge in a cave on the site. He vowed to Saint Catherine that he would build a church in her honor if he was saved.

He initially erected a tiny chapel, but by the 13th and 14th centuries, a monastery had been built. Today it houses a community of Benedictines. Ginger noted that it was accessed by a ferry stop and a climb of eighty steps to the hermitage. *Where is Lake Maggiore?* she wondered.

Her escort, Francisco, the hotel owner, arrived right on time. He was a nice-looking man, short and stocky with a gracious demeanor. He was dressed in a formal, dark suit, and as like so many men in Europe, he wore an elegant scarf around his neck. He introduced himself with the Italian greeting that Ginger had always found so charming. She remembered that it was customary to start with a kiss to the right cheek, and then move to the left. Since they were not acquainted, she appreciated his two air kisses.

"Thank you for inviting me to your Rotary Club," Ginger said. Francisco quickly indicated that he spoke very little English, but he was happy to meet her. He had heard from André that she owned a travel agency. He expressed his hope that she would find her accommodations acceptable and would recommend his hotel to her clients. Ginger assured him that she would do so, and put in a good word for André, who she indicated had been exceptionally professional and helpful.

When they arrived at the hotel where the Rotary meeting was being held Ginger could immediately see that André had not exaggerated or embellished his description of its grandeur. Ginger was in awe of its magnificence. The hotel dining room was filled with luxuriously upholstered high back chairs, the ceiling adorned with chandeliers and the floors covered in plush carpets. She could easily imagine that the hotel had most definitely been a place for the nobility of Venice to congregate. As all of the men entered in their impressive Italian suits, Ginger was relieved that she had dressed well for the occasion.

The president of the Club greeted her with a limited command of the English language. He attempted to apologize that no women were in attendance on that date, but he assured her there were women members in their Rotary Club. It became immediately apparent to Ginger that very few of the members spoke English. *This is fair*, she thought. *After all, it is their country, and I am a visitor from America.*

Francisco spotted Roberto, the Rotary member who had agreed to be Ginger's interpreter. He had been anxiously awaiting his arrival. On their short walk from his hotel, Ginger had become keenly aware of how uncomfortable he was with his inability to speak her language. She could see he was embarrassed. She would have felt exactly the same way if she were to be in his situation in her country. Struggling with his English, Francisco introduced Ginger to Roberto, who had the top law firm in Venice and was fluent in English. She was certain that Francisco was most anxious to pass her off to a colleague who spoke her language. Her instincts were correct. After his informal introduction to Roberto, Francisco disappeared immediately and so did the tension in the air.

Roberto was an attractive man dressed impeccably in a stunning Italian suit. Ginger noticed the touches of class that made her assume he had been successful in his career. He wore gold cuff links and a Rolex watch. His black and white silk tie had a subtle design of a Roman column. Though his presence was almost regal, he exhibited a warm easy-going personality. Roberto was completely at ease with his English language skills and explained that he worked often in the United States. He was even familiar with American expressions and humor.

"Tell me about yourself. Where do you live in the States?" he asked. Ginger was impressed that such an elegant and distinguished man appeared genuinely interested in learning more about her. She replied that she was from Seattle and went on to explain that it was in the northwestern corner near Canada. "Yes, it is a beautiful city." Roberto replied. "Your famous Space Needle is likened to the Eiffel Tower in France."

At first, she was embarrassed to have been explaining where Seattle was located since he had already told her that he visited the United States often. But she quickly regained her composure by asking him a question. "What would you say is your most recognized landmark here in Venice?"

"What a thought-provoking question," he replied with a smile. "You have stumped me there. Perhaps St. Mark's Square or our canals and gondolas."

At that moment, the meeting was called to order, leaving Roberto to ponder her question. She could sense that her quick comeback had intrigued him.

As lunch was served, Roberto acted as her interpreter. Ginger found it amusing to think that amidst these impressive and sophisticated men, the what most interested them was the question of where she had grown up as a child. They seemed truly fascinated to hear that she had grown up on a ranch in Wyoming, a state with less than half a million people. She delighted in telling them that there were more buffalo, deer, and elk in Wyoming than people. She described life on a cattle ranch and shared that the town closest to her family's place was Wapiti, Wyoming, with a mere 100 residents. The town was named after the Cree Indian word for elk, she explained. She laughingly told them that her father used to get upset because the elk would come out of the mountains in winter to eat the hay crop he had put up for the cattle.

Several of the men referred to Wyoming as the "Wild West," and when she explained that Wapiti was near Cody, Wyoming, one older gentleman shared that he had once seen a documentary of Buffalo Bill Cody and found it most interesting.

When it came time to exchange the Rotary flags, the Club president invited Roberto to come forward to introduce Ginger. When he stepped up to the platform, the group members erupted into applause. Not understanding more than a handful of Italian words, Ginger was not sure what this recognition referred to, but when Roberto acknowledged their applause, she assumed by the reaction of the room that he had recently accomplished something significant. When Roberto began her introduction she recognized the word Seattle. However, it was not until she heard the word Wyoming that the men turned around to look at her, appearing to become interested and even possibly impressed. She heard Roberto indicating something about one half a million and the words buffalo and elk, but she could not understand the following words that caused the room to burst into raucous laughter.

As she came forward to exchange flags, she could sense that she had somehow gained their acceptance. They gave her a warm applause. As the meeting came to an end, several of the men even came up to kiss her hand as a farewell gesture. *I can't wait to tell my Rotary comrades in Seattle about this meeting!* she mused to herself.

Several men approached the table to congratulate Roberto as Ginger left the room. However, before she reached the hotel exit, Roberto was at her side.

I'm glad I caught you. May I give you a ride back to your hotel or wherever you are headed?"

"Oh. Thank you," she said with a warm-hearted smile. "I'm staying at a hotel very near here."

"All the better," he replied in his charming, breezy manner. "A little exercise would do me good. May I walk you there?"

"Yes. I am most curious to ask you something."

Roberto loosened his tie and threw his jacket over his shoulder as they began down the street. "What is it you are wanting to know?"

"What was it that made everyone laugh at the end of my introduction?" she inquired.

"Ah, yes," he replied. He threw back his head in a playful gesture. "I told them about Wyoming having a population of only a half million residents with more buffalo and elk than people. I said that it was a fraction of the millions of tourists that invade our fine city each year, and I asked if they thought the buffalo herds would be more well-behaved!"

"That is amusing," Ginger responded. "How many annual visitors do you have in Venice?"

"Over twenty million tourists! It is very crowded in the summer months, and many of us flee the city to our vacation homes. I know you are in the travel business, so don't get me wrong; it is good for the economy, but a bit annoying for us locals. Please know that I am happy that you are visiting, and I especially enjoyed hearing your stories over lunch."

As they approached her hotel, Roberto continued, "Ginger, since you are here in my city, I'm wondering if you would like to join me for dinner tonight, unless of course you are with a gentleman or friends?"

Ginger replied with a hesitant look on her face. "I am here alone, and that is very thoughtful of you, but…"

Before she could finish her sentence, Roberto quickly added, "There is a charming local restaurant around the corner from here. We could meet there, and share a little conversation over some very good traditional dishes."

When Ginger realized it was so close to her hotel, she relaxed. She thought it would be nice to have company over dinner. A local restaurant steps away from her hotel seemed safe and inviting.

"Thank you. That sounds nice," she said.

She and Roberto agreed on a time to meet at the restaurant. "Come casual," he said. "It's a small, traditional family-owned place, very relaxed with excellent food."

When she arrived at the restaurant, Roberto was waiting at a little, corner table for two. It had a flickering candle on the weathered checkered tablecloth, and he was already looking at the wine list. He waved Ginger to the table and stood to seat her.

"Glad you could join me," he said.

"I'm glad to see chivalry is alive and well here in Venice," she teased as he pulled out her chair. She could tell he found her reply to be amusing.

"How was your afternoon?"

"It was great. I took my camera and spent a couple of hours chasing the most perfect lighting in all of the corners of the square. I got some beautiful photos."

"Oh, you are also a photographer in addition to owning a travel company?"

"I'm just an amateur photographer, but I enjoy it." Ginger explained that it was the perfect way to capture memories in the many incredible places she had been fortunate to visit.

"Plus, I suspect you get to relive the experiences when you develop your photos back home in Seattle?"

"You are so right," Ginger agreed. She liked Roberto's relaxed easy-going nature. He made her feel comfortable.

"I'll bet, since you are in Italy, you would prefer red wine this evening," he said with a smile.

"How can you detect my preference in just these few minutes?" Ginger asked in a playful tone of voice. They both laughed and Roberto found one of his favorite wines on the list. At that moment, an older man in a well-worn chef's jacket came directly to their table. He and Roberto hugged and greeted each other warmly. Ginger recognized a congratulatory note in the conversation. Roberto introduced Ginger and the two men continued their conversation in Italian.

Ginger saw the chef look in her direction, and she heard the word "*Bellissima*." She saw Roberto then smile and nod, repeating the word *Bellissima*.

I have to look that word up in my Italian translation book, she thought as the wine was being poured.

"I hope it is agreeable with you that I asked the owner to bring us a sampling of his favorite dishes. As you know, we Europeans like to take our time over dinner. Do you need to be back to your hotel at any particular time?" he inquired thoughtfully.

"No, I also enjoy a leisurely dinner. I suspect it must drive you all crazy when Americans want to make dinner reservations at 5:30 pm?" They both laughed. As they settled into dinner conversation, Ginger said, "On another subject, may I ask you about your recent accomplishment that has garnered so much attention, both here tonight and at the Rotary meeting?"

"Thank you for asking," Roberto replied. "You know I am, as you would say, a lawyer. I just won a landmark case that was advantageous for the working people. It took me well over a year of research and preparation, so you can imagine how thrilled I was to win this case, and how relieved I am that it is over. I feel like a free man."

As he leaned back in his chair, Ginger had a chance to really focus on Roberto. He was good-looking, with dark wavy hair that was greying just enough to give him a distinguished look. She guessed that he was about fifteen years older than she, but it was hard to tell. She loved the way he was dressed in a beautiful linen jacket, crisp laundered white shirt, tailored slacks, and beautiful leather shoes with a matching belt. He was a little taller than she with an appealing physique. His demeanor was natural, and he had a relaxed confident manner about him. She liked the fact that, amidst his obvious success, he appeared humble. He seemed kind and caring, someone who could be trusted. She felt fortunate that he had invited her to dinner so she would not have to dine alone on her first night in Venice. The evening conversation was lively and entertaining. Although they briefly spoke of their personal lives most of the evening was spent discussing their favorite travel destinations, love of cooking and shared interests.

Toward the end of dinner, Roberto stopped the casual conversation, and his voice became noticeably serious. "Ginger, I would like to ask you something, but I would request that you hear my words to the end before you speak. Would you grant me that request?"

Bewildered, Ginger nodded her head in agreement, but she could not imagine what was to come next.

Roberto continued deliberately and slowly. "I find you to be a most impressive woman. I admired your self confidence in holding your own in a room full of men at the Rotary luncheon. Your quick wit is delightful as is your playful nature. And the depth of your intelligence and knowledge fascinates me as well. There is something pleasant about you that is hard to put into words. I suppose it is an authenticity. In one way, it feels like you are almost innocent, and in another way you are a very sophisticated, wise woman. In any case, aside from being most attractive, I am drawn to your zest for life. We have briefly talked of our personal lives. You are single, not currently committed to another, and I am still mourning the death of my beloved wife, Christina, who died of cancer almost two years ago. I am planning to take a few days off for a little holiday trip. I need some relaxation time after finishing this grueling trial. It would also be a time to celebrate. I would like to ask you to join me."

Before she could reply, he stopped her,. "I can see by the look on your face that you are about to say no, but I also saw that same look on your face when I first invited you to dinner this afternoon. I suspected then that you were a cautious woman and would have declined my dinner invitation were it not for the fact that you could simply walk around the corner to meet me here." Ginger nodded as he went on. "I do not blame you for being hesitant. You do not know me, and I'm sure that taking off on a holiday trip with a man you have just met is not something that would make you comfortable. But I can assure you that I am an honorable man. Besides, I have an impeccable reputation in my community. I would never do anything to jeopardize it. I am also the father of a lovely grown daughter who looks up to me with the greatest respect."

Ginger was still looking at him intently and did not interrupt as he had requested. "You may be thinking that I am an older man who would only like to invite you on holiday to have a beautiful woman on my arm and elsewhere. I can guarantee you that this is not the case. In fact I will get you a separate room in the hotels. I just need a break and I would enjoy having your company for a few days. It would be a chance to get away, breathe fresh air, eat good food, drink vintage wine, laugh a bit, and relax."

Ginger took a sip of her wine as her mind raced, and she searched for a response to his request. She liked Roberto but she was stunned to imagine that he would be inviting her on a trip when he hardly knew her.

"Please wait, I have something more I would like to say," he added. "I want to be very clear in telling you that my invitation does not mean that I am hoping to pursue you as a lover. I am not looking for a relationship. I have lost the most wonderful wife any man could ever dream of having. Christina was, without question, the love of my life. In fact, she was my life."

Roberto continued to explain further. "Perhaps, we European men appear to be a bit casual when it comes to matters such as this invitation. We can share a trip with someone we like without any strings attached. When we return home from enjoying ourselves, we can go on as friends. Maybe, a friendship would grow more serious, but maybe it would not. The intent is simply to share a holiday together. To enjoy the moment. I have friends who have dated women from the United States, and they often say that many American women do not date men unless they think it will eventually lead to a permanent relationship or marriage. Ginger, please do not think I am making a judgement about the way women conduct their lives in your country. The cultural norms and expectations here may seem frivolous to you, but to us they are sincere and up-front. I'm not sure if the expectations I described about American women apply to you, so I would not want to mislead you with my invitation. I am asking you to join me because I think you are a unique woman, and I would enjoy your company for these few days on holiday. We could have a good time and return to our respective lives with fond memories, not only of the days we spent together but of each other. Can you understand what I am trying to say?"

Ginger paused a moment before she replied, "Yes, I understand. I am a responsible and prudent woman, but I do feel you are being truthful in your invitation."

"Since you do not know me I would like to invite you to my law office," Roberto continued. "You can see my name on my law firm's door and meet my staff. I would not be disrespectful to you in any way. This truly is an innocent invitation, a time for two adults to just enjoy some time together over a little holiday. And one more thing," he added. "If you are not having a good time, or feeling apprehensive, I will hire a driver to bring you back to Venice. You can make that request at any time, and you have my word that I will honor your wishes."

Ginger smiled kindly but was still deep in thought. Roberto continued, "I know this is a lot to ponder given that we have just met. All I would like to ask is that you think about it overnight. I have some papers to sign at my office in the morning and am not planning to leave until noon. Here is my business card. You can come to my office or call me on the telephone to let me know of your answer." He then stopped with an almost apologetic look on his face, as if he feared that she viewed his invitation as being inappropriate.

Ginger sensed his concern that he had overstepped boundaries. She truly felt he was being sincere in asking her to join him on his holiday trip. He did not want to go alone and having met someone who he found interesting, he asked her to join him. Maybe it was because his wife had died, maybe it was because he didn't want to celebrate his victory alone, or perhaps European men just lived their lives in a more spontaneous and uninhibited manner. She wasn't sure, but she knew he was waiting for her response.

"I appreciate your most kind invitation," she began. "And please be assured, I do not question your character. I actually like you. You seem like an interesting and honorable person." When she looked across the table she saw the look of resignation on Roberto's face. He was ready to accept the answer that she simply could not accept his invitation.

To his surprise, she continued, "Whether it is a skeptical trait of American women or just one held by those of us influenced by nuns and religion as children, it's true that many in my age group would not feel it prudent to take off on a vacation trip with a man they had known for a mere ten hours. However, as I sit here listening to your request it seems most sincere and understandable. Tonight, I am going to call upon my good judgment and inner voice, and I will let you know by noon tomorrow. You see, Roberto, I have been blessed with an uncanny sense of intuition. When I have listened to it, whether it was in business or personal matters, it has served me well. It has been a guidepost in my life. It has never let me down. I will draw upon some intuitive wisdom for my answer."

She saw a knowing look in Roberto's eyes. He nodded as if to say that not only had he heard her clearly, but that he also knew the value of listening to one's hunches and inner voice.

As the conversation lightened a little, Ginger shared a bit of her personal life. "In the past couple of years, I have been on a journey to get to know myself, trying to decide how I want to live the rest of my life. I have found that I rarely slow down enough to stay in the present moment. That is why, when you said that you just wanted to get away to relax, eat good food, and let the wind blow through your hair, it resonated with me. I don't live enough of my life spontaneously or in a carefree manner. I'm always in my head planning my next project, or the rest of my life. I guess I don't know what it means to truly go with the flow." At that moment, Ginger paused. She could see Roberto was listening to her every word and she felt he understood. She then looked at him with gratitude. "I appreciate the opportunity to think it over tonight. I will come by your office by noon tomorrow to let you know of my decision."

Roberto was convinced that whatever choice she made, she would give it her most wholehearted consideration. She was a confident and self-assured woman, and one who was genuinely on a path of self-discovery. He liked the fact that she was practical. He would not have expected less from her. But he did hope that she would decide, as she put it, "to go with the flow." Perhaps, she would join him, but he could not guess what her answer would be.

As the conversation ended Roberto said, "I am so pleased you will consider my invitation, and I want you to know that whichever way you decide, I will be most grateful for this lovely evening we have had together. Let me escort you back to your hotel."

As they walked, Ginger asked, "Could you tell me where you plan to go on your little getaway?"

"To the lake region, about four hours' drive from here. Three beautiful glacial lakes boarder Switzerland and Italy. I have a vacation home near Lake Lugano, and my cousin has invited me to his vineyard resort on Lago Maggiore."

Ginger felt a little spark of recognition. "Lago Maggiore? Is that the same as Lake Maggiore?"

"Yes, *lago* is the Italian word for "lake," but with so many visitors from abroad coming here, most just call it Lake Maggiore. Why do you ask?"

Ginger was now becoming enthusiastic. "Isn't that the lake where there is a monastery that hangs off a cliff high over the water? I think it is called the Hermitage of St. Caterina. Do you know of it?"

All of a sudden she felt a distinct hesitancy in Roberto's voice. Or was it sadness? She wasn't sure, but it was a reaction that she hadn't expected.

"Yes, I know of it," he answered. "Have you been to Lago Maggiore?"

"Oh no. I have never been there," Ginger replied. "But I saw an article about it in a travel magazine in my hotel lobby. The monastery looked so majestic and beautiful. I wanted to photograph it with my new camera but was not exactly sure where it was located."

Roberto's playful demeanor returned. "Well, there is a sign. Do you call it serendipity in your country? It is not located too far from my cousin's place. Now, I am certain you should join me."

When they arrived at her hotel, he walked into the lobby and in a most courteous manner said good night. "I have enjoyed your company. You make me laugh. I like your sense of humor and intelligence."

"I had a great time," Ginger replied. "I believe your intelligence far outshines mine, but thank you for the sweet compliment. Good night. I will contact you tomorrow."

When Ginger stopped by the reception desk for her key, she noticed that André was still working. "My goodness, you certainly work long hours. I hope your evening is going well?"

"Oh, yes, signora, and thank you for asking. Did you enjoy the Rotary meeting today?"

"I enjoyed it very much and the nice gentleman who was my interpreter took me to dinner at the charming restaurant around the corner."

"Yes, it is a traditional family place. I am glad you found it to be satisfying." Ginger smiled at his choice of words. André continued, "I saw the man who escorted you in tonight. His picture has been on the front page of our newspaper because of the important, legal case he just won for workers' rights. Perhaps, I should have thanked him but I did not want to interrupt or to be too forward. How do you say this in English? Is forward the proper word?"

She nodded. "Yes. It is a perfect word for the expression. André, may I take a travel magazine from the lobby to my room?"

"Most certainly, and if there is something in it that pleases you, do take it with you as a remembrance of your time here in Italy."

When Ginger closed the door to her room, she kicked off her shoes and was glad to be somewhere alone where she could think. She changed into comfortable lounge wear and piled her pillows up against the headboard of the bed. "What a day this has been!" she actually said out loud. Her thoughts returned to the moment she said goodbye to her travel clients and entered the hotel.

So many things had happened since then; attending the Rotary club meeting, being introduced to Roberto, joining him for dinner, and hearing his unexpected yet compelling invitation. An invitation that was so far from her comfort zone, but so close to the core of her soul-searching journey. She had been trying to be more open to messages from the Beyond, whether they came in the form of dreams, repeated signs, or premonitions. It was a way of navigating the world that she truly wanted to practice more in her own life.

She wondered if Roberto's invitation was the Universe giving her a chance to accept the subtle messages it was offering. An opportunity to say yes to embracing the unknown and going with the flow. If her intuition said she should go, she wondered if she could muster the courage to follow that nudging from within? As she weighed her options, it was easy to get caught up in the polarity of good or bad. *How can I just take off for several days with someone I have only known for one day?* Not just anyone but a handsome man from a foreign country. And not just any foreign country but the country of Italy, the land of passionate men. Perhaps it was crazy thinking. She started to convince herself that it was a bad idea. Given her religious upbringing it seemed reckless and wrong to go for several days with a man she hardly knew.

But, she questioned, *was it true that she did not know him?* In many ways she knew him better in just one day than men she had dated for months. Roberto had a depth to him. He was sincere and honorable. He fought for the underdog in his law practice. He had many friends, a lovely daughter and a reputation to uphold. She was trying hard not to make her decision based on what others would advise. She knew that her parents would not want her to go. Her friends would share cautionary tales of disastrous calamities. And the nuns would definitely say, "Absolutely not!"

She laughed to herself thinking of her years of growing up with their unwavering, strict, religious beliefs. But tonight there was just one person's advice she should be seeking and it was her own. "What would she choose if not one single person in the entire universe was watching? Did she like him? Did she trust him? Did he make her feel special? Did he make her laugh?" Her answer to these questions was yes.

And if decided purely from a practical viewpoint, there was nothing preventing her from going. She had six days to herself with nothing planned. She had a large suitcase full of fabulous clothes purchased for her cruise. She was single. Roberto was widowed and not looking for a relationship because he adored his wife. She liked his straightforward explanation that he did not wish to go on holiday alone, but would rather go with an attractive woman that he found interesting. Ginger had never thought of herself as being beautiful. It was true that she had a terrific figure, expressive, big blue eyes, and a gorgeous smile, but being stunningly attractive was not an image she held of herself. But she realized as she sat pondering her dilemma that Roberto made her feel desirable. He spoke of her magnetic personality, her positive energy, and her inner beauty. *What is inner beauty?* she thought. Perhaps it encompassed the qualities she had been seeking these past few years in her meditation, spiritual readings, and creative visualizations. All she knew, for sure, was that she would like to be with a man who described her as having inner beauty. She knew that there was no practical or rational reason not to accept his invitation if one dismissed what people might think of her. If she made the decision purely from an analytical framework it could be an opportunity for a lovely Italian holiday getaway. She then realized that she should not be searching for the answer in her intellect; she should be searching for it from her inner emotions. *Get out of your thoughts!* she said to herself. *This question begs its answer from the heart.*

"What was the significance of the monastery at Lake Maggiore?" Ginger said out loud. It didn't seem like a coincidence that the monastery she was so strongly drawn to in a magazine existed in the exact area that Roberto planned to visit. "Was it serendipity at work?" She dismissed his hesitancy when he first heard her mention it. He did say he would love to take her there.

It was getting late, and the time had come for her to make a decision. It was then that she remembered her tried-and-true method of making decisions on the critically important issues facing her life. She would do her T-chart.

It always offered her clarity in written form. Taking a piece of paper from the desk, she drew a line down the middle. The "reasons to go" was written above the left-hand column, and the "reasons not to go" above the right-hand column. Ginger said to herself, "Just write down what you are feeling, both from the head and from the heart. Do it quickly. Don't over-think it." With pen in hand, she started writing in the left-hand column indicating the decision to go. At first, the reasons were of a practical nature; she had the time, the clothing, and desire to photograph the beautiful monastery. But as she continued to write other items came forward on the page. Roberto was a nice man, she trusted him, she had been wanting to make changes in her life related to staying in the present moment and going with the flow. The last item in the left-hand column read: "My intuition says to go."

As she started to write in the column as to why she should not go, she could only come up with three reasons. She had already ruled out danger.

Her intuition told her that she was not putting herself in danger. So what were the three reasons not to go? She wrote three things: what would her family say, what would her friends say, and was it respectable to go with a man she hardly knew? As she stared at the sheet of paper she was truly stunned. The reasons for not going had to do with judgement and guilt. It was true that her parents would be concerned. Her mother always stressed the need to be cautious when in situations that dictated it. But had her family not also trusted her to make good decisions? Her friends would also want her to be safe but had always told her to follow her heart. And regarding being a respectable woman, whose judgement would that be coming from?

She knew she was a respectable woman, and more importantly she was a kind, caring, and loving person. As she looked at the reasons in the columns on the piece of paper before her, it became clear to her that the decision was hers and hers alone. If she went in good faith, if she did not hurt anyone, and if she used her intuition along the way, it could be a wonderful experience. Roberto had been completely honest with her. Yes, it would be a trip taken by an adult man and woman. There would be elements of friendship and maybe even some of flirtation, but all with honesty and sincerity. This could be an unexpected blessing. She wanted to create more expansiveness in her life, and this could be her beginning. *Besides*, she thought, *this is not just about you. Often, we are called upon to consider the feelings and needs of others.*

Ginger closed her eyes for a few minutes to be certain that she was not looking outside of herself for answers. She wanted to be clearly listening to her inner voice. And when she opened her eyes, she had made her decision. "I'm going to Lake Maggiore with Roberto!"

As she settled into bed, she felt a wonderful sense of excitement growing. "This is going to be a very special journey. No more doubts. I am going with the flow." When she awoke in the morning, she felt full of energy. As she repacked her suitcase she saw the Italian translation book she had brought on her trip. "What was that word the chef used when he pointed in her direction?" She recalled it was *Bellissima.* "Yes, that was it." As she turned the pages to the word she smiled. It meant "beautiful." She blushed remembering that Roberto had nodded in agreement. He did make her feel beautiful and there was nothing wrong with feeling attractive and pretty. *If we are going to be driving in a convertible through Italy,* she thought with a playful grin, *I should definitely get a long flowing scarf and a dramatic big hat!*

She checked out of the hotel with two hours to spare, before meeting Roberto at his office. She left her luggage in storage for pick up later and inquired about a shop where she could purchase women's apparel. She was happy to see that the recommended shop was located on St. Mark's Square.

The morning sunlight was flooding the stunning facades of the buildings as she entered the square. She pulled her new camera out of her backpack and began taking photographs. There were couples holding hands and sipping cappuccino at outdoor cafe tables, an elderly woman, in a tattered shawl, was feeding the pigeons, and little children were playing near a small fountain. As one of the most photographed squares in all of Europe, Ginger decided that St. Mark's Square deserved to be eloquently referred to as *The Drawing Room of Europe*.

"Welcome to my shop," a lovely young woman greeted Ginger in perfect English.

"Thank you. I am so pleased that you speak English. I apologize that I know very few words in Italian."

"We have many tourists from all around the world. It has prompted me to learn several languages. My name is Genevieve. What can I help you with today?"

"I'm going to Lago Maggiore, and since I will be riding in a convertible, I thought it would be fun to have a flowing scarf and a big hat for the drive."

"You will love the lake region," the young woman said. "I have been there often. It is so peaceful and relaxing."

Ginger was pleased to find that everything she needed was in the one small boutique. She chose a gorgeous multicolored scarf and a large, movie-star-appearing, white hat. She even splurged on a purely fabulous full length, off-the-shoulder, flower-print sundress. And, of course, Ginger rationalized that she needed to buy a most handsome leather bag, large enough to carry her camera. After all, she concluded, her backpack just didn't seem appropriate for the Mediterranean fashion statement she was creating. Italy was known for fine leather, and it would be the fabulous souvenir. "These will be just perfect," Ginger replied with gratitude.

"They all look stunning on you. I am sure you will enjoy your trip to Lago Maggiore," Genevieve said with a smile.

"Have you ever been to the Monastery of St. Catarina there?"

The young woman became silent for a moment. Her demeanor changed, and she looked somewhat melancholy. Ginger could only wonder why she had reacted in this manner. But, within seconds, Genevieve quickly regained her composure and replied, "Yes, I have been there. It is a most impressive setting overlooking the lake." She packaged up Ginger's purchases and said, "I hope you like candles. I am including a little thank you gift for you. It is a white candle with the most heavenly scent. It will be a little reminder of your trip to our country."

"Thank you. I light candles at my home often, and I will cherish this one."

Back on the square, Ginger got out her map to find the directions to Roberto's office. It was not a far distance, and she always loved walking the little narrow streets of Venice. As she crossed over the canal bridges, she peered down the water-filled streets, hoping to catch a glimpse of an ornate gondola with the gondolier dressed in a red and white-striped shirt. She often looked up in Europe to notice open windows with sheer curtains swaying in the breeze, people standing out on their balcony, or laundry hung drying in the sunshine. Visiting Venice somehow touched her soul. Turning a corner she found herself in a small, well-kept square. There in front of her was a majestic, historic building with the sign of Roberto's law firm hanging prominently near the massive wooden doors.

As she entered, Ginger felt as though she should tiptoe quietly. It was a splendid space of grandeur with an air of refinement. The silence was broken by a pleasing woman who approached her.

"May I help you?" she asked.

Before Ginger could answer, she heard a familiar voice. It was Roberto's as he came down the hall to greet her. He looked even more handsome than she had remembered him to be. He was every bit as gracious as he had been the day before. He introduced her to his administrative assistant and two young lawyers in the hallway on the way to his office.

"Please, make yourself comfortable," he added as they entered his corner office. He steered her to a seating area, away from his desk, and near a window overlooking the gardens on the property. "May I offer you a coffee?"

"No thank you," she replied. "I'm just fine." Perhaps it was the word no in her "no thank you" that made him seem nervous as he sat on the edge of the chair across from hers. Ginger gave him a sweet smile as she began. "I have thought over your invitation, and I would like to accept."

Ginger saw the look of disbelief on his face, and his reply was only one word, "Seriously?"

"Yes. I realize that going on a trip with a man I hardly know is not something that I would normally do, but I have decided to trust my intuition, and I have decided to trust you. So, here I am to say, 'Yes.' I would love to go with you to Lago Maggiore."

"If I were a betting man, I would not have wagered that you would have accepted." He now was smiling and looked very pleased. "The only thing that gave me hope that you might accept my invitation was the incredible serendipity surrounding our meeting."

She briefly thought about his reference to serendipity. It had also not gone unnoticed by her. However, she now decided to make a commitment to put aside any doubt or trepidation. She had accepted, and she had a strong premonition that this was going to be a wonderful trip. Roberto also sensed it was time to put all doubt behind them. He returned to his charming playful nature as he asked, "I suppose this means you will not be needing references from my colleagues here at the firm. I had them standing ready to notarize their statements."

Ginger loved his quick wit. "No, you do not have to get references," she teased. "Being here, I can easily see that you have not built your reputation on shady dealings with foreign women!"

"You are just too delightful!" He laughed. "I can definitely see that I have chosen a feisty, independent woman to join me on this holiday. And a beautiful one at that. Are you ready to depart?"

"Yes, and how do you like the statement that this hat makes?" She removed the elegant white hat from her shopping bag and placed it on her head, tilting it ever so slightly to create a more dramatic effect.

At that point, Roberto noticed the name of the boutique on the large shopping bag. "Now, this is getting to be a little too much for my psyche," he exclaimed. Ginger looked puzzled as he continued, "That bag is from my daughter Genevieve's shop. I knew she was working in her boutique this morning. I can hardly believe that you met Jen. That is my nickname for her. Did you just happen to stop into her shop on the way over here?"

"Well, I didn't just happen into her shop. I was searching for a women's apparel store because I needed a few things to make me feel I belonged in Italy. She was very sweet and helpful. She had everything I was hoping to purchase." With that, she draped her flowing new scarf around her neck with flair.

"I can hardly believe you picked my daughter's shop. I must say your Universe has pulled out all the stops to convince us that this is going to be a great holiday!" Roberto was expressing more animation in his voice than Ginger had heard since meeting him. "Shall we be off?" He smiled and stood to give her his arm.

The drive to Lake Maggiore was enjoyable. Roberto was shedding the stress of his work responsibilities with every turn of the winding road. The peaceful lake was dotted with little towns and church steeples. As he kept his eyes on the hairpin turns of the narrow road, Ginger snapped photo after photo of the breathtaking scenery and a few extras of him.

"Hey," he said when he noticed the camera pointed in his direction. "Why are you taking photos of me? I should be taking photos of you in that hat."

"Compliments will get you nowhere with me," she teased. "Besides, you have encouraged me to go with the flow, and I like this image of the wind blowing through your hair."

Even though the top was down on the convertible, the road dictated a slower speed, so they were able to make conversation. Roberto was the perfect tour guide as he described the attractions along their route. "Lago Maggiore is the largest lake in this region. Its shoreline is actually divided between Switzerland and Italy. I have heard it described as having the sophistication of Switzerland and the passion of Italy. Since you love photography I have a surprise for you. The next little lake-side town is Cannobio. They have a most charming restaurant where we can stop for lunch. Do you know what the locals say their specialties are at the restaurant?" Before she could answer he continued, "Their local sausages, cheeses, fish bruschetta, regional wines, and the clicking of cameras!"

Ginger laughed. She so enjoyed his clever use of words and descriptions.

"I'm serious. Wait until you see how picturesque this restaurant is with its balconies and flowers cascading down the original centuries-old walls. Since it is somewhat hidden from view, just off Cannobio's famous boulevard, one would think that no one would know of it. Trust me, it has been discovered, and it can get crowded. I hope we can capture a table in the courtyard. As a photographer, you are going to love this place."

Amateur photographer, Ginger was going to correct him, but he was already on his way to see about an available table for lunch. As she stepped into the small bustling restaurant, she was awe struck by its rustic charm. Retrieving her camera from her new leather bag she tried to be subtle as to not disturb the patrons. She simply could not resist climbing the stairs to the balcony that overlooked the courtyard. As she snapped a few photos, she saw Roberto giving her a thumbs-up from a table below.

"This is absolutely a dream place for lunch," she shared with great enthusiasm. "I thought walking here, along the cobblestone streets of the historic district was glorious, but this setting is pure magic."

"That makes me happy." He smiled. When the waiter arrived and filled their wine glasses Ginger raised her glass. "A toast to the beginning of our journey."

As they clinked their glasses, Roberto said, "Salute." Then in a heartfelt, caring voice he asked, "Are you glad you came Ginger?"

"Absolutely," she replied with enthusiasm.

Over lunch Roberto told her of the other small towns along the lake. Stresa was a resort town, and it was purported that Hemingway once stayed in the grand hotel there. From the Stresa waterfront, he explained that one could take a boat or ferry to the Borromean Islands. "Islola Bella is one of my favorites," he added. "It is a natural treasure because of its stately gardens. They are Italian-style gardens with terraces, ponds, fountains, and statues dating back to the 17th century. White peacocks even wander the gardens to add to the grandeur of the place."

"Where are we staying tonight?" Ginger inquired as they returned to the car.

"It is a small town called Cannero Riviera. I chose it because one of my favorite lake-side hotels is there. The town is a charming place with narrow cobblestone streets, quaint alleyways, piazzas, and great walking trails along the lake. The ferry stop is directly across from the hotel, and one can take the ferry to all of the stops along the lake, including to the Monastery of St. Catarina. But we will take the car to a closer ferry stop tomorrow. We will need the car after our visit because we will be going directly, from there, to my cousin's place."

"Is it going to be alright that I will be joining you at their home?"

"Well, to start with, it is not exactly just a home. They own a large resort property that includes a historic building that is now one of the area's best restaurants. It is also a working winery with acres of vineyards, a tasting room, and a center for weddings and events. They have several luxurious guest rooms in the main building and private cottages on the property. However, if you are wondering if they will easily accept my bringing a woman, they know I have dated on occasion, but I have not brought a woman to their place since I have been widowed. In fact, Ginger, I have not been intimate with a woman since my wife died. I have asked that we stay in the guest cottage far up the hill right at the edge of the vineyard. It has a fabulous view overlooking the rows of vines. I love it there. I chose it because it has two separate bedrooms. You will like it, especially at night on the balcony. The starry nights are so impressive."

"It sounds lovely, and I look forward to meeting your relatives. I'm sure your wife's death was painful for them too," Ginger said with noticeable empathy.

"Yes, it was. We are a close family, and we were all devastated. I appreciate that my cousin's wife has taken my daughter Jen under her wing. Please, do not feel in the least bit uncomfortable. They will be happy to see you as they have been giving me a hard time recently." Roberto laughed as he added, "They say I am becoming a reclusive hermit!"

Ginger remarked that the weather almost felt like the Mediterranean. The air was so soft and warm. Roberto explained that the weather was one of the appealing things about the lake region. "The winter months are mild, and it is so peaceful on the lake. I enjoy being here anytime of the year."

As they drove along the lake to Cannero Riviera, Ginger spotted something through the trees. It looked like a desolate castle taking up the entire space of a tiny island. It almost appeared that the ruins of the fortress were resting directly on the water. "What is that fortress on such a tiny island?" she asked with excitement in her voice.

"You have a good eye. I didn't know we could see Castille di Cannero from the road. It is the ruins of a Rocca Vitaliana fortress built in the 1500s," Roberto replied.

"Is there anywhere that we can pull off so I can take some photographs?"

"Not easily, but the very best way to photograph it is from the lake. The ruins cannot be visited because of the crumbling walls, but many people take a boat there and picnic on the shore. I'll check with the hotel to see if we can rent a boat to go there before dinner."

Ginger could not believe Roberto's kindness. "I'm really touched that you would go to all that effort for me."

"Your enthusiasm actually delights me. I am enjoying being your host and tour guide."

"I should have hired you in my travel agency," she quipped. "But I'm sure I could not have afforded you." They both burst into laughter.

As Roberto maneuvered around a large bus that was taking up most of their lane on the narrow road, Ginger looked down to admire a delightful village on the water. It had a church steeple and tiny houses dotting the lakefront. "Here we are. This is Cannero Riviera where we are staying tonight. Isn't it a quaint little village?"

They drove down the steep narrow street leading to a lovely hotel on the promenade along the lake. Roberto approached the reception desk indicating he had a reservation for two rooms. Ginger smiled wondering when he had made the reservation. She remembered his offer to have separate rooms if it made her more comfortable. She heard Roberto discussing something with the desk clerk in Italian. She could not understand a word, but after a few minutes he turned to say, "I have just rented a boat to take you out to the fortress. Grab your camera. They will take the luggage to our rooms. We must hurry to capture the early evening light on the lake. The marina is to the right of the hotel. I will meet you there. I want to get something from the car."

As she waited at the dock, Roberto came running with a backpack over his shoulder. Ginger noticed what good shape he was in to have sprinted that fast.

"Ready?" he asked as he dangled the keys and invited her aboard the boat.

"Are you piloting this boat? I didn't know that 'captain' was also on your resume?" Ginger teased.

"There are many things you don't know about me."

Roberto was right, the lighting was perfect. The pristine lake shimmered, as the fortress almost seemed to be floating on the water. Ginger snapped photos from all sides as Roberto steered the boat completely around the tiny island. "I'm going to anchor here by the shore," he said. I brought a bottle of champagne, and it's still chilled. This would be the perfect spot for a toast."

"What a great idea," Ginger agreed. "Could you please hold up the bottle so I can capture a photo before I put my camera away?"

"Does that mean I can add the title of 'sommelier' to my resume, too?" he quipped good-naturedly.

As they sat back on the cushions sipping champagne, Ginger proposed a toast in recognition of Roberto's big court win. In return, he proposed one to her willingness to go with the flow. And as was the tradition in Italy, they toasted to good health and happiness. She also made a silent toast in her thoughts. It was a toast of gratitude to the Universe that she had somehow mustered the courage to follow her intuition and come on this trip with Roberto. She was having such a good time and it was just their first day. Ginger playfully suggested that perhaps he might like to make it a tradition to toast champagne at the fortress every time he won a significant legal case.

"I don't think I have it in me to take on one of that magnitude anytime soon. Remember, I'm just beginning to relax and unwind from this recent one!" Roberto exclaimed emphatically.

"Well, unwinding with you is most enjoyable. Thank you again for inviting me," Ginger said with sincere appreciation.

Roberto then offered a suggestion. "I learned that they are having a special seafood extravaganza tonight at the restaurant next door to the hotel. Dining alfresco with music sounds inviting. The hotel has a fabulous fine dining restaurant, but I thought this might be a nice change of pace. And, besides, if it is featuring seafood it will remind you of Seattle, just in case you are getting homesick."

"Homesick when I am in Cannero Riviera with an attractive Italian man? I don't think so!" she responded with humor.

"Then I'll make reservations for 8:00 pm, so we can have time to freshen up before dinner."

When Ginger entered her room, she was impressed. Roberto had not asked if she wanted a separate room. She felt it was considerate of him. He knew that she was uncomfortable with an assumption of intimacy, so he made a very sweet gesture from the start of their trip. He was every bit the thoughtful man she guessed him to be. The spacious room was decorated with gilded white furniture and an ornate padded headboard that matched the brocade draperies.

She undressed and headed for the bathroom where she found glistening fixtures and a huge wall of mirrors across from an oversized open shower. She was relieved to find that the faucet was not as complicated to operate as some that she had encountered in Europe. The warm water was heavenly, and she indulged herself for several extra minutes. As she went to step out of the shower, she found that the faucet would not turn off. It just kept running, and not just as a trickle, but as a heavy stream of water. She quickly put on the fluffy white robe hanging on the wall and called the reception desk. They apologized and assured her that they had a plumber on the premises who would arrive shortly to make the repairs. There was a knock on her door within ten minutes.

Well, this is great service, she thought.

The plumber was a stocky, short man, almost approaching what she might consider as being chubby. She noticed he had a most endearing, shy demeanor. She noted, by his employee badge, that his name was Alberto.

"Alberto," she started to explain. He immediately stopped her with a gesture of his hand to indicate that he did not speak or understand English. She could easily sense that he was embarrassed to be in the presence of a woman in only a robe. She simply moved aside and pointed toward the bathroom. Or was it called the toilette in Europe? No matter.

She was running late and wished she had retrieved her makeup and personal items so she could continue to get ready. As she looked into the bathroom, she noticed to her embarrassment that she had left her skimpy black lace panties and bra hanging in full view on the towel rack!

Since her extra-long shower had put her far behind in dressing for dinner, she wondered if she could just slip in and gather her makeup and lingerie. On second thought, she sensed Alberto's embarrassment, and she did not want to add to the awkward moment.

Why didn't she dress first and then call maintenance after she had gone to dinner? she chided herself. *Stop to think next time!* She rationalized, though, that the water was not a trickle. It was pouring out of the shower head.

There was another knock on the door. She opened it to find Roberto in a gorgeous cream-colored jacket and light blue shirt. He looked puzzled to see her still in a bathrobe. "I thought, since you are my dinner date, that I would come down the hall to escort you. I know I said we would go casual but…"

Before he could go on teasing her, he saw the frantic look on her face. She stepped out into the hall and explained everything in a whisper; the fact that the plumber was embarrassed to be in the room with her in a bathrobe, that she could not speak Italian to ask him to leave and return later for the repairs; that she needed her makeup; and especially that she was devastated that she had sexy lingerie hanging on the towel rack right in clear view of the gentle, shy plumber. Roberto was more than mildly amused by her predicament.

"Well," he said with a straight face. "You told me you appreciated chivalry in a man, so you can count on me to take care of this; however, I would suggest you come back into the room and not remain out here in the public hallway in a bathrobe."

Ginger agreed and took a seat in a chair at the far corner of her room. She picked up a magazine and pretended to be reading it. She did not want to cause Alberto further uneasiness by making eye contact with him. She could hear Roberto speaking in Italian, and heard the two men laughing.

After Alberto left and closed the door, Roberto came out of the bathroom. His eyes were sparkling, and he could hardly keep a straight face, as he handed her the sexy black lingerie.

"As you say, with your charming American expression, 'the coast is clear.' He will be back to finish the job in one half hour. I can change our reservation. Is that enough time you to get ready for dinner?"

"Yes. Thank you." Ginger knew she had to hurry to put her makeup on and decide on what to wear for dinner. Since she had seen Roberto in a jacket she decided on the flowing vibrant orange dress that everyone had admired on the cruise ship. It clung to her figure, was sleeveless showing off her tan sculptured arms, and even showed a bit of cleavage. It was elegant yet casual for an outdoor setting. When she looked in the mirror she decided it was just right. Roberto was already in the lobby reading the newspaper. He looked up as she came down the stairs, and she knew, by the look on his face, that she had chosen the perfect dress.

"You look particularly stunning tonight," he said as he offered his arm to escort her to dinner.

The restaurant was in full swing when they arrived. The outdoor seating area was blanketed with tiny white lights, and the dining tables were set in a circle, in anticipation of the dancing that would take place later in the evening.

"I'm glad we came here," Ginger said, expressing her pleasure at his choice. "The weather is so warm and balmy. This is just perfect for a girl who comes from Seattle where it rains so often. We actually experience an average of 150 rainy days a year."

"That is a lot of rain in a year," he agreed. "I didn't see your webbed feet, but I did notice as you came down the stairs that you have great legs."

Ginger smiled. She loved the way that she and Roberto shared these little exchanges; sometimes flirting, sometimes humorous, but always clever. They added to the enjoyment she felt in being with him. And she could see by the look on his face that he found them to be entertaining too.

"Would you like an appetizer?" he inquired.

"Since we are relaxing and making a night of it, I would love to start with some calamari. It is a favorite of mine, and I see it here on the menu. Since we had that huge lunch in Cannobio, I think the fish soup you recommended earlier sounds perfect."

Their dinner mood was light and enjoyable. Roberto confessed that he found the incident with the plumber to be endearing. "That kind man was so shy that I couldn't imagine what he was thinking with that sexy lingerie hanging in full view. It was practically over his shoulder!"

"I wasn't sure if I should have tried to thank him as he left," Ginger replied. "But, unfortunately, amidst all of the embarrassment, I couldn't remember the words for thank you in Italian."

"It's *grazie*, but if you really want to show your appreciation you can say *grazie mille*. That means 'thank you a thousand times.'"

"I love that expression." Ginger raised her glass and said, "*Grazie mille* for this most wonderful day." She liked the way the cheerful expression rolled off of her lips. Yes, it might just become her favorite.

As the dinner progressed, the conversation was relaxed and comfortable. Ginger remembered that the dinner pace in Europe was unhurried. The calamari was exceptional, and when the waiter cleared the appetizer plates he returned with their entrees, Ginger could not believe her eyes! It was the largest bowl of fish soup that she had ever seen as a single serving. Teaming with a wide variety of different fish, it was the enough to feed an entire family. As she looked toward Roberto for his reaction, she saw that he had already tasted the steaming broth and gave her a nod of approval. Well, there goes a light dinner she laughed to herself. As they finished their entrée, the band who had been setting up earlier, was ready to offer dance music. Ginger tapped Roberto on the arm to get his attention. "Isn't that the nice man who helped us with the plumbing problem? I almost did not recognize him in that crisp white shirt and his neatly pressed dress slacks."

"Yes, that is Alberto," Roberto replied, as he looked over his shoulder.

"He is a nice-looking guy," Ginger added. "A little chubby, but attractive.

"What is the meaning of 'chubby?' " Roberto asked. "I don't know that English expression."

"Oh, it just means his stature is somewhat stocky. But he's such a sweet, gracious man, I think I will just describe him as being husky," Ginger said with a most sincere look on her face.

"Is it better to be husky than chubby?" Roberto was now in full-on laughter. "If so, I had better tell my daughter that I will have to decline the second helping of her famous pasta. I wouldn't want to get chubby!" Somehow, the word "chubby" was as curious and delightful to him as the words *grazie mille* were to her.

"Look," she whispered. "Alberto is going to ask one of the women at that table to dance." Just then, Alberto, with a hesitant and shy demeanor, got up the courage, and walked all the way across the dance floor to the table where three women were sitting. He asked one of them to dance, but she declined, as did the next one he asked.

Ginger felt sad seeing the look of rejection and embarrassment on Alberto's face.

"Ouch," Roberto replied. "That reminds me of the painful rejections I experienced in secondary school. It's hard on a guy's ego."

At that moment, Ginger could not stand the fact that the kind man she had embarrassed earlier at the hotel was now facing humiliation. No matter how minor his rejection, it was genuinely upsetting to her.

"Could you please excuse me?" she asked Roberto.

Roberto watched Ginger walk directly towards Alberto's table in her alluring, figure hugging dress. When she reached his table, she held out her hand indicating she was asking him to dance. Alberto looked shocked, but Ginger did not move one inch. Again, with a smile, she coaxed him to join her in a dance. Roberto was now somewhere between feeling humored by her crazy spirit and touched by her overwhelming empathy and kindness. Ginger gently smiled at Alberto as they began to dance. She could not speak his language, but she wanted him to know that she was enjoying dancing with him.

Roberto sat back in his chair with his eyes on Ginger. She was indeed a beautiful woman with silky brown hair, big blue eyes and a sublime figure. It was the beauty that was not outward that made him drawn to her; she had a positive attitude that was unwavering. And her sense of kindness had now touched him deeply. He discretely looked over at the table of the women who had declined Alberto's invitation to dance. They were mesmerized and watched Ginger's every step. Roberto also noticed that Alberto was actually a very good dancer. He was light on his feet for a "husky" man, and he definitely had rhythm.

When the song ended, he heard Ginger say, "*Grazie mille,*" at which Alberto seemed genuinely pleased. Alberto then walked Ginger back to their table where he shook Roberto's hand in an old-fashioned gesture to thank him for sharing his lady for a dance.

"You are just one of the most delightful women I have ever met. You keep amazing me at every turn." Roberto felt his admiration grow deeper seeing Ginger so passionately defending Alberto's honor. As he heard the next slow song begin, he reached for her hand to join him on the dance floor. As he put his arm around her waist, she realized that this was the closest that they had ever been. It felt nice to be in his arms. She noticed he pulled her closer as they danced.

It was not Ginger's style to dance without chatting incessantly. She suspected it was a bit of insecurity. However, this time she chose to practice slowing down and enjoying the moment. Putting her head on his shoulder, they danced without a word. She could tell that Roberto was a sensual man. It was true that he had understandably shut down since his wife's death, but she could feel that it was a deeply rooted part of who he was as a man.

As the dance ended Roberto said, "There is a small, lively piano bar in the hotel. Would you like a cognac before we call it a night?"

Ginger nodded and turned to wave goodbye to Alberto, but he was on the dance floor, deep in conversation as he had already found a new partner.

The bar was full of patrons, but Roberto managed to capture a small table next to the piano player. As they sipped cognac from their heated snifters, Ginger smiled and said, "Yum, delicious French cognac while we are here in Italy."

"Yes, it is good. Although we also make cognac here in Italy. It is true most people associate cognac with France because it is a variety of brandy named after Cognac, France."

Ginger liked hearing Roberto's interesting bits of information, especially when they were regarding things that interested her. It seemed especially thoughtful.

As they continued to enjoy their conversation, the piano player leaned over to ask where Ginger was from in the United States. He heard her speaking and explained that his wife spoke fluent English as she was originally from England. Ginger explained that she was from Washington State in the northwestern corner near Canada. Within fifteen minutes the piano player made an announcement. "I see that we have a woman from America with us this evening. I wonder if she would like to make a request?"

Ginger was caught off guard by his question. As he looked in her direction, her mind was racing for a reply. "Do you know 'New York, New York'?" she asked.

"Yes, it is one of my favorites too." As he played the song, several of the people in the bar nodded and smiled in her direction.

Thank goodness, she thought to herself. *If I were in France, they would not be so friendly to know an American tourist was in their midst.*

Ginger had often heard that the French had a definite dislike for American tourists. Although she had good friends in France, and had many positive experiences in their country, she was well aware that there were French locals who resented the visitors from the U.S. She laughed at their reference to the Americans who flooded their cities as visitors with "big, white tennis shoes." She had vowed to always purchase walking shoes in a dark color. Nonetheless, she often wondered how Americans were spotted immediately when traveling abroad. Yes, they spoke English, but so did people from Canada, and those who spoke with the accents of Australia and Great Britain. She did not want to ask Roberto in the middle of her requested song, so she listened intently to the end, clapped enthusiastically, and said, "*Grazie mille.*" She was becoming addicted to the charming phrase of gratitude.

Roberto suggested it was time to depart as they had a very full day coming up. He advised her that they needed to leave relatively early to drive to the town where they were to catch the morning ferry to the Monastery of St. Caterina. He tipped the piano player and walked her to the door of her room where he kissed her sweetly on the cheek. As he turned to leave, he said, "Good night, special lady. Thank you for a most enjoyable day."

They arrived at the ferry terminal the next morning with just enough time to purchase tickets and find seats on the upper outside deck where Roberto suggested she could get some good photographs as they approached the monastery. As they sailed closer, Ginger was awe struck by the magnificence of the Hermitage of Santa Caterina. The sight of it perched on the sheer cliff overlooking the lake was majestic. Her camera was clicking over and over as they approached.

"Thank you for bringing me here. It is far more stunning than I even imagined."

"I'm glad you are pleased," Roberto replied softly. Once more, Ginger thought she noticed a sadness in his voice.

Before she could ask him about her observation, the ferry pilot announced their arrival in three languages. "Watch your step as you exit,"

The eighty steps to the top did not seem daunting as Ginger found different views to photograph at every turn. After paying the entry fee, Roberto highlighted some of the places she should not miss. He recommended the inner courtyard with its Renaissance arches, the bell tower with its spire and cross and especially the views from the curved, arched portico.

"Take all the time you need. I'll just walk a bit and meet you in the church. I'd like to light a candle today."

There is that melancholy voice again, she thought. *I must ask him about it on the way back.*

She headed out with her camera. As he had explained, the portico captivated her. She could hardly believe that she was standing amidst gleaming white columns overlooking the lake below from the site of a 14th century monastery that still housed Benedictine monks. It almost felt surreal. She had been mesmerized by the photos in the travel magazine, but nothing could compare to being there in person.

After an hour of taking photos, she decided to head to the church to find Roberto. Entering the beautiful candlelit church she did not see Roberto at first. When her eyes adjusted to the dim light she caught a glimpse of him. He was sitting on a bench in one of the side chapels. His head was bent forward, and he was sobbing. Ginger realized immediately why he was so grief-stricken. His wife Christina had died less than two years before. Since they had a vacation home in the region, they must have come here often. She knew how much he adored and missed her.

Ginger was flooded with emotion. For several minutes she just stood quietly watching him from behind a pillar. She so regretted that she had not followed her instincts to ask him about his hesitancy. She saw it in his body language, not once, but twice. And she also remembered his daughter's pensive response. *How painful this must be for both of them,* she thought sadly. Roberto lost the woman he loved, and his sweet daughter lost her mother.

Ginger was overwhelmed with sadness to see Roberto weeping in such sorrow. It was as if months and months of grief were spilling out. He had been gracious to bring her to the monastery despite his loss. Roberto knew how enthusiastic she had been to visit the site and did not want to disappoint her. That was the kind of person he was. She now wished with all her heart that he had told her he could not bear to come to the St. Caterina Monastery. She felt deep compassion for Roberto who had lost so much and was now grieving so deeply.

She walked in quietly, sat down next to him and put her arm around his shoulders. They sat there together in silence for what seemed like a very long time. Finally, Roberto broke the silence. "I'm ready to go now."

Without talking, they walked down the steps again to the dock. Since the ferry was not scheduled to arrive for a half hour, they found a bench and sat alongside the lake. Roberto spoke first.

"The cancer was terrible. We tried every specialist, but it just had advanced too far. In the beginning, we used to come here and pray for a miracle. She was so brave, and I felt so helpless."

Ginger reached over and held his hand in silence. When she sensed he wanted to share more, she simply said, "You must miss her so very much."

"Yes, I do. She was the most wonderful person. We met in college and from the first minute I saw her I knew she was the one for me. And she felt exactly the same way. Oh, it wasn't always perfect. We had our arguments, but we always made up. There was never a doubt about our commitment to each other. We had a great life together for thirty-five years, and I wouldn't have traded one of those years for anything. She meant the world to me."

"I'm truly sorry it has been so painful for you to return here. I would never have suggested we come had I known how much sorrow it would have caused you," Ginger said with a tone of regret mixed with compassion.

Roberto's face softened, and he smiled ever so gently. "No, Ginger, I am happy we came here today. I have missed Christina terribly. As I sat in the chapel, I came to the realization that since she died, I have also died inside. My daughter and friends have been very worried about me. Somehow, I just have not been able to move on.

Today, in the chapel, I could feel Christina's presence. It was so strong. It's as if she were telling me to let go of my grief, that she was okay. In the weeks before she died, she kept telling me that when she was gone she wanted me to go on living. I just could not accept her words; it hurt too much. Back there in the chapel, I could hear her saying it was now time to go forward, without tears. Not only for myself but for our daughter."

Ginger whispered softly, "I believe that her spirit will always be with you, Roberto. That will never ever change."

As they rode back on the ferry, she thought about life. She could see that it was a choice to keep living once one had lost someone so precious. It truly was a choice. It must take tremendous courage and faith to choose to go on. Ginger knew, in her heart, that Christina would want that for Roberto. She had told him in the past, and she told him again today.

On the ferry, Roberto apologized to Ginger, "I'm sorry you had to witness my sadness at the beautiful monastery you so looked forward to visiting."

Ginger looked into his eyes; she wanted him to truly hear what she had to say. "You know how much we have talked about serendipity in the last two days. It may not have been a coincidence that we came here today. I saw the picture of this monastery in a magazine, and wanted to photograph it. Then you and I met at a Rotary meeting in Venice. I don't want it to appear that I know of such matters, but I am wondering if there was more of a spiritual reason for you to be here. Perhaps, in ways that we can't begin to comprehend, you were meant to come today so Christina could share her loving message with you."

Roberto was moved by her comment. "That is a touching and sweet way to look at it. I did feel Christina's spirit at the monastery, and it made me so comforted to know she was at peace and happy."

Back in the car, Roberto gave a heavy sigh. He seemed noticeably lighter, and Ginger sensed that he somehow felt better. It still seemed like a time for her to be sensitive and respectful.

"Are you going to feel up to being with your cousin and his wife tonight?" she asked.

"Most certainly, they are family. They loved Christina too. They have been concerned about my well-being since her death. We have had many long talks. If I appear distracted or drained they will understand."

At first they drove in silence. Ginger knew it had been a very emotional day for Roberto. She sincerely felt a deep sense of empathy. The loss of someone that he cherished so very much would take time to heal. But, somehow, she had a strong inner feeling that this day had been a big step forward for him.

After a while, Ginger initiated some light conversation. "What is your cousin's name?"

"His name is Alessandro, and his wife's name is Sophia," Roberto explained. "I was an only child, and he is very much like a brother to me. In fact, I consider his children as my niece and nephew. You may meet their daughter Martina if she is working in the restaurant tonight. You will like them, and they will enjoy your company. Trust me, you are going to love their place. It has been in the family for many years."

"I remember coming here often when I was a little boy. Our grandfather owned the vineyard, and would have us help him prune the vines, or should I say gather the branches? And, when we finished, he would let Alessandro and me take turns driving the old red tractor that pulled the trailer. I have the fondest memories of those days and the many good times we have shared. My cousin has built the property into a successful business. It is an impressive working winery. They actually produce an excellent Sangiovese, but they limit production to use in their restaurant, at wine tastings and special events. Of course, they make enough to gift to family and friends."

As they turned up the road Roberto explained that the old original farmhouse had now been expanded to include a popular restaurant, a terrace bar, wine tasting cellar and lodging.

"The restaurant is named Emilia's in honor of our great grandmother," he added.

As they approached, Ginger could see rows of vines all the way to the top of the ridge. It was an impressive sight. Along the gravelled entry drive were barrels of colorful flowers.

Roberto added, "Sofia has done a lot with flowers on the property. Be sure to take note of the original art in the restaurant. Her grandmother was an art dealer in Rome, and there are several remarkable pieces. One of my favorites is in the guesthouse where we are staying tonight."

Ginger was enamored with the idyllic setting. The original stone farmhouse had been tastefully expanded to include several guest rooms. It looked as if the old stones had been brought in to match from a neighboring centuries old building. The walkways were paved with stone and lined with lanterns. It looked like a property that could have been featured in a wine spectator magazine. She knew this was not the time for photo taking as she was still feeling a need to be sensitive to the experience Roberto had been through that afternoon. Since they were staying for two nights she was sure she could slip away to take a few photos the next day. Alessandro and Sofia came quickly out to greet Roberto as they had seen the car coming up the road. They hugged each other warmly and spoke in Italian. As Roberto turned to introduce Ginger, they all immediately began to speak English. She found it to not only to be a relief, but also a most hospitable gift. She looked forward to visiting easily over dinner. Just then everyone heard a squeal of delight as a young woman came running out of the restaurant and threw her arms around Roberto.

"Ginger, I'd like you to meet my niece Martina," he said.

The young woman was obviously very fond of Roberto and loved being called his niece. When she turned toward Ginger, she realized she was American and also began to speak in English. "I'm so glad to meet you, and relieved to know that my stogy, old uncle is out having fun with a pretty woman." She was laughing mischievously as Roberto gave her a little tap on the behind with the rolled-up newspaper he was carrying. "Is that the newspaper article about your case? Oh, please, let me see it!" Martina asked with excitement. "My friends from Venice have told me that your picture has been on the front page for two days."

"Congratulations," Sofia said in English so that Ginger could understand. "I'm sure you are happy, not only to have won the case, but to finally have it completed. Haven't you spent a year working on this trial?"

"More than a year, but it feels like a decade!" Roberto replied.

"This certainly calls for a celebration," Alessandro said. "I already have a good bottle of champagne on ice." He then turned to address Ginger, "At dinner, we will introduce you to the wine we produce here. I hope you like red?"

Before Ginger could answer, Roberto replied, "You have already won the admiration of this woman. Red is her preference, and I must admit we have sampled a few bottles since leaving Venice. Of course, none as good as yours," he teased.

"You have always been our best critic," Sophia declared playfully. "Why don't you take your things up to your favorite guesthouse. It is ready for you and there is coffee and fresh cream for the morning. Shall we meet in an hour on the terrace? It is so nice to meet you Ginger. I look forward to hearing more about your life."

On the short drive to the guesthouse, Roberto was unusually quiet. "Are you alright?" Ginger asked in a gentle voice.

"Yes," he replied. "I was just thinking about your sensitivity and caring nature. It touched me deeply this afternoon. I'm just feeling a little drained right now, but I will rebound this evening. I will be with people whose positive energy makes me feel good. And, Ginger, I want you to know I put you right there with Alessandro and Sophia."

"Thank you. Your family is gracious, and they have already made me feel welcomed. It is easy to see how much they love you. I'm sure it will be a special evening."

The guest house could not have been more stunning. From the outside the weathered stonework looked as if it had been nestled in the vineyard for centuries. Several steps led up to a magnificent oversized front door with a carved relief of clusters of grapes. The house seemed so far removed from the reality of a bustling world. It was an oasis amongst old vines.

"I think we can make this work for a few days," Roberto commented with humor as he began unloading the luggage from the car.

"That is an understatement if I ever heard one. I'm truly speechless!" Ginger exclaimed. "The location of this guesthouse is amazing."

"If you think the setting is stunning, wait until you see the view from the rear balcony."

As they entered the guesthouse Ginger could see Sofia's decorating talents in every room. And when she stepped out onto the balcony it was every bit as spectacular as Roberto described. Not a bit of humanity in sight, but rows and rows of vines all the way to the top of the ridge with a backdrop of bright blue skies and puffy white clouds. She could hear the birds chirping and the sun was just beginning to set, casting pink streaks across the sky. Roberto brought in the luggage, and Ginger noticed he placed hers in a second bedroom.

"Let's sit out on the balcony for a few minutes," Roberto suggested. "I'll get us a bottle of Pellegrino."

Out on the balcony, Ginger felt that the guesthouse offered the perfect setting for Roberto to finally relax. He seemed genuinely pleased that he could bring her to his cousin's place to experience the beauty and tranquility.

"Do you want to get your camera out?"

"Not tonight," she replied with a kindly tone in her voice. "This evening is for you. Besides, I will have the entire day here tomorrow to drive you crazy with the constant clicking of my camera."

As they sat sipping Italy's favorite sparking water, she realized that she may never drink Pellegrino again without thinking of this moment. She was sitting in the midst of a vineyard in one of her favorite countries in the world.

When she finally noticed the time, Ginger said she wanted to take a few extra minutes to get ready for the evening.

"I always like to dress up a little when I am invited for dinner. It just seems more respectful to the host or hostess."

"I'll sit awhile longer before I change," Roberto replied, leaning back into his chair cushions. As Ginger turned to look back at him, she thought about her trepidation in deciding to come on the trip. How unfortunate it would have been had she declined.

In her guest room, she pondered what to wear. She remembered the elegant outfit she had packed to represent her western heritage on the cruise. How different it was than the ragged flannel shirt and blue jeans she wore growing up on the ranch. This western wear was pure elegance. A fitted black skirt, sandals with turquoise stones, a cream-colored silk blouse and a leather fringed vest. She had also brought her finest turquoise jewelry, a large bracelet from New Mexico and exquisite silver earrings.

"Well, aren't you a stunning reflection of the American West!" Roberto said as he saw her enter the room. "You would have driven those Wyoming cowboys crazy tonight, but you'll just have to settle for the admiring eyes of this Italian guy."

"I'll take him," she said and reached for his arm.

When they arrived at the terrace bar, Ginger realized her attire was perfect. The terrace was casual; paved in bricks, small wooden tables were scattered amongst the beautiful antiques wine barrels and murals of wineries adorned the walls. Alessandro and Sofia were visiting with a few of the guests but came directly to greet them.

"The look you have chosen for the evening is so becoming on you," Sophia commented as they approached.

When they were seated, Roberto handed Sofia an elegantly wrapped gift box. "You remembered my favorite Swiss chocolates!" she declared with gratitude as she opened the box. "Perhaps, I may even share a few pieces with my favorite man," she said smiling at Alessandro. With that Alessandro put his arm around her, gave her an adoring look and a lingering kiss on her cheek. They all toasted with champagne, and as the daylight faded, flickering little lanterns came on to create a warm glow.

Following cocktail hour, they moved into the formal dining room with its crisp, white tablecloths and large wooden chairs carved to reflect the winery scenes. Ginger remembered to comment on the beautiful original art. The fresh fish she ordered was exceptional as was the impeccable service. Roberto encouraged Ginger to re-tell them the story about growing up on a working ranch in Wyoming. And she expressed interest in their life as winery owners. The dinner conversation was pleasantly easy. A friend of Roberto's stopped by the table to say hello, and an older couple came over to compliment Ginger on her western attire. She sensed that Roberto was tired, but he rallied and was warm and engaging.

As the evening came to a close, Sofia explained to Roberto that they would be leaving early in the morning for two days of meetings in Zurich. As they said their good-byes, Ginger shared her sincerest appreciation for a lovely evening. When Roberto shared his farewell with Alessandro, she noticed that their hug was particularly long and caring. As cousins they were definitely as close as brothers. It had been a very emotional day for Roberto, and he looked exhausted. Back at the guest house Roberto walked her to the door of her room. He gave her a sweet good night kiss on the cheek.

"Thank you for your kindness today. It meant more to me than I can put into words right now."

Ginger put her finger to his lips. "No words needed. You just need sleep."

She gave him a caring hug and went into her room. As she climbed into bed, she kept thinking about Roberto at the monastery. Even though she felt it had been a first step toward his healing, she knew it had been extremely emotional and painful for him. Sadness came over her thinking of him being all alone in his room after such a heart-wrenching day. Ginger wished she could think of a way to offer him comfort. Being a naturally compassionate person, in this moment she felt compelled to let Roberto know he was not alone with his feelings. She imagined how devastating it must be. He had offered an apology, concerned that she had been subject to what he considered an uncomfortable situation. However, she hoped that he believed her when she told him that friendship means deeply caring about a person no matter what emotions surface. He was hurting and it was most understandable.

It was then that an idea came to her. It was not something she would have ever done without her overwhelming sense of empathy. Her intuition told her that a caring gesture was needed to assure Roberto that he was not alone and that she understood. She got out of bed and went to her suitcase. Somewhere she knew she had packed the sweat suit set that the cruise line had given passengers as a farewell gift. As she slipped the pants and top on, she was relieved to find they were made of very soft fleece. Roberto was already in bed with the lights off when she tiptoed in. In her fleece sweats, she slid between the sheets and cuddled him, spooning from behind with a gentle hug.

"Is it okay?" she whispered.

"It is so nice. Thank you," he replied, and he fell asleep.

When she awoke, Roberto was already up. She stretched and climbed out of bed to the smell of freshly brewed coffee. Roberto was sitting out on the balcony.

"Good morning," he said in a relaxed and welcoming manner. "Thank you for that very sweet gesture last night. It really means a lot to me."

Ginger acknowledged his appreciation with a sweet smile. "And how do you like this oversized sweat suit I am wearing? They ran out of my size and only had an extra-large left. I have to hold up the pants to walk." She laughed.

"Let me get you some coffee. I wouldn't want you to fall down trying to maneuver in those! I think two of you could fit into them," he commented with humor.

When she settled into a comfortable deck chair with her coffee, she noticed he was writing in a journal.

"I write poetry," he explained. "I have done it for years, ever since my college days. It is a way to be creative and a nice change from writing sterile law briefs. Maybe I will write a sentimental poem about your beauty and kindness. Or, maybe I will write an entertaining poem about you dancing with the chubby plumber," he said, with a twinkle in his eye.

Ginger was pleased to see Roberto returning to his playful self. After a second cup of coffee, Roberto said enthusiastically, "I have a surprise for you. How would you like to go horseback riding through the vineyards?"

"Are you serious? That would be a fabulous experience!" Ginger replied with a mixture of enthusiasm and appreciation.

"Sofia left us a note to say we are welcomed to ride her horses today. They need exercise. I think she may have been prompted by your charming comment last night about growing up on a ranch and riding a horse before you learned to walk. She left you some riding gear at the stables."

"This will be something I will never forget, riding horseback through a vineyard in Italy. How thoughtful of Sofia. You are joining me right?"

"Would I miss seeing a good-looking cowgirl in the saddle?" he said sporting a broad unwavering grin. "And don't forget your camera. The lake views from the top of the ridge are fantastic."

Their morning was truly unforgettable. The views from the ridge were every bit as spectacular as Roberto had described. Ginger was surprised to see how comfortable he was in the saddle. She had also learned that morning that he wrote poetry. Roberto was, indeed, an incredible man in so many ways.

When they returned to the stables Roberto jumped from his horse first. "Let me help you down. I wouldn't want to forget that chivalry is high on your list of priorities in a man." As he lifted her down, with his hands around her waist, they were face to face very close. It was one of those moments that both people recognize as being noticeably significant. "Thank you for sharing this incredible morning with me," Roberto spoke, without pulling away. With that, he bent down and kissed her on the lips. It was such a tender, romantic kiss that she found herself willingly responding as she returned the sweetness of his kiss. When he stepped back she smiled warmly. He nodded with a gentle smile of his own.

Back at the guesthouse, they realized they had just enough time to change for the afternoon wine tasting that Alessandro had arranged for them. Roberto knew his cousin was looking forward to an assessment of the newest blend he had created.

The tasting was held in the wine cellar, and Ginger was glad that she had brought her camera. As she and Roberto toasted one another, a guest offered to take a photo of them. The dark brick walls, racks of wine bottles, wooden beams and large barrels were the perfect backdrop for the wine tasting. Coming back out into the sunlight, Ginger asked, "Do you mind if I just meet you back at the guesthouse? I'd like to take a few photos of the property as I walk back."

"Not at all. I'll see you back there whenever you finish. *Ciao!*" Roberto saw the puzzled look on Ginger's face. "'*Ciao*' is Italian for 'good-bye,' or better described, a casual 'see you later.'"

"Oh. Now I understand. And, by the way," Ginger added, "maybe, you could open one of those bottles of wine you are carrying. It might like to breathe a little."

"Good idea," Roberto replied with a smile.

Ginger spent some time taking photos of the impressive winery and property. As she walked back to join Roberto she saw a small wooden bench under a tree overlooking the vineyard.

She was drawn to it, as if her inner voice said, *Here is the perfect spot to take a few minutes to gather your thoughts.* She sat on the bench and started a little dialog with herself. *What was it that I am feeling?* There was something within trying to get her attention. *What was it?* She realized it had something to do with the kiss that she had shared with Roberto. It felt so wonderful to her. She hadn't wanted to kiss anyone for a long time. Their exchange seemed so natural and so romantic that she found herself wishing for more.

She thought about their earlier discussions. The fact that couples could go on a holiday together with no expectations and with no strings attached. For her, this trip was not a meaningless fling. They were very fond of each other and there was definitely a mutual attraction. Yes, it was true that she did not feel that Roberto was the soulmate she longed to meet. But she was also certain that he did not see her as his forever love either. They were two adults who came together, through a bit of serendipity, and now they had found themselves in a romantic setting with some emerging feelings and desires, stirring in both of them. She reflected on her personal journey. She wanted to stay in the present moment, to enjoy life and to go with the flow. This was a moment that deserved romance. *What a sad thing to let it go by*, she thought.

Out of nowhere, the answer to her quandary came to her in the form of questions. *Why do men have to be the ones to initiate lovemaking? Did he long for intimacy as much as she did?* He had initiated the first invitation with his beautiful kiss. *Why couldn't she make the second invitation, which would be to make love in this romantic setting?*

Sitting on the bench under the tree, she weighed the pros and cons. If she asked, and he didn't feel comfortable accepting her invitation, would she be alright with that? *Absolutely*, she concluded. It would be an honest answer from an honorable man, and it would not change her feelings of friendship for him. And, if he chose to accept, it would just make the trip even more special and enjoyable. She had admired his gentlemanly behavior. He had sensed, over dinner in Venice, that she was hesitant, and he had honored his word.

He had gotten separate rooms without being asked and had never made a sexual move toward her while remaining attentive and a little flirtatious. In the past two days, they not only formed a deeper emotional connection, but they trusted each other implicitly. Roberto had confessed that it had been two years since he'd been with a woman. Ginger was not sure if he was interested in intimacy, but she decided that she wanted to invite him to make love. It was her invitation. After all, he did give her a first sensual kiss at the stables, and she knew that it wasn't a kind of kiss you shared unless you were interested.

When she arrived at the guest house, Roberto was relaxing on the balcony and asked, "Did you get some good photographs?"

"Yes. Every frame was perfect. This is such a lovely, romantic place." Hesitantly, looking directly at him, Ginger then said, "I'm wondering if I could talk to you about something?"

Roberto detected a different tone in her voice, and he leaned in to listen intently. "Uh-oh. I can tell that you have something serious on your mind. I hope this doesn't mean that you are ready to have me call the driver to take you back to Venice."

The twinkle in his eye and mischievous look on his face convinced her that he was certain this was not her request. Roberto paused. He did not want to make light of her question. Ginger seemed a little nervous and this was so unlike her. Having no idea of what was to come next, he asked, "Can you hold the discussion until I get your glass of wine that has been breathing, patiently waiting for your return?"

He brought her the wine, and she pulled her chair closer to his, which got his attention even more. Roberto started by saying, "Tell me what you would like to discuss. I apologize if I was being flippant. I do want to hear what you have to say."

"You know it took courage on my part to let go of my inhibitions and come spontaneously on this holiday."

He nodded without speaking a word.

"I listened to my intuition, and as I sit here today, I want you to know I am so glad I came on this trip with you." Ginger continued, "This has been the most delightful and exciting few days. I have loved every minute of it."

Now, the look on Roberto's face became one of uncertainty. As he surveyed her expression quizzically but most respectfully, he thought, *What is it she wanted to say? What can it be?*

"Since you are the one who invited me on this most incredible holiday," Ginger began, "I would like to now share a personal invitation of my own."

There was a pause, but Roberto did not move a muscle. He just kept his eyes focused on Ginger.

"I want to ask you if you would like to spend an intimate night together. And, please, if you would rather not, I am asking you to be honest and tell me so."

There, she thought to herself. *I expressed my sincere feelings, and I made my invitation. No game playing, no conditions, just honesty and truth.* She made a quick check of her emotions, and they were calm and self-assured. She felt authentic; it was just right, regardless of his answer.

Roberto was silent for just a few seconds, then he stood up, took Ginger's wine glass, put it on the table, and pulled her up to give her the most romantic kiss. He then whispered in her ear, "I accept with pleasure. Your room or mine?"

"Since I invited you, mine," Ginger replied with the sweetest expression on her face. "And why wait for tonight?"

They spent a divine afternoon together. And Ginger noticed they were both noticeably animated and happy when they settled back on the balcony in their bathrobes.

"Thank you for the most unexpected and the most pleasurable invitation. It has been a long time. I almost forgot how wonderful it feels," Roberto said.

"It has been a long time for me too," Ginger admitted. "I totally agree. I have missed those wonderful feelings too." They tenderly smiled at each other.

There was a knock on the front door of the guesthouse, and Roberto remembered the surprise he had planned earlier that day. "Ginger, please take your glass of wine and go into your bedroom. Do not come out until I call you."

She could not imagine what was happening out in the hallway. While she waited in her room she could hear several people speaking Italian and the sound of much activity. After fifteen minutes or so, Roberto knocked on her door. When she opened it he was standing in a lovely casual linen jacket and slacks. He gave her his arm and lead her back to the balcony where she saw the most glamorous, round dinner table set for two. There was a crisp white tablecloth draped to the floor, a bouquet of red roses and candles. The crystal was sparkling in the candlelight, and the table was set with exquisite china covered by ornate silver plate covers. The evening sky was filled with stars making the setting even more breathtaking. Ginger was speechless.

"Dinner is served," Roberto said with a playful bow.

"This is unbelievable," Ginger whispered, truly touched by Roberto's romantic gesture. At that moment, she realized she was still in her bathrobe. "Please, give me three minutes." She disappeared into her room and when she reappeared she was wearing the elegant, off-shoulder, long-flowing sundress that she had purchased in Venice. Perhaps what she loved most was that she was wearing it barefooted.

"You look stunning in that flowing dress," he said, still glowing from their afternoon together.

"Thank you. I purchased it on the recommendation of your daughter at her shop. I just have to say that this is the most romantic dinner setting I have ever seen!"

They dined on short ribs with roasted new potatoes, toasted with Sangiovese wine and watched shooting stars streak through the clear night sky. As the evening closed, Roberto turned to Ginger. "You have added so much more to this holiday than I could have ever imagined."

With a tender look on her face, she replied softly, "Please know it has truly been a shared experience, and I have loved it too."

"Since a discussion of sharing has taken center stage in this conversation, how about we continue this lovely evening? Would you share my room with me tonight?" Roberto asked.

"Invitation gladly accepted."

Over breakfast the next morning, Roberto commented that he felt years younger. Ginger smiled to see that he was in such a good mood. But then she realized she was as well.

As they sipped coffee on the balcony Roberto asked if he could explain something of a sensitive nature with her. She assured him that there was not a thing that he could not talk to her about. He started to approach the subject with delicacy. "Remember that I told you I have a vacation home a couple of hours drive from here in Lugano, Switzerland?" Ginger nodded and listened intently as he continued, "I can't remember if I told you that I intended to include a visit there on this holiday trip."

"What I did not tell you, however, is that I have not been there since Christina died. You may find it to be strange that I have not gone to my Lugano home for almost two years, but it is true. My daughter cleared out her mother's things and goes there often with her husband. She has encouraged me to join them for holidays, but I have somehow found it too painful to return. I would now like to continue my plan to go there. It is a lovely historic home on Lake Lugano that has been in my family for three generations."

"Suddenly, I am missing it. Would you like to go to Lugano with me for a day or two? It is a scenic drive of only a few hours. And instead of going all of the way back to Venice you could fly out of Milano. They have great flights to the west coast of the United States, and it is only an hour's drive from Lugano."

Ginger smiled, realizing that Roberto was starting to move forward in his life. She could tell by the enthusiasm in his voice that he was excited about the prospect of going back to Lugano where his family has owned a home for many decades. She sensed it meant a lot to him and was touched that he felt comfortable in asking her to join him. She had read about Lugano, Switzerland in conjunction with the movie stars who had taken second homes there and at nearby Lake Como. She remembered reading that they had not chosen the region for any glitz or glamor, but because it was so untouched and pristine. If Roberto was now ready to return to his vacation home she was happy to accompany him. She could easily change her ticket to fly out of Milano.

"Are you sure you do not want to be alone as you return to your place after Christina's death? If so, I can try to make some other arrangements," Ginger stated with sincerity.

Roberto softened his gaze. "Ginger, your empathy has touched me deeply these past few days. I am having such a wonderful time with you. I would really like you to come with me. I sincerely mean that."

With a sweet gentle smile Ginger replied, "Then I would be happy to go to Lugano with you."

"Terrific. Then it is set. Instead of driving back to Venice, we are on our way to Switzerland. I will call my caretakers and ask them to ready the house. We will be there by late afternoon. I just know you will love it there. It is situated on the shore of Lake Lugano surrounded by incredible mountains. The setting is truly stunning."

"You have not misled me on this trip so far," Ginger said. "Your description of Lugano sounds so appealing and besides we still have three days, and I am also enjoying our time together."

They packed up their belongings and bid farewell to Martina and the staff as they left for Lugano. Ginger looked back toward the vineyard and smiled thinking of the wonderful time she had spent there. As they drove along, with sunshine and a warm breeze, she let her mind wander a bit. She appreciated the open communication she had found with Roberto. She was sure it was not just because he was Italian, though there was something refreshing and romantic about European men. If Italian men wanted to be with you they made it known in their words and their actions. She did not need to guess what Roberto was thinking. He trusted her, and himself, enough to let her know. It felt authentic and fit perfectly with her pledge to stay in the present moment and go with the flow. She was being totally herself and it felt good.

As they drove and talked, Roberto explained to Ginger that there would most certainly be some curiosity on the part of the caretakers and neighbors when they arrived in Lugano.

"They will be wondering, 'Who is the attractive American woman'? Please, do not be concerned. Many of my friends have been urging me to return and they will be pleased that I am in your company."

"This is your homecoming, and I am sensitive to that fact. You take the lead. I'm sure it will be just fine," Ginger assured him.

As they passed through the immigration check point, Ginger chuckled to herself. The officer looked at her passport, then Roberto's, and then at the two of them.

He must be thinking 'What are these two up to?' she thought At that moment, she was happy she had dressed in a rather sensual summer top. With her dark sunglasses and big hat, she was having fun being the mystery woman.

Rounding a sharp turn in the road, Lugano came into view amidst some of the most dramatic glacial mountains she had ever seen. The town hugged the coastline of the dark blue lake.

"It is incredibly beautiful here!" Ginger exclaimed.

"Yes, and it is curious that you picked that word for your description. Lugano is often described as being 'beyond beautiful.' Many people say it blends Swiss efficiency with the sunny charm of Italy. There are only 65,000 people living here in Lugano, so you can see why I find it to be so relaxing and peaceful. It truly feels like a small village in comparison to Venice. The tourist presence is minimal. If you stop anyone for directions they will go out of their way to help you. They are extremely friendly here and it is a safe city to walk around day or night."

Roberto started his introduction by taking her on a brief drive around Lugano. With camera in hand, Ginger marveled at the main square, Piazza della Riforma, with its pastel-colored palatial buildings and Neoclassical Town Hall. Fortunately, the vegetable market was in full swing, which added to the character of the square, not to mention to the photo opportunities.

Roberto made a quick stop so she could go into San Lorenzo Cathedral. It was built in the Romanesque period and restored in Renaissance style. Her favorite, however, was the Santa Maria degli Angioli Church with the works of Bernardino Luini, the beloved disciple of Leonardo da Vinci. His Renaissance masterpiece the *Passion and Crucifixion* covered most of one entire wall with 150 figures of faces and images, including soldiers on horseback and a throng of people. Ginger was also fascinated by the old town center.

Since it was a pedestrian-only part of town, Roberto dropped her off to walk while he made a few business calls. Via Nassa was the most elegant street in the old town center with long porticoes that gave it a distinctive Italian appearance. Lined with sophisticated shops it was very chic and also charming due to the flower-ladened balconies on the historic buildings along the narrow walking street. When she met Roberto at their meeting place she got into the car and carefully observed his facial expression. There was no hint of sadness or melancholy. He was genuinely happy to be back.

As they left the historic district, Roberto explained that his family home was one of the oldest buildings that sat at the water's edge. "Can you imagine three generations of my family have inhabited that sweet old house? When my parents died I promised to keep it in the family. We have made some great memories here." Roberto's voice trailed off into silence.

Hearing him sigh, Ginger earnestly again asked, "Are you sure you would not like me to take a hotel for the night so you can walk around by yourself to remember those memories. I'm sure you and Christina spent a lot of time here together."

"We did and I will be eternally grateful for those times," Roberto said. "I have been touched by the kind sensitivity you have shown to me regarding the death of my wife. I want you to know from the depth of my being, that I had not intended for you to have to deal with my sorrow when I asked you to join me on this trip. I was just planning to get away from all the stress at the office and to celebrate my legal victory. I actually remembered talking to myself after you accepted my invitation. I said, 'Roberto, do not let Christina's death bring sadness to this holiday. Ginger is a nice person, just relax and keep it light and enjoyable.'"

Ginger remained silent as he continued, "I still can hardly believe my experience in the chapel at the monastery. I am a very pragmatic person, but I truly felt I heard Christina telling me she was at peace, and she was reminding me that I was not keeping my promise to move on with my life. It was real, Ginger. I know I did not imagine it. When I again repeated my promise, I sincerely meant it. It seems as if the dark cloud that had been hanging over me is starting to dissipate. I'm feeling joy again. And there is no guilt because I am fulfilling her wishes. It has truly been a cathartic experience for me. I do not know how to explain it fully, but I sincerely believe it is not temporary. I know there will be sad moments like when I put the Christmas stocking on the mantel, or when Jen has her first child, or even when I hear our favorite song. But I know from the bottom of my heart that she wants me to go on, and these past few days are my first steps."

Ginger gave him a knowing smile to convey that she completely understood what he was saying. "You may not have noticed amidst our playful exchanges," she said, "but I have a strong spiritual side. There is no doubt in my mind that Christina was there to convey her loving message to you. Do you know why she shared that message?"

She paused, giving Roberto time to truly ponder her question. "It is because she loved you so very much. In actuality, she still does. Her spirit lives on in your life Roberto. I truly believe that the most precious gift you received this week is the ability to hear Christina's message."

She gently continued, "I know that you did not intentionally bring me into this healing experience. But for some reason, I am here. Please don't feel that you need to thank me. It is serendipitous that we were meant to take this trip together. I'm really glad that I came."

"And I am also so glad that you are here. You have made such a difference. And regarding Lugano, it would make me feel badly if you were to take a hotel room. I really want you to stay at my home."

"If I stay, I would like you to honor my request. Since we are so truthful and open with each other it is important to me."

"What is your request?" Roberto asked with a questioning look.

"I am willingly stay at your home, but if at any time you feel that you would like to be alone, I want you to tell me, and we can make other arrangements."

"That is an easy request to honor," Roberto answered with a tender smile. 'I believe that we have come a very long way in knowing each other. You can count on me to be totally honest with my feelings, just as I know you will be with yours,"

Roberto pulled into a parking space in front of the most incredibly picturesque row of houses sitting on the shore of the lake. They were stucco and painted in various Mediterranean colors of terra-cotta, light green and pale yellow. Matteo and Bella, the caretakers who watched over the property, came out to greet Roberto. It was touching to see how happy they were to see him. Bella kept hugging him and Matteo had the biggest smile on his face. Roberto greeted them in return with the warmth he would extend to old friends. Ginger could see that they meant a lot to each other. When Ginger got out of the car Roberto introduced her as "his guest." They seemed genuinely pleased to meet her and Matteo helped Roberto carry in their luggage including her heavy suitcase.

As Ginger walked into the main room of the house, she could see why Roberto would want to keep it in the family. It was the type of home that wrapped its arms around you immediately. It reflected a combination of comfortable living with welcoming earth colors, oversized pillows on the furniture and a large country kitchen. But, in contrast, it also had a feeling of grandeur with a Baby Grand piano in the living room, polished marble floors and a swooping, dramatic wrought iron staircase to the bedrooms on the second floor.

Roberto said goodbye to Matteo and Bella and motioned to Ginger. "Come sit on the balcony overlooking the lake,"

Ginger was awestruck by the spectacular view from the balcony. The alpine mountains surrounding the lake were steep, rugged and dramatic. "I can see why your family chose this lot to build their home. The view is dazzling in every direction."

"Yes, it is. One of the original photographs shows the house as the first one built here on this section of the shoreline. Don't you sense the peace and tranquility of this place?" Roberto said taking a deep breath of fresh air. "I've missed Lugano and I'm so glad to be back. I hope you are glad you came too."

Ginger could tell that he was checking to see if she was comfortable being in his home. She found it endearing that he so often considered her feelings. "Oh, yes, Roberto, I am having the most wonderful time. Thank you for introducing me to such a unique region of this country. I always think of Switzerland as trains on time, hikers on trails in the Swiss Alps, cows with big bells clanging from their collars and of course hot chocolate served in little huts with thatched roofs. Lake Lugano is so very majestic."

"Lugano is extraordinary in many ways. We are in the Italian Canton of Ticino, the Italian-speaking region of southern Switzerland, so in many ways it feels more like Italy. Visitors can hardly believe we are on a palm-lined lake with sharp alpine peaks. I'm so pleased you are enjoying being here." With noticeable enthusiasm in his voice, he said, "Hey, I have a great idea. Let's get all dressed up and go out on the town tonight. We have a two-star Michelin restaurant here. It's very elegant and the food is divine. What do you think?"

"It sounds perfect. Besides we have not celebrated your big court win enough. If you worked on it for an entire year, I definitely think it deserves another champagne toast! Besides, upstairs in my suitcase I have the most stunning dress for the occasion. It is absolutely ravishing. I purchased it in the boutique on the cruise ship. It was a stretch for my budget, but when I tried it on all the people in the shop said it was truly fabulous. I'm dying to wear it again! Will there be people at the restaurant who will recognize that you are back and notice that you are not alone, especially if I am wearing this dress?"

Roberto threw his head back in laughter, which delighted Ginger.

"Ah, yes, there will be heads that will turn when we walk in and they see that I am with an attractive younger American woman. But my daughter has told me many times that our friends here in Lugano are concerned that I have not returned. They were worried that I have been depressed and retreating from the world. They will be happy to see that I have returned, and that I am smiling again."

As Ginger passed through the living room on her way to dress for dinner, she took a closer look at Roberto's vacation home. The large room reflected a combination of Switzerland, Italy and the Mediterranean. There were gauzy curtains swaying in the breeze at the large open windows overlooking the lake. Plush carpets covered sections of the marble floors and the furniture looked like it had been designed especially for each room. It was then that she noticed all of the framed pictures.

Since Roberto had stayed on the balcony to answer a call from his daughter, she took a few minutes to look at the photographs. They were of Roberto, Christina, and their daughter, Genevieve, throughout the years. Christina was beautiful and they looked so happy.

When she had finished getting ready for dinner Ginger headed for the staircase. She could hear that Roberto was already downstairs, and he was playing the piano. As she reached the top of the stairs, he caught a glimpse of her and started playing the song, "New York, New York."

She clapped to show her appreciation as she started down the staircase. Roberto suddenly stopped playing and stood up from the piano. She knew he was as taken with her dress as all of the people had been on the ship.

The dress was from the collection of a well known designer in Paris. It was a shimmering midnight black, and it fit perfectly, hugging her body to show off her exquisite figure. It exposed one bare shoulder and draped over the other with a large, free-formed fabric flower of golden threads. Being calf length, it was not too formal for a restaurant dinner. She was wearing it with her black stiletto heels, indisputably one of the sexiest shoe styles in the world!

"There could never be a more gorgeous woman in all of Lugano tonight," Roberto said. "That is indeed a most becoming dress on you."

As they entered the restaurant Ginger saw the impressed look on the face of the maître d and noticed several customers point and whisper something to each other. She wasn't sure if it was the dress or the fact that they noticed that Roberto was with a woman, but she was keenly aware of their reaction. The lights were low, the décor lovely and the tables set with large floral bouquets and candles. It was indeed an elegant setting for a night out on the town. They were seated at an intimate table for two alongside a small dance floor. In a balcony above a five-piece group played soft dinner music.

Roberto looked across the table at her. "I am proud to be escorting the most beautiful woman in this entire restaurant."

"Thank you for the nice compliment. I'm pleased that you feel that way. But I must confess that there is a table of four women, seated across from us, that are gazing at me with jealousy because they sense that I am with the most good-looking man in this restaurant."

They both laughed, but Ginger had to admit that it was actually true. Roberto was dressed in a black silk suit with a crisp light lavender shirt. He looked particularly attractive with a hint of grey in his hair and a relaxed smile. She knew the women had noticed him. "Roberto, the next time you come to Lugano alone, I am certain that you are going to attract the attention of many available single women. It is not just your good looks, but you are kind, attentive, intelligent, distinguished, funny, caring, and…"

She paused for a moment. "And what they might not yet know is that you are a very good lover."

Roberto did not say a word for what seemed over a minute. "I am truly humble hearing your description of me. I know you are a sincere person, so it means a lot to me coming from you. I think I have lost touch with pieces of myself in these past two years. I have felt like a puppet just going through the motions; trying to be strong for my daughter, burying myself in work at the office, eating dinner most nights at home, and all along feeling numb and closed down inside. Your description reminds me of the man I once knew. And your irresistible invitation to make love at the vineyard guest house was something I will never forget. It was so unexpected. Knowing that you enjoyed it too makes it even more precious. Ginger, in so many ways, you are truly an angel."

"I will be sure to share that with my mother because she always said I was a little devil when I was growing up," Ginger laughed.

Roberto gave her a big grin. "I'll bet you were a little hellion!"

"It's heartwarming to hear you say that the man you remember is resurfacing," she replied in a soft-spoken tone of voice.

While they were laughing and toasting champagne the maître d came by their table to tell Roberto that a couple, at another table, wanted to buy them a cocktail. Roberto looked over and waved back to friends he knew. He was especially pleased to see their positive response to seeing him with a woman after Christina's death.

"I'll have a grappa," he told the server who arrived to take their order. "Ginger, you may want to try one since it is a brandy of Italian origin." Ginger agreed and he ordered one for her as well.

When she took her first sip of the grappa she said, "Whew, this is very strong! I'm not sure I can handle it, but I will just leave it here in the middle of the table and slip it to you to finish for me. The champagne is more my style tonight."

"I can taste that they are serving the stronger version of this brandy. Grappa is produced with between 35 and 60 percent alcohol content. This is definitely 60 percent!" Roberto said.

The food was superb. Ginger decided it was high-end French cuisine. In her travels, she had begun to develop a sophisticated palate and she confessed that her main entrée, the classic Boeuf Bourguignon, may have been the best she had ever experienced. She agreed that it most certainly deserved a two-star Michelin rating.

Roberto explained to the waiter that they were in no hurry and would like the service to be slow and leisurely. Roberto finished her grappa and ordered a bottle of red wine with their dinner. When the orchestra began to play a romantic slow song Roberto asked her to dance. Although she noticed he was getting a little tipsy from all the alcohol, she was amazed how quickly he pulled himself together on the dance floor. She smiled to herself when he held her noticeably close. He was, undeniably, being true to the image of Italian men being sensual and romantic. As he turned her in their direction, Ginger observed the looks on the faces of the four women still seated at the neighboring table. Roberto had definitely attracted their interest.

After another dance, they settled back at their table where Roberto ordered an after-dinner cognac. She declined, just sipping slowly on her glass of wine. She loved the fact that he was letting his hair down and having fun. He was disciplined and responsible, not the kind of man to get inebriated, but on this night, she knew for certain that she was driving them home! Outside, the restaurant, Ginger smiled and held out her hand.

"Alright, Mr. Party Guy, hand me the keys. I am driving this Mercedes Benz convertible home with you in the passenger seat." She was pleased that he willingly complied, and she even detected a hint of gratitude.

They returned back to the house safely and Ginger found humor in Roberto's jovial demeanor. As they walked into the house, she noticed he was not steady on his feet. "It is late, so do not ease into the pillows on that comfortable couch in the living room. Even though you may think I am a superwoman, I definitely could not carry you up those stairs to the bed!"

Roberto laughed and allowed her to guide him up the staircase and into the master bedroom. There she helped him take off his shoes and slacks. He removed his jacket and shirt and slid into bed in his shorts and tee shirt. Within minutes, he was snoring quietly and sleeping soundly.

As Ginger turned, she saw a smiling photograph of Christina on the night stand next to the bed. She had grown to feel a connection to this lovely woman who had shared her life with Roberto, and who had loved him so deeply. Standing in the master bedroom they had shared for so many years, Ginger felt an unexpected emotion swell up in her. With tears in her eyes, she turned toward Christina's photo and whispered, "I got your Roberto home safely tonight. I want you to know that he's going to be okay."

Ginger quietly tiptoed as she took her suitcase and wheeled it across the hall to the guest bedroom. As she closed the door, she looked around. It was a most cheerful room with original oil paintings of the lake on the walls, a sky-blue comforter on the bed and a sitting chair upholstered in fabric to match the huge draperies pulled back with tassels. Then she walked into the attached bath to find a long, deep European-style tub. Within minutes, she was soaking in hot water with lavender salts she found in a ceramic jar nearby. Ginger always loved a relaxing bath. Traditionally, it was the place where she got insights on answers to problems, checked in with her emotions, listened to her intuition and became centered. Leaning back into the scented water, she began to retrace the past few days. *What was the meaning of the obvious serendipity that had brought her and Roberto together for this holiday?* She thought about Roberto's healing experience, but wondered what was the significance of this week for her?

As wonderful as Roberto was, Ginger knew he was not the lifelong love she hoped to someday find. He was so special that for an instant she wished he could be the one, but her intuition strongly told her that it was not true. She cared deeply for him but he was not her forever guy. Her heart would have told her clearly if that was the truth. She also clearly sensed that however fond Roberto was of her, she was not his second love.

Intuitively, she was certain that there must be a message in her acceptance of his invitation that day in Venice. Perhaps, it was for her to be helpful to someone needing empathy and kindness, but it felt like there was a deeper meaning. Maybe it was to accept the gifts that the Universe provides without judgement or hesitation. It's true that she was going with the flow and even staying in the present moment when she shared the intimacy that she and Roberto had both missed so much. It was something she would not have ordinarily done, but it felt authentic and right. She would not have traded their lovemaking for a moment.

Adding more hot water to the tub, her soul searching continued. Obviously Christina's death was a reminder that every minute was precious and not to be wasted. Staying in the present moment wasn't easy for her as she had always spent most of those precious moments planning for the next responsibility she thought she should address.

It was at that moment when Ginger came to the realization that she was not clear as to her hopes for the future. *What might I be wishing for?* Her wishes might not materialize if she didn't even know what they were. More importantly, she must allow herself to accept that she deserved to have her dreams come true. Assessing it all, she thought, *I have a great life—caring family, terrific friends, good health, a satisfying career and so much more. So what more could I want?* After being with Roberto the past few days, she realized that she would like to meet her forever soulmate, someone with whom she could share an unconditional, unwavering love like Christina and Roberto had shared. Yes, that was it!

She would like to have a man in her life; not just any man, but the right man, the one destined for her. She became convinced that if so many magical things could fall into place to heal Roberto, why couldn't serendipity and magic be in the air for her as well?

She decided to make that her intention when she returned home. And while on holiday the next two days with Roberto, she would relax and relish every divine moment. Meeting Roberto and spending this holiday together was a very precious gift. With Roberto, there were no pretenses. They were totally enjoying each other in the present moment. It felt natural and honest. She remembered *Anam Cara*, the Celtic philosophy. The words meant "Soul Friend." Yes, she decided, Roberto was more than just a friend to her. He truly was her Soul Friend.

In the morning, Ginger woke to the sound of birds singing outside her window. She stretched her arms high as she sat up in bed. Longing for a cup of coffee, she slipped a fluffy robe over her pink silk pajamas, quietly opened the guest bedroom door and headed downstairs. Roberto was nowhere to be found, and she assumed he was still asleep. She found the coffee maker and when she opened the refrigerator door she was delighted to see that it was fully stocked! There were eggs, fresh fruit and many kinds of cheese and vegetables. She knew that the best way to cure a hangover was to eat a hearty breakfast, so she decided to make Roberto her favorite omelet. She loved to cook and what better place than a charming, big kitchen with a view of a gorgeous blue mountain lake. As she was whisking the eggs, Roberto came into the kitchen. He was in a grey sweat suit, unshaven, hair standing on end and looking ten years younger!

"Good morning," Ginger greeted him with a sunny smile. "I trust you slept well?"

"Please tell me I did not make a fool of myself last night," he said sliding onto a stool at the counter in front of her. "I can't believe how the alcohol went to my head. I never let myself drink that much. It just isn't like me."

"Actually, you were a delightful, funny, inebriated date." Ginger went on to describe the evening. She explained that after half of the bottle of champagne, two glasses of potent grappa, two thirds of the bottle of the red wine, and a cognac, she was worried that when he asked her to dance, she might have trouble holding him up in her very high stiletto heels.

She continued to say that he recuperated amazingly well on the dance floor, and she thanked him, not only for the romantic dances, but also for being cheerful in handing over the car keys so she could drive them home. She then laughingly told him how she helped him get undressed and how it only took a few seconds before he was sound asleep. With an impish look on his face he came around the counter and gave her a big hug.

"Saved by a stunning woman in stiletto heels and a remarkably gorgeous dress. How lucky could I be?" he said in a playfully expressive tone of voice.

Ginger gave him a good-natured grin while offering coffee and breakfast, which he enthusiastically accepted. As they sat at the kitchen table, Roberto changed the topic from one of merriment to one of reflection. "I hope I did not offend you in any way last night. When I got up this morning I noticed that the bed covers on the other side of the bed were unused?"

"No, you did not offend me in the least. It was an enjoyable evening. And we all have had a bit too much to drink, from time to time, so don't give it a thought." Roberto kept his gaze on her prompting a reply to his question. "I thought you might like some privacy, so I slept in the guest room across the hall," Ginger added.

Roberto was not sure that he had still received his answer, but he offered, "That was thoughtful. Thank you for doing that for me."

"Actually, I did not do it for you alone," Ginger confessed. Her reply puzzled him, and he saw that she was tentative in explaining the meaning of her answer. "If I told you the entire story you might think I am crazy. You would order that driver to pick me up and take me back to Venice or Milano."

"Since I am certain that I am not sending you back, maybe you could just trust me with your explanation."

"After I got you into bed, and I heard you sleeping soundly, I noticed the lovely large photograph of Christina on your night stand. She had the most beautiful smile on her face. Somehow, I became overwhelmed with emotion and turned toward her smiling photo and said, 'Christina, I got your Roberto home safe and sound tonight, and you can now be assured that he is going to be okay.'"

Roberto sat quietly for several seconds before he reached out for her hand. The look on his face reflected immense caring and gratitude. The slight hint of tears in his eyes were not tears of sorrow but those of heartfelt emotions.

"Ginger, that is one of the most touching things I may have ever heard. It is not in the least bit crazy. It is so kind and loving."

"I wish I could have known her," Ginger said in a soft, sincere voice.

Roberto squeezed Ginger's hand ever so softly and replied, "She would have liked you."

They cleared the table together and Roberto suggested they finish their coffee out on the balcony. "Ginger, your thoughtful words to Christina are still on my mind. Thank you for assuring her that I am going to be okay. I find it almost miraculous that I feel like a different man than the one you met in Venice so few days ago. I feel at peace, and I feel optimistic for the future. I'm so very grateful to you, Ginger; more than you will ever know. It is hard to believe that you will be flying back to Seattle tomorrow. Maybe, we should see if they can postpone your flight!"

Ginger laughed out loud. Roberto's mood was noticeably playful, and his sense of humor was running high. She then asked, "Since you are feeling so happy and frisky, why don't you tell me what you would like to do on our last afternoon together?"

"I would like to carry you into my bedroom and ruffle up the covers on the unused side of that bed!"

Before Ginger could accept his offer, he continued, "But, as tempting as that is, I was thinking that I would like to make this an unforgettable afternoon of photography for you. I want you to take home some photographs that will impress your family and friends even more than those you have already captured. I suggest we take my boat out this afternoon. It is right outside at my dock, and it is large and comfortable with a galley and sleeping quarters. I'm familiar with some lake views that have earned professional photographers national awards. There is a cove where you can see the Swiss Alps and the picturesque houses along the shore can only be captured from the water. There will be colorful boats out on the water and the sun will be in the perfect location to photograph Mount Bre, with its cable cars. It will be spectacular!"

"It all sounds wonderful. Thank you for thinking about my love of photography. Those views are something I could never see on my own. I appreciate your thoughtfulness."

As Ginger went up to the guest room to change, she thought about Roberto's invitation to spend their last afternoon together in bed; she found his suggestion delightful. Actually, she would have enjoyed it too, but his descriptions of the sights they would see from his boat were so irresistible. Just then, she had a great idea of her own. *Why can't we do both? I could spend the earlier part of the afternoon photographing, and later in the day, we can dock somewhere and ruffle the covers on the bed of his boat?*

As Ginger pondered her plan she became excited. She knew of the perfect way to suggest it to Roberto when it was time. Digging through her suitcase, she came up with the nautical top that she had purchased for the cruise, but thought was too risqué to wear in public on the ship. She found some white sailor pants to match and some tennis shoes. As she slipped the top on, she reminisced about the backless formal evening gowns she had worn in college without a bra. The nautical top had a large sequined anchor on the front, but it was backless. And not somewhat backless. It was backless to her waist. As she looked over her shoulder in the mirror she realized that it was perfect. She would wear her white cotton sweater over it until the time was right.

When she returned to the kitchen Roberto had written her a note: "Come on down. I've packed us a picnic lunch, and I'm getting the boat ready to launch."

Ginger found the stairway down to the private dock. Roberto waved and helped her aboard. "It might be best if you sit up top to photograph. I have a second seat next to mine, and I promise to keep my hands to myself," he teased.

As they set sail, everything was exactly as Roberto had described. She could see why he was passionate about Lugano. The lake region had breathtaking views. She was definitely seduced by its magnificence. Roberto steered the boat in every direction that she asked. She was thrilled when he took her near the Rivetta Tell dock where visitors were renting brightly colored, metal vintage-looking Forsa boats. She included them in several of her photos. The wild beauty of the lake shore was majestic. She captured photos of the cable car taking visitors to the viewing point on top of Mount Bre. She especially loved the picturesque taverns along the shoreline at Gandria, the tiny village at the foot of the mountain. After several hours Roberto suggested that they stop for lunch. He explained that, although Switzerland was a landlocked country, it hasn't stopped them from having some of the best beaches around.

He explained that the beaches near Lugano were even better than those at a traditional seaside. He told her that the water in the lake heats up to around twenty-five degrees Celsius in the summer months, making it pleasant for swimming. After finding a lovely cove, Roberto put down the anchor. They went down to the galley to have lunch from the picnic basket Roberto had packed. Ginger loved seeing the assortment he had artfully displayed on a large ceramic platter, prosciutto, olives, various types of cheeses, salami, and a baguette.

After lunch Roberto asked, "Do you mind if I take a quick dip in the lake? I won't be long. It reminds me of when I was a little boy. My father would playfully grab me and throw me into the lake amidst screams and laughter."

"Please go ahead," Ginger replied. "I love it that you want to relive these childhood memories."

As Roberto swam in the lake Ginger got ready for her surprise. When she heard him coming back on board, she slipped off her sweater and stood looking out a small window with her exposed back in full view. Roberto came down the stairs with a towel over his shoulder and stopped suddenly. He could not believe his eyes, and Ginger heard him gasp. There she was with her suntanned exposed back showing off her lovely curves. She didn't move until she felt his arms around her. He kissed her on the neck and took her hand, leading her to the little sleeping area where he gently closed the door behind them.

The boat rocked ever so slightly as they spent the most romantic two hours together. Roberto turned to her and said, "You are a woman of the most appealing surprises. Making love was something I so hoped we could do together again before you left."

"I actually wanted to as well, and this boat provided an unforgettable setting."

They then piled the pillows up so they could sit and talk. Roberto looked her in the eye for a few seconds before he began. "Ginger, I know you are leaving tomorrow but I can't imagine not having you in my life as a treasured friend. I hope we can stay in touch."

Ginger acknowledged his sentiments. She knew they had developed a profound connection. "Have you ever heard of the term 'Anam Cara?'"

Roberto shook his head. "No." He was now listening intently to her every word.

"I learned of it when I visited Ireland a few years ago. 'Anam' is the Gaelic word for 'soul,' and 'Cara' is the word for 'friend.' So, Anam Cara means 'soul friend.' Soul Friends form a very special bond. The accept each other as they truly are and help each other find their inner beauty. Their connection cuts across all barriers of societal norms, expectation and time. Roberto, I truly think we are each other's Anam Cara. It is more meaningful than just a friend. It represents a bond that is loving and unbreakable.

Roberto looked at her with the most caring eyes and replied, "I have not heard of that expression, but you have put into words the feelings I have been struggling to express. I too see you as much more than a friend. At first, I thought you were sent as an angel to help me move forward in my life, but hearing your words, I believe we are exactly as you describe."

They reached over and embraced each other for the longest time without speaking. It was a hug that confirmed their very special connection.

Roberto broke the silence, "Ginger, I feel I have received more from you than I have been able to give to you. Your delightful, spontaneous personality, your kindness and empathy, and the joyful way you embrace life has been amazing. I have loved our laughter, our flirting, and our lovemaking. I cannot begin to tell you how much it has meant to me."

Ginger put her fingers to his lips to stop him. She could sense there was something he did not realize.

"Roberto, you may not have sensed this, but you have also given me a very precious gift these past few days. It's not only all the remarkable experiences you have so generously shared with me, but it is that you have made me feel cherished every single moment we have spent together. I have felt totally accepted and respected. And you have also made me feel beautiful and desirable. Please, never think that you have not also shared so much with me these days we have spent together."

As the sun started to drop behind the majestic mountains, they headed back to Lugano. Ginger sensed the sweet lightness that had come over both of them. They had finally found the words to express their emotions. To say a final goodbye at the airport did not seem right. They now knew they were Soul Friends. They would keep in touch and wish each other happiness.

"I'd like to make a suggestion," Roberto said as they neared his dock. "Let's make our last night together memorable. Milano is only an hour away by car. What would you think about going there now? We would not have to rush out in the morning to get you to the airport on time. I know of a wonderful boutique hotel. It is such a lovely summer night. We could walk to dinner along the canal. Then in the morning we can have a leisurely breakfast before I get you to the airport. What do you think?"

"I like the idea very much. As with Lago Maggiori and Lugano, I have never been to Milano, and your description of walking along the canal at night sounds so inviting."

"Perfect. We can pack and head out as soon as you are ready. And by the way I would like to say that the nautical blouse you had on this afternoon was over the top. I will never again think that your large heavy suitcase was too cumbersome. I'm so glad I met you coming off a cruise ship. All of the clothing you have worn on our trip has been sensational."

Ginger liked Roberto's honesty. "I had not thought about how difficult this suitcase has been to carry into every place we have visited. You are right. It is huge! So, in honor of our last evening together I will dig deep into it and find another interesting outfit. Do you have a color preference?"

Roberto gave a hearty laugh. "No. Just surprise me."

After a quick shower, Ginger repacked and got dressed for the evening. She chose a vibrant lavender top that was flowing and attractive over a pair of shimmery leggings. She would have worn the outfit with her stiletto heels, but since they were going to walk along the canal to dinner, she found a more sensible pair of sandals. Before leaving the house she asked Roberto for a favor.

"Can I take a photo of you at the piano? I am going to send you a picture book when I get home and I missed a couple of shots that I want to include."

"How very thoughtful. That is why you have taken those photos of me along our trip."

"Well, actually, it is just because you are so darn handsome!" she teased. "Your daughter will love seeing the photo book."

As they drove out of town, Ginger noticed the closer connection that she and Roberto had formed since their time on his boat. People seemed to look up and smile as they drove by. Roberto was still enthusiastic about their plan. As they traveled, he gave her a little information on Milano. "Although you will hear people refer to the city as Milan, it is pronounced Milano in Italy. It is a vibrant, sophisticated city, home to our stock exchange, and considered to be one of the fashion meccas of the world, likened to Paris and your New York City. They even have an opera theatre dating back to 1778, and it is still in use today. You will love the charm of the Navigli district with its cafes, restaurants and bars lining the canals. The city is most alive at night, so I'm glad we will have a leisurely evening in Milano on your last night in Italy."

On their drive to Milano, their conversation was light and easy. Ginger wanted to know how Roberto came to be so familiar with the unusual expressions Americans use on a daily basis. She remembered him saying, "at the crack of dawn," "taking center stage," and many others. He explained that his work-related travels brought him in contact with many Americans and the expressions fascinated him. He enjoyed using them when he was with Americans. He said some of his favorites were, "hit the spot," "made the grade," "fit the bill," as well as "keeping on your toes."

Ginger explained that she could not imagine how difficult it would be for someone to be moving to America and trying to learn English. "If someone said to you, 'Get on the ball,' wouldn't you say, 'What ball?'" They both chuckled as Ginger continued. "My favorite expression you used this week was 'ouch' when Alberto was rejected by that potential dance partner."

"That is one of my favorites too. Doesn't it just say it all in one word!" Roberto laughed.

"Absolutely."

Roberto explained that his daughter had been a foreign exchange student in Chicago and brought home all kinds of American expressions. "Some I approved of and some I did not." His comment tickled Ginger as she remembered her college days.

"I can imagine that was true. Please tell your daughter how much I enjoyed wearing the elegant full-length sun dress she recommended."

"I will," Roberto agreed. "But I might not add that I liked it best worn barefooted on the balcony at the vineyard guest house." Ginger made a playful gesture pretending to zip her lip.

Since they were close to the time of their dinner reservation, Roberto left the car with the hotel valet. Their luggage would be taken to the room so they could head out walking along the canal. Ginger slipped her camera into her large leather bag. She had taken a few moments to study the setting for night photography and was anxious to see the canal district after dark.

"Take my arm," Roberto invited. "It gets pretty crowded with all the young locals and tourists out for the evening."

Ginger took his arm as they strolled along the canal. The twinkling lights of the bars and restaurants made an inviting glow. It was an enchanting setting and Roberto was gracious to stop as she photographed, capturing people dining at small intimate outdoor tables, canal tour boats with their canopy of white lights and second story windows open to the breeze with gauzy curtains.

"That is it! I'm finished for the night. My camera is now going to bed," Ginger shared with a hint humor. She put the lens cover on her camera, turned it off and put it into her bag. "I'm now going to just kick back and enjoy the evening."

"It is appealing here," Roberto commented. "I have always thought Milano did not deserve the reputation it has gotten. People say it is stuffy and business-minded. They say the pace here is too fast to embrace the identity for which Italy is known. But I come here often for business, and I enjoy it every time."

"Well, as far as I can tell, it seems welcoming and most enjoyable. However, might you agree, that our good moods could be attributing to the evening." Ginger noticed there was a relaxed, caring connection between them. There was no more talk of the past or challenges ahead. They were completely in the present moment. Everything seemed unfettered and joyful, as if every pleasure was magnified several times over.

Stopping Roberto remarked, "This is one of my favorite restaurants in Italy. It is a tiny place on the second floor of this historic building. You will love the view of the canal and the seafood entrees are fabulous."

As they climbed the small stone stairs Ginger remembered why she loved coming to Europe. They restored, and still occupied, so many of their centuries-old buildings that add so much character to their cities. When they walked into the restaurant, she squeezed Roberto's arm gently. "This is so romantic and charming. I simply love it here."

Roberto adored her expressiveness and could tell she truly was enthralled. He had reserved a table at the window and made certain that she faced the most appealing view of the canal. When they were seated and their first glass of wine poured, Roberto shared a bit of trivia he knew would fascinate her. "I know how much you love the canals in Venice, so I wanted you to see Milano too. Most people do not know there is another city in Italy well known for its canals. However, the thing you might find most interesting is that these waterways were originally built in 1179 to connect Milano with the lakes in the regions, including Lago Maggiore."

"Our Lago Maggiore?" asked Ginger.

Roberto was a sentimental man and her comment touched him. "Yes, our Lago Maggiore." He then went on to describe how the canals were built.

Suddenly, he was at a loss for words. He could not remember the name of Leonardo Da Vinci. He actually laughed out loud as he said, "It is amazing what a little distraction can do to a man." He leaned over to give her a kiss on the cheek. "How could I not come up with the name of our Renaissance genius, Leonardo Da Vinci! He is purported to have helped plan the renovation of these canals. It's not documented but supposed to be true. I imagine he may have helped plan this very spot where we are sitting."

"That is interesting," Ginger commented. "He gave us a waterway of canals to Lago Maggiore, and one of the most recognized paintings in the western world, *The Last Supper*. Quite a talented man indeed!"

As the conversations and evening progressed it was unforgettable in every respect. The food was delicious, and they toasted wine as they shared stories and relished each other's company. The stars were brilliant in the night sky as they walked back to the hotel. Ginger sensed that it was one of those evenings when one just knew that everything was right in the world.

When they arrived at the hotel, Roberto got the key from the front desk. As they entered the room, Ginger smiled to herself to see the most impressive ornate king size bed. They had come a long way together since their first hotel night in Cannero Riviera.

"I hope a beautiful woman will join me tonight as I see there is only one bed in this room," Roberto teased.

"I'll check with her to see what she is thinking," she shot back in her own playful manner.

In the morning, Ginger woke to the sun shone brightly through a large window exposing a view of one of Milano's magnificent basilicas. Roberto was not lying next to her but was sitting at the desk. When he saw her stir, he quickly stood.

"Don't get up, I'm going to bring you coffee in bed. I just had a little writing to finish, but it is complete now."

It was their last morning together. Ginger leaned back on the pillows and sighed. "Life is good, I feel so contented."

"So do I, and we don't have to rush. Would you like to have breakfast in the historic district before I drive you to the airport? I know of a quaint art-filled café there."

Ginger agreed that it sounded perfect. Lingering over a croissant and cappuccino, Roberto and Ginger relived their favorite parts of the holiday and continued to share their appreciation of each other. "Tell me what you have planned when you return to Seattle?" Roberto asked.

Ginger paused for a moment and then said with conviction, "I have made a very meaningful decision in the last couple of days. I'm going home to put out a request to the Universe." Roberto heard the determination in her voice. He waited with curiosity and anticipation, as he could sense it was important to her. "I am going to look for a lasting love like the one you and Christina shared. I have felt for some time that he is out there. I just haven't slowed down long enough for him to catch up with me."

Roberto spoke from the heart, "There is no doubt that you will find each other. Ginger, you have so much to give in a relationship. You are smart, funny, considerate, passionate and so much more. He is going to be a very lucky man to have you in his life."

Ginger's voice softened. "Thank you. And in the interim I'm going to cast all doubts aside and continue my wonderful life with positive expectancy. There has been so much serendipity and magic here these past few days that I have packed some in my suitcase to take home with me."

As they walked back to the car, Ginger saw an old, weathered fountain in the square. "Do you have a coin so I might make a wish?" Ginger asked earnestly.

Roberto searched through his pockets and came up with two shiny coins, which he placed in her hand. *Perfect,* she thought. She closed her eyes for a moment, opened them and threw the first coin into the fountain. She looked toward Roberto and said, "I wished for my forever love!" Then she did the same thing with the second coin. "And I wished that when we find each other, he has many of the endearing qualities that you possess, Roberto." She saw the tender look of appreciation on his face.

At the airport, Roberto insisted on walking her to security. When they reached the gate, he handed her a sealed envelope and said, "Take this and read it on the plane. I wrote a poem for you entitled *Anam Cara, My Soul Friend.*"

They embraced each other in a long, loving hug.

As Ginger started through security, Roberto called out to her, "Keep going with the flow."

She turned and blew him a kiss as she replied, "*Grazie mille.*"

JESSICA'S STORY

Argentina

lthough Jessica loved to travel, she rarely had an opportunity to get away from the many responsibilities of running her Chicago travel agency. However, luck was on her side when she received a call from the developer who owned the building where she rented space for her agency. He made her an offer she could not refuse. He explained that his contractor would be finishing a nearby project earlier than expected. He had a signed commitment to a painting company for an additional week of work.

He asked if she would like to have her entire suite repainted at no cost to her. It would necessitate everyone vacating the space at the end of the month, but the offer was hers if she wanted it. Jessica called a quick staff meeting and everyone agreed that it was an offer too good to turn down. Within two weeks they would take seven days off and return to a lovely, repainted agency.

Jessica was finally getting her chance for a spontaneous getaway. She was enamored with the idea that she could pick the destination. She would choose a location that she had not yet visited. Being in the travel industry made it easy to book last-minute airline tickets. She started to imagine where she would like to spend a week. She was definitely a Chicago, big-city girl. She thrived on the electric feelings she found walking amongst the skyscrapers, frequenting little wine bars, and shopping the elegant department stores which she especially loved during the Christmas holidays with their window displays and festive decorations. As a city dweller, it wasn't that she didn't admire the beauty of nature. She had many friends living out West and thought the National Parks were astonishingly beautiful. However, walking on a cobblestone street in Ireland, strolling along La Rambla in Barcelona or museum hopping in London were her idea of heaven.

She had tried camping. Her girlfriends teased that it was the invitation from a handsome man that motivated her, not pitching a tent and sleeping in the wilderness. The out-of-doors was not a place where she felt at home. Where someone else might find it frightening to hail a Chicago cab at rush hour or ride the subway at midnight, Jessica found it more intimidating to be hiking in the mountains with bear spray and bear bells hanging from her backpack.

It wasn't that she didn't have a sense of adventure. Where she sought excitement was in taking nature trips that stretched her boundaries. She thought nothing of staying in tent camps when she hiked the Inca Trail of Peru. Asked by a friend why she found tenting there acceptable, but not tenting in the Rocky Mountains, she replied, "I wanted to see the magnificent ruins of Machu Picchu, and it was either take the train or hike twenty four miles on the original stone steps that the Incas used five- hundred years ago. How many people do you know who have hiked over Dead Woman's Pass on the Inca Trail?" It was the intrigue of meeting a personal challenge in a natural setting that appealed to Jessica, not the desire to find peace and serenity in the out-of-doors.

Jessica remembered the time she was sailing on a luxury cruise to New Zealand. While in the Milford Sound, she saw the tiny images of people hiking far up on the mountainside. When she heard that they were hiking the Milford Track, considered to be the most spectacular walk in the world, she made a vow to return. She did so a couple years later, escorting twenty-four of her travel clients. When she returned she gave an account to friends saying, "It was so civilized to arrive at the lodges and be met with a glass of wine at the end of a full day of hiking. The dinners were well-prepared, the beds comfortable and they had drying racks for our hiking boots." She explained that she even learned that the New Zealanders referred to hiking as "tramping." She was so fascinated by the description that she brought back a large tabletop photo book titled, "Tramping in New Zealand."

Yes, it was true. Jessica would be willing to endure bugs, dust, rain and the unknown wilderness if it were a way to find the adventure she was seeking. Undeniably, she appreciated having a bit of luxury along the way. She loved visiting Tanzania in Africa because she would be staying in safari lodges with all of the amenities. She even enjoyed the nights she slept in permanent safari tents alongside the river where one could hear the hippos tending to their babies in the dark of the night. It was not surprising that Jessica chose a hiking trip to celebrate her fortieth birthday. She had not signed up to hike the Swiss Alps because she was an outdoor woman, but because it was a challenge. She marked her fortieth year milestone, not at a luxury spa, but doing something that was a stretch. She sought an adventure that made her feel that she had gotten out of her comfort zone and accomplished something she would not have ordinarily done. When asked by friends how she had trained to hike the Swiss Alps, she smiled and reported that she did a little extra walking on her city streets and then counted on her stubborn tenacity to get her through.

Jessica always appreciated the fact that her travel clients had different interests and preferences. She enjoyed planning trips for the outdoor enthusiast, just as much as she did for those who wished to visit European cities or make Atlantic crossings on luxury cruise ships. But now her enthusiasm was building as she relished the opportunity to design her own personal trip. She would choose a destination that totally met her interests. She knew it had to be in a warmer climate as the winter in Chicago was especially cold in January. She also longed to be in a cosmopolitan city that she had not yet visited. As she as making a mental list in her mind, she suddenly had an idea. *What about Buenos Aires? Argentina?* She had heard that Buenos Aires was considered to be the "Paris of South America." She could not begin to count all the positive comments she had heard from friends and clients regarding their trips there. Everyone expressed delight in the restaurants, museums, Malbec wine, tango shows, friendly people, and especially the architecture which reminded them of their favorite cities in Europe.

Immediately checking airline schedules, Jessica found a non-stop flight and a fabulous apartment to rent in the swank Recoleta neighborhood of Buenos Aires. She remembered that her cousin, Genie, loved to get out and see the world. She would be the perfect travel companion. Excitement was building as she dialed her cousin's phone number. "Hey, Cuz, I've decided to take a little week-long getaway. What would you think about coming to Buenos Aires with me? I have rented an apartment and we could explore a bit of South America. I hear it is a walkable city so we could get off our treadmills and go see the sights."

"I'd love to," her cousin replied. "Interesting you should call. Last night, I watched a program on television about Argentina. The scenes of Buenos Aires were fabulous, and the documentary was about the life of Evita. I was so intrigued to learn that there was no middle ground when it came to how the people in her country perceived her. Either they loved her and believed that she had their best welfare at heart, or they had disdain for her, believing that she and her husband pilfered millions of dollars into their own pockets. It was a fascinating story about Eva Perón and I'd love to see the balcony where she tearfully bid farewell to her admirers."

"That sounds interesting. We can definitely find that balcony while we are there. Can you imagine how good it is going to feel to get out of this cold weather? Chicago has been especially bad this winter, and I'm chilled to the bone. Guess what the temperature in Buenos Aires is today? It is eighty-four degrees and sunny," Jessica said with enthusiasm.

Less than two weeks was short notice, but Genie assured Jessica that she could get away for one week and it sounded like a great destination. "It will probably be your good fortune to meet one of those debonair, Latin men who sweeps you off your feet."

Her cousin laughed. "You had better not leave me stranded on a beach somewhere in Argentina!"

"I would never leave you stranded. Besides, I am not going on this trip to meet men. We are going to explore a fascinating South American cosmopolitan city, which just happens to be sunny, warm, and 2,000 miles south of the equator!

"Count me in," Genie replied.

Jessica's cousin always gave her a bad time about being the one that always attracted men. So many times, she was right. It wasn't just because she was a beautiful woman. It was her natural red hair that garnered the attention. It might be a dashing man who arrived just in time to help her onto the train the time she packed too much luggage, or the one who stepped forward with coins for the parking meter while she was still digging through her purse, or the handsome Parisian who willingly shared a glass of wine from his bottle in a French cafe. It was true that Jessica somehow was always meeting the most wonderful men. They were intelligent, well-mannered, fun-loving, and kind. She would say, "It's not because I'm needy or helpless. I don't need a man in my life, I just would like one."

Although she cherished the time she spent with her women friends, Jessica sincerely enjoyed the company of men. She had a romantic side that was undeniable. Whether it was creating a candlelit dinner on the coffee table over Chinese takeout, dressing up in an evening gown to take the arm of her date at a charity ball, or packing a picnic basket for a surprise lunch in the gazebo of a park, she truly loved the special feeling of creating romance. She was not only the recipient, but she was also the one giving of herself in a relationship. She shared that her mother often remarked, "Jessica, you were born under a lucky star." She agreed and felt that it was luck that brought such terrific men into her life. She truly cared about each and every one of them. She sincerely wanted them to be happy. She was thrilled to explore their world and was delighted when they wanted to explore hers. Even after they were no longer together, she continued to be friends with many of the men she dated.

Destiny is something Jessica believed in. Although she appeared pragmatic, she secretly had a spiritual side that she kept well-hidden. She felt the men who came into her life came not only to share her company, but to help teach her a lesson. She knew the reason may not be apparent at the time, but she truly believed they were meant to come together. She was also unwavering in her belief that when she someday was fortunate enough to meet the man of her destiny, she would know it. She would be able to feel the connection. When dating, she always came in good faith. And, if after a time, she believed the relationship was not the right one for her, she was willing to step up in honesty and end it. She often would say, "Even though we were not for the long haul, I will be forever grateful for the time we spent together." She was sincerely thankful for the men with whom she had shared her life's journey.

Yes, Jessica was an interesting woman. There were so many differing aspects to her. She was definitely analytical. She was not impulsive in her behavior. She would quickly analyze a situation, and if she felt it to be stimulating, safe and interesting, she would be willing to dive in with both feet. It was true that she didn't hesitate often, simply because she could always get herself out of a jam if one presented itself. If a cab driver tried to charge her too much, if a suspicious character got too close walking down a dark street, or if she saw an elderly person being taken advantage of, you could count on her to be bold when needed. Not surprisingly, she always had a back-up plan in mind.

Perhaps, it was her tenacity and self-reliance that contributed to her fierce sense of independence. It was not uncommon for the men who pursued her to say, "Jessica, as much as I am drawn to you, I just don't feel like there is a place for me in your world." She would never allow them to live with her, and she did not live with them. Her friends used to tease her when one of the men she dated from another town complained that she would not even give him one small drawer to leave his belongings during his overnight stay in her condo. Because of it, some of the men left to find women looking for long term relationships, but others stayed because of the exciting romance they shared with her.

As she finalized her travel plans, Jessica was pleased to learn that the Recoleta neighborhood where she had rented the two-bedroom apartment was purported to be the safest area of Buenos Aires. It had wide, tree-lined sidewalks, cafes, elegant shops and was dotted with small parks and fountains. All the plans were made, and her enthusiasm was building daily. Unfortunately, then came her cousin's call.

"I have the most awful news," Genie began with disappointment in her voice. "I can't believe it. I can't go to Buenos Aires with you. I just got out of a meeting with my boss, and he has assigned me to our newest account. The project is so lucrative that it will take our company to a whole new level. They want me in Los Angeles in three days to meet with their engineers for a month. I don't know what to say except I am so sorry. I just can't get out of this assignment. I know we were to leave in a couple of days; our flights are booked, and you rented the beautiful apartment. I was so looking forward to getting away from the cold weather too. Can you find another friend to go on such short notice? I'm happy to pitch in on their costs. Will you forgive me?"

At that moment, Jessica took in a deep breath. She knew that her cousin would not cancel unless it was something very important. "I completely understand and I would make the exact same decision if I were in your shoes. I know how hard you have worked to prove yourself in this company. I'm proud of you for being chosen for this important assignment. We will have many more opportunities to travel. Of course, I forgive you. I would always forgive you no matter what happened."

"Oh. I love you for understanding, Jessica. You are the best cousin, and the best friend in the whole world. I so hope you won't have to cancel on account of me."

"Don't worry. Actually, I may just go alone. I'll have no problem exploring the 'Paris of South America' on my own, and it's only for a week. You just go to Los Angeles and show them what an asset you are to the company, and I'll go to Buenos Aries and learn to tango."

When Jessica hung up the phone, she got to thinking about the upcoming trip. *Should I try to find a friend to go at the last minute, or should I just go solo?*

At that moment, she decided that going alone might be the perfect vacation. She could sleep in until 10:00 am if she felt like it, spend the afternoon exploring neighborhoods from a travel guide book, or just sit in an outside cafe and people watch. The idea of carefree, noncommittal freedom all of a sudden seemed appealing. "Yes." She decided. She would go to Buenos Aires as planned.

The weather was two degrees below zero in Chicago when Jessica arrived at the airport, and she mused to think that she might have considered canceling the trip.

What a bad decision that would have been, she thought as she shivered and wrapped her favorite woolen scarf around her neck. The flight was comfortable, and Jessica felt herself unwinding from her busy days at the office. She deserved this getaway, and she began daydreaming about the many sites she had read about in her new Argentina guidebook. Upon arrival at the Buenos Aires airport, she remembered her friend telling her to arrange for a taxi from the airport kiosk. It was purported to be reliable and safer than taking a taxi on her own. Jessica had traveled enough to know that there were disreputable characters in every country, and it was best to not put herself into precarious situations, especially as a woman traveling alone.

The taxi driver was a pleasant older man who explained that he had been driving a taxi for forty-five years. His English was sketchy, but Jessica's Spanish was even less proficient. However, they muddled through a pleasant conversation on their way into the city. "Very nice part of town," he said as they arrived at her apartment address. Jessica smiled and tipped him generously. She appreciated his confirmation that she had made the right choice in staying in the Recoleta district. The apartment had a security guard who greeted her warmly. After confirming her paperwork, he helped her with her luggage and showed her to her unit.

She closed the door and took a long look around the apartment. It was perfect! She winced to think of some of the hotel rooms or apartments she had rented in previous travels. There were times that she could not even recognize the property from the photos she had seen in their glossy brochure. To her relief, the apartment was just as she hoped it would be. Crisp white walls, comfortable modern furniture, a sparkling small clean kitchen, a balcony with patio chairs and a small tree with pots of flowers. She opened the door and walked out onto the balcony to feel the warm breeze. *Yes*, she thought to herself, *this will be a great place to hang out in for a week.*

It was still early afternoon. Jessica decided to unpack her suitcase and go for a walk to exercise her legs after the long flight. It was definitely time to get out of the warm clothing she had worn on the plane from Chicago. Jessica wore a down vest and woolen scarf on international flights because the air conditioning was always blowing cold air overhead. Now, these items would find their way to the back of the closet until it was time to fly home to Chicago, with its snow and ice. She chose the bedroom with the king size bed, hung her clothes, and filled all of the dresser drawers. Since she was not certain of the types of clothing she would need, she overpacked. But she knew it was not a problem because she would be taking a taxi back to the airport.

The weather was warm and sunny, so she chose a bright turquoise top and a colorful multicolored swish skirt. It was the perfect compliment to her red hair. As she checked herself in the mirror, she smiled to think of how she hated her red hair and freckles when she was a child. Her classmates always teased her, and she dreamt of being a brunette or blonde. Anything but a redhead! But as she grew older, she realized that her natural red hair was considered attractive.

It always drew attention from people. Interestingly, from men in particular. It was true that she had the gorgeous looks to add to the equation. A perfect figure at 5'7" she could wear all of the newest clothing styles and look as though she stepped off a fashion runway. She had amazingly long eyelashes, alluring hazel eyes, and a lovely creamy skin tone in keeping with her Norwegian heritage. Perhaps the most noticeable trait she inherited from her ancestors was a feisty Viking warrior spirit. Even though she had a kind and sensitive heart, she kept it well hidden behind her tough outer shield.

As she headed out for the afternoon, Jessica was happy she had exchanged money at the airport. She was always more comfortable using the local currency, although she always carried smaller U.S. bills so she could tip in a rush without trying to calculate the exchange rate in her head. She found a most charming outdoor café steps away from the apartment. Sipping a cappuccino, she looked over her city map to decide where she might like to spend a few hours. She would be certain to memorize the directions. As a single woman, traveling alone, she didn't want to be standing on a corner looking at a city map and telegraphing that she was a tourist. She always walked confidently as if to say, "I live here, I know my way around, and don't mess with me."

Looking over the map, Jessica saw that the Recoleta Cemetery was only a few blocks away. Although she was not one to seek out a cemetery as a tourist attraction, she had read in the guide book that the Recoleta Cemetery was ranked number four in best things to do in Buenos Aires. As the resting place of many notable political figures and elites of Argentina, it was considered to be one of the most unique and grand cemeteries in the world, containing no less than 6,400 graves. Each grave site was distinctive, from Greek temples to miniature Baroque cathedrals. Most of the tombs were made of materials imported from Paris and Milan between 1880 and 1930. The guidebook stated that the cemetery encompassed 14 acres, and one could spend hours winding through the mausoleum lined passageways. Jessica remembered that she had promised her cousin that she would take a photo of Eva Perón's grave. She wondered how many tourists actually recognized Evita's married name? With the magnitude and vastness of the cemetery, she pondered how she would find one grave site. Hopefully, they will have a sign or map, she thought.

After she got her bearings, Jessica headed for the cemetery. She liked the feeling of the big wide sidewalks and noticed the lovely architecture of the buildings. The Recoleta district certainly earned its reputation as the most stylish neighborhood in the city. She passed parks with little children playing in the grass, colorful flower stands, outdoor cafes, and boutiques carrying the most exclusive brands in the world. It was only a few blocks before Jessica rounded a corner to see a large, elegant hotel with many flags lined along the canopy. *This must be the famous Alvear Palace Hotel,* she thought. She had once read about it in a travel magazine and remembered that it was purported to have the most beautiful lobby bar in the world. As she admired the hotel's magnificent architecture, she thought to herself, *I'll be sure to stop by for a drink in the bar one evening.*

Jessica remembered that the cemetery entrance was only one block away from the Alvear Palace Hotel. She passed several restaurants filled with people dining and enjoying themselves under colorful umbrellas. She felt immediately at ease. It was true that she would keep up her guard, as she would in any foreign city of millions of people, but her first impression delighted her, and she looked forward to spending a week in Buenos Aires.

The entrance to the Recoleta Cemetery had a small gift shop on one side and a room with historical information on the other. There was no fee. It had remained an active burial site for over 200 years. As she stepped inside, she quickly saw its enormity, with rows and rows of graves and passageways leading in all directions. It was easy to detect the graves of prominent and wealthy residents. They were covered with carvings of angels and saints and were massive structures nestled amongst the more modest ones.

What an absolutely amazing cemetery, Jessica thought. She sidestepped one of the cats that lived there and was fed by caring locals. There were visitors respectfully walking about quietly taking photographs. In keeping with an active cemetery, there was not a directional sign to be found. It suddenly dawned on Jessica that one could actually get totally lost in the maze of passageways. *How will I ever find Evita's grave?* Maybe, if she made her way back to the entry, she could find a map or at least a display outlining the direction she should take. Looking completely lost, she headed back. As she neared the entry gates, she heard a man's voice.

"I'll bet you are looking for Evita's grave."

Jessica turned quickly, looking directly into the captivating brown eyes of a man sitting on a bench nearby.

Being fiercely independent, she hated to think she needed to be rescued by a man in Buenos Aires, especially on her first day in the city. As she looked at him, now smiling somewhat mischievously, she thought to herself, *He might be attractive, but he is definitely not my type.*

He had wavy, thick brown hair pulled back in a ponytail. His attire was casual, a wrinkled light blue shirt with sleeves rolled up, a pair of shorts, and sandals.

She thought, *There is something appealing about this guy, but I'm definitely not interested in these Bohemian types.* She quickly changed her perceptions from those of judgement, when she realized he was correct in assessing that she was lost. As a local, she was certain he had seen her bewildered look before amidst the maze of passageways. Maybe she should accept his help.

"Seems like you've encountered my dazed look before," she replied, trying to project a bit of gratitude in her voice.

"Absolutely." He grinned. "If you are looking for Evita's grave, let me tell you the foolproof way to locate it. I'm assuming that is where you are headed."

She nodded in agreement, and he continued. "See that tour group coming through the entry gate? Just follow them. No. A better plan is to walk alongside of them, and when you hear the tour guide say, 'We are approaching Evita's grave on the left,' you quickly and nonchalantly,walk ahead of the group. You can get a photograph before they catch up with you. If you don't have a camera and want a remembrance, there are only 10,000 postcards for sale on every street corner in the city."

Jessica was now intrigued. Who was this playful guy with a great sense of humor? She liked his clever choice of words. She was amused by his confident, unabashed behavior. This was certainly a man who did not need assertiveness training.

"Thanks for the tip, I'll actually give it a try," she said in a flippant tone of voice.

"Let me know if it works out," he called to her as she walked away.

This guy is too much! She laughed to herself as she walked alongside the group of tourists. Strange as it may have appeared, his advice was spot on. She was able to slip in ahead of the large group, and they were indeed courteous to let everyone have a few minutes to read the plaque at Evita's grave and take a photo. How interesting, she thought when she saw three or four fresh flowers at Evita's modest grave site.

"It must be true that people still revere her," she whispered to herself. Having read that she was a champion of woman's suffrage, Jessica decided she was worthy of her respect. Imagine, as the First Lady of Argentina, she died at only thirty-three years of age from cervical cancer. It all seemed sad. She decided that during her visit she would try to ask a few locals of their impression of Evita.

After taking a photograph for her cousin, she spent about twenty minutes walking through the narrow passageways and observing the graves. Several were of young children with sweet cherub carvings. Others were modest and unkept as though the last family members had died years before, and no one was there to pull the grass that was beginning to grow between the crumbling bricks. And then there were the towering mausoleums rich in art deco, baroque and neo-gothic architectural styles. As Jessica strolled back to the entry, she shook her head in amusement that the Bohemian, good-looking guy was still sitting on the bench.

"How did it go?" he asked.

Jessica now could not resist a little jest since he was obviously a prankish character. "It was the perfect advice." She then continued in a teasing tone, "You are certainly a good tourist cemetery representative!"

"Oh, I'm actually not with the tourist board. They just let me out of prison for the afternoon to clean up the place," he said in a joking manner.

"Well, thank heavens they let you change out of your striped prison suit. It certainly would have frightened the tourists," she replied with a straight face. She could see that he was impressed and amused by her snappy comeback.

"Touché," he replied with an engaging smile. "Actually, I must confess that I am a respectable citizen. I was waiting for my friends from Europe, but they missed the ferry from Uruguay, so I will have to be their tour guide another day."

"Since I am now free, how about you join me for a coffee or wine? There is a popular outdoor cafe right across the square. I promise I don't bite, and I'll treat." He was not about to give her an easy out so he waited patiently for her reply.

Jessica was not as quick with her comeback as she was earlier. She was silently weighing the pros and cons of his request. *What the heck*, she thought. *It's just across the plaza, I have no plans, and maybe I'll learn about the city from this playful, outgoing guy.*

"Okay, if you promise you are not a con artist who will slip away to the restroom and leave me with the bill," she said, accepting his offer.

Laughing out loud at her reply, he said, "No worry about that."

He was right about the outdoor café. It was directly across from the cemetery, and charmingly picturesque with little tables scattered under leafy shade trees. They were seated at a small table near colorful flowers overflowing from a wooden wine barrel. Jessica relaxed. There was no concern. She could walk back to her apartment at any time. For some odd reason, she found her new acquaintance to be delightful, in a quirky sort of way. He was so opposite of her, a free spirit who seemed to just say whatever he was thinking without reservations. She sensed that he may be from the United States because he did not have an accent. But on the other hand, he had dark brown eyes that made her think perhaps he was from Argentina.

"My name is Will," he said as they were seated.

"I'm Jessica."

"Where do you call home, Jessica?"

"Chicago. I'm just getting away from the snow and cold for a few days. Are you from here or the States?"

"Very good question," he replied in a breezy manner. "I grew up in the United States. My father is American, but my mother is Argentine. They met in Philadelphia while she was attending college."

"So which side of the pond do you call home now?"

Will looked at her with increasing interest. He admired her wit and intelligence. "I'm living here for now." Before the waiter arrived, Will asked, "So what will it be for you now that it is 4:30 pm here in Argentina? Coffee or wine?"

"What would you suggest?" She smiled and directed her question back to him, not sure if he wanted to spend a bit more on wine or stay with coffee.

"Frankly, 4:30 pm is the start of happy hour in the States. I'd suggest you try our fabulous Malbec unless you drink white wine."

"Actually, I prefer red," she responded. "I suspect I have picked a great destination, not only for its sunshine and warm weather but also for its noted red wines."

When the waiter appeared, Will requested a bottle of his favorite reserve Malbec. Within minutes a handsome older man came directly to the table. He gave Will a warm greeting, and they spoke for a few minutes in Spanish. Will then said, "Meet Jessica, she is visiting from Chicago. Jessica, this is Tomas, the owner of this fabulous restaurant."

As Jessica acknowledged him, Tomas quickly changed to English. "I am so glad that you have come to our city. I think you will enjoy the wine that Will has chosen for you."

"I'm sure I will. Malbec is one of my favorites. Thank you. You have a lovely restaurant, and I appreciate your gracious welcome." He smiled and left the waiter to open and serve the wine which Will tasted with a swirl of his glass.

Impressive for a casual, bohemian-type guy, Jessica thought. After the wine was poured, the conversation went back to a typical first date genre.

"So, what do you do here in Buenos Aires?" Jessica inquired.

"You mean, what is my profession? I just knew that would be one of your first questions of me. I could have predicted it. I wish I would have written it on the back of this cocktail napkin ahead of your question. I could have then shown it to you, to prove my point."

"Why is it that women ask men that question before anything else? It almost feels like the answer determines whether you stay or not. What if I said that I worked as a dishwasher at the Alvear Palace Hotel? To be fair, perhaps, you are inquiring as to my intelligence level, but it always feels to me, personally, that you are hinting to learn my income or level of prestige."

Jessica found Will even more of a challenge than she had even initially imagined. He was definitely a handful! "I suppose I see your point. I'm now searching my mind, wondering what the first direct question a man would ask of me. I could be prankish and tell you what I guessed a man was thinking, but that wouldn't be fair would it?"

Will threw back his head in laughter, and she noticed a more flirtatious look in his eye. "Well, let me ask you then, since you are visiting Buenos Aires, do you prefer beef steak, pasta or fish at dinner?"

"I can see you have obviously changed the subject. But, since I am in Argentina, I think the correct answer would be steak. However, whether steak is the expected answer or not, I would still say it is my preference."

Will continued with a hint of a smile, "Your answer has led me to think about the dinner reservation I have at Fervor tonight. It is my favorite restaurant in the city, and since my friends are not making it over from Uruguay, I would like to invite you to be my guest for dinner. It's a shame to cancel the reservation at such a popular restaurant."

He could tell by the look on Jessica's face that this was far too forward a question for a single woman who he had just met that afternoon. So he quickly added, "Unless, of course, you have a gentleman waiting for you."

The question kept Jessica from immediately saying "no" to his invitation. "I actually am not seeing anyone right now, so there is no one waiting for me."

Before she could politely decline his invitation, Will interrupted with another question, "Do you play backgammon?"

Jessica was now becoming completely intrigued by this crazy outgoing man she had just met. "Yes, I do play a mean game of backgammon. I am good at it. Why do you ask?"

"Because you seem like a woman who would accept a wager. I sense that competitive spirit in you. So, here is my proposition, we play a game of backgammon now, right here over Malbec, and if I win you join me for dinner. And, if you win, you can decline. What do you say?"

Will was like no man she had ever met. He was so open, so audacious, and so unapologetically forward. "You're on," she said. "But I don't want to hear any complaints when I beat you."

"That's fair. Give me a few minutes. I'll go next door. There's a great leather shop, and I know they have some high-quality backgammon boards. Only the best for this competition." He grinned broadly.

As he left to purchase the game board, Jessica had a chance to think over what had happened in the past two hours. She had to admit to herself that she actually felt an attraction to this outgoing, playful man.

Will had a sweetness that she found appealing, and she had to admit that his sense of humor and engaging personality kept her on her toes intellectually. She somehow trusted him, and she decided to not ignore the chemistry she felt when they first said hello.

Could it be less than a coincidence that her cousin canceled, and she came to Buenos Aires free to do whatever she wished with whomever she chose to spend her time? She and Will had a nice connection. She liked him, but decided that it was far too early to let him guess it. Besides, a backgammon competition was about to start and she was happy that it was one of her favorite board games and that she was a darn good player.

Will returned with a package under his arm and unwrapped the most impressive backgammon case Jessica had ever seen. The leather was soft and smooth. It had real silver corners and a stunning clasp. She was sure the discs were made of marble.

"You were certainly right about the quality of this board. I think it's the most handsome backgammon board I have ever played on," she said. As he set up the board, Jessica shared a bit of trivia. "Did you know that backgammon is one of the oldest games in existence. It's dated back around 5,000 years and originated in Mesopotamia. The earliest dice discovered by archaeologists were made of human bone."

"Yikes!" Will said emphatically. "That's certainly the way to show off one's warrior skills. Are you trying to intimidate me, Jessica?"

"I had not thought of it that way, but let the battle begin."

As they drank Malbec over their backgammon game, the conversation settled into a relaxed exchange. Jessica purposely did not make reference to Will's profession. She would not fall into that trap again! With each move, Jessica could see that they were equally matched. There were no mistakes, and their win would literally come down to the luck of the dice.

"Aha, I win," Jessica declared as she completed her final play.

"Congratulations," Will conceded with gentlemanly grace. "You are a tough competitor indeed. I suppose now you are going to decline my invitation for dinner?"

There was a long pause on Jessica's part and then she spoke. "Yes, I am sorry you cannot take me to dinner. However, since I have won the match I have the prerogative of inviting you as my dinner guest." She was curious to see Will's reaction. It was pure shock, but she also noticed a hint of delight.

Since the dinner reservation was in keeping with South America customs it was not until 8:00 pm. Will announced that he needed to go home and change his clothes for dinner. He offered to walk Jessica to her apartment but she explained that it was only a few blocks away. And, since the restaurant was only around the corner from the Alvear Palace Hotel, she also offered to walk back the ten minutes to the restaurant and meet him there.

He could sense that she was still being cautious and he thought that it was certainly understandable. "Great, I will see you at Fervor. And, by the way, thanks for the invitation. I don't suppose you would agree to an arm wrestling match to see who pays the check?" he said with a grin.

"No, I would not. Remember I won the backgammon game fair and square, so you are my guest."

He gave a warmhearted smile. "Fair is fair. See you at 8:00 pm"

Jessica was surprised at the level of excitement she was feeling. She had been fortunate to date many exceptional men in her lifetime. They were interesting, gracious, and kind. The problem was that they just weren't the kindred spirit she longed to find. There was something special about Will. She was glad she would have the opportunity to get to know him better over dinner.

Back at the apartment, she pondered what the appropriate attire should be. She did have an off the shoulder, short black dress but wondered if it might be too dressy for his casual appearance. On second thought, she decided that he did say it was one of the most popular fine dining restaurants in the city. She was the host, and she was in the mood to dress up and look elegant for her first night out in Buenos Aires. She would pay special attention to her makeup and hair and wear the little black dress for the evening. Whether she ever saw Will again didn't matter, this was a special occasion. Although, in her heart, she had a funny little premonition that it would not be their last night together.

When Jessica arrived at the Fervor restaurant, Will was waiting for her, sitting in the entry lounge on a leather couch. He looked comfortable and handsome. When he saw her he immediately got up to greet her. "You look stunning," he said with an approving smile.

"You clean up pretty nicely yourself," Jessica replied. She took note that he did not look exactly like the man who had been sitting on the cemetery bench that afternoon. He was wearing a crisp white untucked shirt, a light gray jacket, and pressed slacks.

Just then, the owner of the restaurant appeared. As Will began to introduce Jessica, he realized he did not know her last name.

"Jessica Hansen," she said with a smile as she extended her hand.

Alan, the restaurant owner, extended his hand to introduce himself. In English, he replied, "Will always brings the most beautiful women to our restaurant. It is nice to meet you."

Turning toward Will, he said, "We have changed your reservation from a table of four to your favorite table for two. Welcome, Senorita Hansen. I hope you will enjoy your evening with us."

As they were escorted to the table, Jessica could not believe that she actually felt a pang of jealousy at hearing that Will often brought attractive women to his favorite table at this most posh restaurant. *What a foolish emotion*, she thought to herself. And it certainly was not fair as she had dated often. She tried to brush it away, but it lingered in her mind.

When they were seated, Will looked into her eyes, and Jessica felt he read her mind.

"I don't want you to the assume from Alan's comment that I am some sort of a playboy escorting gorgeous women about town."

"Since I don't know your profession, I could surmise that you are a mob boss who spends time with glamorous women dripping in diamonds and furs, but I will assume tonight that it isn't the case."

Will shook his head and chuckled. "Your assumption is correct. It is true that I have dated good-looking women and also escorted several in my profession, but I assure you that I'm not a player. I'm actually kind of an old fashioned, ordinary-type guy."

The dinner was relaxed and pleasurable. The steak was delicious. She marveled at the size of the piece of meat served, it almost filled her entire plate. The wine at dinner was perhaps one of the best Malbec's she had ever tasted. She noticed that the waiter did not ask her to choose a bottle from the menu, and she hoped that it was not terribly expensive, since she was the host for the evening. She thought perhaps it was the specialty house wine, but her palate for fine wines told her otherwise.

Will wanted to know all about her. She started by telling him she was an only child and was surprised when he told her he was also an only child. She said that her parents gave her a secure and loving upbringing. They owned a bookstore so introduced her to the joy of discovery through reading. As a toddler they brought her to the store, and she had a little room in the back with lots of toys and a tiny, white ornate bed for her naps. She would wander through the book store interacting with the customers who were enamored of her curly red hair. Jessica laughed when she confessed that as a school girl she was teased unmercifully because of her chubby cheeks and long red pigtails. "Perhaps, the fact that those schoolboys gave me such a hard time is why I am so feisty and independent today."

"I'm not sure that being a skinny kid with braces helped my self-esteem," Will replied. "But I did learn to become self-reliant in dodging the rulers wielded by those nuns in Catholic school."

They told humorous stories about their growing up years. She had a cat named Spot, and he had a talking parrot named José. She loved his story about taking José to the Christmas pageant at school. He had spent months training José to offer a holiday greeting and was pleased that he could mimic "Feliz Navidad" quite well. It was to be the last scene in the program. He was to come on stage alone, with José on his shoulder, and his parrot would then wish everyone a Merry Christmas. Will's eyes sparkled playfully as he told the "rest of the story," as he put it. José was sitting on the shoulder pad of his brand-new blue blazer. Right on cue he mimicked his line perfectly. But before the audience could burst into applause José deposited right on his shoulder, and bird poop dripped down the front of his jacket!

"Can you imagine the humiliation of that skinny, awkward eight-year-old boy?" he said.

Jessica loved his sweet remembrances and especially his ability to follow her story with a delightful one of his own. She was still amused when Will interrupted with an apology, "I'm sorry this is not an appropriate dinner topic of conversation."

"No problem, I have an ironclad stomach," she shot back with a grin.

Will was especially interested to hear what career path Jessica had chosen. She told him that she had attended the state university earning an undergraduate degree in journalism. At twenty years of age, and directly out of college, she had gotten a job with the local television network reporting the nightly weather. "Can you imagine me in a very short skirt, talking about rain, sleet and the freezing temperatures in Chicago?" she asked with a wrinkled-up nose.

For some reason, Will found the idea of Jessica as the local television "weather girl" to be terribly amusing. He actually turned aside with his shoulders shaking in laughter. He found it both charming but also so unlike the woman he was coming to know. It made him even more fascinated to hear more. She explained that she only lasted a year in that job. The network producers wanted her to wear shorter skirts and smile more. She decided it was time to do something more intellectual.

She landed a job at the local newspaper covering the city commission meetings and political news. She found it interesting at first, but she became tired of all of the infighting and angst. She wanted a job in journalism that was more rewarding and challenging. On a whim, she sent her resume to a nationally acclaimed travel magazine. They requested a 400-word article written on a local destination. She remembered writing hers on an afternoon spent exploring a Polish neighborhood in Chicago. She got the position and spent seven exciting years traveling the world as a journalist.

"I am hesitant to break the sequence of your life history," Will interrupted. "But I would be interested in hearing about your favorite assignment during those years?"

Jessica was touched that he was interested in learning of her preferences. "I particularly liked writing about Africa. It seemed to call to me. I have read many novels about Africa, and the female characters confessed to have had the same kind of reaction. I think my favorite experience was the time I covered a story about hot air ballooning in Tanzania. My style is not to engage in early morning activities, and it was barely breaking daylight when we headed out in our jeeps to the site where the balloons were being filled. The sun was just starting to peek over the horizon, and I remember the beautiful colors of the sunrise. When the brightly striped balloons were filled and ready, we entered the baskets, and, swoosh, up we rose over the Serengeti, the vast land famous for its annual migration of over 1.5 million white-bearded wildebeest and 250,000 zebras. My most vivid memory is of when our balloon dipped close to the river over a herd of hippos. They all opened their mouths wide and pushed their young underwater for protection. My photographer captured the most fabulous shots."

"I'd like to see those photographs one day. It seems like a country that could touch your soul with its wild and untamed beauty. I have not been to Africa yet, but it is definitely on my bucket list," Will replied.

He and Jessica spent quite a while talking about Africa before he brought the conversation back to asking about her career.

"It's interesting how life offers opportunities in strange ways," Jessica continued. "I booked all of my assignments through a travel agency in my neighborhood. I liked the energy of the company. Everyone was extremely professional, yet fun-loving and engaging. One day, the owner asked me to lunch. She explained that her husband had just been offered a lucrative promotion with his company. They would be moving to the west coast and she was planning to sell her agency. She asked if I might be interested. When I asked why she thought of me she said that she saw something special in me. It was an entrepreneurial spirit and a determination, which she felt would help in taking the agency to a whole new level. She explained that her manager was highly qualified in running the agency and supervising the agents. What was needed was creative marketing. She felt my reputation as a travel journalist would also add to their success. Strange as it happened, shortly thereafter, a great uncle of mine died and left me a fair amount of money. I decided to buy the agency, and years later we are still experiencing success beyond my wildest dreams. Luckily, my manager is committed and excellent, so it gave me an opportunity to go back to the university to get my master's in journalism. I guess I have always considered teaching at the college level, but I've also wished I could just take a leap of faith and try my hand at writing a novel. I don't remember if I told you I have an especially high energy level?"

"Somehow, I'm beginning to get that feeling," he responded good-naturedly. "But I actually like your energy level. It matches mine."

Jessica noticed that Will had steered the conversation in her direction the entire evening, and she had not had an opportunity to learn more about his life. She sensed that he was purposely keeping it a secret. At least, for now. When the waiter brought the check, Jessica reached across the table to retrieve it. As she looked it over she noticed it was not correct.

"Will, this is only the amount for the food. I don't see a charge for the wine?"

"Oh, that is because I wanted to share a vintage bottle from my private wine locker here at Fervor. This Malbec is from one of my favorite old wineries in the Mendoza region. I hope you liked it."

"It was truly exceptional. That was most gracious of you. Thank you," Jessica added with a gentle smile of appreciation

As they were leaving the restaurant, Will asked, "May I walk you back to the apartment?"

"I'd like that very much."

As they began down the street, Jessica took his arm and smiled. She wanted to convey to him that even though they had just met, she felt a connection, and she hoped that they might continue to get to know each other.

"Are you free tomorrow evening?" Will asked. "I'd like to cook dinner for you."

"What a wonderful invitation. I would love that."

"You might want to wait until you taste my cooking, but given the many positive comments I've received from friends, I must humbly admit that I'm a very good cook. I actually inherited my love of cooking from my favorite aunt. We used to laughingly say that 'she could make soup from a shoe.' I think the most important element in cooking is that you are passionate about it. And that, I am."

"I look forward to seeing you in action in your kitchen," Jessica teased with a grin.

"Get ready. I also dance in my kitchen, and I may even ask you to join me!"

"As long as it's not the tango," Jessica exclaimed. "I have not yet had the time for lessons."

"Not a problem, I prefer a slow dance," he offered with a flirtatious smile. "I'm tied up most of the day tomorrow. It's just a suggestion, but you might want to take a tour to get an overview of the city. They offer a great, English speaking, half-day sightseeing tour from the Alvear Palace Hotel. They use a small, air-conditioned van, and I hear their tour guide is most knowledgeable. You can call them in the morning to make a reservation."

He oaused. "On second thought, I forgot you are not a morning person. You may want to sleep in."

"How thoughtful of you to remember," Jessica replied with a little squeeze of his arm. "Mornings are my time to ease into the day on vacation. But an afternoon tour sounds perfect. What time shall I come for dinner?"

"How about 7:00 pm? We can have cocktails before dinner."

Jessica shared her business card and cell phone number. Will said, "I will call you around 6:00 pm, and we can discuss getting you over to my place. I live in San Telmo. It's a funky old part of the city. It used to be where the dock workers lived at the turn of the century. It appears a bit shabby and eclectic but there are some hidden gems there. Several 'ex-pats' have purchased beautiful historic mansions and restored them into town homes. Argentina has the most talented tile layers, wood carvers and builders in South America. They are so affordable. I have had a couple of properties restored. I'll tell you all about that tomorrow night."

As they approached the lobby of her apartment building, Will lingered a moment. "I've had the most wonderful day with you Jessica. You appear to be a remarkable woman in so many ways. When my friends had to cancel this afternoon, I was left sitting on a bench in the Recoleta Cemetery. Of all places to have met you. It certainly feels like a bit of luck dropped in." Will drew her close and gave her a tender good night kiss. "See you tomorrow and sleep well."

When she entered her apartment she suddenly realized she was indeed sleepy. Between her international flight, having gotten up so early that morning in Chicago, and the time change, she was ready for bed. She had her makeup off, teeth brushed, night shirt on, and her head barely hit the pillow before she was in slumberland. In the morning, she was surprised when she awoke earlier than usual. It wasn't like her to be wide awake at 7:00 am on vacation. She suspected that it had something to do with having met Will, and her anticipation of dinner at his home that evening. As she sat up in bed, she suddenly realized that she did not stop to purchase coffee and cream for the apartment on her way back from the cemetery. Darn, she thought. I was looking forward to sitting on the lovely balcony sipping coffee in my robe. She made her way into the apartment kitchen and was immediately thrilled to see a package of complimentary coffee next to the coffee maker. *Please, let there be cream or milk in the fridge,* she thought as she turned to open the refrigerator door. There it was, a small carton of cream on the shelf! All she could think of was gratitude, and Will's comment about a bit of luck in the air.

Out on the balcony, in her robe with a steaming cup of coffee, she felt a growing sense of happiness and contentment. Could these emotions be tied to the free-spirited, tender and romantic man she had met less than twenty-four hours before? Her mind was racing as she began to analyze her feelings. She knew that her nature was to be more guarded with her emotions than she had been with Will. She wasn't one to open up so easily to a man she had just met. But it was different with him. He was not like any man she had ever dated. He was so transparent with his feelings, having the innocence of a child. Not that he was immature in any way, but that he was so comfortable with expressing his feelings. If he was happy, he openly showed joy in his expressions and words. It was crystal clear to her that he would share a truthful emotion in any situation.

She found it refreshing, but she also started to notice a feeling of hesitancy surfacing. Wasn't he the type of man she longed to meet, one who was genuine who unconditionally liked her just the way she was? Why were these feelings of doubt creeping in? Thoughts that it was too good to be true. That Will was too good to be true.

Just then Jessica wanted to talk to a trusted friend. She thought of her cousin. They had a sincere bond and her cousin knew her inside and out. She would be truthful and straightforward in her advice. It wasn't too early to call her, as she was an early riser.

"Good morning, Cuz," Jessica said as Genie answered the phone.

"Wow, you are sounding chipper this morning."

"Do you have a minute to talk?" Jessica asked. "I could use some of your good advice."

"Uh-oh. Are you in a jam? Is there a problem?"

"Actually, there isn't a problem. It's just skittish me calling to talk. I actually met someone here. Not just anyone, but an amazingly wonderful man named Will. He is kind, intelligent, and funny."

"And you need my advice?" her cousin said with a laugh.

"Seriously," Jessica continued. "I met him yesterday, almost by accident. We had a good time last night and he has invited me to his home tonight to cook me dinner."

"So, what is the concern? A great guy who is kind, funny and cooks!" she replied with a bit of humor.

Genie got serious. "I'm sorry to make light of your call. Tell me what is bothering you."

Jessica softened and tried to put her feelings into words. "He's just so different than any man I've ever met. He's so open and himself. I just don't know if I'm the right woman for him."

"I can't believe it. It sounds like you actually want to protect this nice guy from you. It is true that you are a control freak, independent to a fault and tough as nails, but I know you, possibly better than anyone else. Down deep you are a sweet, soft and loving person. Is the problem you don't want to give up your independence for a relationship, or is it you are just getting cold feet?"

Jessica listened intently to her cousin's questions, but before she could answer, her cousin continued, "Hey, wait a minute. I'm just going to ask you the exact question you asked me when I met my husband, Dan. You asked me, 'Did you feel an immediate spark of connection when you first met?'"

As she thought for a moment, Jessica replied, "I did feel a definite attraction when I met him, and every minute I'm with him I feel alive and excited. It's not that I'm afraid of giving up my independence. Will isn't the type of man who would want that from me. He actually likes my independent streak. I guess it's just my intense skepticism resurfacing."

"Jess, just remember that you are not only lovable, you are also deserving of love. I think if you are as attracted to this guy as you say you are, you should take a deep breath, muster up some courage and see where it goes. Just be yourself. If he really is the right man, all he will expect from you is that you be yourself. That is all he would want. And you are enough."

"Thanks for the good advice. I love you, Genie."

"And I love you. Maybe there is a bit of universal destiny at play here given the fact that I had to cancel this trip leaving you alone to meet this fabulous South American guy."

"He grew up in Minneapolis. But that's a long story for another time."

I hope it has a happy ending, Jess. I must confess I have not heard you so excited and animated in a long time. Go for it, and call me again to add some excitement to my mundane business trip."

They both laughed and bid each other goodbye, but not before Jessica inquired about the progress on her cousin's new contract, which she learned was going very well. As Jessica finished her coffee, she felt her energy level rising.

"I think I am ready to take a tour of the city," she decided. When she called the hotel, they advised her that they had availability on the late morning tour. Perfect, she thought to herself. I'll get a little breakfast at the hotel and be back in time to change for dinner. She was out of the shower in a flash and into tennis shoes for her day of touring. When she exited the elevator, the doorman approached her with an exquisite bouquet of flowers.

"I was just about to deliver these to your apartment, señorita" he said.

Jessica was surprised. "Oh! Thank you," she replied and accepted the colorful floral arrangement.

A card read, "Thank you for being you. Looking forward to tonight. Will."

Jessica's eyes teared a little as she thought about her cousin's advice. How could his message be almost written in her cousin's exact words? Perhaps it was the sign she needed. She would be her authentic self, and go forward to see where this new path might lead her.

At the hotel, she grabbed a little breakfast, exchanged more dollars into pesos, and joined the tour group. Will was right; their tour guide, Carlos, was entertaining and knowledgeable. Since there were only eight participants, it was easy to ask questions, and touring the city flowed effortlessly.

Their first stop was the Plaza De Mayo, named as the Symbolic Heart of Buenos Aires. Originally, during Spanish rule, it was an unpaved marketplace for sailors, colonial officials and traders.

Today the plaza is often the site of political rallies. Jessica noted that there was still a small group of protesters occupying one corner of the public square with signs and banners.

Everyone in the tour group was interested in seeing the Casa Rosada, located at one end of the plaza. It was the presidential palace where Maria Eva Duarte de Perón, better known as Evita, delivered her farewell speech to the Argentine people. Jessica remembered that her cousin had hoped to see the balcony, and she took a photo. Even though most people in America were familiar with the song, "Don't Cry for Me, Argentina," Jessica wondered how many people actually knew the many details of Evita's life.

While in the square, Carlos also told the group about the Mother's of the Plaza de Mayo. It was a movement started by Argentine mothers who still keep up the pressure to find out information on the 30,000 protesting students who suddenly disappeared during the military dictatorship in the 1970s. For years, they have marched every Thursday in the plaza, wearing white head scarves to symbolize the diapers of their lost children. They remain today protesting the human rights violations committed in what was called the Dirty War.

Jessica couldn't help feeling sad for these mothers. She had never had children of her own, but she could not imagine the pain these mothers had endured. She was a generous benefactor of her local women's shelter and felt it was her small part in helping women and children.

As the tour continued, Carlos pointed out several main attractions: the fourteen-acre Recoleta Cemetery, which brought a smile to Jessica's lips and a little skipped beat of her heart, the modern art bridge designed by a Spanish architect to depict a couple dancing the tango, and the many buildings on the Avenida 9 de Julio, described as one of the widest avenues in the world and named to honored Argentina's Independence Day, July 9, 1816. Undoubtedly, the most elegant building on the avenue was the Teatro Colon, the magnificent opera house. Considered to be one of the top three in the world in terms of acoustics, it was famous, not only for its size, but for the classic decor dating back to its opening in 1908. Carlos went on to say that it had attracted the world's greatest artists, not only to perform in its symphonies, but also in its operas.

Jessica raised her hand with a question. "Are there scheduled tours to visit the opera house?" Carlos sadly answered that although tours were usually offered twice a day, the opera house was closed for two months for cleaning and restoration. Several of the tour participants gave out loud sighs of disappointment. They did not want to miss it while in Buenos Aires. Jessica was also crushed. She loved her local symphony performances and would have relished telling her friends, and symphony director, that she had toured the halls of the famous Teatro Colon in Buenos Aires.

Carlos' description of the opera house's splendid European marble, Versailles-like mirrors and 2,500-person main hall only served to enhance their disappointment. He told the group that at one time, as a college student, he was invited to sit in a balcony box at a performance. He said that when the 700-bulb chandelier was turned on, it took his breath away.

The tour continued, and when Jessica heard mention of San Telmo, she paid particular attention. It was the neighborhood where Will lived. In his commentary, Carlos explained that San Telmo was the site where the first Europeans made their 1536 arrival in what is now the city of Buenos Aires. In its earliest days, it was the area where dock workers lived in tiny wooden and tin houses. By the mid-1800s, wealthier residents moved in and built beautiful mansions. But when yellow fever swept through the area, the wealthy fled, and the mansions became homes for the immigrants who arrived in the late nineteenth century.

It must be one of those original mansions that Will had restored, Jessica thought. Her guidebook painted a picture of San Telmo as being a historic neighborhood of cobblestone streets, raucous local bars, and couples dancing tango day and night in the small square. It was home to the famous San Telmo Sunday Market, where antiques, handicraft items, old books, jewelry clothing and more were sold.

The guidebook description included phrases referring to faded elegance, crumbling buildings, antiquated hardware stores, and a community that stubbornly remained unchanged. There was even a section describing the graffiti covering so many of the old buildings along San Telmo's narrow streets.

For all of the questionable comments, the area was loved by the residents and the visitors alike. Jessica especially delighted in a references to San Telmo having a Bohemian vibe. She smiled to think that it was the exact description of Will that she had first used in her mind. She even looked up the dictionary description on her cell phone. The word "Bohemian" referred to a socially unconventional person, especially an artist or writer. *Perhaps, he is an artist or writer,* she thought. If so this would be the perfect neighborhood for him.

One of the passengers asked, "Is it safe to walk around the San Telmo market?" She had a friend whose wallet was stolen while there.

"The Sunday market has become one of the most popular attractions in Buenos Aires," Carlos replied. "The streets are lined with stalls selling antiques, jewelry, old books, and handcrafted souvenirs." He advised not to wear expensive jewelry or watches and to keep one's money in a safe place to discourage pickpockets. With a slight grin he added, "They actually say that the San Telmo Market is the training ground for pickpockets in the city."

The last stop on their tour was Caminito. Although originally a traditional alley, it was now listed as a street museum. Amidst brightly painted zinc dwellings, the alleyway was filled with artists selling their original paintings, jewelry, and handicrafts. Jessica purchased several small paintings for friends, a lovely large woven bag for her cousin, a shawl for herself, and several small leather coin purses for her agents. She found a small shop selling shirts and caps with the logo of the soccer club Boca Juniors, Argentina's professional sports club based in the neighboring La Boca district. She knew gifts from there would make her very popular with her manager's sons. The tour ended back at the Alvear Palace Hotel where Jessica generously tipped the tour guide, indeed most knowledgeable and informative. As she walked back to her apartment, she felt grateful for Will's suggestion to take a city tour. She had gained a good overview of the city in just a few hours.

Will called exactly at 6:00 pm as promised. "How was your day?"

"It was fantastic!" Jessica could not contain her enthusiasm. "Thank you so much for recommending the tour. I'm already in love with Buenos Aires. What an amazing city. And we even visited your neighborhood of San Telmo."

"I'm so glad you enjoyed it. And speaking of my neighborhood, I'm calling to suggest your transportation to my home for dinner. I could drive over to pick you up, but since we are planning a longer evening, with lots of wine, I would rather send a private taxi. Is that okay with you?"

"That's just fine, and I want to tell you how much I appreciate your thoughtfulness in sending me the lovely bouquet of flowers. It was a most romantic gesture."

"I'm glad you took it as the romantic gesture I intended. I've already got the grill going to prepare our dinner. I'm making our country's national specialty. And we'll have traditional empanadas for our appetizers on the roof. Be sure to come hungry." he advised. "The taxi will pick you up at 6:45 pm"

Jessica changed into some stylish black palazzo pants. She liked the way they showed off her long legs and swirled as she walked. She felt sexy and festive in them. She chose a fuchsia figure fitting top and a large silver pendent necklace. With her new South American shawl over her shoulders, she was off to meet Will at his home.

The taxi arrived on time, and the driver got out to display his sign with her name printed on it. When they arrived in San Telmo, Jessica noted that the area seemed as ramshackle as she remembered it. The taxi driver turned onto a narrow cobblestoned street and stopped, indicating they had arrived at their destination. *Could this be Will's house?* she thought. The large windows of the tall, modest appearing building were all shuttered for the evening. As she noted earlier there was graffiti on every structure, including his. The taxi driver indicated that he would remain until she was safely inside. Jessica walked up to one of the most massive, wooden doors she had ever seen and noticed a security buzzer on the wall. She pressed it and heard the familiar voice she had come to recognize and enjoy.

"Hi. I'm on my way down. Be there in a second." As Will opened the door, she waved the taxi driver on and stepped inside.

After receiving a warm, welcoming hug she turned from the entry and gasped. Inside his home, away from the dingy street outside, she found herself in the most gorgeous setting. It took her breath away. The entry was a large space with marble floors, impressive columns and three steps leading up to an outdoor dining area right in the middle of the town home. The open-air room had a large grill vented to the outside. The walls were covered with most exquisite tiles. And in the middle of the room was a huge antique table and ornate high back chairs. She wondered if this was one of the original mansions that Carlos had described on her city tour.

"Come on in. I have a great Malbec breathing in the kitchen."

As Jessica followed, she could tell that to Will, this was his home. He was impervious to the awe-struck expression on her face. The kitchen was directly off the dining courtyard. It was like walking from the 1800s into the most modern high-tech kitchen imaginable with stainless steel appliances, black glass-fronted cabinetry and stone countertops.

"Your home is gorgeous," Jessica said, still a bit overwhelmed and surprised given the appearance of the San Telmo neighborhood.

"I'm glad you like it," he casually replied. Will poured two glasses of wine into elegant long-stemmed glasses. Before he handed her a glass, he said, "Let me take a minute to look at you. Not only are you beautiful, but you look like you belong here in Buenos Aires."

Swirling around in a circle, Jessica replied, "I'm glad you like these palazzo pants. They do remind me of South America."

"Can you carry the wine bottle and your glass so I can carry the empanadas?"

She nodded and followed him up a stairway that led past several guest rooms on the second floor, and onto a third floor, outdoor terrace with trees, flowers, and a gurgling fountain.

"What a perfect spot for cocktails!"

He placed the platter of appetizers on a small glass table. "Have you had an empanada yet?" he asked. "They are an Argentine staple, brought over by

Spanish immigrants during the 16th century. They translate to 'wrapped in bread,' and are usually filled with all sorts of meats, rice or beans. I made us a little assortment for our happy hour."

"Well, you are spoiling me, and I have only just arrived," Jessica exclaimed with gratitude. As they enjoyed their appetizers and wine, Jessica told him about the tour and all of the places she had visited. "I was so sorry to hear that the opera house is closed for renovations while I am here," she lamented.

"Do you enjoy classical music?" Will asked inquisitively.

"Oh, yes, very much. I have had season tickets to our Chicago Symphony for years, and try to never miss a performance. I was really looking forward to visiting your opera house because it is so well known. My friends would have been impressed. I'm so sorry I will miss seeing it."

Will acknowledged her disappointment. Then he smiled with a particularly interesting look on his face.

After a carefree hour of conversation Will announced it was time to start their dinner. "Would you like to sip your wine downstairs and keep me company while I do some grilling? We are having Argentina's national dish, asado. In English, asado is known as barbecue, but since we have more livestock in this country than people, it is a bit more extreme here. We grill all sorts of meats at once, pork, sausages, chicken, and churrasco which is beef sirloin. Since we are only two people, I reduced it to beef and pork. I think you will like the sauce I prepared to go with our meat. You can't leave Argentina without trying chimichurri, our famous accompaniment made with parsley and herbs. I'm also making a grilled dish called provoleta. It's made with lots of cheese."

"I'm impressed just hearing the menu," Jessica commented with enthusiasm.

Down in the open air courtyard, Will put on a big apron and started grilling. Jessica had to admit she had never thought that a man could be so good looking in an apron. He asked her to light the candles on the table, and around the courtyard on magnificent iron sconces. As they were seated, Jessica thought their dinner setting may have been one of the most unique she could remember. Will was an excellent cook and seemed to enjoy, not only preparing the food, but also seeing how much Jessica enjoyed it. The meat was grilled to perfection and they spread their bubbly hot provolone cheese on crusty bread. During the candlelit dinner Will interrupted their light, breezy conversation.

"Jessica, I'd like to tell you more about myself. I know it has been playful and mysterious to keep you guessing about me, but I like you, and I want you to feel that I will always be truthful and honest with you."

Jessica held her breath. *Oh, please, be about his profession,* she thought, *and not the fact that he is engaged or in a seriously relationship.*

He saw the terror in her eyes. With a bit of humor in his voice, he said, "Please, relax, I'm not going to tell you I'm married or an ax murderer. I was being elusive yesterday regarding my profession, just as a sportive game, but I want you to know that I'm a reputable man. My father is a noted physician in the States, Minneapolis to be specific. I followed in his footsteps and became a physician too. I love medicine, but it is not my primary career here in Argentina. I'll share that with you tomorrow night if you are free."

Jessica nodded that she was free to join him, and he continued, "I think you will like the surprise I have planned. But let me get back to my career in medicine. I worked in the States in pediatrics at the major hospital group where my father is still a surgeon today. I love children, although I have not had any of my own. Youngsters are so open, trusting, and innocent. Being around them and helping the little ones heal brings me great joy and satisfaction. I've been back in Buenos Aires five years now. Since living here, though, my schedule does not allow me to practice medicine full time. I help out part time as a doctor in a low-income children's clinic.

I think I told you my mother is from here. She comes from a musical and artistic family. My great-grandfather and grandfather were internationally accomplished musicians, and my mother is now a professional artist. Later, I will point out her pieces here in my home."

"I noticed the quality of your artwork earlier," Jessica commented. "The large oil paintings in the hallways are truly impressive, I look forward to my personal gallery tour." She smiled softly. "Thank you for sharing your story with me. You actually did not convince me, for one minute, that you were a disreputable, sleazy character. Knowing you have a heart for healing children makes me feel an even greater admiration for you. It blends beautifully with the many qualities I like about you."

Will took a minute to reply. He was pleased to hear her comment on the characteristics she admired in him. He was not sure if the tough independent woman he had just met would emotionally let him in. "Thank you. I appreciate the compliment."

Jessica looked at him with a softness that she rarely displayed. "I see you are a perceptive man, and you may have noticed I have a tendency to keep my feelings, as they might say, 'close to the vest pocket.' Actually, although I have dated several terrific men in my lifetime, I tend to be fiercely independent. My women friends tease me because the last man I dated left because he said I would not give him even one, small drawer in which to keep a few personal items for his overnight visits.

My cousin says it will take an exceptional man to earn that precious piece of real estate in my home. I guess I'm considered to be a pretty tough woman. But I feel myself letting down my guard a bit with you. I do not want you to think that in past relationships I was demanding or placed excessively high standards on the men I dated. I really enjoyed the times we spent together, and I truly cared about each and every one of them. It's just that I never felt that important magical connection. I just knew they weren't my forever sweetheart."

Jessica noticed a look of understanding on Will's face. She saw him nod a couple of times while she was making her heartfelt confession. It was as if he realized that, although strongly independent, she had been true to herself. With her last sentence spoken, she thought she caught a glimpse of a smile on his lips.

"I'm smiling because I appreciate your use of the word "sweetheart." It seems loving and romantic. In the States, you often refer to your lovers as partners. When we hear someone say, 'I'd like to introduce you to my partner,' we consider that to be a business partner. I guess we South American men are just hopeless romantics. Sweetheart is tender and sentimental. I like it a lot. So, my question to is, are you actually saying you are open to finding a sweetheart?"

His question was a fair one, and one that should have been easy to answer, but her hesitancy got Will's attention. He didn't take his eyes off her as he waited for her answer.

"As hesitant as I appear to be, yes, I am longing to meet a man that I can open my heart to." *There, she had actually said it out loud.* A feeling of authenticity come over her. Being transparent was not her nature, but she trusted Will and she trusted herself in that moment.

"I'm pleased to hear that, Jessica, because I would very much like to get to know you better. I have enjoyed the brief amount of time we have spent together." Will paused to pour her another glass of wine, and she noticed a lightness in his demeanor. He added with a mischievous and playful grin. "Well, at least, you will have a sign when you meet your perfect sweetheart."

"What sign would that be?" Jessica inquired, looking rather puzzled.

"Your willingness to offer him an empty drawer," he replied. He'd found the comments on the dresser drawer to be charming and almost comical. Yet, he truly understood the significance it held for her.

Noticing the lighthearted nature that had returned to their conversation, Jessica raised her glass high. "Yes, when I am lucky enough to find my forever sweetheart, I will even share half of my entire closet with him." She smiled to think she had actually admitted to that fact. And to her astonishment, she felt it to be true.

"Wow, now there is commitment!" Will laughed as he lifted his glass to toast with hers.

Having finished dinner, they moved to the living room to finish their wine. As they sat together amidst the multitude of colorful woven pillows on the massive couch, Jessica looked around the room. It most definitely reflected the image she held of Argentina. Everything was bold and vibrant. Will's mother's original paintings were of market scenes, the faces of people and historic monuments. The living room seemed to be decorated around the paintings. The fabric on the furniture was complimentary, as well as the draperies. Because of the sixteen-foot ceilings, the room had a presence of grandeur, but in reality, it was welcoming and comfortable.

"Look up," Will said. "I was so excited the day I found those huge, carved beams in the back room of an antique store."

"I think I will add interior decorating to the list of talents you seem to so easily possess," Jessica replied.

"Actually, my mother helped me decorate, but I have enjoyed restoring this place. It is like a piece of history. Imagine how sad it would be to have all these gorgeous old mansions torn down to build a modern hotel. What did you think when the taxi driver stopped out front?"

Jessica paused, and Will grinned because he already surmised her answer. "I'll bet you would never have guessed what was behind the graffiti splattered walls." She nodded as he continued. "All of us neighbors were advised not to make any changes to the outside of the building for two reasons.

First, was that we do not want to call attention to the fact that we have beautiful objects in our homes. The second reason was because the minute the graffiti was painted over it would be back the next night." He went on to explain that their street art was not likened to the graffiti in the States which often signifies the territories of gangs. Much of the graffiti told a story; revealing love for someone, possibly honoring a family member or, sometimes, just representing an expression of art.

"That is so interesting. I will look differently at it with this in mind. Who are your neighbors?"

Will went on to describe his neighbors on the narrow, cobblestone street. There was Michael and Alena, a retired couple in their sixties. He had worked for an international company in Brussels, and she was Argentine. They wanted to return and restore one of the old mansions, and Will explained that Michael had been so helpful in assisting him to find the best builders and artisans.

"These craftsmen are so affordable in Argentina that we can take on projects of this magnitude. Even when Michael and I pay them generously, it is far less than the expense we would incur in the States."

Will went on to explain that another couple, Kirk and Kathleen, were from Los Angeles in the entertainment industry. They became enamored with Buenos Aires and now consider it their second home. They are extremely talented and interesting." It was, however, Will's description of the elderly man who lived directly across the street that most touched Jessica. Sebastián grew up as a little boy in that exact house and had lived there all of his life. Will described him as a kind older gentleman who liked to come out on his second-floor balcony to check out the happenings in the neighborhood. He always had a bit of history to share about San Telmo. At eighty-six years old, he had outlived two wives and was dating again. "You'd like him," Will commented with a smile.

Jessica immediately caught his reference that she might return. It thrilled her to think he would like to have her visit again.

They shared several kisses on the couch before Will spoke, "It's getting late. I have a busy day tomorrow so we should end this delightful evening."

"Let me help you clear the table," Jessica offered.

"Next time," was his reply. "While I call for your taxi, may I tell you about our plans for tomorrow night?"

"Ah, yes, your surprise. I can't wait to see what it is. And if it's Tango lessons, I want you to know that I have two left feet."

Will chuckled. "No Tango lessons, but I can't let you get out of town without taking you to the most authentic tango dinner club in the city. Just then he stopped suddenly. "I hope I am not monopolizing your time or making assumptions that we can spend your evenings together this week?"

Jessica liked the open and candid way he checked in to clarify things. "Actually, you have already made my trip unforgettable. I would be disappointed if it ended now."

"Good, because I really want to share a surprise with you tomorrow night."

"Can I have a hint?" Jessica said in a flirtatious manner. "I'll trade another kiss for a hint."

"It's tempting. But how about I just steal one instead?" He snatched her around the waist and laughingly pulled her toward him. He loved the fact that she did not resist his kisses.

"I'll pick you up at 7:00 pm. Please dress formal for the occasion." Will indicated that he would be in black tie. "Afterwards, I know of a small, intimate Italian restaurant for a late dinner."

The taxi arrived to take her back to her apartment and she left with both a sweet good night kiss and a list of museums to explore the next day while Will spent his morning at the children's clinic.

Jessica enjoyed a lazy morning reading and sipping coffee on her balcony. In the afternoon, she took a taxi to a small decorative arts museum and had lunch in the charming café located in the small gate house on the property. The entire day she reminisced about the prior evening at Will's home. It was perfect in every way, lighthearted and so very romantic.

Back at the apartment, she remembered that she had brought a marvelous, calf-length black lace dress. She had packed it in hopes that she might be able to attend a classical music event or tango show. She also picked out a lovely pearl necklace, which she had carried safely in her purse on the plane. As she looked in the mirror, she decided that it was indeed elegant. Just perfect to fill his request for her mystery event.

What could it be? she thought. *Maybe a work-related cocktail party where she might meet his friends. Or perhaps a fancy tango show?* She had no clues as to where she would be going in her black lace dress.

Will arrived to pick her up, and when she slid into her seat, she saw that he was wearing a tuxedo.

"You look formal and handsome tonight," Jessica started the conversation.

"Hey, wait a minute!" she exclaimed. "You cut your hair? Your ponytail is gone? This is indeed a surprise!"

"That is not my surprise for the evening, but yes, I did give up my ponytail. I went to my favorite barber for a trim this afternoon. He's a charismatic old guy. I'm certain that he has been in his corner barbershop for decades. He even cut my grandfather's hair and gave me my first haircut. My mother still has the photo of me getting my curls cut off when I was a toddler. The guy is an icon."

Will continued. "I swear he's not only a barber but a psychologist, marriage counselor, career coach and more. We are all so fond of him and everyone calls him Gramps. When I went for my trim, he asked if I would like a little professional advice as to how I was wearing my hair. Somewhat puzzled, I agreed, and he jokingly patted himself on his balding head. He told me that if I kept pulling my hair back, my forehead would begin to look like his, since a ponytail promotes a premature receding hairline. I immediately decided that if I was going to be courting a beautiful redhead, I should consider his advice. As you can see, I couldn't resist leaving it longer in the back."

Jessica actually thought he looked even more attractive as his natural curls were more pronounced. She reached over and ran her fingers through the wavy hair on the back of his neck. She affirmed his decision. "I think it's sexy."

"Well, I made the right choice in following Gramps' advice," he shot back with a smile. "Sexy eh? I like that."

"You look most dashing for a Wednesday evening," she said, hoping it might prod him to explain more about their forthcoming plans.

"Yes, I wanted to dress in the correct attire." It was all he said as they drove down the bustling Avenida 9 de Julio. Will turned into the parking lot of the opera house Teatro Colon.

"I thought the opera house was closed?" Jessica commented with a puzzled look on her face.

"It is," Will confirmed. "But I have a little pull with the janitor and thought you might like to see the interior."

"This is indeed a most wonderful surprise," Jessica said, indicating that she was truly grateful that he remembered that she was disappointed to have missed seeing it on her city tour. "You are just the best! I can't believe you have somehow arranged this for me."

Will greeted the gentleman who opened the door upon their arrival, and they spoke for a few minutes in Spanish before he took Jessica inside. Will was pleased to be her tour guide as he explained that the first performance was held in 1857. A new updated opera house was opened in 1908 with a performance of *Aida*. In the beginning, he explained, Buenos Aires recruited opera companies from other countries, but as of 1925, it now had its own permanent orchestra, opera and ballet company. The performance seasons have been ongoing since 1930 and are funded by the city. He proudly told her that throughout the history of the theatre, every worldwide twentieth century artist of importance has appeared on its stage.

"All of them?" Jessica marveled. "Do you mean Placido Dominico, Maria Callas, Pavarotti and all of the others?"

"Yes, and dancers such as Valav Nijinski, Margot Fonteyn and Mikhail Baryshnikov. Plus, my favorites, the accomplished composers and conductors who have come. It is common for composers to arrive at the theatre to conduct or supervise the first performances of their productions. Can you imagine that this tradition was established by Strauss?"

"How very impressive," Jessica remarked. "I can't wait to tell our Chicago Symphony director all about your famous opera house. I am so very appreciative of your kindness in arranging this surprise. Look at these marble columns, the staircase, and windows. It is magnificent. Thank you so much."

Will quietly looked at her for several minutes. It was as if he knew that she truly saw what he saw in the splendor of the building and the importance of its impressive history.

"Come with me. I want to show you the symphony hall from upstairs. It holds 2,500 people and the balconies are impressive." As he opened a door and led her into a balcony box, he paused again to get her reaction.

"This symphony hall takes my breath away. Look at the size of the chandelier. Our tour guide Carlos told us it holds 700 bulbs. It is truly stunning."

"Not as stunning as you are tonight," he graciously remarked. "Please, sit here at the railing. The lights will go out for a minute, but don't be frightened. Just wait. They will come on momentarily." Having imparted his directions he quickly left. Jessica could not imagine what was about to happen.

She waited patiently in the dark theatre. When the lights came back on suddenly, she could not believe her eyes! Will was alone on stage with the spotlight directly on him. He began to play a most impressive cello. His fingers moved like magic, as he filled the entire hall with sounds that only a master cellist could deliver.

She had read once that cello was considered one of the most soulful instruments, and Will seemed to play every note from the heart. Not once did he look up in her direction. He played a fabulous piece from Bach as if no one was listening. Tears gently rolled down her cheeks as she gazed at Will on stage alone and totally in the moment with his cello. It was as if time was somehow standing still.

Jessica was overcome by emotion. The moment felt almost surreal. Here was the man who she had met only a few days before in the Recoletta Cemetery. He had reached deep into her soul, not only with his music, but also his kindness, generosity and his unconditional caring. When he finished he looked up in her direction, bowed and blew her a kiss. Jessica could hardly regain her composure enough to stand and clap, but she did as he bowed again and left the stage. Jessica sat quietly alone waiting for Will to return. She was still overwhelmed with emotions. When he came through the door, she melted into his arms.

"Your music brought me to tears," she said softly. "I'm so touched that I am at a loss for words."

Will was noticeably moved. He had not seen this vulnerable, emotional side of her. His eyes met hers in a way that said thank you for truly seeing me and letting me truly see you. As they made their way to the first floor, Jessica began to feel that she was finally coming down from a cloud. She felt her feet beneath her again.

"I so appreciate this most unexpected surprise. I will never forget this evening. Not for the rest of my life." She could tell that Will was truly pleased with her reaction.

He stopped by a playbill displayed on the wall to show her that he would be the featured soloist when the symphony orchestra began their season in the fall. He shared that he so hoped that she would come back for the opening night. She assured him she would. As they were departing, Will thanked the man who had assisted in his surprise. She saw him hand him an envelope as he shook his hand again in gratitude.

At the restaurant, Jessica wanted to know more about Will's musical career and talents. He explained that he truly believed he had inherited his ability and passion from his mother's father, who was an internationally renowned cellist. He started playing when he was seven years old, and he said he felt from the very beginning that it came naturally to him, "from deep inside of me."

He had attended one of the best schools of music in the States and never doubted his commitment to playing the cello. But, he explained, he also felt a calling to be a doctor, so he actually pursued both careers. At times, one would take center stage and then the other would surface to consume more of his time.

Right now, he said he was concentrating on his music, but kept up his medical license and worked at the clinic a few mornings a week.

Jessica was moved by Will's humility. She could sense that he was about to change the subject. He smiled as he humbly changed the subject from his own accomplishments.

"Did you know that the word 'cello' is of Italian origin? You may notice that I am keeping the theme going in choosing this post performance restaurant."

Jessica could see it was time to lighten up again. "I just thought it was because you liked pasta."

"I won't pretend that isn't true."

They both ordered the tortellini. It was Will's recommendation since the stuffed pasta was so popular in the Tuscany region of Italy. "Did you know that Italian is the largest ethnic origin of modern Argentines? It is estimated that over sixty- percent of the total population have some degree of Italian ancestry."

Jessica found the fact to be most interesting, but she noticed Will was holding back a yawn.

"No more history lessons," he said. "I think it is time to call it a night. I'm bushed. What about you?"

"It's been a full day to be sure."

In his car, outside her apartment, they shared good night kisses.

"I love these passionate kisses," Will whispered in her ear. "They remind me of when I was taking my high school date home. We had those last few minutes together in the car before we made it to her doorstep, just within seconds of the midnight curfew."

"I remember those times too. Sometimes, it seems like yesterday and other times like so many years ago. Perhaps since we are now adults, it might be time to use these seductive kisses tomorrow night as a prelude to something more," Jessica said with a sparkle in her eye.

Will responded with both surprise and delight, "Are you suggesting what I think you are?"

When Jessica nodded he continued, "Well, keep that thought in the forefront of your mind."

"You can be assured I will ."

As Jessica unlocked the door and entered the apartment, she felt it wrap its arms around her. It was a cheerful place, and she was so pleased she had chosen it. In some ways, she felt as though she had been there for months, not just a few days. She changed into a cozy sweat suit, made a cup of tea, and went out onto the balcony. The balmy breezes of Argentina's summer felt good. She took a deep breath, exhaled, and just knew that life was good. She was still marveling at Will's amazing surprise, let alone all of the incredible times they had spent together. It truly was beyond her wildest dreams that she could meet someone so special, and with whom she was so completely relaxed and herself.

Could destiny be a real phenomenon? she wondered. Was she somehow meant to meet Will? She retraced in her mind the circumstances that had brought them together: the need to vacate her travel agency suite for a week, her cousin's sudden cancelation, and her decision to visit the Recoletta Cemetery on that very afternoon. As she was daydreaming, the phone suddenly rang loudly, jolting her into reality. She picked up and heard Will's voice.

"I hope I'm not interrupting anything?"

"No, not at all, I'm just relaxing on my balcony with a cup of tea."

"I wanted to call to tell you that on my drive home, I decided I must be deranged. To think that an irresistible woman propositioned me tonight, and I didn't stay. It made me want to turn my car around and come right back to your apartment."

Jessica laughed, but her voice then softened. "How sweet of you to call. I can assure you that I did not take it as a rejection. You put a great deal of energy into my surprise tonight, and I can certainly understand your wanting to get out of your tux and into bed. I've been sitting her thinking how much your music moved me. Thank you again for such a magical evening."

"You are so welcome. I got to thinking. Since you have not seen a Tango show yet, would you like to go tomorrow night? My favorite tango club has two dinner shows. We could choose the early one and go back to my place for the night. Would you enjoy that?"

"I would like to see a Tango show, but could I take you as my guest, since you have been so generous to me?"

"No. You have given me the best gift that I could ever wish for, your company. It is my pleasure to take you. I want to share my city with you this week. By the way, what are your plans during the day tomorrow?"

"I was just going to take a nice long walk and do some shopping."

"If you have a free hour in the afternoon, I am going to be coaching a youth soccer team. We could use a cheering section. These little guys are from the local orphanage and don't have parents to attend the game. We could use all the encouragement we can get."

Jessica's admiration for Will shot up another notch, and she assured him that she would love to come and cheer on his team.

He seemed pleased. "Great. Since you wanted to get a walk in, you can kill two birds with one stone and just meet us at the soccer field. It's only a thirty minute walk from your apartment. I'll give you directions tomorrow. I'm glad you can join us. Sleep well. I can't begin to tell you how much I look forward to being with you tomorrow night."

"I am looking forward to it too. Good night, Will."

When the phone rang at 9:30 am, Jessica smiled to think that Will remembered she was not an early riser.

"Good morning. I wanted to catch you with the address of the soccer field before you headed out for the day. I'm just on my way to a symphony meeting so I'll meet you there."

"That is perfect. Before you go can I ask you a question?"

"Sure, what is it?" Will responded in a tentative tone. He was hoping she was not going to change their plans for the evening.

"I was thinking that there will be plenty of time to see a tango show when I return in the fall. What would you think about our grabbing some takeout Thai food and staying in tonight?"

"That is a wonderful suggestion. I can't tell you how much it appeals to me."

He was truly pleased to think that they could just kick back and enjoy an evening alone. "I'll see you at the game. Tonight, why don't you count on my picking you up at 7:00 pm Don't forget your overnight bag."

"It's already packed," Jessica replied in a playful tone. Will gave a noticeably robust laugh. She found it so appealing that he always caught her quips. He liked her sense of humor as much as she enjoyed his.

Since she had time, Jessica decided to take a few minutes to call her cousin and see how the project was going in Los Angeles. She was surprised when her cousin immediately answered.

"Hi, Cuz," she began. "I was just thinking of you. You have caught me at the perfect time. I'm taking a coffee break. How's it going with that interesting new man you met?"

"It is going so well that I'm actually smiling just thinking about him."

"That sounds sweet and unlike you. Are you sure you haven't been bitten by an exotic, dangerous mosquito down there in South America? You haven't contracted some strange fever, have you?" she asked teasingly.

Jessica burst into laughter at her cousin's clever question. "No, I haven't, but I cannot tell you how happy I am and how truly extraordinary Will is. I've never met anyone like him. He's unbelievably wonderful, and I think his feelings for me are mutual.

"Oh, my goodness. I love hearing this, Jess. I can't wait to tell Dan all about it; he's coming this weekend to help me celebrate. I did such an exceptional job on this project that I got a promotion!"

"That is so good to hear. I knew you would impress them. Congratulations."

"And congrats to you, Jess, for having the courage to open your heart to this guy. He sounds remarkable in every way. I've got to run, but before I hang up, I want to read you a meaningful little quote that I have carried for years, inscribed on my key chain." Jessica could hear Genie digging through her purse. "Here it is. This little message applies perfectly to you right now. It says, 'Destiny dictates who comes into your life, but your heart decides who stays.'"

"I love that," Jessica replied. "Genie, can I ask how long it was before you knew that Dan was the one for you?"

"About ten minutes to know, and three days for verification."

Jessica shared a heartfelt goodbye and hung up the phone. She liked to think this was true. Her cousin was so in love with Dan. It had been ten years, and they still acted like newlyweds. Maybe it was possible to meet someone and know within days that they were the right person for a lifetime. She planned to hold that thought.

Before heading out for the morning, Jessica flipped through the pages of her guidebook to the section on shopping in the Recoleta area of Buenos Aires. Yes, there were high-end boutiques carrying Gucci, Dior and Armani brands, but she was thrilled to see that there was a craft market in front of the Recoleta Cemetery on that very day. She slipped into her tennis shoes and a casual sporty outfit for the soccer game. She would spend the entire day enjoying herself.

Out on the street, Jessica remembered why she loved the hustle and bustle of big cities. They were full of energy; taxis whizzing by, people rushing for appointments and others filling their shopping bags with colorful fruit and vegetables from the corner street vendors. She was always comfortable in the city because she knew how to be safe and careful. She secured bigger bills of money in a hidden pouch, carried her small shoulder bag close to her body, and was always alert to where she was walking. The panhandlers did not intimidate her. Sometimes, she would put a few smaller bills into her jacket pocket to help out someone in need, especially a woman. She did not open her wallet in public and carried her credit cards in a metal lined security sleeve. She knew that taking these precautions was just as important in the city as carrying a flashlight and compass were to a hiker in the wilderness.

The craft market was located in a large grassy area directly in front of the Recoleta Cemetery. It was a bustling place filled with stalls selling every imaginable handicraft item. Jessica's first stop had been at the Alvear Palace Hotel to get more pesos in smaller denominations. She knew the local craft markets rarely took credit cards and often could not easily make change. Besides, she loved the idea of being sensitive to fitting into the surroundings of the foreign country she was visiting.

The guidebook described the craft market as an upscale version of the one near Will's home in San Telmo, and the artists were vetted before given a booth. She purchased a lovely, large, hand-crafted woven bag and began to fill it with all of the items that called to her. She could always use little items to share with friends as hostess gifts. And her mother's birthday was coming up so she would look for a more expensive silver bracelet with a matching ring. The market was filled with every imaginable artist's creation. There were earrings with colorful stones, little dolls made from modest pieces of fabrics, small hand-painted leather shoulder bags, and animals carved from wood. She even purchased a *maté* cup made from a gourd.

The merchant told her it was pronounced "ma-tay." The first day she arrived she had noticed people drinking something out of metal straws from small round vessels. One group of people in the park was actually passing it amongst themselves, and there was a little old lady sipping hers at the produce stand. Jessica learned that these cups held *maté*, the traditional drink of Argentina. It is a caffeine-rich infused drink made from dried Yerba leaves and mixed with hot water. Many locals did not go a day without drinking it, and as she wandered through the market she actually saw several vendors sipping from metal straws in their *maté* cups. Jessica found there were so many *maté* cups to choose from. Some were wooden and engraved, others metal, but the ones that she liked most were the ones made from a round gourd and rimmed in silver with a silver straw. She also purchased several boxes of Yerba leaves and hoped that the American customs officials would recognize them as the drink of the region! She planned to make it for friends when she returned home. She would tell them about the friendship ritual of passing the cup from person to person. Since everyone shared the same straw, she decided to reserve the tradition for her very closest friends and family.

Jessica stopped for lunch in a quaint neighborhood café and tried the traditional empanada again, but decided she was partial to the ones Will had made for her. As she sat at the small wooden table, she pulled out her city map to find the best route to the soccer game. To her delight, she would pass directly by her apartment, so she could drop off her shopping bag. She refreshed her makeup and decided to change into a lively top with big red poppies, which she felt might be fun since she had learned that the team color was red.

She arrived at the soccer field to see Will huddled with his young players. It warmed her heart to see how carefully the boys were listening to his every word. They could not have been more than seven or eight years old. It broke her heart to think of them, without parents, living in an orphanage. She was sure that there must be many different stories and all of them tragic and sad. Will came over to give her a hug and suggest where she could stand to be supportive of the team. As the players kicked the soccer ball back and forth, she reminisced about the times she played soccer in grade school. She cheered enthusiastically for every goal that was in their favor and was especially thrilled when they won by two points.

As she went up to the team to congratulate them, she overheard one of the little boys asking, "Doc, is that pretty lady your girlfriend?" She also heard Will answer him by saying that he hoped so.

Jessica purchased ice cream for each of the players from a street vendor nearby. She was so touched when they all vied to stand next to her as they enjoyed their treat. Their innocent little faces were so endearing, and Jessica smiled broadly every time they called Will "Doc."

"Thanks for coming to cheer on the team. And thanks for the ice cream treats," Will said as he juggled his own melting cone in the blazing sun. "I need to drive the boys back to the orphanage. Are you okay walking back to the apartment?"

"Absolutely, I've had the best day. I'll tell you all about it tonight."

As she began to leave, she noticed that the little boy who had been quizzing Will about their relationship turned to her and waved goodbye with an endearing grin that revealed two missing teeth.

On her way back, Jessica decided to take a different route. It only added a little extra time, but it was an opportunity to see more of the neighborhood. She had read that Recoleta was the district that most deserved the city's title of "Paris of the South." The streets were lined with beautiful trees and the buildings reflecting the opulent architecture of the homes of wealthy families who populated the area after leaving San Telmo during yellow fever epidemic.

Around almost every corner was a small square, some adorned with fountains and statues. One short street was lined with antique shops and boutiques. There she saw a sign that read, "Elegant World Market." In the window was a collection of masks from Africa. Jessica remembered how interested Will was in her trips to Africa and even expressed an interest in visiting Tanzania. Having several masks hanging on the walls of her own condo, she felt that they added interest and a reverence for past cultures. Masks also represented an aspect of spirituality that Jessica found compelling. She had learned that the symbolism of masks was different in every country around the world.

They served an important role in rituals and ceremonies to ensure a good harvest, address a tribal need, aid in a healing, or convey spiritual presence. Deciding that an African mask would be a perfect thank you gift for Will, Jessica entered the little shop. She explained to the shop owner that she would like to purchase an African mask as a gift for a man who was currently a healer but one who also exhibited strong traits of compassion, honesty and integrity.

"He sounds like an exceptional man," the shop owner said with tenderness. Jessica appreciated her comment and agreed. The shop owner showed her several masks explaining that the images from the Ivory Coast have eyes half closed, which symbolized patience, self-control, and a peaceful nature. In Sierra Leone and other parts of West Africa, small eyes and mouth represented humility and a protruding forehead represented wisdom. Along the Atlantic coast of Central Africa a large chin and mouth represented strength. Jessica pondered all of the options as the owner brought out several masks for her consideration.

Jessica surprised the woman by saying she was going to purchase three masks. It was indeed a major purchase, but Jessica loved the two that represented patience and humility. They would be impressive hanging side by side in Will's home. And since she did not have one with a large chin in her collection she decided that she could certainly use some strength of conviction as she fought her impulses to dismiss the strong feelings she now felt for Will. She was beginning to care deeply for him.

As she walked back into her apartment, she thought about Will's reply to the little boy when he asked, "Is she your girlfriend?"

Will had said, "I hope so."

It was then that she realized that there was no way that he could know the depth of her feelings. It was true that she had accepted his invitation to return for his opening performance, but she knew there was much more she could convey to assure him that her feelings for him were becoming stronger each day.

As she looked at the clock, she was delighted to see that she had almost two hours before Will would pick her up. She would do some packing since she would be flying home in two days. She could hardly believe that the next day was the last one of her visit. Opening her large suitcase on the bed, she wrapped her new mask carefully in her excess clothing. She was grateful that she had packed more than usual. Perhaps it was the enthusiasm she experienced in pulling summer items from the back of her closet, she was thankful that she had brought so many different outfits to wear for the times she had spent with Will. Jessica wanted to dress a little sensual on this particular evening, since she would be staying overnight. But she had suggested take-out food so she decided casual was more in order. She dressed in a comfortable, plaid blouse with distinctive copper buttons down the front, a pair of skinny jeans, and a brightly colored cotton sweater over her shoulders. She separated her winter clothing in the closet for her trip home and emptied all of the dresser drawers. As she did so, she paused to reflect on the standing joke amongst her friends about her not wanting to share a drawer in her dresser. She was becoming convinced that one day that might change.

Will was in the lobby visiting with the security guard when Jessica came down the elevator. He greeted her with the warm long hug. "That casual look on you is becoming. What is that big box you are carrying?" he asked.

"It's a surprise for someone very special to me," she replied provocatively.

In the car, Will thanked her for coming to cheer on the soccer team. "You made quite an impression on the boys. And it wasn't just because you treated for ice cream. They thought you were pretty and loved your red hair. I told them I did too."

Jessica reached over to squeeze his hand in appreciation. He did not let go as they traveled to pick up the Thai food.

Will said, "I have a great idea for tomorrow, your last day here. If you are up for it, I would like to take you to Uruguay? I cleared my calendar for tomorrow and thought it might be fun for us to take a little trip out of town together."

"How can we go all the way to Uruguay and back in just one day?"

"Our neighboring country is not far away. We can take the high-speed catamaran to Colonia del Sacramento. It's just across our river, the Rio de la Plata, and only an hour in each direction. If we catch the 10:00 am departure we could have lunch there and spend the day exploring. There is not a lot to see in the sleepy little town, but you will have another stamp in your passport. I will put a dinner jacket and slacks in the car and then change from my jeans at your place when we return to the city. I definitely don't want you to miss having cocktails at the infamous Lobby Bar of the Alvear Palace Hotel tomorrow night. You know, it is purported to be the most beautiful lobby bar in the world, so it's the perfect spot for our last night."

When they arrived at Will's home, he carried in the large box. He questioned her again as to what was in the box. She said that he would have to wait until after dinner so their Thai food did not get cold. Agreeing that was a good idea, Will suggested they eat at the little round table on the roof garden.

"You are pretty good with those chopsticks," he commented.

"Chicago has a sister city in Japan," Jessica explained, "and we have hosted many delegations throughout the past couple of years. I traveled to Japan a few years ago with an Illinois woman's delegation. And speaking of women, I just got to thinking about something this afternoon. When I get back and tell my mother that I met someone special she is going to ask me all about you. Unlike the inquiring women who ask a man's profession, my mother is going to ask if you have been married before and whether you have children. I know you do not have children, but as strange as it seems, I never did hear you say whether you have been married before?"

Will told her that he had not been married, but that he had been engaged. Her name was Cindy and he met her in undergraduate school in the States. He said she was a great person, but he explained that she was an extreme introvert and rather timid. When they were alone together they had enjoyed each other's company, but she was uncomfortable around his friends and wanted him to spend all of his free time with her. When he brought her to Buenos Aires, she was frightened by the city and would not go out of his apartment without him.

"I guess it was such a change from the small town in upstate New York where she grew up and lived most of her life. As I look back I can't believe that we actually got engaged. We really hardly knew each other, and we were so young. We just drifted apart and went our separate ways. Since then I have had several relationships but none that I felt were the person I wanted to spend the rest of my life with. What about you? Have you been married before?"

Jessica smiled and shook her head. "No."

"Have you been engaged?"

Again she shook her head to indicate a no answer.

"Ever been asked?" he inquired with a sheepish grin.

"Yes."

"More than once?"

She simply nodded an affirmative "yes," as she smiled coyly.

"Well, you certainly are holding onto that empty dresser drawer!" Will laughed in a playful way. They finished dinner and went downstairs to the living room. Deciding to watch a movie, they chose a lighthearted romance comedy and cozied up on the couch together.

"Hey, wait a minute," Will interrupted. "Don't I get to see what is in my surprise package?"

Jessica loved the look on his face. It was as if he were a little boy waiting to open the biggest package under the Christmas tree. She loved his carefree nature. The exuberant little boy had grown into a wonderful man who never lost his sense of wonder.

"Yes. I almost forgot your surprise." She got up and went out to the entry to retrieve the box. As she walked into the room holding it, Will looked up in anticipation. But he did not say a word, knowing Jessica's sense of humor. For all he knew, it could be a joke of some sort.

They sat back on the couch as he unwrapped the two masks inside. Will was noticeably moved by her gift. She explained why she had chosen each mask for him personally, and she showed him the certificates of authenticity. They documented the countries of origins and the meaning of each mask's symbolism.

"I don't know what to say. These masks are so remarkable." Will found them to be exceptional in every sense. "It means so much to me to think you believe I possess these qualities. This is a very precious gift. I can't thank you enough." His emotions were so sincere and humble that Jessica became emotional herself. It was one of those times where you just want to savor the moment. They held each other and began indulge in the most passionate kisses; the kind of kisses that come from the heart and are full of meaning and intimacy. As their passions grew, they melted deeper and deeper into the couch. Will then whispered, "Let's forget the romance movie and go to the bedroom. I have created a romantic setting of our own."

Jessica had not seen the master bedroom suite before, and it was indeed a romantic setting. The king-sized bed was covered with the most elegant satin coverlet, and there was a large bouquet of red roses in a cut-glass vase. The lights were dimmed and there was a candelabra on the sideboard that Will went to and lit the six long tapered candles. The candlelight made the room glow. Will walked up to her and began kissing her on the neck. He unbuttoned her blouse, ever so slowly. There was no hurry. This was their night to enjoy.

When Jessica opened her eyes in the morning, she smiled to find she had been sleeping with Will's arm around her. She stirred, and he awoke with a glowing appreciation in his eyes. It conveyed that he had enjoyed their first night together, every bit as much as she had.

"Ready for a little coffee or shall we cancel Uruguay and just pretend that we are on the catamaran here in bed?" he playfully asked.

"Now there is an inviting idea," Jessica agreed.

"On second thought, we could do both." Will was suddenly animated with his brainstorm. "We could take the 1:00 pm departure and spend the entire morning right here."

"Delaying lunch sounds perfect. Aren't you South Americans known for dining late anyway?"

Will relished the way he and Jessica playfully bantered back and forth with each other. "Yes we are, and we are also known for being extremely passionate."

"Oh, that's right. You told me so." Jessica teased.

"Told you! Just told you?" His eyes crinkled at the corners as he began to laugh and pulled the sheets back over their heads.

After spending a glorious love-making morning in bed, they still somehow made it to the ferry terminal in time to catch the 1:00 pm catamaran. The terminal was bustling with people traveling to the well-known beaches of Montevideo, Uruguay, and others opting for their chosen destination, the picturesque small historical port town of Colonia del Sacramento. They found a window seat on the catamaran and Will purchased two coffees and croissants to tide them over until lunch. He put his arm around her shoulder and again became her tour guide, telling Jessica about the destination they were about to visit. He explained that they would cross the muddy La Plata river which forms part of the border between Argentina and Uruguay.

"Colonia is just a modest little historic city of cobblestone streets. You'll see buildings dated back to the time when the city was a Portuguese settlement. It actually has been declared a World Heritage site by UNESCO, but the reason I like to bring visitors here is because it is so peaceful. My friends can't believe that such a lovely, quiet, small town could exist just an hour away from Buenos Aires."

"Is this where your friends from Europe were arriving from the day we met?"

"No, they had rented a place in Montevideo. I'll take you there another time when we are in the mood to soak up some sunshine on a beach."

Upon arrival in Colonia, they walked into town from the terminal, and Will advised Jessica to watch her step as many tree roots were growing through the cobblestone cracks along the main avenue. "Can you imagine that these are still some of the original bricks used by the Portuguese in the 17th century? There is a grassy area by the wooden drawbridge and the City Gate. Since we are in jeans, let's get a *chivito* and a *medio y medio* and have lunch on the sprawling lawn. We city dwellers rarely get an opportunity to run our toes through soft green grass."

"That sounds inviting, but what is a *chivito?*" she asked with a bit of skepticism in her voice. She was averse to cilantro and spicy food.

"Come on, Jessica, you don't think I would offer my new sweetheart a lunch that isn't edible, or better yet, not delicious?" he replied with a smile. "Honestly, it is my favorite Uruguayan sandwich. It's made with thin pieces of steak. And the drink is half white wine, and I'm not sure what the other half is, maybe juice. But I do know it is very good."

Will's favorite local restaurant packaged up their lunch, and they found a perfect shady spot to sit on the grass. Jessica explained that, on the way over, she had read that eighty percent of Uruguay is grasslands. "You certainly are introducing me to this country in a hands-on way." Jessica eyes twinkled as she grinned at Will. "

Seriously, I really do appreciate you bringing me here today. I'm not sure that I know anyone in my group of friends who has ever been to Uruguay."

"It isn't a large country, so that's not surprising. As a comparison, the entire country of Uruguay has just a little over three million people and my hometown has almost 15 million. What do you think of Buenos Aires?"

"I am enamored of your city," Jessica truthfully shared. "It really calls to me. Yesterday, when I visited the craft market, went walking through the neighborhoods and sat in a corner café, I decided I could not wait to return. I'm not just saying that because I want to impress you."

"Let me assure you that you can give up that endeavor right now. You impressed me within the first few hours that I met you." He laughed with the air of a man who was being spirited, but who also wanted to make be sure she caught the meaning behind his humor.

With a few hours to explore, Will took Jessica walking along the streets of the historic barrio, a UNESCO protected site.

Why did they choose it as one of their sites?" she inquired.

"UNESCO wanted to protect the historic structures; the homes dating back to the first colonial period, the wedge stone walkways and the drawbridge which led to a fortress. Are you up for a bit of a climb? There is a panoramic view of the surrounding area from the lighthouse. It is the city's landmark that was built over the ruins of the San Francisco convent in 1857. It is a climb of over 100 steps, up a narrow staircase, to the very top."

Jessica just couldn't resist a little humor at that point. "If I run out of breath will you give me CPR?" she asked with an impish grin.

Will burst into laughter. "You are just too much!"

When they returned to the waterfront, Jessica saw several couples having their photos taken overlooking the river. "Do we have time for a photo?" she asked.

"In front of this muddy brown river?"

"It's not the scenery I'm interested in," Jessica replied. She asked a nice gentleman to take their photo.

"Remind me to take a photo of us in the Alvear Palace Lobby Bar tonight," Will said. "I want to be cleaned up with my jacket on, so I look more presentable in the photo you show your mother."

When they arrived at the ferry terminal in Buenos Aires, they drove directly to Jessica's apartment to change for the evening. She had saved her favorite lilac purple silk dress for their last night in the city. Will looked handsome in his navy jacket, grey slacks, and crisp white shirt. She had invited him to stay overnight at her apartment, as he wanted to drive her to the airport for her flight the next day.

"I'll just valet my car overnight at the hotel and we can walk back to your apartment after dinner. It is safer than leaving it on the street."

"That's a good plan," Jessica replied. "It is better to be safe than sorry."

When she looked at Will he had the sweetest look on his face. "My grandmother used to always use that phrase. I like the reminder of her."

Entering the Alvear Palace Hotel, they made their way directly to the infamous Lobby Bar. Jessica had not gone into it when she took her city tour from the hotel a few days earlier. When they walked in she stopped to take in its grandeur. The room was decorated with French style wood paneling. There were marble columns in every corner and behind the magnificent bar were two floor-to-ceiling windows draped in brocade. Everything was stunningly elegant. The marble floor was immaculate and shiny, there was a large crystal vase of flowers on the bar and the red fabric on the chairs was crushed velvet. The side doors opening on adjoining private rooms, were mirrored, making everything in the room sparkle. Will paused to take in her reaction. Having been there so many times before, he realized he had become too accustomed to its unrivaled magnificence. He quietly made a vow to keep his sense of wonderment alive. Jessica was giving him a new enhanced perspective on his surroundings and even more so, on life in general.

The evening could not have been more enjoyable. They talked, held hands, and toasted their new relationship. Will remembered to ask their server to take several photos of them, and everyone seated around them smiled noticing the loving glow they emitted as a couple. They decided to have dinner in the intimate restaurant on the eleventh floor overlooking the city.

"Thank you for this most incredible final evening," Jessica said softly as they began to walk back to the apartment. "I have had such a good time tonight."

"I know it may sound like mushy sentiment, but I am really going to miss you when you leave tomorrow," Will said in a loving tone. "I'm glad I'll be staying here tonight with you at the apartment."

"I'm glad, too. It certainly is not as beautiful as your lovely master bedroom, but there is a king bed and amenities like a clean bathroom. I even have an extra toothbrush from the airlines in case you forgot yours," she teased.

Their intimate time together was as magical as the nights before, and as they cuddled to fall asleep, Jessica started thinking about their future. She truly believed she was falling in love with Will. It was as if all of her hesitations about relationships had faded away. It was almost incomprehensible that she and Will could have become so close in such a short time, but she was now ready to commit to opening her heart to him. She wished that he could somehow find a way to let him see that her affection for him was sincere and true. Suddenly, in that moment, she thought of a way she could give him an undeniably clear sign before she flew back to Chicago. Sensing that Will had fallen soundly asleep she quietly slipped out of the sheets to prepare her statement that would be her way of telling Will of her deepest feelings for him. She then climbed back into bed for the night.

As the morning sunlight started to fill the room, she awoke to look into Will's eyes focused on her.

"Good morning, Sweetheart. I hope you slept as well as I did," he said.

"Umm, yes, I did," Jessica replied and kissed him sweetly. She noticed that he called her "sweetheart" and she loved it.

"How about I walk down to the corner bakery and bring back cappuccinos and croissants?" Will suggested.

"That would be so nice. I can almost smell the aroma."

As Will stood up to get dressed, he started searching around the room for his clothing. "That is strange." he said. "I know I hung my pants and shirt over this chair last night."

As he turned toward Jessica he saw a soft loving look in her eyes as she turned her gaze toward the dresser.

Will turned to see his clothes folded neatly in the open top drawer. He walked toward the dresser with an awestruck look of disbelief on his face. In a minute his expression turned from astonishment to one of deep emotion. He looked toward Jessica who was still sitting in the bed.

"Are you sure?" was all that Will uttered as he looked at her intently.

"I am completely sure," she said with unwavering certainty.

Will realized the significance of her gesture. It was a fortunate turn of the tides of destiny, and it was spinning in their direction. He walked over and sat down on the edge of the bed. He took her face in his hands and gave her the most tender loving kiss. Jessica then pushed back the covers of the bed with a come-hither sweet smile. Will gave a gentle laugh. He knew that hitching his wagon to Jessica's star was going to be the trip of a lifetime. Now, he knew they were both ready for the ride!

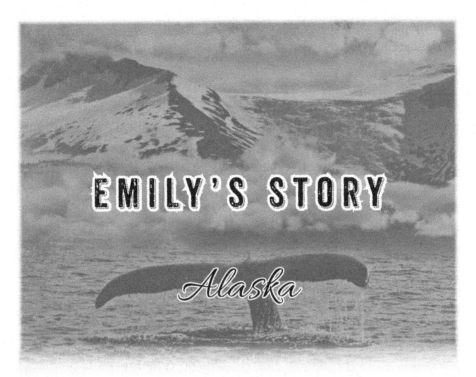

EMILY'S STORY

Alaska

Emily grew up in Southern California, and she looked like a pin-up poster model of a surfer girl. She was petite at 5'2" and had the perfect athletic body; long, silky blonde hair; and a creamy complexion. Her green eyes were as captivating as her engaging smile. She was definitely a natural beauty. Emily's friends always commented that her outward appearance did not match her serious, exacting nature. She was conscientious and disciplined in every aspect of her life. Her parents taught her the values of integrity, honesty, persistence, and generosity.

With a mother who was an accountant and a father who was the vice-president of the local bank, she accounted for every penny of her savings as a little girl. She was drawn to numbers at an early age and excelled in math in elementary and high school. Emily also loved athletics. Because she was so petite, she did not participate in girls' basketball or volleyball, but instead joined the swim team and soccer league.

She was extremely athletic and coordinated, so she excelled in both sports. Her soccer team called her their 'little bullet'. Not only was she exceedingly fast, she was smart. She anticipated her opponents moves. She was humble ,and had no need to claim the glory,. She would pass the ball to her teammates, who scored. Her talents did not go unnoticed by coaches, and her parents were constantly receiving calls from select teams wanting to recruit her.

The fans in the stadium were also drawn to Emily because of her small stature. Her blonde ponytail was always blowing from side to side as she covered the field. Her mother smiled when she would hear someone in the stands behind her say, "Look how tiny that number 12 is, but watch how good she is." Her team won the state championship when she was a sophomore, and she still had her uniform tucked in a trunk in the family attic.

However, it was her talent as a swimmer that earned her a college scholarship. She loved competing in an individual sport. Her strong determination and willingness to strive for perfection helped her win many trophies. Her girlfriends laughingly said that the only reason the high school football players came to cheer on the swim team was because they wanted to see her accomplish one of her amazing feats from the diving board.

Emily was blessed with many friends. She had a set of values that she lived by. She was loyal, caring, and unselfish. Her friends always knew they could count on her, and she did not disappoint them. Whether it was lending a helping hand to decorate the gymnasium for prom night, tutoring a freshman failing in math or standing up for the rights of disabled students, her core values always guided her behavior, decisions, and actions. Empathy came naturally to her. She was always cognizant of other people's feelings. When her best friend's dog died, she went to her house and stayed overnight to be of comfort. Her understanding and sincerity were especially appreciated by her high school girlfriends. If they were jilted by a boy at school and needed a shoulder to cry on, Emily was always the one they sought out. She was the best listener and gave the wisest nonjudgmental advice.

In college, Emily continued to enjoy life to the fullest while earning a 3.9 GPA. She loved her courses in statistics, mathematics, research and accounting. When it came to elective courses she always chose areas of study that interested her, such as art, literature, geography and world religions. It was an easy choice for her to major in accounting and finance, and she decided to continue her education to earn a master's degree in accounting. It prepared her well for the CPA exam, which she passed with flying colors.

Men seemed to naturally gravitate to Emily, and she dated often in high school, college and beyond. When she would walk into a party in a short dress with her beautiful athletic legs and long blonde hair, it only took minutes before an interested fellow was introducing himself to her. She always wore high heels because she wanted to appear taller, but they also seemed particularly appealing to the guys. It only took a short conversation before the men realized that this attractive blonde did not match the dumb blonde jokes that had gone around campus. Emily was exceedingly intelligent, but in a humble sort of way. She could engage in conversations easily, but her introverted personality that made her also seem a bit mysterious.

It was as if there were two sides to her. One was a confident, assured woman who knew exactly what she wanted in life, and the flip side was one of a gorgeous, petite blonde who was breezily following the universe in the direction she felt it was leading her. She was a sweet person; not sweet in any sappy helpless way, but rather in a kind, thoughtful and giving way. She was never demanding or selfish. Being with Emily was always pleasant and easy. It was no wonder that every time a young man took her home to meet his parents, they fell in love with her! Throughout the years, Emily had significant relationships with wonderful men, but in her heart she knew they were not her Mr. Right. Her mother had always said it would be worth the wait and she was committed to waiting.

There was a side to Emily's personality that few got to see. She had an unwavering feeling that there was magic in the universe. When she was a little girl she believed in Santa Claus much longer than any of her classmates. On the grass of her front lawn, she searched through all the clover to find the lucky one with four leaves. Emily never passed up a penny on the sidewalk, considering it to be a sign of good luck. And she always threw a coin in the wishing well at her family's favorite Chinese restaurant. When girlfriends came to her home for slumber parties she would get out her Ouija board. She loved the mystifying process of asking questions and was convinced that the answers she received held clues to her future.

Renée was Emily's older sister, her best friend and confidant in many way. Her brother Joseph was five years older so when she was in junior high he was already in high school and then off to college. She worshipped him as a little girl; begging for piggyback rides, constantly following him around, asking questions and pleading to sit next to him on long family road trips. Being a really good guy, he was a devoted, loving big brother to her and her sister, who was only eighteen months older than she.

Reading fairy tales was a pastime of Emily's, and the pages of her books were worn thin. As a child, her nightly bedtime stories were "The Little Mermaid," "Sleeping Beauty" and "Cinderella," which was her very favorite. When they were little girls, she and Renée, would reenact the story with paper dolls. They took turns being Cinderella. They would never choose their second character to be the ugly stepmother or nasty stepsisters. Instead, they would choose the Fairy Godmother.

These characters, combined with Emily's belief in magic, formed her feelings about love and relationships. She believed, with all her heart, that when she met her Prince Charming, she would know him at first glance. She was convinced and not to be dissuaded. Throughout her dating years she kept the faith. She called it "the knowing," and referred to him as Mr. Right. When her friends asked, "How will you know he is the right man for you?" She would sincerely and convincingly explain to them that she would just know. In her mind, the sign would be clear.

As she dated throughout the years, she kept looking for her Mr. Right. It wasn't that the suitors she dated were not exceptional. Because of her strong ethics and values she always chose good men who were smart, kind, honest and respectable. Their values and integrity matched hers. They enjoyed each other's company, took lovely trips together, and were committed and supportive throughout their relationships. Unfortunately, Emily had to tell them, at some point, that they were not the love of her life, as much as she might wish it was so. When they parted, they both felt grateful for the wonderful times they had shared and they often stayed good friends.

Emily's belief in destiny was confirmed when she and her sister, Renée, went on a vacation trip to Hawaii celebrating the completion of her master's degree. They had booked a hotel right on the beach. On their first day, they put up an umbrella, got out their towels, and were sipping margaritas when, all of a sudden, a huge beach ball slammed into their space. The umbrella tipped over spilling their drinks. Suddenly, out of nowhere, an attractive man came running up to explain that he was playing ball with his little nephew when it got away from them. He was apologetic and sincerely sorry for what had happened. He offered to help them relocate and ordered new drinks for them. It was when he handed Renée her margarita that Emily saw the sparks between the two of them. It was so noticeable to her, as if the sparks shot high above them in one fell swoop of colors. His name was Paulo, and he was also from Los Angeles. He was in Hawaii at a family reunion, celebrating his grandparents' 50th wedding anniversary.

After a brief conversation, he asked if he could extend his apology with buying them another drink at the pool later that afternoon. Emily laughed to see how quickly her sister accepted. Fortunately, Emily had a close college friend who lived in Maui, and had planned to join them for a few days. It turned into five days because Renée and Paulo were inseparable for the rest of the holiday. Emily was the Maid of Honor when they married six months later and her toast at the wedding was so charming. She described the moment her sister met Paulo and the fact that they immediately knew they were meant for each other when he handed her a replacement margarita. It was truly love at first sight.

After college, Em, as her family and friends called her, moved into a lovely two-bedroom apartment with her best college comrade, Joan. They had met at the university, and their friendship was deeply rooted. Joan earned a combined major in political science and economics. She had landed a great management position in city government. As roommates, they were perfectly suited. They both loved to cook, they respected each other's privacy, and they had great conversations over wine during major political events and elections in their community. After getting settled, Emily was anxious to begin applying for openings at local accounting firms. She actually had an interview the next day, when she received a frantic call from her favorite aunt, Marjorie. She was her mother's sister, they lived only a few blocks from each other, and they practically raised their children together. Emily loved her Aunt Marge and considered her to be a second mother.

Marjorie was patient and easy going. Many days her entire house would be filled with cousins running from room to room, as she lovingly made cookies and hot chocolate in her big kitchen. When all her children entered high school, she decided to concentrate on finding a career that brought her joy. She loved geography and people so decided to become a travel agent. Within a few short years, she ended up purchasing an agency and steadily grew it into a very successful business.

Emily could hear the stress in her aunt's voice. "Are you alright, Aunt Marge?" she asked with concern.

"Yes, dear. It is not a family emergency. Your uncle Albert is fine, as are all the cousins, but I have a serious crisis at my travel agency." She then went on to describe her dilemma. The woman who managed her accounting department was moving. Her husband had taken a job transfer and they had to move immediately. Marjorie said that she was struggling to find a replacement on such short notice.

She explained that the "back room," as she called the accounting department, was an extremely technical operation. There were not only the normal accounts payable, receivables, and payroll but there were major procedures needed to satisfy the airline industry regulations. These were complicated, and she had just had her second hire resign in frustration. She was truly at wits end as she lamented that she could not find anyone knowledgeable in the financial workings of a travel agency. She said that she had spent the last week at the agency until past midnight, trying to keep up by working on the finances herself. Her situation seemed dire.

"Emily, I know you are ready to begin your career as an accountant, but is there any way that you could please come help me for a couple weeks until I can find someone? You are so smart and resourceful. I know you could pick it up quickly. I would not ask you except that I am truly desperate."

Emily could not refuse. She loved her aunt dearly, and she simply could not live with the image of her working all day managing her agency and then staying to do the finances until midnight!

"Aunt Marge, I will come see what I can do. I don't know a thing about the workings of a travel agency, but if it is in what you call the back room, I do know about finances. I can put off my job search to help you for a month or two."

As Emily sat in her office at the agency, she smiled to think that it had been four years since she had gotten her aunt's frantic call for help. She could never have dreamed that she would still be at the travel agency. In fact, she found maneuvering all of the financial challenges to be rewarding. Every day tested her skills in problem solving, her knowledge of finance, and her innovative spirit. Marjorie was thrilled to see how quickly she was able to train Emily on the ins and outs of the complicated airline reporting process. Within a month Emily had the agency's "back room" in perfect order. She also found that she enjoyed the staff of travel agents her aunt had hired. They were bright, positive, and enthusiastic. Emily felt herself to be a key part of the team and her aunt paid her well. She also found that she could successfully accomplish the needed workload four days a week, so she joined a local accounting firm on Fridays. She wanted to keep up her knowledge of the changing tax laws. It was the perfect combination to keep her stimulated and satisfied in her field. Since her friend Joan had moved in with her partner, Gary, Emily found an attractive loft apartment in a hip Los Angeles neighborhood, developed an interesting group of new friends, and even joined a local adult soccer team.

One day, Marjorie asked Emily to join her in her office. "Em, I am sorry to always be leaning on you, but I need your help again."

"What is it, Auntie?" she asked in a helpful tone of voice.

"You know how busy every one of my agents is these days. Now I have one going on maternity leave and another on her honeymoon. With these two agents gone next month, I will have to roll up my sleeves and take care of their clients. I won't be able to escort my favorite travel group on their cruise to Alaska."

Marjorie explained that her senior travel group had grown to forty-two participants for the upcoming cruise. A popular five-star ship had just added Alaska to their itinerary, and due to the relationship Marjorie had built with the line she had been able to secure cabins at a substantial discount. "Within two days of the flyer going out to the senior travel club at our favorite bank, all the cabins were booked," Marjorie explained.

"Is that favorite bank you are referring to the one where my father is the vice-president?" Emily inquired with in a joking manner.

"Yes, and the travel club is a delightful group of people. Every year I go as their agency escort, because I so enjoy their company. They are seniors like no other seniors you will ever meet. They are fun-loving, adventuresome and always up for a good time. The group is too large to not send a representative from the agency. Could you escort this travel group for me? It isn't that you would need to do anything too time-consuming or complicated; just be available if there are any problems at check in, host the agency cocktail party and be their contact should any emergencies arise. It's only an eight-day sailing, and I just can't get away this year."

"I'd be happy to accompany them," Emily enthusiastically agreed. The idea of getting out of the office to explore the wilds of Alaska sounded like a great idea. She loved nature, and she had never seen a glacier calving or kayaked in the waterways of Alaska.

"Oh, thank you, Em. You will be the perfect escort for this group. I will plan a pre-sailing gathering so you can meet some of the main travelers. There are many couples, but there is also a group of women who are particularly delightful. Sylvia, Carol, Emma Lou, Cathy, and Donna have been repeat passengers on these tours for a couple of years; you will like them. Most of these clients are experienced travelers so it won't be difficult. As the escort, you will have a private cabin, and are free to participate in cruise activities as you wish. Join the group when you are inclined and enjoy your private time as you choose. It's a bit of a vacation for you even though you are on call."

"I'm sure I will enjoy the cruise and also the group's company. Do they all know each other?"

"Not all of them. We started the "Travelers on the Go" travel club through the bank several years ago. They are a loose knit group who receive our travel fliers with lucrative discounts. Most are retired but a few are still working. Don't let their ages of seventies and eighties lull you into thinking this is an inactive crowd. You'll soon learn that they know how to have a good time in life and don't waste a moment in grabbing the gusto."

Emily smiled to think of a group of senior citizens out enjoying their retirement years. At twenty-eight years of age, she imagined a more subdued group than her aunt was describing. She was actually looking forward to being their group escort. She would make herself available as needed and be responsible in any unforeseen emergency.

"Please enjoy yourself on the ship," her aunt urged. "You aren't there to be a nurse maid, just to represent our agency and serve as a point of contact. Be sure to pack some dressy outfits and feel free to book any shore excursion that interests you. Do enjoy the ship's activities. You might even be asked to dance by a handsome ship's engineer."

"Is that allowed?"

"Heavens, yes. There is a late-night disco on every cruise ship. The executive staff and young engineers go there to relax and mingle with guests on their time off. Sylvia loves to dance and goes there often.

"Is Sylvia in this cruise group?"

"Yes, she may be seventy-two years old but she is young at heart. She's a great dancer, and all of the Gentleman Hosts are thrilled to see her on a sailing."

"Gentleman Hosts? Who are they?"

"My dear, they are the men who come on the cruise ship to dance with the single women. They are often retired professionals, always single or widowed and lovely conversationalists. They are considered staff in many ways but are not exactly."

Emily decided she would have ample time aboard the ship to learn more about cruising. For now, she would be sure she had the agency's finances in order so everything was covered in her absence.

At the pre-sailing cocktail function Marjorie introduced Emily and explained to the travel group why she could not be their escort on this sailing. Everyone teased her saying she should retire early, so she could get out and have more fun in life. Emily immediately liked the fun-loving nature of the crowd. She also was amazed at how young they all appeared, not only in their looks but in their energy levels and personalities. She would have easily put their ages as early sixties.

Marjorie assured them that they would be in good hands with Emily as their travel escort. They all nodded their heads in agreement. Sylvia jokingly added, "Don't worry about us Marjorie. It is your niece you should worry about. We can be a bad influence on a pretty young woman." Everyone laughed. Emily was convinced without a doubt that this was going to be an enjoyable travel group.

The flight to Vancouver, British Columbia went smoothly as did the check-in onto the cruise ship. She could see by the look on the faces of her clients that Margorie had not exaggerated the splendor of the five-star ship they would be sailing on to the Inside Passage of Alaska. Before everyone scattered to explore the public rooms and their cabins, Emma Lou approached Emily with a request.

"Dear," she said in the most elegant voice. "Could you please make some arrangements for me on the ship?"

"Most certainly, I would be happy to help. What is it I can do for you?"

"We have several people who enjoy playing bridge. Could you arrange for us to reserve the card room for Tuesday and Thursday afternoons so we can keep our competition going?"

"That will be no problem. What time would you like?"

"How about 1:00 pm? We wouldn't want it any later because several of the players will want to participate in the pre-dinner activities of teatime dancing and, of course, happy hour cocktails in the lounge," Emma Lou replied.

Emily assured her that she would check with the activities director and would leave her a note of confirmation. As Emma Lou walked away, Emily broke into a big smile. She was wearing an attractive pair of tight capri pants, a colorful tunic top, and sandals. *I hope I will look like her when I'm in my seventies and eighties,"* Emily thought to herself.

The first evening was enjoyable. Everyone was relaxed and liked their cabin assignments. Emily joined several members of her group at the open-seating dinner in the main dining room. As dinner ended and she bid everyone good night, she overheard several of her group members making plans to meet in the piano lounge for after-dinner drinks. Entering her cabin Emily felt that it suited her perfectly. The color scheme was green, one of her favorites, and she was thrilled to have a balcony. She unpacked her suitcases and settled into a comfortable chair to peruse the daily briefing for their first day at sea. She was looking forward to participating in the activities that were offered aboard. The afternoon cooking class caught her eye immediately. She called to the desk to see if there was still availability.

"You are one lucky woman," the cheerful front desk receptionist replied. "We have one opening, and I will sign you up right now. Please come down tomorrow to get your ticket before class begins at 1:00 pm."

"Thank you so much. I love to cook, and there is always something new to learn." Emily replied.

"Oh, yes. You will learn many useful cooking techniques. The rating of this class has been among the highest on our sailings. I suspect it is attributed to the personality of our young executive chef. We were so lucky to recruit him. He was highly trained both in America and Paris. You will enjoy his class," the receptionist assured her.

"I'm certain that I will. Thank you for the recommendation." Since Emily was on a roll, she continued to inquire into the availability of the game room for her bridge players. She was relieved to hear that Tuesday and Thursday afternoons were available. *The woman at the receptionist counter was right. I am on a lucky roll.*

Emily awoke rested and full of energy. After a light breakfast she went to the front desk to retrieve her ticket before deciding to take a brief swim in the outdoor pool on the Lido deck. She had purchased a new swimsuit for the trip. It was beige with a hint of light green seaweed cascading down one side. She questioned whether it was a bit too sheer, but since it was one piece she decided it was fine. She was the only one in the pool, so she enjoyed doing flips and diving to the bottom of the pool to retrieve a colorful plastic ring she found there. The kitchen staff was constantly coming and going, setting up the outside lunch buffet. After an enjoyable forty-five minutes in the water, she slipped on her long colorful swimsuit cover-up and ordered a quick lunch from the pool bar. She needed to get back to her cabin to change clothes. She did not want to be late for the cooking class. As she entered the auditorium she was surprised to see the size of the crowd. Almost every seat was taken. Just then, she saw one of the members of her group waving to her from the front row. There was one seat available directly in front of the chef's demonstration table. *Another lucky break*, Emily thought to herself.

When the chef came out on stage, Emily was amazed. He was so young, maybe only a few years older than she and so attractive in his white chef coat. Indeed, the chef was extremely good-looking with curly sandy-colored hair, bright blue eyes and an athletic build with broad buff shoulders. He wasn't tall, maybe 5'7", but the way he confidently carried himself across the stage made him seem much taller.

"Good morning everyone, my name is Eric Olsen. I am the Executive Chef on this ship. I hope we will meet your highest expectations on our sailing of this wild and scenic 50th State of the Union." He smiled broadly as his eyes scanned the audience. When he saw Emily in the front row, his blue eyes focused directly on her and stopped. As the class progressed Eric said he needed a volunteer to assist him. Without another word, he quickly said, "How about you in the front row in the orange shirt? Would you please come up on stage?"

Emily was surprised to be singled out, but she willingly made her way to the steps and joined him on stage. "You'll want to wear this apron," he said as he slipped it over her head and tied it behind her waist.

The appetizer to be demonstrated was seafood in a phyllo pastry. Eric asked her to roll out the dough as he prepared the filling. Emily almost stopped breathing as he came up behind her and put his arms around her to give directions.

"This thickness will work," he said as he rolled the dough a few times.

She felt herself begin to blush, but she was not going to lose her cool in front of seventy spectators. She prepared the phyllo dough to his specifications, and he gave her a big smile as he said, "You've got it. It's just perfect." As she finished he thanked her and said, "Please keep the apron as a souvenir."

Her legs felt weak as Emily descended the stairs to return to her seat, and she noticed several people smile at her, as if to acknowledge a job well done.

At lunch, Sylvia chimed in to comment on the cooking class experience. "You did a great job up there assisting the chef this afternoon, Emily. Not only is the food on this sailing exceptional, but I must say our executive chef is also handsome. Wouldn't you agree?" She looked directly at Emily who tried to casually respond.

"Yes, I would agree."

Cathy, who was one of the other women in her group, remarked. "I missed the demonstration, I'll have to check him out at the captain's formal welcome reception tonight."

As Emily began to dress for the captain's reception she hesitated. She had brought an elegant full-length, black dress, but as she looked at herself in the mirror, she wondered if it was too dressy. It had quite a plunging neckline, and she didn't want to appear too suggestive were she to Chef Eric, at the function. However, she decided that it was a formal affair, and it was her only formal dress. She would wear her highest heels and stand tall in confidence, even though she was only 5'2". Besides, she said to herself, *I look pretty darn good in this dress, I'm going to wear it and have fun tonight.*

The captain's party was in full swing when she arrived. The line to have one's photo taken with the captain was not long and she decided to join in the tradition. When the captain saw her next in line he gave a look that assured her that he approved of her attire.

"You look lovely tonight," he said as he shook her hand and their photo was taken. With a glass of champagne, Emily walked around and joined in conversation with members of her travel group. With the clinking of a glass, the captain requested everyone's attention. "I would like to introduce the men and women who will make this a memorable week for you aboard our beautiful ship."

When Chef Eric took his bow, everyone clapped a little more loudly to show their appreciation for the superb dining experiences they had already enjoyed since coming aboard the ship. Emily thought she had caught a knowing glance from Sylvia, but she pretended not to notice.

Following introductions, the band began to play dance music. Emily felt a tap on her shoulder.

"I'm wondering if I might request a dance from my able and willing volunteer from this afternoon?"

As Emily turned around, she was looking directly into Eric's eyes.

"You are looking stunning tonight, I'm Eric again," he said smiling. "And I didn't get your name at the cooking demonstration?"

"Emily Anderson. My mother is Swedish so we may both have some Viking roots if I read your name Eric as being Scandinavian?"

"Very good assumption. You have half of the equation right. My mother is of Swedish descent, but she fell in love with a Scotsman."

"A perfect combination. The good looks of a Swede and the bravery of a Scot," Emily shot back playfully.

"Thank you. I will take that as a compliment," he said with a chuckle.

As the dance ended, Eric thanked Emily and moved on, circulating with the other guests. It was then that she noticed a beautiful woman approach him with a kiss on each cheek. She was elegant with long hair tied back in a French braid, exotic makeup, and a gorgeous figure. As the music ended, the dinner bell chimed calling everyone to the sumptuous welcome aboard dinner awaiting them. As Emily looked over her shoulder, Eric was gone, as was the elegant woman.

Everyone at her dinner table commented on their choices as being delicious and outstanding. Emily had ordered the braised lamb shank and noted that the sauce was out of this world.

"Would you like to join us for the show tonight, Emily?" one of the women in her group asked.

She welcomed their invitation and the opportunity to get to know them better. The show was taking place in the palatial showroom. The decor was magnificent, sparkling chandeliers, polished brass, and semicircular booths. Richard, the Cruise Director, came on stage to welcome everyone. He was the epitome of what you might expect in a cruise director, handsome, silver haired, polished, and confident. One could tell that he had been in the business for many years. He knew exactly how to set the audience at ease while building enthusiasm for the show that was about to begin. The production was professional and well-presented. Emily loved the theme songs from the '30s and '40s.

So romantic, she thought to herself — just like the dance she had shared earlier with Eric. She wondered if he was traveling with that beautiful woman. Being practical as she was, she concluded that a man as charming as he would not be without the attention of women. She was a bit disappointed. She knew that she sensed an instant spark when she first saw him. It was the feeling of 'knowing' that she had so hoped to experience when she found her Mr. Right. Being a realist, she knew that the emotions would need to be mutual, so she dismissed it as wishful thinking on a vacation holiday.

The next morning, Emily had just finished breakfast when she heard the ship's announcement that they had entered Alaska's Inside Passage. The commentary said that their cruise would travel over 500 miles up the passage and advised passengers to keep an eye out for dolphins, killer whales, and the flukes of humpback whales.

What am I doing sitting inside reading a book? Emily thought to herself as she headed to her cabin for a sweater and her yellow rain slicker. She hadn't been out on the deck but a few minutes before she felt a hand touch her arm.

"Come quickly Emily." It was Eric. He directed her to the opposite side of the ship. "Here, use my binoculars," he said and he put his arm around her shoulders. "A pod of humpback whales have been spotted. Their tail fins are called flukes. Watch for their flukes when they dive down for food."

At exactly that moment, the whale's fluke surfaced above the water. Emily was fascinated. She had never seen a humpback whale before, even if it was only its tail fin.

She turned to Eric, "Thank you. That was so exciting! I'm sure if we wait a few minutes we will see even more of the whale."

"I'm sorry to tell you that when you see those flukes, it means that those big fellas are diving deep to feed. They won't surface for quite a long time."

"Where's your sense of optimism?" Emily coaxed. "With a little magic we may even get to see the whale's hump."

And, at that very moment, to the complete amazement of everyone, a humpback whale launched itself out of the water and landed back onto the surface with a huge splash! The crowd of passengers went wild with excitement. Everyone kept saying that the event they just witnessed was almost impossible to see in the wild. Many had seen whales breaching at Sea World in San Diego and Orlando, but it was a rare and perhaps once-in-a-lifetime experience to see a whale propel itself so high out of the water in the Inside Passage. Everyone was sharing photos on their cameras and telling others who had just arrived of their good fortune. Having witnessed the incredible spectacle, Eric was curiously looking at Emily with wonderment.

"Well, your sense of optimism is most impressive," he said, still a bit amazed. Emily smiled to imagine that he could possibly think that she created the magic to make a whale do such an acrobatic feat, but she could tell by the look on his face that he was still pondering the thought. "I wish you could sprinkle a little of that magic on the soufflés I am preparing for tonight's dinner," he said with a twinkle in his eye.

"I wish I could," she replied. "But you're now on your own."

"Darn, too bad," he laughed. "I'm sorry I have to run,. Duty calls, but I must say that I look forward to more of your magic soon."

"Anytime."

"I'm going to hold you to that," he replied as he waved goodbye. "Keep the binoculars on loan, I'll get them back from you later."

As she watched Eric depart through the doorway, Emily felt a warm glow come over her. She thought for a moment that he might feel an attraction for her as she felt one for him. *Could this shared experience be a sign?* she wondered.

The rest of the afternoon flew by quickly with an interesting lecture on the Inuit people, an hour on the treadmill in the gym, and cocktails at the Lobby Bar with members of her travel group. When Emily returned to her cabin to dress for dinner, she found a note at her cabin door. It read: "Do you have space on your dance card tonight? I'd love to get to know you better. Can you join me in the disco later? If so, see you there at 10:00 pm. Be sure to try my chocolate soufflé at dinner tonight. Eric."

Emily could hardly believe her eyes as she read Eric's note. Maybe, he wasn't with the beautiful exotic woman. Maybe they were just colleagues or friends? In any case, Emily decided to gladly accept his offer. She would ask him about the woman, and she was most excited to experience the disco that her aunt had told her about. She felt almost euphoric knowing that in a few hours she would be in Eric's company again. And this time, it felt like a first date! As the dinner hour approached, Emily hoped there might be an empty seat available at the big round table occupied by her single woman travelers. She secretly had to admit that her favorite dinner conversations were shared with them. They were, in her mind, simply amazing.

The women were so full of life, flirting with the single men on board, always on the dance floor with the Gentleman Hosts and constantly laughing and sharing stories from the past. Emily marveled that when she was with them, she often forgot that she was far younger in age. She felt that true friendships knew no boundaries, and she was having so much fun with her group members who called themselves the Dazzling Dames. When she had asked earlier where the name came from they told her that several years before, they had all participated in a fund-raiser for their local hospital called the St. Joseph's Follies. They loved their wild, sparkling flapper outfits and the name just stuck. *I would love to have their energy and zest for life when I am their age,* Emily thought to herself. And then she unexpectedly added, *And, why not?*

As she entered the dining room she noticed Sylvia chatting near the doorway with Richard, the handsome Cruise Director. She also notice that there were two distinguished older gentlemen standing next to the table occupied by her group. They were engaged in lively conversation with Emma Lou and Donna.

"Emily, come meet our newest bridge players. This is Hank and Ted. They just stopped by to visit on the way to their table." She expressed her pleasure in meeting them and moved on to find a seat next to Donna.

"I don't recognize Hank and Ted as members of our group?"

"Oh, no, they aren't," Donna replied in a particularly cheerful tone of voice. "A university alumni association is sailing on the ship this week, and there are several very handsome single men in the group. We got to visiting with Ted and Hank in the lounge, and they love to play bridge. We have a game planned for tomorrow afternoon."

"Actually," Carol, another member of the Dazzling Dames, added, "I'm surprised how many gracious and intellectual men we have already met in our age group." Carol was a retired judge, recently widowed. Although, somewhat reserved, on this evening she seemed particularly animated. "Often, there are very few single men on sailings, so it is nice when the cruise line arranges to have Gentleman Hosts on board to dance with us women."

"Have you met any of them yet?" Emily inquired.

"Yes, I danced with Charles several times last night at the Captain's Gala. We shared some interesting stories about criminal law. He is a retired defense attorney from Maine and very charming and intelligent."

Emma Lou asked, "Does he play bridge?"

"The question is not whether he can play bridge, but whether he can dance!" Sylvia chimed in with her engaging sense of humor. Everyone laughed. The dinner conversation was especially lively. When the dessert menu arrived, Emily mentioned that the chef had recommended the chocolate soufflé.

"I noticed you on deck today with that dashing, young executive chef," Sylvia said coaxing a reply.

Emily tried hard not to seem flustered or interested. "Yes. He loaned me his binoculars to view the humpback whales."

"Well, if you were to ask me, I would say he might have been more interested in you than the whales," Sylvia said with a mischievous smile.

"Sylvia, please give our new, young friend a break from your prodding. Besides, we have all noticed that a good looking, silver-haired man seems to be interested in getting to know you better on this sailing," Cathy teased her good friend.

"Yes. Richard is handsome isn't he?" was all that Sylvia would say.

Following dinner, Emily joined members of her group to listen to a quintet, entertaining in the Observation Lounge, before she returned to her cabin to freshen up prior to meeting Eric in the disco. She was glad that her aunt had explained the acceptable protocol for passengers, ranking officers, and staff who wished to spend time together at the disco in the late evening hours. She decided to change into something a little more festive than her dinner attire. Being uncertain of the best outfit to wear, she chose a silky pair of skinny black pants, a long, flowing multicolored tunic top and a black pair of heels that she knew she could dance in comfortably. She had recently broken them in, dancing the night away at a friend's wedding reception. No necklace, she decided, but only a big pair of sparkling earrings.

As she entered the disco lounge, her eyes slowly adjusted to the low lighting. The DJ was already spinning a familiar tune, and the place was packed with late-night revelers. Eric saw her enter and immediately waved from his table. As she approached, he stood to greet her. She liked seeing him out of his official chef coat. He was dressed in a casual linen jacket over a collarless shirt, and she loved the fact that he wore his loafers without socks. It had become popular attire of men who wanted to signal that they were savvy.

"I'm so glad you could join me," Eric said with an engaging smile.

Emily took a seat in the small booth that Eric had chosen for the evening. It was in the perfect location, on the second tier overlooking the dance floor, but removed enough so they could carry on a conversation. "This disco is quite the place," Emily said, breaking the silence after the waiter had taken their drink order.

"I hope you like it. It's a great spot for us to unwind after our busy workdays, and the engineers especially appreciate the opportunity to mingle with attractive female passengers like you."

"Thank you for those flattering words."

"I mean it sincerely, Emily. You are a most beautiful woman. When you ended up sitting in front of me at the cooking demonstration, I thought to myself, 'Now, here is someone I would like to get to know.' And here we are. I hope there isn't a special guy waiting for you back home?"

"Actually, there isn't," Emily replied and instantly realized that this was her opening to ask about the person she had seen Eric with at the captain's party. She quickly continued, "And what about you, Eric? I couldn't help notice how enthusiastically that gorgeous woman greeted you at the captain's reception."

Eric threw back his head and laughed. "You are being kind in using the word "enthusiastic." I might have used the words undeterred. Her name is Katarina, and she just came aboard as the new spa manager. She is attractive and seems to be a good person, but she has been flirting non-stop since she learned that I was single and one of the chief executive officers. Somehow, I just didn't feel that special connection when I met her, and I don't feel a romantic pull. Besides there will be no problem now. Tomorrow, when she hears that I was at the disco holding hands and dancing with a beautiful blonde woman, she will focus her attention elsewhere. There are several engineers who would be happy to line up in my place."

"Will she really hear about our being together tonight?"

"Without a doubt. Living on a cruise ship is like being constantly on live television. Everyone knows about everyone else's business. At first, I found it intrusive, but actually it's harmless curiosity. The ship is like a very small town, and there isn't a lot that slips under anyone's radar. Truthfully, people do sincerely care about each other. I've seen many acts of kindness amongst the staff and crew."

"I like hearing that." Emily nodded.

"You would," Eric replied. "Because you seem to be an especially warmhearted person. I'm glad you could join me this evening. I really look forward to getting to know you better." Emily gave him a tender smile. "Hey, perfect timing, it's a slow dance, and I like this romantic song." He led her onto the dance floor and held her close. She was happy she had worn her high heels so she could rest her head on his shoulder. As the song ended she heard a familiar voice call out her name.

"Emily, so nice to see you here." It was Sylvia looking particularly ravishing in an off-the-shoulder, tight-fitting black dress.

"Oh. Hello, Sylvia."

"You remember meeting Richard, our Cruise Director?"

"Yes," she replied. Eric joined in the conversation to compliment Richard on his particularly humorous commentary in the morning briefing. Emily was still smiling to herself when she and Eric settled back into their booth. "I see what you mean about the ship being like a small town. That was one of the members of my travel group."

"I know," he replied with a wink.

The evening seemed to fly by quickly between slow dances and hours of conversation. They both talked about their loving parents and the experience of growing up in a middle-class neighborhood where everyone knew their neighbors, and even the names of their family pets. Emily told him about her love of sports, and Eric found humor in thinking that her summer job was as a lifeguard at the beach. He couldn't imagine a 5'2" blonde keeping all of the unruly teenagers in line. She explained that being the youngest child in the family, one learns a bit of assertiveness. Eric laughed to admit that was true as he was the little baby brother of two older sisters. He told her that he never dreamed that, at thirty-four years of age, he would have finished a liberal arts degree at the university, completed the master courses at the culinary institute, interned with some of the best chefs in Paris, and now found himself exploring the world during the past three years as a chef on a cruise ship.

Emily asked if he liked it. He smiled to say that he wouldn't have seen so much of the world were it not for the experience, but it was not something he aspired to do for the rest of his life. The conversation was easy and personal. They could hardly believe it when the DJ announced the last song. As they danced, Eric whispered into her ear, "I never skip the last dance with someone I would like to see again."

It was 2:00 am as they departed the Disco. "I left my little Fiat back in the lower 48," Eric said in a kidding manner. "So, since I can't drive you home, we'll just have to walk."

Emily took his arm, and he walked her to her cabin door. He paused and bent forward to share a romantic good night kiss.

As Emily closed her cabin door, she ran in and fell back onto the bed. *I adore this guy!* she thought. *I must say thank you to the Universe tonight!*

Emily woke early, filled with the energy of a teenager who had just been on her first date. As she enjoyed her morning coffee on her balcony, she heard the telephone ringing.

"Hi, Em, how goes the cruise?" It was her sister, Renée. Emily was so pleased she had called while the ship was docked in Sitka. The phone coverage was crystal clear.

"It is not only going well for the travel group, but Sis, I think I met him, my Prince Charming."

"Oh my gosh, so soon? You have only been on the ship for three days!"

"What about the fact that you met Paulo, the love of your life, and knew you would marry him within two days?"

"You're right, Em, I did, and I am so happy and in love. I bless my lucky stars every night. Please forgive me for any doubts. I know how long you have waited to meet your Mr. Right. I'm so excited to hear this news. Tell me every detail."

Emily explained everything to her sister, Renée.

"He sounds wonderful! I can't wait to meet him, and the folks will be overjoyed."

"Let's wait just a little while so they don't get worried that I'm moving too quickly. But there is no doubt in my mind that he is the one."

With a cautionary tone in her voice, Renée said, "Because I love you and never want you to be hurt, I just have to ask if you are sure he feels the same about you?"

"Thank you for being honest enough to ask that question. Since it has only been three days, I have not said anything to him about my conviction and my belief in love at first sight, but he is being very attentive, and I can feel our mutual attraction."

"I'm so happy for you. I promise that I will keep it to myself until you are ready to share it with the folks. If Paulo promises not to say a word, can I tell him? He will be so thrilled."

"Of course, you can tell Paulo. And I can't believe the fact that you called this morning. Just when I wished I could share the incredible news with you," Emily replied.

"Is there any doubt why this happened? You know how our strong bond is. Keep me informed," Renée said with the most loving tone in her voice.

"One more thing, could you please call Aunt Marge to tell her that the cruise is wonderful, and everyone is having a great time?"

Just as Emily hung up the phone, it rang again. She recognized Eric's voice immediately. "Good morning. I hope you slept well. I'm wondering what your plans are for today? I thought if you enjoy it, we could do some kayaking this afternoon. My assistant chef, Michael, is willing to cover for me during lunch since I will handle dinner without him tonight. He is celebrating his girlfriend's birthday. Sitka has a great rental shop close to the dock, so we could get a couple of kayaks and have a little fun together."

"That sounds wonderful. I was so hoping that I could do some kayaking on this trip," Emily replied with enthusiasm.

"Knowing it is something that you hoped to do makes it perfect. Meet me at the kayak shop at 1:00 pm. It is just off the ramp on your left when you disembark." After a brief, but noticeable pause, Eric added, "I look forward to being with you again."

Emily was certain she had heard it in his voice. She could sense that his feelings for her were growing stronger. She dressed and joined a few of her group travelers by the pool for an early lunch, and rushed back to her cabin to change clothes for her kayak adventure. Emily loved to kayak; it was such a relaxing way to connect with nature. Eric shared her sentiments as they both paddled alongside each other, pointing out various birds in their path. They heard the loud, distinctive honking of the snow geese, and Eric shouted to her that he was pointing at the Willow Ptarmigan on the hillside. It was the state bird of Alaska and was rather difficult to catch a glimpse of on land. Emily heard him say, "It's your magic again."

As they turned to head back, Emily spotted a bald eagle souring overhead. She had always felt it was a sign that the Great Spirit was watching over her. When she pointed to it she blew a kiss to Eric. He put his hand into a fist and taping it twice on his chest. She knew it as a gesture of gratitude and affection among those in their generation. When they returned to shore, Emily gave him a big hug of appreciation. She had fulfilled her dream to kayak in Alaska, but she knew she had gotten much more that afternoon. It was a confirmation that Eric was beginning to care deeply for her too.

As they walked back to the ship, Eric said, "Any chance I can cook dinner for you tonight? If you can wait until 9:30 pm, I can be finished with the second seating entrees, and my staff can wrap up the rest. It would be just the two of us. There is a private dining room off the wine tasting salon."

"I would love to have dinner alone with you tonight."

"Good, I'll pick you up at your door. Your group won't even notice you are gone after dinner, because tonight's entertainment is the ever popular performance of local native dancers."

"You are so thoughtful to be concerned that I remain attentive to my travel clients, but I assure you that they are having a good time on their own."

"Yes, so I hear. Especially Sylvia, that lively one in your group."

"Has she already worked her way into the grapevine?" Emily laughed.

"Yes, but it's all positive; she's an attractive woman with a fun-loving, likable personality. She is also fabulous on the dance floor. I hear all of the gentleman hosts are getting in line. See you at 9:30 pm."

Emily joined her travel group members for cocktails at happy hour. She was interested in learning more about Sitka, since many of them had participated in various shore excursions that afternoon. Dan and Jim had gone on the city tour exploring Sitka's Russian heritage. She learned from them that Sitka was located on an island. It belonged to Russia until 1867.

They had visited St. Michael's Cathedral, built in the nineteenth century, when Alaska was still under the control of Russia. As the earliest Orthodox cathedral in the New World, it's green domes and golden crosses had become a prominent landmark of Sitka. Dan was quick to add that the structure today is a rebuilt version as the Cathedral burned down in 1966. Some of the icons in the cathedral were saved and date to the mid-17th century.

The tour to the Sitka National Historical Park had sold out early, but several of her group had taken taxis to the walking trail that was home to many magnificent totem poles. Emily listened carefully to their descriptions. Because of her spirituality, she was interested in the meaning the ancestors conveyed in carving the wooden poles. She learned that they often symbolized characters in mythology such as the popular supernatural being, the Thunderbird. Some symbolized beings that had transformed themselves into various forms, many as a combination of part animal and part human. It was also noteworthy that some poles simply conveyed the experiences of the recent ancestors. The meanings of the designs were as varied as the native peoples that made them. Emily decided that, on this trip, she would definitely purchase a few small totem carvings for her family members back home as well as one for herself. In keeping with the discussions on culture, Emily reminded her group of the evening show featuring local native dancers who had come aboard the ship to perform.

At 9:30 pm sharp, Eric arrived, looking casual in slacks and a crisp blue and white striped shirt with the sleeves rolled up. He had a bottle of wine under his arm.

"The sommelier wanted me to sample this new wine, I thought you might offer a second opinion." He smiled. "I noticed you were drinking red last night, so I suspect you'll like this one."

"I admire an observant man." Emily smiled as he stepped aside to let her pass ahead of him. "And one with manners too."

They took a staircase that was not in full view of the crowds in the lobby. Eric used a key to unlock the lovely wine tasting room. As they stepped inside he said, "I thought about serving our dinner under these stunning chandeliers, but a table for fourteen seemed a little much. Let me turn the lights on before you step into the smaller, private room."

Emily waited as he opened an adjacent door and stepped into the room for a couple of minutes.

"Dinner is served, my lady," Eric said, making a bowing gesture as she entered the most charming small space with a lovely little table set for two. It was a tiny room, but palatially decorated, causing her to suspect it was used for the honeymoon couples or those celebrating a very special occasion.

"How very romantic," Emily exclaimed. "This is perfect in every way."

"I thought you might like it. Besides, it is so private. No peering eyes watching our every move. I'm pleased we can be alone tonight." He seated Emily at the table and began to open the wine. "I brought a decanter, so it is not as necessary to wait for this fine wine to breathe. I also made a big seafood salad with homemade bread and some good cheeses. Dinner will not get cold, and this way we do not have to be in a hurry. We can stretch our evening out as long as we like." He poured her wine and, once seated, smiled and held his glass high. "A toast to meeting you," he said in a confident tone of voice. "And might I add that you look especially pretty tonight. I like that off-the-shoulder red blouse. I'm not sure if you wore it to match the wine or to tempt me into kissing you on your bare shoulder?"

"Both," she replied with a grin.

They talked about many personal things. The movies and books they liked best, the places in the world they had visited, and the activities they enjoyed on their time off from work. They also shared some glimpses into their experiences in former relationships. "Those guys were very lucky to have had you in their lives. You are a special woman; intelligent, funny, and caring. You truly listen when we talk. You seem to understand what I'm trying to convey. I must say that your gentle, easy going nature has not gone unnoticed on the ship. Several people have already mentioned how sincere and beautiful you are. I am grateful that we met early on, as I know that Kyle, the gym manager and fitness instructor, already had his eye on you. I'm surprised he hasn't offered to be your personal trainer this week."

Emily became silent and looked down at the floor avoiding his gaze. "He already did didn't he?" Eric laughed. "Well, lucky me that you came to the cooking demonstration."

"Remember, I am a woman who has to feel a magical connection," Emily began. "He seemed nice enough, but he's not the guy for me. I'm glad you have asked me to dinner tonight. I like you and appreciate your belief that I possess these many positive qualities. However, I must confess that it is far too early for you to have discovered my annoying and ill-natured side."

"Oh, a woman who is human and has faults! I'll take it since it will allow me to divulge my shadow side. We all have one, don't we?"

"Yes, we do," she replied with a smile.

"Tell me more about the power of magic you referred to on deck the other day," Eric asked. "Your eternal optimism intrigues me."

"I suppose it is just a trust in the Universe. I count on it to bring positive loving things my way. Because of my unwavering faith, it always delivers. When I was a little girl my mother taught me about the power of positive thinking. She said it would create magic in my life. Every time I would see a shooting star I would make an intention. Every time I would see a rainbow, I was convinced that good things were coming my way. One could call it 'wishful thinking,' but I like to think of it as positive expectancy. Maybe it is naive, but it is my belief that my life is going to be truly wonderful."

"Hearing you describe it touches me. I do not believe it is naive. There is so much chaos in our world today. Greed, fear, and suffering are so commonplace. A bit of positive thinking, or should I say believing, is refreshing," Eric said in a kind voice.

"Eric, tell me something of your hopes and dreams related to your personal life."

He took a few minutes to think over his answer. "I see my future spending my life with a woman who is my equal, a playmate and a trusted partner. It has to be someone whom I'm attracted to in the deepest sense. There has to be a conviction that says, 'she's the one.' I know that it may seem romantically corny, but my father once told me that he knew my mother was the one for him within hours of knowing her. They were college students attending an international youth convention on world hunger. They met on the first evening at a welcome dance. Even though they were from different backgrounds and parts of the country, they transferred to the same college to be together. They have been happily married for over forty-five years. They are as much in love today as ever. My father said he just knew, and trusted his instincts. My mother told me she felt exactly the same. They have never doubted their love, and I'm certain they never will. I suppose it is what I would like for myself."

"That is very sweet story about your parents. I also believe that my partner will be the man of my dreams. I can't imagine not having kids. Plus a big house with a backyard for grilling and a basketball hoop in the front driveway. I know it sounds old fashioned but it's what I see or, at least, what I wish for in my future."

Eric looked more seriously into her eyes. She felt like he wanted to say something personal regarding their relationship, but retreated, thinking, as she did, that it was too soon to reveal his feelings.

"You might be wondering how I'm going to fulfill my future dream from the galley of a cruise ship? It doesn't quite go together does it?" Emily laughed but remained silent, intently giving Eric her total attention. "I actually have a goal of owning my own restaurant. I'm just not sure if I can pull it off. It seems like a daunting concept and an investment banker once told me that restaurants have a very high rate of failure. They are considered to be a risky business. In fact, they are one of the most speculative ventures for loan officers."

Emily was truly surprised that Eric would think he could not succeed in his own restaurant, yet he was right in quoting those statistics. She had been introduced to them when she earned an accounting degree at the university.

"You won't believe this, but my thesis in college was writing a business plan for a high-end, fine dining restaurant," Emily added.

"Are you serious?" he said with a surprised look on his face.

"Yes, I am. When I studied all of the financial possibilities, including the risk factors, I discovered something encouraging." Eric was waiting expectantly. "In my final analysis, I proved that, although risky, it is possible to be profitable in the restaurant business, if…"

"If what?"

"If the chef was highly trained and educated, experienced in all aspects of the kitchen, and notably talented. It is proven that the most popular, and most profitable fine dining restaurants in the country are chef owned. The chef owner has to possess a high degree of passion and determination. He or she must be willing to roll up their sleeves and put in extra hours in the first years of operations. They would have to pay careful attention to the bottom-line, plus be meticulous in their training of the kitchen staff and servers. Bankers will loan money for restaurants if the business plan is solid, and they sense that the passion is there."

Emily continued with a curious smile on her face, "There is something more that I would like to add. What were the last two words you just said to me?"

After searching his memory, Eric said, "I remember, I was waiting for you to finish your sentence. You stopped with the word 'if,' I then asked you, 'if what?'"

Emily gave a gentle smile. "Give me your hands? In one hand, I will put the simple word if."

She smiled as she pretended to place something into his hand. "And, in the other hand I will put the word what." Eric nodded with a look of anticipation. These are two very simple words that we use in our conversations every single day. But, if you switch their order, they convey two completely different messages."

She made a little gesture to indicate she switched the objects in her hand. "They become 'what if.' What if you could get the loan, and what if you could fill the restaurant every night with happy customers, and what if you could do it all and still have a home and family you love? Put in reverse order, these two little words become powerful."

Eric was visibly moved. "You are right. 'What if' creates the feeling of possible success."

"Yes, it does. I saw this scenario in an old movie once, and I never forgot it. It is just two little words that if reversed, have a completely different meaning. 'If what' is negative and fear based, and 'what if' is optimistic and hopeful. I'm sure you know the one I would chose. Perhaps, you might too. Think about it." Emily said.

With a pensive look on his face, he replied, "I will think about it."

Eric turned to Emily as they ended their evening and exited through the lovely wine tasting room. "Would you be my date here tomorrow night? The captain's wife is flying into Juneau to join the sailing for a few days, and I have offered to prepare her favorite dish, Coq Au Vin. There will be fourteen of us around the table. Staff and guests of the captain's choosing. I prepare the seven various courses from the kitchen, but when the main entree is served, the captain's wife insists I join the dinner party. It's usually an interesting collection of guests."

"Who will be attending?" Emily asked.

"I'm not sure, because the captain makes the invites. But I think Richard has asked your friend Sylvia. And Austin, our chief engineer may bring Katarina. Remember her? The spa manager who you suspected might be with me at the captain's party."

"Thank you, I would love to be your date, and I'm most certain your Coq Au Vin is every bit as delicious as Julia's." Eric loved her clever reference to one of the world's most beloved chefs, Julia Child.

"We are sailing through Glacier Bay tomorrow morning on our way to Juneau, so be sure to get out on the deck early. With your luck, you will probably see a glacier calving." Eric put his arm around her shoulders as he walked her back to her cabin.

Since it was past midnight, and no one was in the hallway, he nuzzled her neck and gave her a kiss on her shoulder as he worked his way up to give a passionate good night kiss on the lips. Before leaving, he whispered, "I hope you will wear this red, off-the-shoulder blouse again when we have more time."

Emily smiled. She loved his romantic nature. He noticed when she put extra effort into looking pretty, but in her heart, she knew that he would be attracted to her if she was in sweatpants and a tee shirt. This was the connection she had always longed for, and on this evening she was feeling especially cherished. Remembering her childhood fantasy, she imagined this might be how Cinderella felt as she danced with her prince at the ball.

The next morning, Emily was up at the crack of dawn. She ordered breakfast to be delivered to her room and turned on the cruise channel to check the outside temperature. It was definitely a morning for her wool sweater and scarf. She took a few minutes to step out onto her balcony.

She could already hear the loudspeaker. A local naturalist guide and Park Ranger, who was expert in glaciers, had already come aboard the ship. Emily had read, in her cruise brochure, that Glacier Bay National Park was the highlight of an Alaska cruise. It was listed as a not-to-be-missed wonder, covering 3.3 million acres of rugged mountains, snow-capped peaks, active glaciers, and deep sheltered fjords. President Jimmy Carter had expanded the land mass in 1978, and it was declared a National Park in 1980. Emily was interested to learn that the Park was actually named a World Heritage Site in 1993 and joined neighboring Alaska parks in combining over twenty million acres to become one of the largest internationally protected ecosystems on the planet.

Out on deck, Emily marveled as their large cruise ship maneuvered through the heart of the Fairweather Mountains. With Eric's binoculars she was constantly scanning the shoreline for wildlife. Toni, the naturalist guide, helped her spot a brown bear on the shore. It was thrilling, as was seeing large sea lions basking on the rocks in the sun. One of her favorite wildlife viewing moments was when an iceberg came floating by with a native bird standing proudly on it.

It was a black legged kittiwake, and Toni explained that they were a common variety of gull that live in the Northern oceans. Emily was certain that it was the most photographed gull that day! The Park Ranger announced that they would be arriving shortly at Margerie Glacier. He explained that the glacier was a 21-mile-long tidewater glacier. It was just one of the more than 1,000 glaciers in the National Park, but the favorite since it had the most active glacial face. It offered the greatest chance to see ice calving, the dramatic breaking off of chunks of ice from the wall at the edge of the glacier. The ship turned 360 degrees so everyone would have an opportunity to see the glacier, especially those in the upper lounge. Those who decided not to brave the elements would most certainly be toasting a calving event with Bloody Marys and Mimosas.

As Emily waited patiently on the public deck, with camera in hand, she felt a sweet familiar arm around her shoulder.

"Any calving yet?" It was Eric, who had heard the ship's announcement about the arrival to Margerie Glacier. "I'm sure with your luck it will happen soon." He smiled warmly and gave her shoulder a little squeeze, trying not to be obvious to the hundreds of passengers on deck.

"Not yet, but I can't wait until I tell my Aunt Marjorie that they named a glacier after her! I hope I can find a post card of Margerie Glacier so I can send it to the agency."

She saw Eric laugh. He loved her enthusiasm and zest for life. She relished gathering facts that she found curious. "Did you know that Glacier Bay National Park has something in common with the Tower of London, the Galapagos Islands, the Taj Mahal, and the Great Wall of China?"

"I haven't the faintest idea," Eric replied with a big grin. "No, wait let me guess. I'll bet it has something to do with birds. There are bald eagles and sea gulls here in Glacier Bay National Park, Darwin's finch are in the Galapagos Islands and black ravens frequent the Tower of London. But I suspect that is not the answer, because I don't know about birds at the Great Wall of China or Taj Mahal in India."

"You are not correct, but that was an impressive guess. They are all World Heritage Sites."

"Well, aren't you just the cutest walking encyclopedia." Just as Eric uttered the words, the crowd gave a big whoop as a huge piece of the ice wall broke from the face of the glacier. "We did it, Em. We saw a glacier calving!"

Emily looked at Eric with the most loving expression. "You called me, Em. It is what my family and dearest friends call me."

"Hopefully, that is okay? It just sort of rolled off my tongue. It seems more personal to me."

"I love it," Emily replied as she snuggled a little closer to him.

"Have you seen lots of wildlife? I heard there was even a bear on the shore. Hope he isn't eating too many salmon. I will be buying some in the morning at the Fish Market in Ketchikan," Eric shared.

"I did get to see the bear, because you so kindly loaned me your binoculars. We also saw a sea gull riding along on a floating iceberg. Sadly, I did not get to see a loon. I have never seen one in its natural habitat. When I was a little girl, I had a favorite bedtime story about a loon called Lucky. Silly I admit, but I've wanted to see one ever since."

"Well, guess what? I can make that wish come true for you. Since you have been educating me this morning, did you know that Minnesota has more Loons than any other state except Alaska? My uncle has a lake house there. I'll take you next summer so you can see your first real, live loon. And, with that piece of trivia, I had better get back to work. This is a very busy day in the kitchen. We are serving three international entrees at dinner in the main dining room, and then I will be preparing the seven course French dinner for the captain's private party. Don't forget it is at 8:00 pm in the wine tasting salon where we were last night. I won't be there when you arrive, but they are expecting you. I have my seat reserved next to yours. Luckily, Kyle, the gym trainer won't be there," he joked. "Have a good time. I know you will charm them. See you there."

As Eric left, Emily smiled to think that he was as jealous of Kyle as she had been of Katarina. As silly as it may appear, she knew it was a sign that they felt the same for each other.

Emily met her delightful women's group for lunch and signed up to join them on an afternoon shopping tour of Juneau. It was a tough decision for her to make because she was torn between two different tours offered in Juneau. Hugh and Mary, a couple in her group, had asked if she might like to join them for the Alaska Dog Sled Tour. They were going to experience an authentic sled ride in the Tongass National Rainforest with a team of huskies. Being a woman of adventure, Emily so hated to decline their invitation, but the tour did not return to the ship until 7:30, and she did not want to chance being late for the captain's dinner party. Besides, she had been wanting to make some purchases of Alaskan art, and this seemed like a great opportunity.

As the shopping tour participants disembarked the ship, they found the waterfront bustling with various cruise ships, fishing boats and float planes zipping in and out. On the motor coach, their tour guide, Diane, shared a little of Juneau's rich history. Emily smiled at her use of the word "rich," since the city was built on gold discoveries. In 1880, a native Tlingit Indian chief lead two prospectors to what later became Gold Creek, where the men discovered gold nuggets laying on the open ground. Considering that the big Klondike Gold Rush didn't start until eighteen years later, these early prospectors most certainly 'hit pay dirt,' as the expression goes.

The travel group was amazed to find that Juneau had no highway access It is the only capital city in the United States than could only be reached by air travel or by water.

Juneau was a mecca for those who loved nature. There were helicopter sightseeing tours providing the chance to walk on the Mendenhall Glacier, at the city's edge, hiking trails, whale-watching tours, and fishing excursions were also plentiful. In the motor coach, they passed the state capital building, Saint Kristoff Russian Orthodox Church, and several museums. As they turned onto historic South Franklin Street, Diane explained that they had two hours to shop in the turn-of-the-century buildings that now held lovely boutiques and art galleries.

"The coach will pick you up here at 6:30 pm to go directly back to the ship," she announced to the group.

Emily finished all of her shopping in time. She got a postcard of Margerie Glacier, some bone jewelry earrings for her sister, a tee shirt for Eric with the image of a breaching whale and aprons and coin purses for friends. For herself and parents, she purchased totem pole carvings by a local native artist. She also found a hand-painted box of note cards as a hostess gift for the captain's wife. *After all*, she thought, *it is, in a sense, her dinner party.*

On the way back, she told everyone about the international dinner entrees that Eric was preparing. They could choose from Smoked Pork Shoulder with spätzle from Germany; Roesti, a potato pancake with veal from Switzerland; or Osso Bucco alla Milanese from Italy. Everyone teased Emily saying that she and the handsome young chef must definitely be spending some time together if she were to learn all of these details. When asked if she was joining their table that night Emily simply said she had other plans, but would be with them for lunch the next day.

When they returned to the ship, Emily decided to take a little rest before the dinner party. She thought about how hard Eric must be working in the kitchen, with so many commitments, including the many courses for captain's dinner. Seven courses seemed daunting, but she had read somewhere that it was the tradition for a formal French dinner. She was glad that her grandmother had taught her about fine dining and the utensils used for each course. But she wasn't sure that she would be familiar with all seven pieces of dinnerware. She would just wait patiently and observe the others for her cue. Searching through the closet she found a kelly-green dress that matched her eyes. She liked the fact that it was mid-calf, flowing, and elegant. She decided on some drop earrings, a gold bracelet, and a large green turquoise ring.

At 8:05 pm, Emily arrived at the private wine tasting room. Several people were already standing around the room visiting over a glass of champagne. She made her way directly to the captain and his wife. Captain Smith saw her approach, and explained to his wife, Madame Analie, that she was a passenger on the sailing and a guest of Chef Eric. When Emily offered her hostess gift, she received the reply, "How very thoughtful of you, my dear. I appreciate your kindness."

The dinner was planned for fourteen people and Emily made her way around the room introducing herself. She smiled to see that Sylvia was the invited guest of Richard. They greeted her warmly and introduced her to Jack Burg, who was the cruise doctor, and his partner Marybeth, the ship's chief purser. Also standing with them were two women who owned a large cruise agency in Miami and a couple from France who were passengers on the sailing. As Emily made her way to the next couple, she recognized Katarina. She was on the arm of Austin, the handsome chief engineer and was even more stunning up-close as she was from across the room. She seemed genuinely pleased to meet her, explaining to Austin that she was the woman that Eric had met on the ship.

As the dinner progressed, Emily counted the seven courses in her mind. Not only was she interested to see what Eric and his staff had prepared, but she also knew that he would be filling the empty seat next to her, as the main entrée was served. She had tasted the first course, Brie and green olive Canapés that were served with the champagne. They were delicious, and she mused to think it was one course down.

Emily was seated at the end of the table occupied by the captain, his wife, the doctor and the purser, as well as the French couple. When the second course arrived, it was a beautifully-served bowl of chilled Vichyssoise. Madame Analie was thrilled and stated that it was her very favorite chilled soup. Emily replied that it was also well liked in the United States. She then went on to describe how it became so popular. She explained it was purported that New York City's famous Ritz Carlton Hotel hired a French chef named Louis Diat in 1917. One day Louis prepared the potato leek soup that his mother had made for him as a child. He put the leftover soup in the refrigerator. On the next morning, he remembered that on a hot day, his mother would chill it with cold cream.

He had been searching for chilled entrees to serve the customers dining in the hotel's new, outdoor roof garden restaurant. He decided to serve chilled Vichyssoise, a soup he named after Vichy, France, a town near where he grew up as a boy. The soup became an overnight sensation. Emily continued, "I do not know if it is true, but it is said that the chef of the Waldorf Astoria was a friend of Louis Diat and asked him if he could introduce the soup on his weekly radio talk show. Since household refrigerators were just being introduced in America, it would be a chance for people to show off their sophistication in serving chilled Vichyssoise."

Madame Analie loved hearing America's introduction to her favorite soup. And the couple from France said they knew where Vichy was located. Emily ended by saying that she had actually visited Vichy two years prior, and could not find one restaurant that served Vichyssoise or even had heard of it! Everyone laughed and said they thoroughly enjoyed Emily's story.

The third course was fish. Emily was impressed that Eric had used Alaska's local fish in a delicate buckwheat crepe stuffed with dill, salmon, and briny capers. She was relieved that the fish was wrapped in a crepe. Being left-handed, she would have struggled with the traditional fish flatware. It was designed for those who were right-handed!

A lime sorbet was served next as a palate cleanser before the main course. It was then that Eric arrived to join them. He was wearing a formal chef coat with long sleeves, a black collar, matching cuffs, and six offset black buttons. When he walked through the door, everyone cheered. He went directly over to give Madame Analie a kiss on both cheeks and to shake the hand of Captain Smith. When he approached his empty chair, he gave Emily a sweet kiss on the cheek before being seated. She could hardly believe he was so open with his affections toward her. She was thrilled and saw it as another sign that he felt comfortable letting others know that they were a couple.

Madame Analie announced to the entire table that Chef Eric had pleased her again, by making not only her favorite chilled soup, but also Coq Au Vin, the French dish of chicken braised in wine with lardons and mushrooms. Emily found that the chicken melted in her mouth and the sauce was divine.

She was thrilled to have Eric seated next to her for the last three courses: a light salad with vinaigrette dressing, a traditional cheese course, and the chocolate soufflé. The soufflé was perfect, high, light and decadent. It got all kinds of compliments from around the table. Eric was humble as usual. He did whisper to Emily, "I saved some of your magic from the other day and added it before baking."

Emily smiled and squeezed his hand under the table. She noticed he did not let go but continued to hold her hand on his knee.

When the dinner party was coming to an end, Madame Analie spoke to Eric directly. "Chef Eric, we are all so pleased that you invited Emily to join us tonight. She shared the most delightful story about Vichyssoise, and we have so enjoyed her company."

"I am happy to hear this, because I too think she is very special," Eric replied. It was almost midnight, so everyone departed with warm hearted goodbyes and kind words of appreciation for a lovely evening. Emily felt a warm glow. She was grateful to be accepted so graciously by everyone. However, she was especially glowing because she now truly felt that she and Eric were a couple. And down deep in her heart, she knew it was for real.

TRAVEL AGENT ESCAPADES

As Eric walked her back to her cabin, she said, "Would you like to sit out on my balcony for a while? Maybe we can catch sight of a shooting star." When they entered and closed the door to her cabin, Emily turned the desk lamp on low, saying, "This is more romantic, isn't it?"

Eric was not sure if the look she was giving him was an invitation or simply a question. Not being certain, he decided that a kiss was a perfect place to start his inquiry. Within seconds, they were lying on the bed, kissing passionately. At their ages, the hormones were already raging. They were both certain of their feelings for each other. There had never been a doubt from the moment they met, and there were certainly none now.

Eric had the most loving look on his face when he turned to ask, "Em, are we ready to take the next step?"

Emily nodded sweetly.

The next morning, Eric awoke at 5:00 am "Em, I am going to slip out now, so as not to bump into anyone in the hallways, and because I have a very busy day ahead. Remember, we are having the big fish fry around the pool tonight. I'm taking a couple of my best crew with me to the Fish Market this morning. Kristoff, Levi and I have a mission to pick out the freshest salmon available in all of Ketchikan. I sure hope the bears left us some of the big ones," he joked.

"You certainly are in a lively mood this morning," Emily replied, still half-asleep.

Eric leaned over and gave her a most amorous good morning kiss. "Why shouldn't I be? Last night was wonderful. I cannot begin to tell you how much you mean to me. Your magical Universe has somehow brought us together, and I truly believe this is just the beginning."

Emily was not a morning person. She turned over and went back to sleep. Around 8:30 in the morning, she awoke to a very loud blast. It actually felt like it shook the ship. She thought maybe it was one of the ship's engines, but it seemed to be much more powerful, like a violent explosion. She looked out her window and could see that the ship had already docked in Ketchikan. Several minutes later, she heard a strong knocking, almost a pounding, on her door. She quickly threw on her robe and opened the door. It was Katarina, she looked frantic and was out of breath.

"There has been a massive explosion at the local fish market. I think they suspect it was a faulty gas pipe. The entire building is engulfed in flames. You can see it from the other side of the ship. Captain Smith is terribly distraught because Eric, Levi and Kristoff have not returned from the market. It's awful, it's so awful. We could see the people running from the building."

"Please, no." Emily was almost in tears and her heart was racing. Katarina then gave her a hug, which made her even more frightened. "I'll throw some clothes on and be up on deck right away."

Within seconds, she was into her blue jeans and a sweater and out the door. On deck, people were already gathered watching the huge flames shooting stories high from the Fish Market. It was only located two or three docks away, so it was frighteningly close. Black smoke was billowing into the sky and the sound of sirens were everywhere. The worried looks of the passengers made Emily even more fearful. Captain Smith, Richard, and Dr. Burg were all standing on the dock at the bottom of the gangway.

As Emily stood at the railing in shock, all she could say to herself was, *No. Please no, God, don't let Eric be killed.*

Just then, Donna and Sylvia came running up to her and threw their arms around her. The looks on their faces made Emily feel even more panicked. The magnitude of the fire was overwhelming and right there three docks away, in clear view of the ship! Emily could hardly get her words out. "Eric hasn't come back from the market yet."

Donna said, "We know, dear. We all heard and are praying for him."

Emily did not hear the words she so desperately wanted to hear from them, "He will be alright he will make it out." The blaring of a fire engines, ambulances and police sirens were deafening. *This is such a small town,* Emily thought. There were only 8,000 residents. *How could they fight this blaze? Please, God, bring him back. We have just found each other,* was all she could say over and over again in her head.

Captain Smith was now pacing, and the waiting seemed to go on forever. Emily could see all of the kitchen crew in their white uniforms standing on the bow of the ship. The looks on their faces were of concern and shock. Several held their hands over their mouths. No one was saying a word. *What if he was killed? Or severely burned or injured his hands? How could he fulfill his dream?* Emily choked back tears. She was now in complete anguish and sheer terror.

Everyone waited. Emily knew that it was not a good sign that thirty minutes had passed since the blast. Tears started to stream down her face. Just then a sheriff's vehicle drove onto the dock in the direction of the ship. Donna put her arm around Emily fearing the worst. Captain Smith, Richard, and Doctor Burg all approached the sheriff's vehicle. The back door opened, and Kristoff and Levi stepped out. They had soot and cuts on their faces and arms.

Emily then saw Eric getting out of the passenger's side of the front seat. She could not hold back. She burst down the gangway steps and started running toward him with tears streaming down her face. When Eric saw Emily, he began running towards her. They locked in an embrace, both with tears flowing. They were holding each other as if no one else was there, as if they were the only ones on the dock. Everyone was completely silent, as if out of reverence for their heart-wrenching embrace.

As he regained his composure, Eric turned to Captain Smith who gave him a big hug. Eric then reached for Emily's hand and would not let go. He held it tightly in his. It was then that she noticed his arm was bleeding through his blood-soaked shirt. Eric motioned to Kristoff and Levi to come forward and join him. They linked arms and Eric raised his hand in the air as if to say, "We made it." Kristoff and Levi waved, and the crowd erupted! The kitchen crew was shouting cheers of joy and twirling their hats and aprons, and the passengers waved, wearing smiles of relief.

Back on the ship, Captain Smith made the announcement that Eric and his crew were now safe on board. He explained that the reason there was a delay in returning to the ship was because they heard cries for help as they ran from the explosion and stopped to assist in saving the lives of three people. He briefly described that the people were trapped on a fourth story ledge, on the south side of the building. The explosion had dislodged the metal fire escape stairs, which were then dangling from their hinges.

With the help of others, Eric, Levi and Kristoff were able to push the metal structure back up against the building for an escape route. The captain said he was proud of their unselfish bravery and assured everyone that they were not badly injured. They were headed to the infirmary for treatment of cuts from flying glass and debris. He ended his presentation with a touching remark about those on his ship being like one big family. He expressed heartfelt gratitude for the safe return of Eric, Levi and Kristoff.

Eric asked Emily to wait for him in her cabin while he got stitches and treatment for the gash on his arm. When he returned she could see that he unsteady on his feet. He looked pale and was shaking.

"I'm afraid you may be in shock. I think you should get under the covers where it is warm. You have been through so much. You could have been killed in that explosion," Emily said. She was still unsettled.

"Let me shower this soot and dust off first. The doc said I could shower with this waterproof bandage."

Emily had a second fluffy white robe hanging in her closet. Eric appreciated its cozy texture and climbed into bed. Emily slipped off her sweater and jeans, put on her robe and cuddled with him under the warm covers. "Are you okay?" she asked gently.

"I think so, but I still feel shaky. The thought of those flames right on our backs and the bricks and glass flying everywhere was horrible. Levi slipped and fell. We didn't notice right away, but we hurried back to get him. It was awful hearing those people crying for help. Thank goodness we were able to somehow push the fire escape frame toward them."

With a huge sigh, he said, "I'm just so thankful that we made it. As I was running from the building, all I could think of was you."

"I know Eric, and all I could think was that we finally found each other, and it just couldn't end this way. I prayed so hard. I cannot begin to tell you how much you mean to me and how grateful I am to have you back safely. Is there anything you need right now?"

"Just you, Em. Just you."

Within minutes, Eric had stopped shaking and had fallen asleep bundled under extra blankets. Emily was jolted back into reality by a knock on the door. She quickly threw on some clothes and answered it. There stood Captain Smith, Dr. Burg, and Richard.

"We came by to see how Eric is doing?"

"He is sleeping now," she whispered. "He was actually quivering and pale when he first got here, and I was worried he could be in shock."

Dr. Burg explained that people can experience symptoms likened to Post Traumatic Stress. "I checked him out thoroughly. He doesn't have any internal injuries. I think with his age and fitness level, he will be just fine, but let's keep an eye on him for a day or two. Let me know if anything changes."

Emily nodded and assured him that she would.

Captain Smith said that Eric was not allowed back in the galley for two days. With a twinkle in his eye, he said, "Tell him it is under captain's orders."

As they left, Richard told her that the crew and passengers alike were sending their best regards. "We have brought you a platter of breads, meats, and cheeses, plus a full bar cart just in case you want to stay in for the evening. Please call room service for dinner delivery." He added with a grin, "Don't let Eric critique the room service food. He's off duty tonight!"

They all smiled in agreement as Richard added, "Oh, by the way, I'll assure your friends that Eric is in good hands so they should not be expecting you at dinner tonight. Sylvia and the other ladies were concerned, not only for Eric, but also for you."

Emily nodded in gratitude. "Tell them I appreciated their support up on the deck this morning, and I hope they enjoy the salmon bake at the pool." Emily then suddenly realized she wasn't thinking clearly, "Oh, no. I'm sorry, I meant . . ."

Richard interrupted her in mid-sentence. "Tell Eric the most touching thing happened this afternoon. A group of fisherman heard about the accident and brought a boat load of fresh salmon to the ship. Eric's assistant chef has it all under control."

"Thank you for coming to check on Eric. That was so thoughtful of you. I'll tell him you came by."

When they left, Eric poked his head out of the covers. "I didn't want to greet them in a bathrobe," he said with a gentle smile.

"I hope you heard their words of concern and the captain's orders? You are to stay in and take it easy tonight." Emily stood alongside the cart. "I never was a bartender in college, but can I get you a drink? It is 4:30 pm and almost cocktail hour in Los Angeles?"

Eric gave her a feeble smile. "The doc said I could have a drink, and I could use a bourbon on the rocks. Maybe even make it a double."

After the day you have had, I heartily agree." She also opened the bottle of wine and poured herself a glass. They sat up in bed with their drinks and finally felt their bodies relaxing. Eric's playful nature was returning. "If my buddies heard I was in bed all afternoon with a beautiful blonde and didn't even…"

Before he could finish, the sentence Emily put her finger to his lips and said, "We have the rest of our lives to make love. This most definitely isn't the time, is it?"

"No, it isn't. Thank you for cuddling with me. I was feeling shaky and a little disoriented when I got back to the ship."

"Maybe you should call your parents to let them know you are okay?" Emily suggested.

"It's early evening now in the Midwest, and I don't want them to go to bed with this on their minds. There's no way that Ketchikan's news will spread east that quickly. I'll call in the morning."

"Would you like to go sit on the balcony and get a little fresh air?" Emily asked

"I think I'd like to wait till it's dark. I wouldn't want to be spotted on the balcony of your cabin in a bathrobe. Hey, how come you are dressed?"

"Remember the captain and your comrades came by to check on you. I wasn't going to answer the door in my robe."

"The idea of you in nothing but a robe is getting me excited," Eric said with a half grin.

"Obviously, you are no longer in shock, and I can see that you are getting back to your old self." Just then, there was another knock on the door. "See? Grand Central Station! I'm glad I'm still dressed to open the door."

It was her cabin steward, Guilherme. "Is there anything I can get you Miss Emily? Would you like me to gather up these cards and notes on the floor outside your cabin?"

"Yes, thank you." When Guilherme handed her the collection of mail, she said, "I think we have everything we need right now." Emily refreshed their drinks and climbed back onto the bed. She asked, "Would you like these? It looks like fan mail. And by the way, how did they know to deliver them to my cabin? Oh yes, how could I forget. A cruise ship is a small town where everyone knows everything." They both laughed.

As they nestled in for the evening, Emily could sense that Eric was going to be just fine. He had narrowly escaped a horrific accident with just a few stitches. Doctor Burg was right, being only thirty-four years old was a positive factor in his speedy recovery. *Youth did have its advantages*, she thought. As they talked and cuddled, it felt like her cabin was their own little nest away from the distractions of the world. Although Emily laughingly commented regarding all of the interruptions that were taking place, the extra attention they were receiving from the staff and friends made both of them grateful that so many people did care. Guilherme came in with a heating blanket in case Eric was still cold. No doubt, when he was refreshing towels, he had noticed Eric's soiled clothes on the bathroom floor, so he delivered a men's sweatshirt and lounge pants compliments of the gift shop. They were a much-needed gift so that Eric could join Emily in sitting out on the balcony. The timing was perfect. Her cabin steward was now free to make up the room for the night.

When they came back into the cabin, they were both touched. Guilherme had noticed the room service menu on the bed. He ordered a small dining table and set it up with a crisp white tablecloth and a small vase of red roses. They ordered dinner and Eric was moved to see the special attention they received when the cart arrived. There were several items that were not on the normal room service menu; two chilled lobster starters, his favorite soft wheat dinner rolls, perfect medium rare steaks, served sizzling on metal platters, and a little note that read: "If you would like a soufflé for dessert, please just call to order." But without doubt, the things that got Eric teary-eyed were the notes from the kitchen staff. They were written on the back of paper towels, kitchen order pads, and on edges torn from boxes. In all sorts of languages, they expressed their heartfelt gratitude that their executive chef had survived. Many of them had personal messages: "We really miss not having you as our boss tonight"; "It's too quiet without your laughter down here"; "I appreciate all that you have taught me"; "It's just not the same without your leadership"; and "My best isn't as good without your encouragement."

"These messages are so sincere and caring. You really have made a positive difference in their lives," Emily said. She and Eric also looked at some of the other cards that had been delivered. She noticed that Madame Analie had written her message on one of the note cards that Emily had given her as a gift.

In an 8 x 10 envelope was a pencil sketch of the two of them embracing on the dock that Shirley, a member of her travel group, had done. She was a professional artist and captured the moment beautifully. There were so many more cards, but as she looked over at Eric, she could see he was fading. He seemed tired all of a sudden.

"I'm thinking we should go to bed early," she suggested. He nodded in agreement. It had been a very emotional day, and they both needed sleep. "If you would like to just stay here again tonight, I have a tee shirt I purchased for you in Juneau and an extra new toothbrush in my bag."

Eric was most grateful. While he was in the bathroom getting ready for bed, Emily put the heating blanket over the covers and turned it on high. When he came out and slipped between the sheets, he commented on how good the warmth felt. Within minutes she was also ready for bed in her little pink night shirt. They cuddled for a few minutes. Eric then turned toward her and said, "I love you, Em."

"I love you too, Eric."

When they awoke in the morning, Eric seemed very much like himself. His energy level was back, as was his romantic nature. "I think this image of a breaching whale on my tee shirt is giving me ideas."

Emily began to laugh out loud. "What would those be?" she asked. She glanced over and saw him pulling the shirt off over his head. She smiled and put the Do Not Disturb sign on the cabin door. With her night shirt now on the floor, she climbed back into the bed.

After making love, Eric turned to look her in the eye. "Em, I don't want you to think that when I told you last night that I loved you that it was just because of the emotional day I had come through. I truly do love you. You are the woman I want to share the rest of my life with."

"And I am certain that you are the Prince Charming I have waited for all of my life. I could not be happier. I dearly love you too."

"Since I am not supposed to work today, let's just relax and bask in our afterglow. Would you like to have breakfast in bed together?" Eric asked.

"That is a fabulous idea. I like it. I'll call room service. What would you like?"

"A ham and cheese omelet, home fries, wheat toast, and black coffee." Eric replied.

When the person on the phone asked for her order, Emily began, "I would like to have two eggs over easy, but not too runny please. Then an English muffin toasted crisp with butter and one extra pat of butter and raspberry jam on the side. Could I have my hash browns extra crispy and no peppers? Tomato juice and a bowl of plain yogurt with honey and walnuts. Oh, and coffee with cream please. Yes, that is all for the first order." And she then gave them Eric's uncomplicated order. She ended with a cheerful, "Thank you so much, I appreciate it." When she looked over at Eric, he had the most sheepish grin on his face.

"What?" she asked.

"You are the most interesting person I have ever known! Being with you is like putting together a giant box of puzzle pieces. That breakfast order tells me you are definitely a woman who knows what she wants. I'll call that piece decisiveness, and add it to the puzzle pieces of kindness, empathy, and caring for the emotions that you exhibited yesterday. And, of course, this morning, I'll add the pieces of passion and sensuality. And how can I forget optimism, a belief in magic, and spirituality? It will take me a lifetime to gather all the pieces that make up the person you are. It actually delights me to see all the different aspects of you."

Emily grinned. She had heard comments such as these many times before from her lifelong friends. They were not unfamiliar. She was never described as complicated, but rather as multifaceted. She looked up the definition in the dictionary once to find that the word multifaceted meant someone with many features, perspectives, and talents. She had long ago decided to accept who she was in life. And now, she also learned that Eric loved her just the way she was. He had sincerely shared that he would not change a thing about her. She laughed to herself thinking that, throughout the years, he would undoubtedly discover many more puzzle pieces to add to his collection.

As they sat in bed together eating their breakfast from trays, the telephone rang.

"The phone is for you, Eric," Emily said while she made a hand gesture to indicate that she did not know who the caller was.

Eric recognized the voice on the other end of the line. It was Jonathan, a chef who he had been mentoring on the ship for the past three months.

"Hey, Jonathan, why are you calling from the ship's inside line? I thought you were still up in Denali National Park communing with the caribou?"

Jonathan replied, "Well, I'm glad your sense of humor was not damaged in that awful explosion yesterday. Captain Smith called me. I've never heard him so shook up. It must have been terrible. He asked if I could cut my trip short by two days. When I assured him I could, he even sent a private float plane to pick me up. I felt like a VIP. He said you were not to work for a couple of days, so I'm back. Don't panic, you have trained me well and I'm on it!"

With a chuckle, Eric replied, "Panic? You are a fabulous chef, way better than me when it comes to fish entrees, so I suspect there will be a couple on the menu tonight."

"On a more serious note Eric, I heard about your near-death experience yesterday. Are you alright?"

"Just a gash to the arm and a few stitches, but it was terribly frightening. How are Levi and Kristoff? Have you seen them?" Eric inquired.

"Yes. Kris looks a bit worse for wear, with little cuts all over his face, and Levi had a pretty bad sprained ankle from the fall. But you wouldn't believe how they are lapping up all of the attention. Last night they were served Filet Mignon and a good bottle of Chianti in the wine tasting room. And today Katarina has arranged a complimentary massage for each of them at the spa."

"That was kind of Katarina. She sent a certificate to Emily and me too."

"Who is Emily?"

"Oh, I forgot you have been gone all week. I have met the most wonderful woman in the entire world. She is a passenger, escorting a travel group from Los Angeles. I can't wait until you meet her. You won't believe this Jonathan, but I'm convinced She's The One."

"The one, like in forever?" Jonathan asked with wonderment in his voice.

"Yes, like in happily ever after."

"Wow. I love hearing this. But you had better not go off in a Pumpkin Carriage until you teach me to perfect that Roquefort dressing that you make. I'm happy for you, Eric. It really is a bit of fate to find the right partner. Having dated as much as I have, I know!"

They both laughed and Eric shared that he was sorry that Captain Smith had cut his vacation time short.

"No problem, five days in the wilderness was getting a bit long. Except I'll miss the gorgeous Russian girls who were working in the lodge."

"I'm sure they will miss you, too." Eric teased.

"Well, glad to hear you are okay. Reading the front-page of the newspaper gave me chills. That was nice of them to feature you in the articles. I'm proud of you guys for rescuing those people from the burning building. That takes guts my friend. Hey, if you are up to it, why don't you take your new lady to the Silk Road for dinner tonight? Chef Kai would love to have you."

"I'm up to it. Remember, I am not injured seriously. Thanks for the idea, and I'll see you back in the galley tomorrow. Could I ask a favor? Would you get me a copy of that newspaper? I want to see it before I call my parents."

"Sure, I'll bring one right down and put it in front of the cabin door. Are you in your cabin or hers?" Jonathan said with a smile in his voice.

When he hung up, Eric shared that Jonathan was a highly experience chef who he was mentoring on the ship for several month. Emily asked, "Why would he be training with you if he is already a successful chef?"

Eric explained that being a chef on a cruise ship is much different than a restaurant. "Can you imagine, on a ship of our size, we are feeding 2,000 passengers and 750 crew three meals a day at a minimum. On a seven-day cruise we use over 20,000 eggs, 3,250 pounds of chicken, 4,000 pounds of beef, 7,000 pounds of potatoes, and much more. It is the magnitude of ordering supplies, feeding so many people on a time schedule and the many specialty parties that makes the job challenging. Jonathan is smart and he learns quickly. When he finishes here he will be granted an assignment on one of the ships in this line. It will be much easier when I just have to manage the kitchen in my restaurant."

Emily looked at him in surprise. "Your restaurant?"

"Yes, Em, I've been thinking a lot about your 'what if' scenario. I'm getting excited about the possibilities. I'll tell you more later. I need to call my parents."

He went to the door and brought in the newspaper, and also more cards and messages from well-wishers. Reading the three pages of newspaper coverage, he was shocked to see his name mentioned several times. There was even an article, that read: "Executive Chef of nearby cruise ship saves lives."

"I've really got to make that call now. I'm going down to my cabin. What are your plans? We will be sailing back through the Inside Passage all day, so it is essentially a sea day."

Emily explained that she was going to go to the main dining room to join her woman's group for lunch. She was a little concerned that she had not been attentive in following up with the plans for her hosted travel agency party. It was a combined cruisers party and a celebration of her clients Steve and Laurie's 50th wedding anniversary. She needed to check on the function, which she had reserved for the Observation Lounge at 4:00 pm. The invitations were sent before the accident, so at least that part was taken care of earlier.

"Eric, would you be able to come to my agency party? I would really like you to be there."

"Sure, I would be glad to come. Remember, this is my day off," he said with a tongue-in-cheek grin. "And don't worry about the party. After I call my parents, I'm going to go down to the galley, to say hello to the crew. I'll put a bug in their ear to give a little extra effort to the food for your party."

She came over to give him a big hug and kiss of appreciation.

He then added, "It is the least I can do for all of the things you did for me yesterday. How about we meet back here at the cabin around 2:30 pm? You might want to call your aunt in addition to your folks. Word does spread quickly in the cruise industry."

When Eric entered his own cabin, he stopped to notice how lonely it seemed all of a sudden. He had only been staying at Emily's cabin for two nights, but it seemed much longer. And it felt more like home. He noticed that his clothes from the day before were laundered and folded on his bed. The tear in his shirt sleeve was mended and there was no sign of blood. For a moment, the day before seemed almost surreal. However, as he glanced down at the newspaper he was holding, he knew it was indeed real. It had been a frightening day. Fortunately, it had not turned into a disaster for him personally. But sadness overcame him as he thought of the eighteen people who lost their lives in the blast.

"Hi, Dad," Eric said when his father answered the phone.

"Son, how great to hear from you today."

"Good to hear your voice too. Is Mom home? If so, could you get her on the other line?"

"Hi, Honey," his mother lovingly greeted him as she picked up the second line.

"Mom and Dad, don't get worried. I'm okay, but yesterday I had a near-miss experience that could have been tragic. I could have easily been killed."

"Oh, Eric. What happened?" his mother replied in a frantic tone of voice.

Explaining the events of the explosion in detail, Eric shared the fear he felt as he ran from the building and rescued survivors.

"What survivors?" his father prodded for details. Eric explained about those he, Levi and Kristoff had rescued from the burning building.

"Were there people who died?" his father asked.

"Yes, eighteen people. I just didn't want you to see it on the national news before I had a chance to call. Our cruise ship was docked relatively nearby, and all of the passengers and crew watched the flames from the deck." He explained that he had not gotten back to the ship right away, because of the rescue, so everyone waiting on the ship's deck thought he might have been killed. "I should have called you yesterday, but I think I was in shock. Emily helped me get under warm blankets and I fell deeply asleep. With our time difference I didn't want to share the news with you right before bedtime."

"Is Emily the young woman you told us about? The one you met from California?"

"Yes, she was so distraught she ran down the gangway crying. I was so happy to see her that we both held each other with tears streaming down our faces."

Eric's mother was a retired nurse, so her next questions were, "Are you sure you aren't injured? Did the ship's doctor check you out? How did this young woman, Emily, know to keep you warm? The idea of you holding this dear girl on the dock in tears makes me realize how serious this explosion and fire must have been. My heart is still racing, but I am so relieved. Are you sure you are okay?" his mother asked again.

"I'm sure, Mom. I just have a gash to my arm and a few stitches. Emily and I had dinner in her cabin last night and got to bed early. I feel more like my old self today. I could easily go back to the galley, but Captain Smith forbids me to do so, at least for today. I'm feeling settled now, and will be attending Em's agency party this afternoon. I also plan to take her to the Silk Road for dinner tonight."

"This relationship seems to be getting serious rather quickly," his father began. "Don't you think you should slow it down a little?"

"Dad, I have fallen in love with Emily. I've never been more certain about anything in my entire life."

"But you can't really know her in less than a week? Or be sure of your feelings?"

Before Eric had a chance to respond, his mother spoke from the second line. "Thomas, Darling," she began. "When did you know I was the woman for you? I realize it has been many years ago, but how long was it before you were sure?" She didn't wait for his answer. "I think you said it was within a few hours. I also fell in love with you on the first day we met, and I still adore you today."

"Nancy, I still adore you too, Sweetie, but…"

His mother interrupted again, "Eric, Honey, we have raised you to make good decisions, whether it was in your choice of friends, colleges, or career. You have a great head on your shoulders. If this dear Emily has captured your heart, as your father captured mine so many years ago, then we can't wait to meet her. Everyone is not lucky enough to find their forever love so quickly, but it can happen. It did for us, and it sounds like it has for you too. I'm so happy for you son."

Eric's father realized that his initial reaction was perhaps too cautionary, or maybe just a parental concern. "I'm sorry, son, if I was seeming stern and negative, I'm just an old worry wart but your mother is right. Finding the love of your life can happen at first sight. We certainly are proof of that. If you and Emily have as wonderful a life together as your mother and I have had, you will be a very lucky man. Forgive me for giving you a hard time. I'm relieved that you are safe. And believe me when I say, I am pleased that you have found a girl who means so much to you. She sounds like an amazing person. Please bring her to visit soon."

"Thanks, Dad. I'll fax you a copy of the newspaper article on the explosion, but please be assured I am just fine."

They talked a little longer about family matters. Eric chuckled as he hung up the phone thinking that his mother, once again, reminded his father of the day they had met. He had heard their love-at-first-sight story so many times during his growing up years. Now he was certain it would be the story that he would someday tell his children, about the time he met their mother, on a cruise ship in Alaska.

While Eric was making his call, Emily was off to find her travel group for lunch. She was fairly certain that the news would not reach her aunt or parents so quickly. She felt a need to touch base with her clients and check on the agency gathering. When Emily walked into the dining room to join her women's group, they all got up and gave her a big hug. As she looked around the room, she also noticed passengers giving her an especially tender smile.

"How are you doing today?" Cathy said. "We are all so relieved that your sweet guy was not seriously injured."

Emily smiled. She loved hearing Eric referred to as *her* sweet guy.

"Thank you. I can't believe that I ran to him crying with so many people watching."

"Don't be embarrassed for a moment," Carol replied, "It reminded me of the day my fiancé, Ray, returned from the war in Vietnam. The minute I saw him at the airport, I burst into tears. I couldn't stop crying. I guess they are tears of joy, but I remember their intensity to this day."

Sylvia was especially quiet and finally spoke, "My heart was beating so hard I thought it would burst. I kept praying that Eric would come back safely, but the magnitude of the flames and the waiting period almost killed me. When I saw him get out of that sheriff's car, I shed a few tears too."

Emily was touched. Sylvia outwardly appeared so confident and strong that one would not imagine her shedding a tear for someone she hardly knew. Emily had always sensed that she had a heart of gold.

"Where is Donna?" Emily asked. "Is she alright? I hope she doesn't have sea sickness?" They all laughed and looked at each other with a playful look, which puzzled Emily.

"Not sea sickness, but she's lovesick!" Cathy exclaimed. Emily then learned from the women that Donna had been spending the last several days nonstop with Ted from the university alumni group.

"I saw it immediately the first time they were bridge partners. It was like a 'dance' between them. Smiling, complimenting each other, and teasing." Emma Lou continued, "It was like sparks came out of nowhere and surrounded them!"

Cathy added, "I'm thrilled for Donna. She's been widowed for seven years and always hoped to meet someone special. Ted is a great guy. He's been alone since his wife died three years ago, and they make the cutest couple. They are acting like teenagers. I've never seen Donna so happy."

"Didn't she call you, Emily?" Sylvia asked.

"No, I don't think so. I'm sorry I didn't check my voicemail in the cabin yesterday. I'll check it as soon as I finish lunch."

"She is going to ask you if you can change her flight at the end of the cruise. She's not going to return with us to Los Angeles."

"Is there a problem?" Emily inquired, looking most concerned and serious.

"Oh no. It's happy news. She is going to fly to Boston and drive on to Cape Cod to meet Ted's family," Cathy said.

"Is it that serious?" Emily inquired.

"Honey," Emma Lou replied with a lighthearted look on her face. "When you are our age, time gets to be more precious, and you don't hesitate to grab the golden ring, if you know what I mean?"

Emily nodded. She knew well that it was good advice, at any age.

"We almost forgot to tell you. We planned a little 50th Wedding Anniversary party surprise for Laurie and Steve."

Sylvia went on to explain that Richard had assisted in the planning. There would be a baby grand piano available for the music. Emily looked puzzled as Sylvia continued to describe the surprise. "Valerie, Fran, Bobby and Kari are members of the Symphony Chorale and have beautiful voices. We called Steve and Laurie's daughter to ask her what song was played for the first dance at their wedding reception. It was 'Fly me to the Moon,' so we're going to recreate the moment."

"What a clever and wonderful idea. Thank you so very much for planning this tribute. They will love it," Emily said. She assured them that Eric was feeling well enough to attend, and she would see them at the Observation Lounge.

Returning to her cabin, Emily realized she had an hour to call her aunt and parents before Eric arrived. She decided to call her aunt first and was lucky to find that she was not on the phone with a client.

"Aunt Marge, it's Emily. I know you are busy covering for the agents, so I will be brief. I wanted you to know that there was a terrible tragedy yesterday in Ketchikan. Don't worry it did not affect the passengers on the ship, but there was a terrible explosion at the Fish Market. Our ship was docked only a few piers away so we could see the flames from the ship. Eighteen people were killed, and it was so awful because my new sweetheart was there and narrowly escaped."

"Oh my, that sounds so tragic. I am sorry to hear this news. It must have been so frightening, especially knowing that someone you care for deeply was in harm's way."

Emily then explained that Eric was the executive chef, and they had met and fallen in love in only a few days.

"Nothing could make me happier, unless he invites you to move away, and I lose my very best back room wizard."

"You know, I am kidding dear. I'm delighted to know you have found that special guy you have so longed to meet. See? There are no accidents. You were meant to escort this cruise. I believe in destiny as you do, Em."

"You're so right. But I want to assure you that I am not planning to run off to elope and leave you stranded!" Emily said teasingly.

"I'm relieved to hear that news. And tell me, have you had a nice time with the travel group?

"They are the most caring and fun-loving people. I have especially enjoyed the Dazzling Dames. We are having the agency party tonight, and I will report back. Also, Donna is not seasick but lovesick. I'll contact you about her change of plans tomorrow. I just did not want you to hear about the explosion near our dock and worry. We are all fine."

Her next call was to her parents. She knew it was easiest to reach her mother at the accounting firm, so she called there first. Luckily, her mother was free answer her call.

"What a nice surprise to get a call from you this afternoon. Are you having a good time on your trip to Alaska?"

"Mom, although I am calling to tell you about a tragedy in Ketchikan, I have something more to share. It has been the most magical week of my life."

She told her mother all about the terrible explosion and assured her that everyone on the ship was safe. She explained how she had met Eric and that, in one short week, they had fallen in love. She ended by saying that she had finally met the man she wanted to marry, and she could not stop smiling.

Emily's mother's voice was especially gentle and caring as she replied, "Em, I have so wished this for you. My heart is now smiling with yours. Since you were a little girl, you have been looking for your Prince Charming. Hearing the certainty in your voice makes me realize he has finally arrived. Nothing could make your father and me more pleased. We can't wait to meet him. And your sister will be ecstatic to hear the news."

Emily smiled, knowing that her sister had kept her promise to not tell her secret until Emily shared the news with her parents.

"Mom, I will be home in just a few days, and I will bring pictures and tell you all about Eric then. He is so wonderful. I know you all are going to like him a lot."

"Em, the important thing is that you love him."

"I do, Mom, more than I ever thought possible."

Within moments of ending the call, she heard a knock on the door. She opened it to see Eric's smiling face. "Why didn't you just come in?" she asked.

"Because you have not yet entrusted me with a key to your cabin."

Emily pulled him in and closed the door behind them. She then gave him the most romantic kiss. "I am the doorman, or should I say the doorwoman? Please, do come in."

"With that kind of welcome, I don't need my own key! Come, tell me how your afternoon has gone. Did you have a good lunch with your comrades?"

"Yes, and they have added a few special musical touches to the party."

Eric explained that he also had some surprises to report. Because Jonathan heard it was her function, he was preparing a buffet table of exceptional appetizers. And Eric said he wanted to also contribute, so he personally upgraded the wine list and champagne offerings. Emily realized that she could now relax. Everything was in place for her agency gathering. They decided to sit out on the balcony and take in the views as the ship made the return voyage through the Inside Passage. Emily shared her conversations with her mother and aunt. She told him how much they looked forward to meeting him. Eric also told her about his father's caution on moving too quickly in the relationship. But he immediately added that his mother reminded his father that when they met it was love at first sight.

Looking at him, with a most sincere gaze, Emily asked, "Do you think we are moving too quickly?"

"Not at all," he replied emphatically. "I am so in love with you that I could call Captain Smith and ask him to marry us tomorrow. That is how sure I am. But why do you ask? You aren't getting cold feet are you?"

"Are you kidding? I have waited for you all of my life, and I would accept your invitation to contact Captain Smith, except my sister would disown me if she was not the Maid of Honor in my wedding!"

"Does this mean that I have to replace your puzzle piece marked 'spontaneity'?"

Emily laughed. "I hope not, however, you could replace it with loyalty to family. And speaking of family, my mother is already asking me when you will come to Los Angeles to meet them. Perhaps, you might want to add impatience to your puzzle pieces. I have inherited it from her."

Out on the balcony, they marveled at the sheer beauty of the rugged snow-capped mountains. The water was calm, and Eric commented that he could see why the passage offered a safer route for ships who were traveling to Alaska. Emily smiled as they held hands while they talked. Eric seemed to be in a particularly good mood.

"I have something important to tell you, Em. I have scheduled a meeting with Captain Smith for tomorrow morning. I am going to give my notice. I have decided to open my own restaurant. In the last few days I have given it a lot of thought, and I am now more and more convinced that it can be successful. I hope you still have a copy of that business plan. I will need your help."

Emily's eyes opened wide. "Wow, this is big news. I have to say I'm thrilled to hear it, but I hope I haven't coaxed you into it in any way."

"No, Sweetie, you haven't pressured me. This afternoon, I got to thinking about our finding each other, and what I would like the next steps to be. I'm glad we have these few minutes to talk. We can discuss it further over dinner, but I truly want to start a life together. I've enjoyed the adventure of being on ships, earning the title of Executive Chef and seeing so much of the world.

But it doesn't work for me anymore. It is not what I want in my life. My thought is, I could finish out the Alaska sailings and then come to Los Angeles to see if it would be a good fit for the new restaurant. It seems like a city that is alive and eclectic. With the movie industry crowd, business folks, and trendy up-and-comers, there should be room for another high-end restaurant. I know I am a very good chef, and I'm willing to put in the extra effort. I've made a lot of great contacts in the food industry. With your encouragement, I know that it will work out. I'm convinced of it."

"You can be assured of my help, every step of the way. I can assist with the business plan, but more than that I am educated and experienced in finance and inventory control. And, yes, you can add those qualities to my puzzle pieces," Emily replied in a teasing manner. "They are qualities that I am certain of, and you can be too. I know I am being selfish in asking, but how long does the Alaska cruise season last?"

"I'm not going to add a selfish nature to your puzzle pieces, because I am touched that you want me to come sooner than later. We have sailings throughout August and a couple in early September. But, with my brilliant idea, I may be leaving the ship earlier than expected." Emily's anticipation was growing as she waited to hear more.

"I had a flash of genius when I went down to the galley to speak with Jonathan about your party appetizers. I took him into my private office and asked him an important question. I wondered if he would like to accept this ship as his first Executive Chef cruise assignment. He is familiar with the set up and already knows the crew, captain, and staff. They all like and respect him. He said he would love to be considered for my position. I think Katarina may have helped him make that decision."

"What does Katarina have to do with his decision?" Emily asked with a puzzled look on her face.

"Remember I told you that she had recently come on board as the spa manager? Well, she has decided that Austin and she are best suited as good friends. Jonathan got to visiting with her last night in the disco. Their paths had only crossed briefly in her first weeks here, but they have found they have many things in common. I think it is rather sweet, don't you?"

"Yes, and now, I will be forever grateful to her for two reasons. Did you know that it was Katarina who thought to come get me when the explosion occurred?"

"I heard that, and I now feel badly having described her the way I did when we first met. She really is a thoughtful and caring person. Maybe we should take her up on that couple's massage tomorrow night after the farewell dinner."

"Hey, it is getting late, and we have your travel agency party coming up soon. You go ahead and get dressed here, and I will go down to my cabin. I think the captain would prefer I wear my formal chef's coat, even though I am officially off duty tonight."

Emily chose her favorite stylish white dress with the sheer sleeves. She wanted to arrive early to check out the arrangements before her travel group arrived. Entering the Observation Lounge, she noticed that it appeared especially festive. She suspected that Richard had assisted in the decorations. There was a lovely welcome sign stating the name of the agency. A banner also hung on the wall congratulating Steve and Laurie on their 50th wedding anniversary. The shiny stainless-steel buffet cart waited for the appetizers to arrive. She said hello to the bartender and servers giving them her thank you envelope, ahead of time as not to forget.

Everyone arrived promptly at 4:00 pm, and she was pleased to see that her group had felt comfortable enough to invite a few guests. Richard was there as well as Ted and Hank. Carol had even invited Charles, her favorite dance host. When the appetizers arrived it was obvious that Jonathan had wanted to please her, and possibly impress Eric, with his display of scallops wrapped in prosciutto, little cream puffs filled with exotic cheeses, a baron of beef, and other delicacies. The crowd was mingling and enjoying themselves when Eric arrived, looking dashing in his formal chef's jacket. Emily felt a warm glow seeing everyone giving him personal hugs to express their concern and gratitude that he survived the explosion. She was also delighted to see that Captain Smith had come to her gathering. He shared a few words of congratulations for Steve and Laurie on their anniversary and presented them with a lovely crystal vase with a logo of the ship. He also stopped by to acknowledge Emily and put his hand on Eric's shoulder to ask how he was doing. He indicated he would see him at their meeting in the morning. Midway through the party, there was a clinking of a glass to get everyone's attention.

"We have a little special surprise for some of our favorite people today," Sylvia began. She looked especially gorgeous in a long black skirt with an off the shoulder shimmering silver top. She went on to explain that four group members were going to share their beautiful voices in a musical tribute. She introduced Valerie, Fran, Bobby, and Kari, explaining that they were members of the Los Angeles Symphony Chorale. With a mischievous smile, she explained that the group had secretly learned of the first song that Steve and Laurie had danced to at their wedding reception. She invited them to come forward to share an anniversary repeat. As they stepped onto the small dance floor, located in front of the baby grand piano, Emily almost gasped at what she saw next. Sylvia sat down at the piano and began to play with the composure and skill of a professional.

Everyone was mesmerized. Sylvia had always just seemed like the sophisticated woman about town; dancing beautifully with all of the dance hosts, flirting with the officers, and being somewhat mysterious through it all. When Emily glanced in Richard's direction she could see he was extremely impressed as he shook his head with a big smile on his face. Even Eric gave her a look that indicated he was noticeably surprised. She played the introduction and then the singers lent their voices to the song, "Fly Me to the Moon." The ship's professional photographer was even present to capture the moment.

"We have one more rendition we would like to perform," Sylvia announced. "It is to recognize a very special couple that we have become most fond of and to acknowledge that we are relieved to find them safe-and-sound in our midst."

She then asked Eric and Emily to come forward. Emily was in a mild state of shock, but she could tell that the group had worked hard to make the moment a surprise. On the dance floor, she looked up at Eric. The relaxed smile on his face made her realize that he was also in on the planning. Sylvia played the piano and the singers did a rendition of Emily's two favorite songs, "Somewhere Over the Rainbow" and "When You Wish Upon a Star." As she and Eric danced, she saw a couple of people getting as teary eyed as she was. When they finished, everyone applauded enthusiastically.

Emily went up to share her appreciation with Valerie, Fran, Bobby, and Kari. When she came to Sylvia, she gave her a big hug and whispered, "Thank you, I will never forget this dance."

With a most tender look, Sylvia replied, "I am certain that it will be the beginning of many more for you and Eric."

As the party was about to end Emily addressed the travel group on behalf of her agency. She told them that she never could have dreamed how much the cruise has meant in her life. She shared that, in just one week, she now saw so many of them as friends and relayed that she would be forever grateful for their kindness in the past two days. It pleased her to know that they had enjoyed the cruise and she looked forward to saying hello when they dropped by the agency. The party ended with everyone feeling warmhearted and connected.

The reservation at the Silk Road was imminent, so Eric and Emily headed directly to dinner. Upon arrival, Chef Kai came over to welcome them. He told Eric how proud he was of his bravery in rescuing the stranded people from the burning building. He escorted them to a lovely table for two, at a window overlooking the water. It was in a private section surrounded by beautiful etched glass panels. Emily appreciated the choice of tables so they could be alone and talk privately.

"Doesn't it seem like the explosion is now so far in the past? I can't believe it was only two days ago," Emily shared.

"I agree, except for a little reminder in my sore arm, it really does seem like it was at least a month ago."

"Maybe, it is because so much is happening in our relationship that we have a distorted sense of time. And, by the way, that was such a touching dance we shared at the party. I am wondering how they possibly could have known my favorite songs?" She looked directly into Eric's eyes, and she could tell that there was no way that he could dodge her question.

"I must confess that I was in on the surprise. The ladies got in touch wiht me this afternoon through Richard. They gave me your aunt's number at the agency, and when I reached her, she told me where I could contact your sister who provided the names of your favorite songs. I must say that your family all seem like especially warmhearted people. They were so charming and said they could not wait to meet me. I almost felt like I was being welcomed into your family."

"In a sense you were because I told them that I was in love with you, and that I knew you were the one I wanted to spend the rest of my life with." Eric moved his foot closer to touch hers under the table. Emily continued, "I can hardly believe that we first saw each other, at a cooking demonstration on a cruise ship to Alaska."

When Eric began his confession he had the sweetest impish look on his face. "I didn't want to embarrass you, but that was actually the third time I saw you." He went on to explain that the first time he had seen her was on the dock the day she was arriving with her travel group. "I was just returning to the ship, having had lunch with friends in Vancouver when you arrived. I actually stood back to watch you walk up the gangway to see who you were having your welcome-aboard photograph taken with."

"When I saw you were not with anyone, I was thrilled. Most of the younger beautiful women who come aboard are either on their honeymoon or married and traveling with extended family. I was instantly taken with your appearance; you were so attractive. But it was the easy way you laughed, interacting with the passengers and crew, that really got my attention. I said to myself in that moment, 'I would like to get to know that beautiful woman.' I vowed to try to find you on the ship to start a conversation."

"That doesn't seem like an embarrassing situation?" Emily replied with a puzzled look.

Eric then continued to say that it was the second time he saw her that was, in his words, magical although it might make her blush. He said, on the morning of day two of the cruise, all the guys down in the galley were twitterpated about a gorgeous, young woman who was swimming in the pool on Lido deck. They said she looked like she was nude at first because her swimsuit was the color of her skin. They were all taking turns going up to fill the condiments at the pool bar. After the fourth group of guys went up, I decided to see what all of the excitement was about. When I came around the corner the sunlight was reflecting off the glass windows, and I actually thought I was seeing a mermaid!"

"You were swimming so gracefully, diving and coming up with your hair all wet and shiny. As you did flips and twirls, you looked so at home in the water. It actually did take my breath away, and I could see why my crew was so enamored. At that moment, I then recognized you as the woman I had seen coming aboard solo on the day we embarked. I wasn't going to tell you this because I didn't want to embarrass you into thinking that all of the crew were spying on you, but I guess, in a way, they were," he admitted.

Instead of being aghast, Emily burst into uncontrollable laughter. Her expression was one of total amazement and delight. It took several minutes before she got herself back together enough to reply. "This is indeed a moment of magic. Yes, it is in the air!" She then told Eric that several months prior she and her sister had gone to the beach. They saw the small tent of a fortune teller on the boardwalk and decided to have a reading. She said the woman looked exactly as one might imagine a fortune teller to look, with a turban, rings on every finger, and lots of eye makeup. But Emily felt that there was something authentic in her demeanor. She looked right into her eyes with a strange knowing smile. When Emily asked about her future love life, the woman told her that she was not like everyone else. She was different. She would have to find a man who could love a mermaid.

"I can't believe that! It makes the hair on my arms stand up," Eric said in astonishment.

"Those were her exact words. The fortune teller went on to explain that, because there were so many facets to my personality, I would need to find a man who could not only accept that I was unique and different, but also see it as a positive aspect of who I am. A man who could love a mermaid."

Eric was quiet and looked out the window for a few moments before he answered. "Well, all I can say is that I am ready to prove to you that I am a man who can love a mermaid."

She looked at him with the softest eyes and reached across the table to hold his hand. "I could call it another sign, but I am now convinced that we are the right people for each other. I know you will love me unconditionally."

"I will most certainly, you can count on it. I was just thinking of another curious aspect to this story. It just dawned on me. It is my earlier references to the puzzle pieces that make up the astonishing woman you truly are. Never in a million years would I have guessed that when I put the last puzzle piece into place I would see the image of a mermaid!"

They both laughed, and Emily told him that her sister had given her a painting of a mermaid. It hung on the bedroom wall, over her bed. "When you come to stay at my condo you will see it."

"The idea of being with you, in your condo bedroom, is giving me romantic ideas. It might be time to head to your cabin, wouldn't you agree?" Eric teased.

"Absolutely, but not until I give you your little gift." Emily opened her evening bag and waved an extra cabin keycard in front of him. "Now, you have your own key," she said with a come hither grin.

They awoke the next morning, wrapped in each other's arms, but quickly realized they needed to get up and get going. He was on his way to the galley. The kitchen would be busy with the captain's farewell cocktail party, the gala farewell dinner, and those ordering dinner in, while they packed for departure the next morning. He also had his important 10:00 am meeting with Captain Smith. Emily was booked on the shore excursion tour of Victoria, the capital of British Columbia. She was happy that she would have plenty of time on the tour to visit with various members of her large travel group. When does the tour return to the ship?" Eric asked.

"We will be back on the ship at 3:00 pm so people can pack before the evening's farewell activities."

"The thought of you packing is already making me miss you. How about I carve out an hour and meet you here at the cabin when you return. I will want to report on the meeting with the Captain and steal an afternoon kiss," Eric said.

"I hope Captain Smith will be understanding," she said in a hopeful tone.

When Emily entered the touring motor coach, she noticed that one of her group members, Sandee, had an empty seat next to her. "Is your husband not joining you today?" she asked politely.

"We have been here twice before, and when he saw that the tour included High Tea at the Empress Hotel and a tour of the flowers at the Butchart Gardens, he decided to take a pass and play gin rummy with friends. Truthfully, I think it was because he noticed that Texas barbecued ribs were on the lunch menu," she said with a laugh.

Emily enjoyed sharing the day with members of her group. She joined a table of six avid travelers at High Tea. They told her about the afternoon they had been invited to tea at a castle in England. The Butchart Gardens were the world-class botanical spectacle she had read about. As she roamed the various paths in the fifty-five acres of floral displays, she made conversation with several different clients. It was a good opportunity to ask how they had enjoyed the cruise. Every person she spoke with shared their satisfaction with the splendor of the ship and great service.

Emily warmed when they gave extra accolades for the quality of the food. A few even felt comfortable in sharing the fact that they were so relieved to see that the executive chef she had met was not injured in the explosion in Ketchikan. She was pleased to catch up with Dan and Jim at the Royal BC Museum. They helped educate her as to the history of the collection in the Totem Hall, the central exhibit in the First People's gallery. She was impressed to see the quality of the totem poles and realized she was happy to view them since she had missed the tour in Sitka. But she thought to herself, *Would I have traded seeing totem poles for an opportunity to kayak with a good-looking cruise chef? Not on your life!* As she returned to the ship, she was confident that her Aunt Marge would be pleased with her clients' responses.

Emily was elated to see that Eric was waiting in the cabin when she returned. "I'm so glad you are here. How did the meeting with the captain go?" Eric then immediately came over to say they could not discuss business until they had kissed hello. Afterwards, she said, "I like that idea. Let's make it a tradition."

"Captain Smith was most understanding of my decision to leave the ship. It's not an unusual happening in the cruise industry. People rarely stay forever. A few years and they move on. But some, like captains, cruise directors, and engineers make a career of shipboard life. I think he was actually proud of my determination to open my own restaurant. He said he was going to come to dinner when the ship lays over in Los Angeles. You should have seen the look on his face when I told him I had an idea to make my departure easier. I told him about Jonathan, and suggested he stay on this ship instead of taking a placement elsewhere. Captain Smith said he admired his work ethic, and the crew liked him. He was thrilled with the idea and said he would get a firm confirmation from Jonathan before he contacted the corporate office. He said that he would like to keep it confidential until everything is in place, so mum is the word."

"How can you keep it a secret on this ship?" Emily teased.

"That is true, but I'll do my part. Let's see how long it lasts! If Jonathan accepts the position, which I already know he will, that means I could be leaving the ship in two or three weeks. I will fly directly home and ask you to come to meet my family. I'll pack up my things and then, if you have a few extra days, we can drive back to Los Angeles together. One good thing, about having lived on a cruise ship these past few years is that I don't have to dismantle an entire apartment of furniture and kitchen supplies. I'll just have my clothes, a couple pieces of original artwork and my set of knives."

Emily was puzzled regarding the knives. Eric explained that accomplished chefs often have an expensive set of knives that they take with them from place to place. "I'll use them in our new restaurant," Eric said watching for her reaction.

Emily looked at him with a twinkle in her eye. "Since you now refer to it as 'our restaurant,' does it imply that you are going to put me to work?"

"Yes, but not peeling potatoes in the kitchen. I hope you will be the hostess for the first couple of months. With your beauty and charm we are certain to fill the house every night!"

"I'd love to dress up and greet the patrons. And I can't wait to fly out and meet your family. I'm happy to know that you won't be bringing a U-Haul full of furniture. My apartment is already furnished from corner to corner." Emily laughed.

"Will your parents be comfortable with our living together so soon?" Eric asked.

"Absolutely, my folks know how committed we are to each other, and besides, haven't we already been living together in this cabin for several days?" Emily reached over to give him a loving hug and beautiful kiss.

"Hey, you can't get me all excited now. I have to go back to the galley filled with those guys who remember you in the sheer swimsuit. Hold the thought until tonight!" he ribbed her as he headed toward the door. "Oh, and I forgot something. Since you are making all of my wishes come true, when you come to Minnesota, I promised to make one come true for you. We will go to the lake region and find you a loon."

"I love you for remembering, and for so many other reasons," Emily said as she blew him a kiss goodbye. "See you at the captain's farewell reception." She took a few minutes to make a quick call to her Aunt Marjorie at the agency. She thanked her aunt for participating in the surprise dance with her two favorite songs. Her aunt said Eric sounded like a wonderful man on the telephone. Marge confirmed that Donna's ticket was successfully changed. She was on the same flight as Ted and seated next to him.

Emily shared again how much the group enjoyed the cruise. With a sense of humor, her Aunt Marge said, "It sounds like some enjoyed themselves even more than others. Sylvia called this morning, and she, Cathy, Emma Lou, and Carol are taking another cruise in three months. It is a Fall Foliage itinerary on your exact ship. I got them repeat passenger discounts, and they are all booked."

Emily was tempted to say something playful, but decided it would remain her delightful musing.

The captain's party was an elegant affair. It was obvious by the look on the faces of passengers that they had all enjoyed the cruise. When Emily saw Madame Analie, she went over to say hello. They greeted each other warmly, and Emily told her how much Eric appreciated her lovely card. She then said, "Dear, come talk with me outside in the hall. I would like to tell you something in confidentiality." She and Emily found a private place to have their conversation. "My husband confided in me that Eric is going to leave the ship to start his own restaurant, and we wish him the very best. But I wanted to tell you that I do so hope that this change also means that you two will be together. I feel an affection for both of you, and I believe you two would make a wonderful lifelong couple. I apologize if I am being intrusive in commenting, but I saw the beautiful connection between you two at dinner the other night."

"I have a fondness for you too Madame Analie, and it touches me that you care enough to share your feelings. I am happy to say that Eric and I have fallen in love, and he is coming to start his restaurant in my city of Los Angeles. We are moving in together, and I am certain we will marry within the year."

"This makes me happy to hear. I know you are well aware of the good man that you have found in Eric. He has been one of my favorites since he joined the ship. I am delighted that he has found such a lovely woman in you. I wish you all the happiness in the world. And now, we had better return to the party. I swear these walls have ears."

Emily chuckled and replied, "I understand. Thank you for your most kind message. I have appreciated knowing you for this brief time. I will not forget your kindness."

As they walked back into the gathering Emily thought about the fact that such a gracious elegant woman, who hardly knew her, was considerate enough to share such an endearing sentiment. With a smile she said to herself, *One can never have too many Fairy Godmothers!*

The farewell dinner was especially grand. Lobster and Filet Mignon were on the menu, and Emily smiled to see Vichyssoise listed as a starter. The parade of Baked Alaska was a huge hit at dessert time. Eric led the sparkling parade and gave her a little wink as he passed by. When dinner ended everyone scattered, many to pack for their morning departure, some to say a final goodbye to newfound friends, and even a few, to share a last dance with the Gentleman Hosts. Emily went back to her cabin to finish packing and wait for Eric. Shortly after she arrived she heard a knock on the door. She was surprised, since she knew Eric has his own key. She opened the door a few inches to peek out and heard Eric's voice.

"Are you still dressed, Em? I have someone I would like you to meet."

Emily shook her head yes as she opened the door.

"I wanted you to meet Jonathan because there won't probably be a chance amidst the morning rush."

Emily gave Jonathan a big smile and indicated her delight in meeting him. Just then, Eric put his finger to his lips to indicate quiet, as he and Jonathan both stepped into her cabin and closed the door behind them. "We have good news to share," Eric began. "Captain Smith already put the wheels into motion. He got a call back from the corporate office right before the farewell party. They approved Jonathan's placement. He is going to be the ship's new Executive Chef."

Emily was so overjoyed that she jumped into Eric's arms with a big hug. And as she turned to Jonathan, her enthusiasm was still running so high that she gave him a hug too.

He was at first caught off guard, but found it charming and said, "I can imagine how pleased you are to get him back to LA sooner than planned." And then, with a tender grin he added, "It is nice to meet the woman who has kept my friend smiling all afternoon."

When Jonathan left, Emily wanted to hear all of the details. They sat on the couch, and Eric told her that it was still a secret for a few days, but that he would be staying for only two more Alaska sailings. He said he had another piece of good news. After sharing his plans with his parents, he received a call from his grandfather who indicated that he wanted to be an investor in the new restaurant. His grandfather had said not to worry about paying him back. He would just make it part of his inheritance as long as he was always guaranteed a reservation! "We now have our seed money for the bank loan," Eric said with excitement.

"Em, I've been planning in my head all afternoon. What would you think about getting engaged at Christmas and married in the spring or summer?"

"If you are you telling me that you are ready to marry a mermaid, my answer is yes to a holiday engagement, and yes to a spring wedding," she replied with a loving expression on her face.

Eric laughed and pulled her toward him to share a most romantic kiss. It was at that moment he noticed her silver high heels on the floor nearby. "Wait, I want to make it official." He walked over, picked up one of her shoes, knelt, and slipped it onto her foot. "Emily Andersen, I'll be doing this again, with a proper diamond ring in December, but for now, will you be my Happily Ever After?"

She whispered in his ear, "Absolutely, yes!"

EPILOGUE

Escapades, Travel, Romance and the Rest of the Story

As Emily finished the last story of the evening, a silence fell over the table. And then, smiles started to reappear on everyone's lips. "I loved hearing your story Emily," Ginger said. "It gave me an insight into so many things I did not know about you. Also, being a hopeless romantic, I just feel badly that you and Eric didn't stay together. You were so sure. I know you dearly love Tom and your boys, but you just have to tell us what happened."

Jessica immediately and emphatically interrupted. "Wait a minute! We all made a pact, and we are going to abide by it. We said we would wait until each one had a chance to share her story, and then we would go back, in the same order, to hear the rest of the story. We don't want to shortchange anyone, and don't worry, you all will have your opportunity to ask questions." Everyone nodded their agreement and Jessica continued, "Victoria, since you were the first one to tell your story, you'll now go first again."

Everyone refilled their wine glasses and became intent on hearing what happened to Phillip after returning from Mongolia.

As Victoria began, everyone could sense sadness in her voice. Being a group of close friends, the playful mood quickly changed to one of caring and empathy. "When Phillip left the Mongolian archaeological dig, he went directly home to London, and I flew over shortly thereafter. We had the most romantic week together. He was everything I remembered him to be and more: kind, playful, smart, sensitive, and loving. We were so happy going forward in our relationship. It was definitely with the conviction that we would become a committed couple. Neither of us was concerned about how we would navigate two continents because we knew we would find a way."

She told them that Phillip came to Boston. Her family adored him and, of course, he completely charmed her friends with his British accent and his rugged attractive looks. She explained that they flew back and forth, across the ocean, almost every six weeks. Suddenly Victoria's tone of voice changed. There was sadness and even regret as she continued. "Things were so amazing until I received his unexpected call."

She revealed that he had been invited to be the expedition leader of an archaeological dig in Egypt. He had already established a name for himself in the Middle East, and the offer was a prestigious honor. It was an eight-month commitment. She said that Phillip wanted to know what she thought. He explained that it was going to be his last hurrah. He surprised her by saying that he was then ready to see if they couldn't come up with a plan to live together on either side of the pond. Phillip described the excavation site in great detail. It was five hours from a major city, making it extremely remote. He would not be able to call, except when he went into Cairo for supplies."

Victoria admitted that she was emotionally torn. "I knew it was a dream come true for Phillip, so I accepted the news willingly." Sadly, after he left, she explained that she was lucky if she heard from him once every six weeks. Then she received the call that changed everything. Phillip started by telling her how much she meant to him.

Apologetically, Phillip explained that he had been asked to stay on in Egypt to see the project to its completion. It would be a commitment of another seven to nine months. Victoria was in anguish as she told her friends that she could hardly believe it. It had already been eight months.

"He told me if the additional separation jeopardized our relationship that he would turn it down. But you all know me, I wouldn't stand in the way of someone's dream, especially Phillip's."

Everyone was completely silent as she went on to describe the situation. As the months dragged on, Victoria started thinking that they were from different worlds, and doubts about their relationship started to creep in. When he called two months later, he caught her at an especially vulnerable time. Unfortunately, she told him that she did not think it would work between them, and that her feelings for him had changed.

"I could hear the deep sadness and disappointment in his voice. Being the wonderful person he is, Phillip said he wished me only the best. When I hung up the phone, I knew it was not truly how I felt, but somehow I just couldn't take it back. I never heard from him again. I've shed a million tears. The undeniable connection that Phillip and I shared is what I miss the most. Knowing that I wasn't truthful when I ended the relationship is something I will regret for the rest of my life. I didn't want to burden all you with my heartache, but I feel my life has broken into a million pieces."

Seeing the tears welling up in her eyes made Victoria's friends feel incredibly sad for her.

"Do you know when Phillip will return to London?" Ginger asked.

She listened carefully as Victoria explained that she surmised Phillip had returned approximately six months ago, but she was not sure. "Have you considered calling him, to tell him how you really feel? Maybe he continues to care for you. It could still work out. By the tone of your voice, I am guessing you have never tried to reach out to him."

"I have wanted to contact him so many times, but to be brutally honest, I guess I haven't called because I fear that he will tell me he has moved on, and he is no longer interested. I know he will be polite and nice about it, but hearing those words is more than I can bear."

"Would you feel any worse than you do now?" Jessica asked. "Falling in love takes courage. You have talked about the pain of carrying regret. What about the regret of never reaching out to Phillip to tell him that you were feeling uncertain and that you do care deeply for him? All you can do at this point is make the call."

Everyone could sense Victoria's deep sadness and knew it was time to move on. All eyes were now on Ginger. She explained that over two years had passed since she and Roberto shared their holiday in Italy. He absolutely loved her gift, the photo album with images of himself. She marveled at how well it had turned out, not just because he was such an attractive man, but because it highlighted so much of his endearing personality with the wind blowing through his hair, his laughing eyes, and sweet smile. Ginger shared that at Christmas he thoughtfully shipped her a case of wine from his cousin's vineyard.

Emily then asked, "Do you two ever talk with each other?"

Ginger smiled warmly. "We check in with each other a few times a year. Roberto really is my Soul Friend. In fact, the last time he called, he told me that he had met someone special, and they were dating seriously. Hearing his news made me feel happy for him."

Jessica was particularly moved. "There is something so genuine and authentic about Roberto and your time in Italy. Your story touched me deeply. In the truest sense, it is a remarkable tribute to giving and receiving. Somehow, it just makes me feel good knowing there are relationships that can become loving friendships. The playful romantic exchanges sounded so sweet. Thank you for sharing your story Ginger. I think the true ending will be when you meet your soulmate; the one you wished for when you threw that coin into the fountain."

Jessica was particularly animated and excited, as it was now her turn. Her announcement was the most life-changing news. So many amazing things had occurred since she and Will connected eight months prior in Buenos Aires. Her women friends were completely mesmerized. One could have heard a pin drop as she started to describe what had transpired in just a few months.

"I have fallen madly in love, and you all know that I wouldn't say it if it weren't wildly true. I have never been happier in my entire life! Every single day I'm with Will, I find more reasons why he is the man with whom I want to share the rest of my life. It has been a glorious whirlwind. It's impossible to count all of the airline miles I have logged, not only between Buenos Aires and Chicago, but also to the international cities where Will has performed with various symphonies."

Jessica went on to explain that she was not going to forgo one moment of the bliss she had found. She was already making plans to sell her travel agency to her manager. "Don't think for a minute that I'm going to miss our yearly reunion. I'm staying on the agency's Board of Directors. I have already told them that I will take on the responsibility of representing the agency at our yearly ASTA convention." Everyone was still in total wonderment as she added, "And are you ready for this news? Will and I are planning to move in together."

"Where in the world will that be Jessica? And I do mean it literally," Ginger asked playfully.

Jessica described the plans she and Will were making for their future. She already had good friends who wanted to rent her place in Chicago. She and Will were going to spend some of their time in the United States at his family's guest apartment in New York City. The majority of the time would be spent in Buenos Aires.

Emily could not resist asking her a tongue-in-cheek question. "We know you are not going to stay home and build a love nest all day long. So what are you going to be doing with your many talents, not to mention your high energy level?"

"Well, actually, for starters, I plan to check off a couple of things on my bucket list. I always wanted to do 'a little give back', so I've begun volunteering at a women's shelter in Buenos Aires, where I'm teaching English. Don't roll your eyes at me," she teased. "It's true. I'm also learning Spanish from these women, but that was not my main intent!"

Everyone burst into laughter knowing that Jessica always found a silver lining in all of her endeavors.

"Seriously, these women have moved to the city from impoverished rural communities in Argentina. Their stories would break your hearts. I'm going to spend some additional time writing grants for their program. If you have any extra funds to share, they really could use your financial help." Jessica went on to tell her friends about another one of her goals. She reminded them that she actually earned an advanced degree in journalism. Many years ago she had started a novel, but never had an opportunity to devote serious time to completing it. Full of enthusiasm, she explained, "I will take my laptop when I join Will on the road. While he practices for the symphony performances, I'll stay at the hotel and write. Oh, and speaking of performances, I have a surprise for all of you." Jessica opened her purse and fanned out five symphony tickets. "Will is the featured soloist at the Chicago Symphony next month, and we all have box seat tickets. Emily, I have an extra one for Tom, if he would like to join us."

Everyone was thrilled and Ginger said, "I am only coming if I get to meet the man who has amazingly stolen the heart of our most independent friend.

I am so pleased for you, Jessica. I'm not sure I can fall asleep tonight thinking of how just one turn of the wheel of destiny has changed your entire world. It makes my heart sing!"

It was hard to come down from all of the excitement that Jessica's revelation had generated. Ginger would finally get back to her original question of Emily. "What happened to Eric?" It was not her intention to dredge up old memories. From Emily's loving and devoted comments about Tom, it was easy for her friends to see the depth of their love and commitment. It was a relationship built on trust and loyalty. Emily shared that she and Tom still held hands when they walked down the street, gave each other a kiss as they left the house, and stayed firmly committed to their weekly date nights.

Knowing of their commitment, Ginger softened her voice as she began, "Emily, your romantic story was so endearing. I loved hearing of your magical search for your Prince Charming. You seemed so certain that Eric, the cruise chef, was the one. What happened to that romance?"

Due to Ginger's question, Emily realized in that moment that there was something very important that her friends did not know. Smiling broadly she replied, "I did fall in love with Eric, and I still adore him today. Tom is Eric!"

Everyone seated at the table looked at each other in disbelief. Emily went on to share that Tom's grandfather was Thomas James Olsen. His father is named Thomas Daniel Olsen. When Emily's husband was born, his parents named him Thomas Eric Olsen. As the years went on his mother found it humorous and confusing. Each time she called for "Tom," she summoned both her husband and son.

In time, the family started calling Tom by his middle name, Eric. It just stuck and he used it until the time he moved to Los Angeles to start his new restaurant. As he signed his given name on legal contracts, agreements with vendors, and even on his wedding certificate, he decided he liked it. He felt Thomas seemed more adult and professional than Eric. Since he had just arrived in Los Angeles, and was starting a new phase of his life, it was easy to change.

"His old college chums and parents still, on occasion, call him Eric but all the rest of us have transitioned to Tom."

Ginger's eyes grew wide as she exclaimed, "Wow, that is a relief, and it makes me feel so much better. Listening to your story, I so wanted your belief in a Prince Charming to be real. As I go out to find my 'Mr. Right', I'm taking your unwavering convictions with me. And speaking of being open to meeting a good guy, I had better get going. I have an eight o'clock dinner date. What are the rest of you planning for the evening?"

"I'm off to call Tom to see if the boys won their soccer game and how our new puppy is surviving. Thank you for letting me share the story of how Tom and I met. It brought back so many wonderful memories," Emily replied with an endearing smile.

Jessica told them that she was off to meet some college friends for dinner.

When everyone looked at Victoria, she paused and replied. "I remember something Phillip told me in Mongolia. He said, 'Victoria, we are all human, we all make mistakes.' I'm going to my room to place an international call."

— *The end* —